W9-BSK-516

All the Beautiful Girls

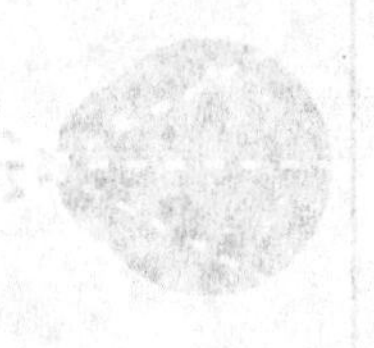

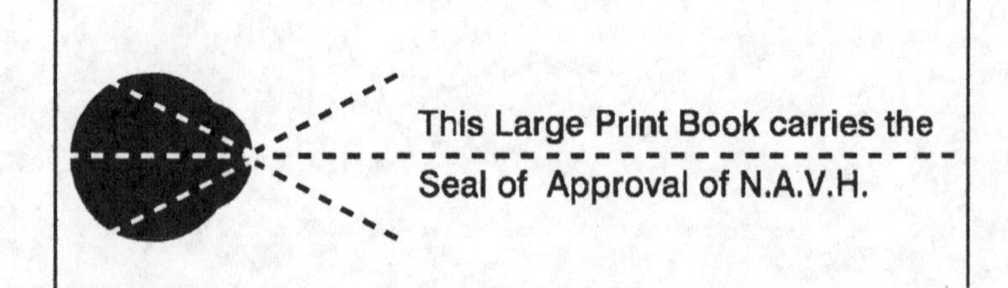
This Large Print Book carries the
Seal of Approval of N.A.V.H.

All the Beautiful Girls

Elizabeth J. Church

THORNDIKE PRESS
A part of Gale, a Cengage Company

Farmington Hills, Mich • San Francisco • New York • Waterville, Maine
Meriden, Conn • Mason, Ohio • Chicago

All the Beautiful Girls is a work of fiction. All places, incidents, dialogue, and characters, with the exception of some well-known, real-life places and persons, are products of the author's imagination and are not to be construed as real. Where real-life places and persons appear, the situations, incidents, and dialogues concerning those places and persons are entirely fictional and are not intended to depict actual events or to change the entirely fictional nature of the work. In all other respects, any resemblance to places and persons living or dead is entirely coincidental.

Thorndike Press® Large Print Basic.
The text of this Large Print edition is unabridged.
Other aspects of the book may vary from the original edition.
Set in 16 pt. Plantin.

**LIBRARY OF CONGRESS CIP DATA ON FILE.
CATALOGUING IN PUBLICATION FOR THIS BOOK
IS AVAILABLE FROM THE LIBRARY OF CONGRESS.**

ISBN-13: 978-1-4328-5009-8 (hardcover)

Published in 2018 by arrangement with Ballantine Books, an imprint of Random House, a division of Penguin Random Publishing Group, LLC

Printed in Mexico
1 2 3 4 5 6 7 22 21 20 19 18

Dance, when you're broken open.
Dance, if you've torn the bandage off.
Dance in the middle of the fighting.
Dance in your blood.
Dance when you're perfectly free.

— Rumi

Lily Decker

1

The line of Aunt Tate's jaw was fierce and unyielding, like a hammered steel length of railroad track, but her eyes were soft and puffy from furtive crying. "You can keep what you can carry," she said and handed eight-year-old Lily a cardboard box. Lily stared into the shadows of the empty box as if it held answers to all of the mounting uncertainties that frightened her.

It was June 1957, and Uncle Miles and Aunt Tate were in Lily's house in Salina, Kansas, picking through things like crows at the town dump. Lily wanted for them to leave everything the same as it was before, not to move her father's copy of *Andersonville* from the nightstand or her big sister Dawn's toothbrush and pink pajamas with the elephants that danced and wore silly hats. Mama's dresser scarves should not be folded and packed in a box, and her hat with the white netting should not be wrapped in tissue paper and tucked away for Aunt Tate's church bazaar. Lily's whole life was disappearing — all of her history, everything that fixed her feet to the earth and held her safe.

"C'mon, honey," Aunt Tate said, trying to prod Lily into action. "The longer we stay here, the more it's going to hurt. Let's just get this over and done with, all right?" Aunt Tate clumsily patted Lily's shoulder and picked up a box she'd packed for Uncle Miles to load onto the back of his pickup. "Get a move on, Lily," Aunt Tate said, this time firmly, and then headed down the hallway.

There was no place Lily wanted to be, to stay, other than home. *This* home. Her home. But, standing in the middle of her former life, Lily realized she didn't have a choice. She looked at her bed with the deep purple bedspread, the curtains Mama had made with the purple fringe running along the hem. Her stuffed animals, still sitting in a row on top of her pillow, just as she'd left them in her Before Life. Raggedy Ann and Raggedy Andy, the gingerbread man with the nap rubbed into nonexistence by her love. The deliciously soft pink bunny rabbit that had appeared in her Easter basket one year. The desk her father made that was just her size with a cabinet door she could open and close. Her red leather jewelry box with the mirror inside the lid and the ballerina that twirled on one toe while a tinkling, silvery bell played "Frère Jacques."

When Lily had asked Aunt Tate what would happen to the house and everything in it, Aunt Tate said, "That's for the adults to decide." Lily knew better than to push her luck, and so she let it be.

Dangling her legs in her apple-red pedal pushers, Lily sat on the edge of her bed and picked up the pink rabbit, tugging gently on his long satin ears. The things she wanted to put in the box wouldn't fit. Her family couldn't fit. The only home she'd ever known could not be wedged within those four cardboard walls. Her swing set, the toy telephones she and Dawn used to call each other. The familiar view out her bedroom window, the way the leaves on the elm tree turned their silvery backs to the breezes just before a rainstorm. Her parents dancing in the living room while Brook Benton sang "Love Made Me Your Fool," his voice rumbling smooth and low on the hi-fi; her father's hands threaded into Mama's thick gold hair; Mama's full-skirted pastel dresses. The cool, apricot-colored satin lining of Mama's best coat, and how it smelled of ripe pears and wisteria. No one was going to call Lily *Scallywag* — not anymore. And Lily couldn't fold and pack Dawn's skinny ankles turning cartwheels or her sister's voice reciting the endless "Paul Revere's Ride" until Lily wanted to scream. Nothing fit, including Lily. Lily no longer fit anywhere.

While Daddy had brylcreemed his wavy hair and worn a suit and tie to work as manager of the rail yards, Uncle Miles was a diesel mechanic who wore overalls and plaid shirts and rolled his own cigarettes and later stuck his rough, callused fingers inside Lily and whispered with his sour breath, "Our secret."

As for Mama's older sister, Aunt Tate was too tall with wide shoulders and so maybe secretly a man, and she moved ponderously, as if someone had hit a slow-motion button on her life and put her at permanent half speed. She wore loose-fitting, pastel cotton housedresses that hung limp and lifeless below her knees, and sensible black lace-up shoes with low heels. The only jewelry Aunt Tate allowed herself was a plain gold wedding band, and she kept her lusterless brown hair short and tightly curled. She was formidable, strict and austere in a way that had always made Lily both shy and wary. "It was the Depression," Mama once said. "It made your Aunt Tate hard. Deprivation made her think that being rigid was the only way to survive. But there's a soft center there; she has a heart, I swear." Still, Lily thought that even Mama had been more than a little cautious when faced with her sister's perennial judgment.

Within two weeks of the funeral, Aunt Tate had enrolled Lily in the July session of summer school, "To keep you out of my hair." Lily's aunt and uncle lived several blocks from Lily's old house on Sycamore Street, but to Lily's relief, she would still be able to attend her familiar elementary school. Before class on the first day, the kids gathered around Lily on the playground. "Did you see their guts?" "They said your sister was all tore up! Ground chuck!" Lily's best friend, Beverly Ann, hung back from the others, seemingly frozen in place, nervously watching Lily's reaction.

Lily ran into the breezeway, squeezed herself between a cool concrete pillar and the prickly leaves of a sumac bush, and waited until the bell rang. Mid-morning, Mrs. Tobias had the class put away their books and pencils, and then she conducted a ceremony in which Ray Bellamy carried a cage with a bright red bow and presented Lily with a chubby brown hamster bought and paid for with the sympathetic nickels and dimes of her classmates. Shannon Leary followed Ray, carrying a bag of wonderful-smelling cedar chips and a box of hamster food.

"You'll have to keep his water bottle filled," Mrs. Tobias said, her cool, composed hand on the back of Lily's neck. "And take really good care of him."

"What's his name?" Lily asked, looking around the room at her classmates.

"That's for you to decide, honey." Mrs. Tobias walked to the blackboard. "But we can list possibilities, if you'd like." She picked up a piece of chalk and began writing as Lily's classmates shouted out suggestions.

When all was said and done, Lily chose Pickles. Dawn had loved the vinegary saltiness of their mother's homemade pickles, and she'd sucked on them until her mouth was funny-looking, smoochy and all scrunched up. Dawn made the best faces, and the sisters would laugh until they got the hiccups. Pickles was a happy name. When Lily pressed her index finger between the bars of the cage, the hamster put his whiskery face up close, sniffed. It made Lily smile. Pickles let her stroke his soft fur, and with his little, rough tongue, he licked her finger.

The moment Lily walked through the kitchen door, Aunt Tate spotted the cage and said, "Not in my house. What were they thinking? Rodents? Your Uncle Miles will have something to say about this." When Lily started for her room, Aunt Tate added, "Leave the cage here. The food and all, too. You won't be needing it."

As soon as Uncle Miles got home, he took the hamster cage to the backyard. Lily knelt on her bed and watched from the window as he cornered Pickles and pulled him from the cage. He twisted the hamster's neck in a swift motion, and the little animal's body wilted in his beefy hands — the same way the pullets did when he killed them for Aunt Tate's soup pot.

Lily was breathing fast, and she wanted to cry. Her stomach hurt. She sat back on her bed and found a tender spot on the inside of her thigh, just above the cuff of her seersucker shorts. She pinched it as hard as she could, watched the skin turn white, then a deep, purply red. She did it two more times, in different places. But Lily didn't cry. She'd made herself a promise while sitting beneath the green awning in Gypsum Hill Cemetery where strangers — people who hadn't lost what she'd lost — cried until their noses ran ugly and red and full of snot. Lily decided, then and there, that crying was weak, an unaffordable loss of control. *No crying. Not ever again.*

When it was nearly time for supper, Aunt Tate appeared at Lily's bedroom door, wiped her wet hands on the front of her red-and-white-flowered apron, and looked at Lily wordlessly. Finally, she said, "Child, he only did what had to be done," and Lily knew it was a sad excuse for an apology but likely the best she'd get. Avoiding her aunt's gaze, Lily pushed out her lower lip and blew so that her dark cherry curls lifted briefly from her forehead. Aunt Tate continued, "Life is hard. You've had it easy, up until now. But —" Aunt Tate stopped talking.

Lily looked up at her aunt, who stood frozen in place like King Midas' daughter in the aftermath of her father's royal embrace. She watched her aunt frown briefly, as if she were suppressing tears, and then Lily saw real tears traveling down her aunt's cheeks.

Aunt Tate cleared her throat. "It's for your own good. Your mother didn't do you any favors by coddling you all the time, and if you don't toughen up, the world will eat you alive." She sighed and perched on the bed beside Lily. Absentmindedly, Aunt Tate played with a length of Lily's hair. "Look, honey, I know I seem mean to you, but I'm not. Neither is Uncle Miles. That's not it, at all." She let go of Lily's hair and folded her hands in her lap. "You can't let what's happened make you a victim. People will want to see you that way; they'll say, 'Oh, that poor little girl. She's so pathetic. Let's just let her get away with anything and everything.' But I don't want for you to live your life trading on being a victim. I will not let that happen. You have to face life, head on." Aunt Tate stood and squared her shoulders as if preparing to march. She held out a hand to Lily, who took it. Aunt Tate's tone was softer now. "Come set the table. It can be your job from now on."

Lily dutifully laid out four places, just as she'd done at home. Four plates. Four water glasses. Knives on the inside, sharp edge toward the plate, napkins folded neatly.

"Moron girl can't count," Uncle Miles said when called to the table for macaroni and cheese topped with a crisp bacon crust. "One. Two. Three," he said slowly, pointing to Aunt Tate, Lily, and then his own broad chest. "Sister, did you check this one out of

2

Lily lived for *The Dinah Shore Show,* starting with the NBC peacock, followed by the brass-heavy orchestra and the singer's wide-toothed rendition of "See the U.S.A. in Your Chevrolet!" . . . Lily would hum along, "Da-dadadadadadadadadah!" Dinah Shore had a tiny waist just like Mama, and Lily thought the television star seemed really happy.

They watched on the black-and-white set with Aunt Tate's milk-glass collection balanced precariously on top. Lily imagined the colors: Dinah Shore's long, elegant gloves must be emerald green, her fine net flounces would be sparkly deep blues and greens. Fuchsia silk scarves, silver and gold sequins, beautiful high heels dyed to match Dinah's gowns. Slit skirts revealing long legs, whirling skirts that flew up to show dancers' underpants and elicited the occasional *"Shameful!"* from Aunt Tate.

But, oh, the best part was the dancing!

Maracas and mambos and cha-cha-cha, handsome men lifting Dinah in the air and carrying her around the stage, her smile never faltering. The dancers' hips swaying, feet moving in rococo patterns. It was a world mercifully far removed from the martyred, blood-red edges of Aunt Tate's Bible, her thick support hose, and Uncle Miles' weight on the edge of Lily's bed, the way he pulled down the covers, a prelude.

Lily first ran away when she was nine, the summer after third grade. She climbed up on a chair and pulled her suitcase from its shelf high in her bedroom closet. It was made of cheap, pressed cardboard painted in pastel shades, with a lamb that had a yellow bow perched gaily in the curls of each ear. Lily flipped the latches so that the case opened to its pink-and-white-checked interior, and then she looked around to decide what to pack. She put in *Black Beauty* and two of her Nancy Drew mysteries, followed by the miniature porcelain elephant her father had won at the state fair. She filled the rest of the space with plain white Carter's panties and undershirts, a nightie decorated with daisies, a comb, and a cylinder of scented talcum powder that had belonged to her mother.

The last thing Lily included was her mother's big black palmistry book with the line drawings of hands, the mounts of Jupiter, Mercury, Apollo, and Venus. Mama used to run a ruby-red, manicured nail along the lines of Lily's palm, pointing out the differences between what she'd been born with and what she would do with whatever the Fates sent her way. Lily had loved her mother's touch, the way she prodded the pads of Lily's fingers. "You have psychic hands, too, my Valentine's Day child," Mama had said, noting Lily's long, tapered fingers and holding her own hand up for comparison. "Now, your sister Dawn, she's a Leo — her hands are square, like your daddy's. Practical, no nonsense. You're the one, baby girl. The one like me."

Lily got as far as the Petersons' house, two streets away, before Uncle Miles happened by on his way to the drugstore for rolling papers and beef jerky.

"Get in," he said, pulling over and pushing open the passenger door to his pickup truck. Lily hesitated, holding the hard plastic handle of her suitcase with both hands, already weary with the weight of it. She looked around, hoping someone would see her there, marooned in the shimmering summer heat. "Now," her uncle commanded. Slowly, Lily climbed in, set the suitcase at her feet, and pulled the door shut behind her. "Don't try that again." He squeezed her upper arm until she cried out. "It'd be the death of your Aunt Tate."

As he pulled away from the curb, Lily curled in on herself, trying not to smell Uncle Miles' body next to hers. She glanced at his hands on the steering wheel, his thumbs like stubby, rounded clubs. When he said, "Stay put or else" and left her sitting in the truck while he went into the drugstore, she pulled out her mother's book. Uncle Miles had what palmists called a clubbed hand. Such people, the book said, lacked willpower and were prone to criminal behavior.

She closed the volume when she saw her uncle lumbering back across the parking lot. He sat heavily behind the wheel and turned toward her, smiling so that his canines showed long and sharp. "You're so sexy," he said, using his husky, nighttime voice. "You make me lose control." He scanned the parking lot and then crept his hand across the front seat toward her. Lily scooted so that her back was pressed against the passenger door. Surreptitiously, she tried to find the handle. "You're not going anywhere," Uncles Miles said as he started the truck. "You hear me?" He looked straight ahead through the windshield splattered with dead insects. When Lily failed to answer him, he slapped the seat between them, making dust rise. "Hear me? I said 'NOWHERE.' "

"Yes," Lily said, her voice small.

"Sir!"

"Sir," she squeaked.

"Or else!"

"Or else," Lily confirmed.

On the way back to the house, Uncle Miles took a detour. "Got something to show you," he said as if he were giving her a gift. He drove until they reached a neighborhood of homes with big, welcoming front porches and shadowy green lawns. Uncle Miles slowed the truck, looking at house numbers. Finally, he stopped in front of a pale gray, two-story house with elaborate white trim. He let the engine idle and pointed.

"See that one?"

Lily nodded. It had broad flower beds with lilies, roses, and Mama's favorite — peonies.

"That's where he lives. The man who killed your family."

Lily stared at the contrasting charcoal-gray front door with its inset diamond panes of leaded glass. She saw a lush fern hanging from the porch ceiling and two white wicker chairs angled toward each other, as if they were friends. Everything she saw from the window of Uncle Miles' truck only deepened her curiosity about the man who'd collided with Lily's family on that June night when dry lightning raked the horizon.

"You listening? I'm telling you that a murderer lives in that fancy house. These air force pilots think they can come to our town and lord it over the rest of us. You just remember," Uncle Miles said as he took the truck out of neutral and slowly pulled away from the curb, "when you hear those sonic booms it's probably that aviator, flying over you. The man who killed your family."

Lily looked back at the Aviator's house for as long as she could. She wanted for him to come out of the front door, to see her. She wanted to sit on his front steps and ask him things like *Why?* and *How come?* She wanted to beg *Save me.*

She had few memories of the night that broke her life into *Before* and *After.* She remembered that her allergies had been so severe that her nose bled, and so Mama made Lily lie down in the backseat, wrapped in a blanket patterned with stars and moons.

As Lily drifted off to sleep, she watched Dawn stand, reach over the front seat, and begin to braid their mother's hair.

Lily remembered waking up on the side of the road, curled into the arms of a stranger and seeing the Aviator standing near his car — the one with taillights set in wildly exaggerated fins that looked like some beast's red, wicked eyes. She remembered her family's motionless car, sparks of insects flashing in the headlight beams. Redwing blackbirds rising from fields of summer wheat, panicked by the commotion. The hiss of whitewall tires as they sighed last breaths; a violent whoosh of steam erupting from the radiator.

The Aviator had knelt beside Lily, holding a handkerchief to the top of his head. A thick shock of black hair hid his eyes. Lines of blood painted the contours of his face and ran into his mouth.

"What have you got there?" he had asked Lily — just as if he'd met her on the street outside Hutchinson's Ice Cream Store in downtown Salina.

Lily handed him her bouquet of four crayons, the ones she'd held on to, tight, when the stranger lifted her from the car's wreckage. "These ones are my favorites," she said. Periwinkle, Carnation Pink, Cornflower, and Pine Green.

Mostly, Lily remembered that the Aviator hadn't felt like a bad man. He felt like a sad one.

There were intermittent pools of rainwater relief, times when Lily smiled. Those times came when the parcels arrived in the mail, wrapped in brown paper, tied with twine, and addressed in bold black ink to *Miss Lily Decker.* The first was Gene Stratton-Porter's *Freckles.* It was an old book from 1904, with a battered cover and fine engravings of trees, cattails, birds, and clouds. Before beginning the novel, Lily hoisted herself onto the kitchen counter and sneaked exactly ten saltines from Aunt Tate's larder. Then, she propped herself up on her bed with the book, eating the saltines as slowly as possible. As she sucked the salt from each cracker, she knew she was just like Freckles — crippled and unlovable. Still, she felt a little less lonely.

The mysterious books smelled of time, somehow held the breath of another reader, someone before Lily. The secrecy surrounding the identity of the book-giver made Lily feel special, somehow deserving. The books also let her travel far from the relentless flatlands of her life with Uncle Miles and

Aunt Tate.

Pragmatic Aunt Tate didn't abide mysteries, but if she wondered about the books' origins, she never said anything to Lily. Aunt Tate dealt with the tangible world, the only exceptions being Jesus, the disciples, and the New Testament miracles. As for Lily, she thought the books might be from her elementary school librarian, who'd often commented on Lily's avaricious appetite for books about pioneer girls who were held captive by Indians, or the wildly vengeful myths of the Greeks and Romans. In a way, it didn't matter who sent the books, as long as whoever it was kept sending them.

It took some convincing, but finally Aunt Tate agreed to let Lily sleep over at Beverly Ann's. The girls had been friends forever. They traded Cherry Ames books, shared after-school snacks of apple slices loaded with peanut butter, and played Chinese jump rope.

"We've missed you, sweetheart," Beverly Ann's mother said, kissing Lily good night and promising that they'd have French toast in the morning.

When Mrs. McPherson pulled the door nearly closed so that only a thin pillar of light shone from the hallway, Lily felt a sudden moment of panic. She audibly sucked in her breath as a fleeting image of Uncle Miles' probing hands crossed her mind. The image was there, *he* was there, even though she knew that at least for tonight she wouldn't have to fear the drop of his weight on the bed like a gunnysack of river rocks.

"What's wrong?" Beverly Ann asked, her voice sleepy.

Lily thought about telling. She could tell Beverly Ann about what happened in her bedroom, when the only noises in the house were crickets and the hum of the refrigerator. Sometimes the furnace clicking off or on. And Uncle Miles' breath, his *huh-huh-huh* that got faster and faster.

But she couldn't tell. It would make her sick to tell. Sicker to tell than not to tell. Beverly Ann would know how disgusting Lily was, and Lily would lose her best friend. And if she did tell, then what would happen? She had nowhere else to go.

"Nothing," she said, finally, but Beverly Ann had already fallen asleep. Lily listened to her friend's deep, regular breathing, the breathing of a girl who could trust, even in the dark. Lily felt her own eyes fluttering closed as she nestled in sheets that smelled of a sun-kissed clothesline.

The next morning, Lily came home from

Beverly Ann's begging for a pogo stick, but Aunt Tate said it was "too dear," and Lily nearly stomped her feet. Beverly Ann got to have *everything*! Lily's friend's life was a constant reminder of all that Lily had lost, and sometimes — like this time — Lily felt her cheeks flame hot with jealousy and anger.

But a few weeks after the sleepover at Beverly Ann's, Uncle Miles beckoned a hesitant Lily to join him in the backyard beside his workshop. In his hands, he held a pair of homemade stilts.

"I sanded the handles real good so you won't get splinters," he said, turning the stilts so that Lily could admire his workmanship. "And I know these aren't the same as a pogo stick, but you can learn to do tricks on them. Here," he said, motioning to Lily to come closer. "I'll help you get up on them. You'll learn fast cuz you're real coordinated."

He was right; it took Lily no time to learn how to walk steadily, and soon enough she could balance on one stilt and even hop on a single wooden pole while holding the other one in the air. She sang songs and made up dances she could do balanced high on the stilts.

"I still think they're dangerous," Aunt Tate

said after one of Lily's stunt shows, performed just before dinner.

"Lord, Tate. Let the girl have some fun," Uncle Miles had said and then winked at Lily, which made her nervous, not a happy co-conspirator. Lily became convinced that Uncle Miles wanted something in exchange, that he was incapable of a simple kindness. Eventually, that persistent knock of fear led Lily to abandon the stilts next to the woodpile, against the back fence where the squirrels lived.

Maybe Uncle Miles loved Aunt Tate. Lily didn't know. He did love his raspberries — all forty-eight bushes, lined up in rows like soldiers on parade. He inspected them for infestations, dusted them with a white powder that poisoned any bugs bold enough to alight on the sharp leaves. He fertilized. He shooed away sparrows who dared to feast on the ripe fruit. When frost was predicted, he used old pillowcases to shroud the bushes so that they stood like an eerie battalion of child-sized ghosts.

They weren't pretty plants, not like the boldly bright dahlias that had filled Mama's flower beds. They were thorny creatures that protected themselves by being nondescript, unwelcoming. But when the fruit came —

the faceted gemstone berries with their lush lobes, the juice running down Lily's chin — it was heavenly. Aunt Tate would ladle the berries over vanilla ice cream, and they'd sit out back, watching the soft evening descend. It was a puzzle Lily couldn't solve — the fact that something delicious came from her uncle's devotion.

3

Lily's fourth-grade school portrait showed a tall, gangly ten-year-old with a long neck and indentations at her temples as if someone had pressed his palms to the sides of her skull and squeezed until the bone succumbed. The generous spread of her cheekbones gave her a clear, open gaze. Her indigo blue eyes were large, her child's lips surprisingly luscious, and she faced the camera without flinching. If Lily had held a numbered placard in her hands, the school photo almost would have passed for a mug shot.

It had been nearly two years since the accident, and from time to time, she saw the Aviator around town. Lily liked to imagine that he was watching her, a presence like God or Jesus or Zeus or Santa Claus. Someone who knew her secrets but wouldn't tell. He was a potent mystery — not an enemy, not quite a friend. Just there.

She discovered, finally, that it was the Aviator who was sending her the old books. When *How They Carried the Mail* arrived, it had the Aviator's name in it, written elegantly in what Lily's teacher called copperplate calligraphy. His name was Stirling Sloan, and he had once been a boy living on Magnolia Street in Dormont, Pennsylvania.

Holding the books from the Aviator's childhood, turning the pages of his memories, Lily sent her mind to the places where his mind had been. She dogged his steps. And although she thought Stirling was a nice name, to Lily he remained always and forever the Aviator.

Mostly, it was curiosity that led her on a warm, late-April day to pedal all the way over to the Aviator's street, put down her kickstand, and leave her bicycle tilted on the sidewalk that bordered his front lawn. She'd dressed up for him, pulling her hair back on the sides with a pair of pink butterfly barrettes, and she wore her best smocked cotton dress — the yellow one with a big sash she'd tied in back all by herself. Still, she was feeling less bold, now that she was actually at his house. Lily used the rubber toe of her Red Ball Jets tennis shoe to kick at a tuft of crabgrass that grew up through the sidewalk crack like a patch of unruly hair.

If she continued to linger out front, Lily realized, one of his nosy neighbors might come out and ask her questions she didn't want to answer. Lily took a deep breath, marched up the front steps, and pressed the doorbell.

Nothing happened. She wasn't sure how long she should wait. Feeling a nervous queasiness begin to slosh about in her stomach, she pushed the buzzer again. Again nothing. She saw the Aviator's mail stuffed into his mailbox and realized he must still be at work. Maybe he was busy flying one of the jet-propelled B-47 bombers, part of the country's Strategic Air Command they'd learned about at school.

Slowly, Lily descended the front porch. She hadn't gotten what she wanted — an audience with the Aviator — and she couldn't leave. Not yet. Maybe she'd just circle around back. Maybe she could wait there until he came home.

As Lily rounded the house, she could smell something overripe, on the edge of decay. Her tennis shoes slid on rotting apricots that had dropped from the neighbor's tree. Lily picked up a piece of the fruit, brought it to her nose and grimaced.

There were speckles of fruit flies all over the mushy flesh, and she dropped it quickly. She wiped her sticky fingers on some long, wet grass and then dried them on her dress.

Boldly, Lily climbed the Aviator's back steps and sat on his porch swing. She pushed off with her feet and could hear the groan of the bolts that held it aloft.

He was taking forever to come home, and Lily wished she'd brought along *Jane Eyre* or *A Girl of the Limberlost.* She twiddled her thumbs for a while, and then she tried whistling. It came out slender, ineffectual. She wanted to learn to whistle so loudly that hordes of dogs from all over town would come running to her. She wanted to be able to whistle a tune when Dinah Shore came on the television and sang "Shoo-Fly Pie and Apple Pan Dowdy."

"Lily?"

She hadn't heard his car. The Aviator pushed open the screen door and came out onto the porch. Lily stood guiltily.

"What are you doing here? Lily, does your aunt know you're here?"

He'd said her name, twice. He did know her. She was so full of emotion that she was having trouble finding her voice.

"Sit down a minute," the Aviator said, gently taking her arm and leading her back to the porch swing. "How did you know where to find me?"

"Uncle Miles showed me."

"That's your bike out front?"

"Yes."

"But, Lily — do they know you're here? They can't possibly know you're here."

Lily shook her head.

"Oh, this is a bad idea," he said. "You can't be here. I'm so sorry. You just can't be here."

"But I came to ask you," she said before he could make her leave unsatisfied. "I have to ask you something." Lily clenched her fists in the way her mother had always said proved *just how stubborn you can be, Scallywag.* She was determined not to leave without asking him.

The Aviator took a deep breath. He was a handsome man with an omnipresent five-o'clock shadow, a nose so straight it looked as if it had been drawn with a ruler, and bruised-looking blue eyes. He sat with a ramrod-straight back, and he was wearing a military green flight suit that zipped up the front. On one sleeve was an embroidered patch picturing an armored fist that clasped an olive branch and three bright red lightning bolts.

"You may have three questions," he said at last.

"Like three wishes with a genie?"

"Yes. And then you go home." She could see he was afraid of her questions, but still he said, "Go ahead. Ask me."

"My school is having a dance. Fathers bring their daughters." She opened her hands, wiped her sweaty palms on the skirt of her dress. "I get to dress up and everything. And I wanted for you to take me."

She'd been so happy when she'd concocted this plan to avoid humiliation. The other girls would be so jealous — even Beverly Ann. Lily would dance with a handsome pilot, handsomer even than the men on *The Dinah Shore Show,* and the fact that she had no father to take her would be completely overshadowed by the splendor of the Aviator.

The Aviator's face went from one expression to another in an instant — as if clouds were first blotting out the sun and then letting it shine full force. She saw him pained and surprised and then frustrated. Maybe even angry, which scared her a little.

"I wish I could," he said at last. "But I can't."

"Why not?" Lily stood and faced him.

The Aviator bit his lip, and for a minute

Lily thought they both would cry. She felt violent and crazed disappointment thrashing about in her chest.

"Please," she begged.

The Aviator stood quickly and pulled her into a hug. She pressed her face into the dark solidity of him, felt the zipper of his jumpsuit chafe her cheek.

"They would never let me," he said, still holding her.

"Because they hate you," she said, raising her face to look up at him.

"That's right."

"But wasn't it an accident? Like when I spill the milk? Or when I trip and fall?"

He put his hand on the top of her head, as if blessing her. "I wish it were that simple," he said.

"You didn't mean to kill them, did you?"

The Aviator released her. "Come sit back down for a minute. Are you thirsty? Do you want a glass of water?"

Lily shook her head. What she wanted was answers.

"Okay. Well . . ." The Aviator rubbed his jaw with his knuckles. Lily thought she could hear the rasp of his beard's stubble. "I was driving fast. Too fast. I do that sometimes — go out on the highway and fly along the asphalt, blow off steam. And I didn't see them — you. There was a dip in the road, and I hit your car. I'd take it all back. I can't —" His voice broke.

"If you really were a murdering bastard, you'd be in jail. That's what I think."

"Bastard?" She saw a fleeting smile cross the Aviator's face. "Lily." He shook his head.

She wouldn't apologize for quoting Uncle Miles. "But you're not in jail," she repeated. "So it wasn't on purpose."

"I'm not in jail because it was an accident. But that doesn't mean that I'm not sorry each and every day."

They sat in silence until the Aviator said, "Lily, I'm so sorry I can't take you to the dance. I would be honored, really and truly. Nothing would make me happier. But I can't. It just won't work, for reasons I can't explain to your satisfaction."

"I just wanted. I just wished."

"I know," he said, taking her hand in his. "But I will always do what I can. I am your friend, forever. And let me make you a promise, all right?" Lily looked up at him. "I will find a way to make it up to you. For the dance, I mean," he said and then released her hand. He made an X across his heart with his index finger. "I promise."

"I love the books you send me," she said and smiled in a way she hoped would convey how much they meant to her. Then Lily took a deep, resigned breath. "Okay," she said, grudgingly agreeing to his promise. "But don't wait too long!"

He smiled and stood. "You're a pretty good bargainer, you know that? But now you need to get home before it starts to get dark. Promise me you'll be safe?"

"Umm hmm," Lily said and instead of using the steps hopped off the side of the porch to show him how agile she was.

"You could come through the house," he told her, but she'd already started to round the corner. The Aviator followed her out front, and Lily felt him watch her climb on her bicycle and ride away.

Lily pedaled as fast as she could — not to rush back, but just to feel the wind blow her clean. She decided she wouldn't tell her aunt about the dance. She just wouldn't go. Lily knew no one would have the nerve to ask why the fatherless girl had chosen not to attend.

And maybe in the Aviator's promise she had something even better than a stupid old dance with a bunch of stupid old girls and their stupid old clumsy fathers. Lily believed the Aviator would come through for her. It felt glorious once more to believe in someone.

4

Aunt Tate said, "HOW COULD YOU?" and roughly flipped Lily over on her bed where she'd been reading the Aviator's latest gift, *Beautiful Joe.* Aunt Tate held Lily by the arm and struck her with the gut-flecked flyswatter. "That was my mother's pitcher! My mother's! You!" — *whack* — "ungrateful" — *whack* — "child!" *Whack.* "After all I've done for you!" *Whack whack whack!*

Lily had no idea what Aunt Tate was talking about. "I didn't do anything!" Lily protested. "Aunt Tate, I didn't do anything!"

"Don't add the sin of lying." Aunt Tate let go of Lily's arm and gave Lily's backside one more good *whack.* "No supper. Why I took you in is beyond me." Aunt Tate slammed, opened, slammed the door several times. *Bang!*

Lily stayed still, as if she were playing freeze tag at school. She sucked in her cheeks and bit down, wondering if she could bite hard enough to tear out the sides of her mouth, chew and swallow the flesh. Her body burned in all the places where the flyswatter had landed. Lily remained there, perfectly still, breathing scant breaths. She fought back tears, ever mindful of her vow to keep control.

Later, when it was nearly dark and Lily was wondering if it might be safe to go pee, Aunt Tate came and stood beside Lily's bed. "Uncle Miles told me."

What? Lily panicked. What exactly had Uncle Miles said?

"He knocked the pitcher off of the mantel when he was looking for his matches. He told me you didn't do it."

Lily didn't understand why Aunt Tate automatically believed such awful things about her. What was it about her that led Aunt Tate to assume the worst about Lily? Lily had never been a liar. Why didn't Aunt Tate believe her?

Aunt Tate crossed her arms and held them against her middle as if she were suddenly cold, or maybe trying to hold something in or even protect herself; as if Lily might stand up and try to punch her in the stomach like they did sometimes on *Roy Rogers* when there was a fight in a saloon and cowboys smashed each other over the head with wooden chairs.

"I made a mistake," Aunt Tate confessed. "I jumped to the wrong conclusion."

Lily thought about the Aviator's *Beautiful Joe* and how Joe's cruel master cut off his ears and hurt him even though Joe was a kind and loyal dog. A good dog. Then Joe got rescued and lived in a good home where people loved and understood him. Beautiful Joe's life was the opposite of Lily's. But why? What was wrong with her? What had she done? What could she do differently so that Aunt Tate wouldn't call her *"The cross I have to bear"*?

"Aunt Tate?" Lily dared.

Her aunt tightened her arms about her middle. "What is it?" she said, not unkindly.

"Why can't you love me?"

"Honey." Aunt Tate took a step toward Lily but stopped herself. "It's because I love you that I'm hard on you. If I didn't care, I wouldn't bother."

Even though Aunt Tate had half-buried "love" in that brief statement, she had at least admitted it. Still, it didn't feel like love to Lily. There were no soft, rounded edges to Aunt Tate's love. It was uneasy, all spiky and fearful, like the sea urchin Tom Bradstone had brought back from his vacation in California.

"I know I'm not very patient with you." Aunt Tate sighed. "To be honest, Lily, I don't have much experience with children. Just watching over your mother when she was a young brat." Aunt Tate nearly smiled. "But now come have a sandwich, and then we'll get you ready for bed." She extended a conciliatory hand.

"Can I have tuna fish?"

"You *may* have grilled cheese."

"Oh, with Velveeta." Lily sighed with pleasure. Her aunt's hand in hers was neither warm nor cold. It was like dry newspaper, and Lily almost thought she could hear her aunt's skin crinkle when she squeezed it.

That night, Lily dreamed that she was sitting at the top of the playground slide, looking down the length of it. The polished metal chute went on for miles — down, down, and down to an abrupt end where children dropped off into some kind of a crack in the earth. Someone was behind her, prodding her to release her handhold and let gravity take her. She felt the insistent push of a hand. *Tap. Tap. TAP!*

Lily awoke to the deepest part of the night. Half asleep, she swatted at something wet that was touching her under her bunched-up nightie.

Uncle Miles clenched her wrist like a slave's clevis and held it immobile until he finished. After he was gone, Lily fed her pillowcase into her mouth, bit down, and swallowed her cries so that they filled her stomach like sharp gravel.

When she came home from school the next day, there was an entire box of cherry suckers on the nightstand beside her bed. The kind with the looped rope handles she liked best.

"Go ahead and have one," Aunt Tate said from the doorway. "But just one, or you'll spoil your supper."

Lily stalled, looking uncertainly at her aunt. A part of her was afraid the candy was from Uncle Miles.

"Adults make mistakes, too," Aunt Tate said. "I made a mistake yesterday, when I blamed you. I'm sorry for that."

"It's okay," Lily said because she could see how badly Aunt Tate needed to hear it.

"And, I've made your favorite chicken and dumplings for dinner. Wash up and then come help me with the snap beans. It's about time I taught you to cook."

While Lily sat on the kitchen stool and broke the crisp beans into pieces in a big white mixing bowl, Aunt Tate told Lily stories from when Mama and Aunt Tate were girls. She even showed Lily a little sickle-shaped scar on the back of her left hand where Mama had used a willow whip to attack her big sister. "We didn't always get along," Aunt Tate said. "But I always loved your mama. I just want for you to remember that she was a real person, with real faults. We always put the dead on a pedestal, but they were real humans, just like us. They made mistakes, just like us."

Lily had just finished setting the table when Uncle Miles came through the kitchen door carrying a teeny-tiny guitar under his arm. Lily couldn't help but hope it was a gift for her, a reward for keeping their secret.

"Oh no! You didn't!" Aunt Tate said, laughing. "Oh, this is just plain funny!"

Lily had never before seen her aunt get the giggles. Aunt Tate used the hem of her apron to wipe the tears from the corners of her eyes. "You don't have a musical bone in your body, old man. What on earth possessed you?" To Lily, she said, "Don't forget the bread."

Lily opened the bread box and stacked six slices of Wonder Bread on a plate. She twirled the plastic bag closed and used Aunt Tate's wooden clothespin to reseal it. From the corner of her eye, she watched as Uncle

Miles set the child-sized guitar on the chair next to the prayer shawl Aunt Tate was knitting. He rolled up his sleeves before washing his hands.

"Got it at Pawn City," he said, lathering his hands. "Dirt cheap." He was clearly more than a little pleased with himself.

"It shoulda been free," Aunt Tate said, carefully ladling the chicken and dumplings into a deep white tureen. "No one in their right mind would buy that. A ukulele, Miles?"

"This is a ukulele?" Lily asked, gingerly plucking a string on the instrument.

"It's *Hawaiian.*" Uncle Miles pushed Lily's hand away. "And it's not a plaything."

"You can't even read music." Aunt Tate sat down and scooted her chair in. "Here," she said, handing him the tureen. "And what were you doing at the pawnshop?"

"Stopped in on my way home. Just lookin'." Uncle Miles gave himself a generous helping of chicken and dumplings.

"Talk about money down the drain." Aunt Tate shook her head.

Lily found it strange that any part of her could feel sorry for Uncle Miles. And to realize that it was Aunt Tate who held the upper hand, not her uncle.

"You'll see," he said. "And you'll be begging me to serenade you." Uncle Miles laid aside his knife and fork, floated one hand in the air, and began singing a Patsy Cline song.

His voice was awful, and Lily couldn't help it — she laughed into her hand and looked across the table at her aunt, who stuck her fingers in her ears, rolled her eyes, and smiled right back at Lily.

Aunt Tate had been wrong about Lily being able to leave her sorrow behind in the house that used to be home. Sorrow was not so easily fooled; it stuck to the soles of Lily's feet and dogged her every step. It was an undercurrent to every breath.

Lily stood on the sidewalk in front of Aunt Tate's American Beauty rosebush. Making sure that the coast was clear, she dropped down on all fours and began dragging her right knee along the rough pavement, shredding the skin. It burned, but she kept going, checked the raw skin often, and only stopped when she was certain that the wound was serious enough to merit Aunt Tate's attention. The blood ran down Lily's leg, into the top of her knee sock. Straightening her cotton twill dress, Lily picked up her schoolbooks and went inside.

Aunt Tate said, *"You need to be more care-*

ful," as she painted Lily's knee with the bright red Mercurochrome that Dawn had called *monkey's blood.* When Aunt Tate softly placed a square of gauze over the skinned knee, when she used the fingernail scissors to cut strips of white adhesive tape and was careful not to hurt Lily as she pressed the tape to Lily's leg, Lily felt cared for, reassured. As if she mattered.

Lily created other injuries. She "fell" off of a curb and for good measure bravely struck her ankle three times with the heaviest rock she could find. She knocked her forehead against a doorknob. She burst her lower lip and gave herself a black eye on a rung of the playground ladder. Yet, it wasn't until Aunt Tate taught Lily how to use a razor blade to scrape hard-water stains from windowpanes that Lily realized she could turn the blade on herself, at last finding blissful release.

Lily's teacher announced that there was a special, last-day-of-school assembly. Along with her fourth-grade classmates, Lily sat on the polished gymnasium floor and then looked up to see the Aviator standing at the podium. He wore his navy blue dress uniform with the gold wings and rows of medals and ribbons, and in his hand was his uniform cap.

"I'm here today as the special guest of Lily Decker," he said. "Lily, please stand and let your schoolmates thank you for making this happen."

Basking in the glory, Lily stood, thinking her mouth could not stretch widely enough. All the kids who'd pointedly skirted around the girl of contagious calamity now cheered loudly.

The Aviator spoke about flying bombers over Europe during the war, of the new aircraft he was testing high above the plains of Kansas and the entire Midwest, and he cited facts and figures about the speed of the planes, what he saw when he catapulted beyond the clouds. The boys shouted questions about how many enemy cities he'd destroyed, and the girls — who were for the most part absurdly shy — asked questions about whether people on the ground really looked like ants, if the Aviator could see into windows and know what families were having for dinner.

When it was all over, the Aviator asked Lily to come up and stand beside him. She made sure her bobby socks weren't drooping and smoothed her green-and-blue plaid dress as she walked to the front of the gymnasium. The Aviator held a small corsage with two white roses and some airy greenery.

"This is for my good friend Lily," he announced as he pinned the corsage to the collar of her dress. Lily's heart soared — high, into the stratosphere, venturing far beyond any altitude even the Aviator had ever sought.

Aunt Tate said Lily could go look at the elephants, but she had to be back in ten minutes. Lily hopped down the bleachers, holding her paper bag of popcorn against her chest so that she wouldn't spill any. She could hardly wait for the show to begin, because there would be trapeze artists in sparkly costumes and maybe those girls in leotards who twirled on ropes.

Lily made her way past the man selling chameleons tethered on lengths of red thread, and then she stood in the straw in front of the elephants. She decided she liked the one named Bruno best. Lily wanted to run her hand across the terrain of his gray skin, to smooth away his wrinkles and try to make his eyes look less sad. Other kids were holding out fistfuls of peanuts, but Bruno ignored them all. He turned his head and stared morosely at the red-and-white wall of the canvas tent.

"How are you, Miss Lily?"

It was the Aviator, standing at Lily's elbow. He wore a ball cap and a forest-green T-shirt, and Lily saw half circles of sweat beneath his arms. July's heat was upon them. Soon enough, there would be days in a row of 100-degree temperatures that left everyone in Salina wet and wilting.

Lily grinned. "Hi," she managed and then offered the Aviator some of her popcorn. He accepted a few kernels.

"Are you shy today?" he asked. Lily nodded, and he continued. "Well then, how about I ask you questions? All right? Let's see," he said, putting his finger to the center of his chin and pretending to be deep in thought. Lily giggled. "Tell me what you like to do. What's your ten-and-a-half-year-old heart's favorite pastime?"

Lily was thrilled that he knew enough to add that half year to her age, but she wasn't used to being asked what she liked. She was used to doing what she was told or suffering the hairbrush — Uncle Miles' favorite form of punishment, one he reserved for offenses like sassing back or stealing nutty chocolates from the box next to his ugly brown turd of a recliner.

"I like to dance," Lily said, and then feeling braver, she handed him her bag of popcorn, wiped her hands on her purple shorts, and stepped back from the elephant enclosure. Lily showed the Aviator some of the steps she'd copied from Dinah Shore's show. She pointed her toes, held her breath, and performed a passable pirouette.

"What's your favorite kind of dance?" he asked.

"All kinds. Any kind," she said. "I love the June Taylor Dancers. I've seen them on *The Ed Sullivan Show.*"

"They're pretty good," he said, munching on a few more pieces of her popcorn.

"They kick like this." She turned sideways, kicked as high as she could, kept her balance. "And when they make those patterns, like a kaleidoscope — I love that. They're magic. Oh," she added, "and the outfits. Sequins and feathers. Headdresses!" Lily could hear how fast the words were coming out of her mouth.

"So, dancing makes you happy."

"More than that," Lily said, looking up at him. "When I dance — when I dance, nothing else matters. Everything else disappears. There is only dancing." That was it. Dancing took her to another world, a world that Uncle Miles could not reach. A world where her lost family was a faint shadow, not an omnipresent, weeping wound. When Lily danced, she was not a misfit. She belonged.

But she couldn't bring herself to say all of this to the Aviator. Instead, she simply said, "I feel happy when I dance. Free."

"All right then," he said, just as the band began playing an upbeat song. Lily was torn — she had to get back to her aunt, but she wished she could ask him to come sit beside her.

"Here." He handed her the popcorn. "You can't miss the show." He held out his hand, and she took it. "I was very glad to see you, Lily Decker. Now, you go have fun, and later you can tell me what you think of pink and green and blue and yellow trained poodles, all right?"

Lily laughed. There couldn't possibly be such a thing. The Aviator was funny.

"I'm not kidding," he said, touching the brim of his ball cap in a mock salute. "They dance, too, but not as well as you! Now, promise me you'll have a good rest of the summer, all right?"

"I will!" Lily skipped a few steps toward the bleachers and then turned to wave to him one more time. She watched him cross the parking lot, stand beside his tuxedo-black Corvette, and light a cigarette.

A week later, Lily received a card in the mail that said she'd been given a *Tah-Dah!*

Dance Studio scholarship, along with a stipend to pay for a leotard, tights, and appropriate dance shoes. It was signed "Your Secret Benefactor." Aunt Tate said, "Someone has money to burn" but otherwise manifested no curiosity. And so after school Lily rode her faded red bicycle to the studio. It gave her two days a week when she was out of the house, free from chores and the lead-weight sensation of knowing Uncle Miles was due to come through the kitchen door, smelling of oil and diesel and sweat.

Uncle Miles said, "Tonight we experiment."

September's full moon through the window made everything silvery bright, lit the edges of things, made silhouettes of her desk lamp and her bureau with her ballerina jewelry box. Lily jammed the ends of her fingers into her mouth, bit down to keep quiet. She squeezed her eyes shut, tight. Warm tears eased their way from the corners of her eyes, ran into her hair, and wet her pillowcase.

Uncle Miles put his mouth to the center of her. He was moaning, which made a buzzing bee vibration that journeyed from his throat, his lips, to her core. And then she felt the growing heat of her own flesh in response. She fought against it but couldn't help it. "Oh!" she cried, a surprised baby-bird voice. "Oh, oh, oh!" He held her pelvis as if it were a bowl.

She thought that she might explode, that she was descending, plummeting, and it was release and good and hot and out of her control and sick and bad a disease and the worst thing ever that Uncle Miles had done but it felt good. It felt good. It felt good. Oh, *no* — it felt good. How could her body betray her?

"You like it." His whisper left a hot brand of accusation against the side of her neck.

Once he was gone, she told herself that tonight was the exception to the rule. Tonight, it was okay to cry. With her face pressed into the wet pillow to muffle the sound of her confusion, Lily cried her shame. Her need. She cried a poisonous blend of gratification and disgust, of wonderment that Uncle Miles had given her pleasure, which was more frightening than any of the painful, awful things he'd done in the past. She cried her rupture, her irreparable breakage.

5

The light from the gooseneck lamp on top of the church organ turned Mrs. Olson's face cadaver white as she played "O God of Mercy, God of Might." Seated next to Aunt Tate in the unforgiving wooden pew, twelve-year-old Lily wrapped her arms around her gut, which had harbored a deep, persistent ache since before the second hymn. Finally, Pastor Lester intoned the benediction and released the sanctified congregation.

Lily immediately headed downstairs to the church bathroom, which wasn't much more than a stingy coat closet. When she looked at the crotch of her panties, she saw blood. *Oh no oh no oh no oh no.* A string of dark, thick blood dripped from inside her, and there was more blood in the toilet bowl.

Was this God's doing? Was this one of the things that the all-powerful, vengeful God did to punish bad girls? She knew that what she did with Uncle Miles was evil, and God did seem so very fond of bloody atonement. Lily wadded toilet paper into her panties and then sat uncomfortably through her sixth-grade Sunday school lesson.

Aunt Tate was waiting in the car when Lily finished class. "What did you learn today?" she asked, waving to some of her Bible-study friends like Margaret Steepleton, who kept a handkerchief tucked between her bulwark breasts and blew her nose loudly at least seventeen thousand times during the pastor's tedious sermon.

"The story of the prodigal son," Lily dutifully reported. Then she took a deep breath, steeling herself to tell Aunt Tate about the blood and possible impending doom. "Aunt Tate? I'm bleeding."

Aunt Tate turned to look at Lily. "Where? Did you fall?"

"No." It was hard, but Lily knew she needed help, that something was horribly wrong. "Down there," Lily whispered, looking out the windshield and across the street to the Texaco station, thinking about the smell of gasoline, the way oil puddles on the asphalt formed galaxies of rainbows. "It hurts," she said, still avoiding her aunt's stare and holding a hand to the ache in her belly.

"Between your legs."

"Yes."

Aunt Tate closed her eyes and leaned forward until her forehead rested on the steering wheel.

So, it was true. Lily was going to die. Or at least she was very sick, and there would be hospital bills. She'd *bankrupt them.* They would be roaming the streets, *penniless.*

Margaret Steepleton knocked on Aunt Tate's window. "Tate, honey? You all right?"

Aunt Tate rolled down her window. "She's got the curse," she said, tipping her head in Lily's direction. "First time."

Mrs. Steepleton leaned in the window and beamed across the seat at Lily, "Congratulations, sweetheart! Now you're a woman!"

The curse? Since the accident, Lily had always known she was cursed. But was it a curse simply to be a woman?

"Lord, help me." Aunt Tate sighed as Margaret Steepleton trundled off to join her husband and two boys. Her aunt's voice was flat and unyielding, like the iron skillet that wouldn't fit in the cupboard and so sat on the stove's back burner, black, heavy, and inert.

They stopped at the drugstore on the way home, and Aunt Tate bought Lily a sanitary belt and a big box of napkins with a picture of a dreamy woman strolling through meadows of flowers. She showed Lily how to wear the belt low on her hips and had Lily practice attaching the napkin tabs snugly to the belt's metal fittings.

"You're growing up so fast. A young woman, nearly," Aunt Tate said wistfully. "So much ahead of you," she summed up.

"Does the aching go away?" Lily asked, and for a moment she saw confusion on her aunt's face.

"Oh, the belly pain, you mean. Let's get the hot water bottle." Aunt Tate helped Lily lie down with the soothing heat of the pig-pink water bottle planted squarely over her belly, and they split a special Almond Joy candy bar Aunt Tate called "medicinal under the circumstances."

Lily fell asleep wondering about the connection between blood and womanhood. She hadn't been able to make herself ask Aunt Tate *why* she was bleeding, if it had a purpose, other than inconvenience and ignominy. Was it something to do with God's unending wrath toward Eve, the curse Aunt Tate talked about? Was that why only women harbored secret, open wounds?

On Saturdays Lily swept and dusted. She got down on her hands and knees and scrubbed the kitchen's green and white linoleum. In the bathroom, she held her breath and washed away the yellow splashes of urine Uncle Miles left on the porcelain toilet bowl.

Alongside Aunt Tate, she learned how to make stew and soups, chipped beef on toast, casseroles, and hash from leftover pot roast. She mastered pastry, crimping a perfect blanket of crust over apples, cherries, or peaches. Aunt Tate taught her to fold laundry properly, how to iron simple things like sheets, pillowcases, and dresser scarves. When Lily conquered the straightforward items, she moved on to more difficult things like Uncle Miles' work shirts and Aunt Tate's cotton blouses.

One afternoon, Lily opened the linen cupboard and shifted a pile of sheets to make room for her fresh ironing. Beneath the sheets, she found a cardboard folder that held a portrait of her parents. Her mother wore a light gray suit with a big chrysanthemum corsage, and her father had his arm about her mother's shoulders, an unmistakable flash of joy in his eyes that Lily thought she remembered, even if she could no longer hear his voice.

There was a newspaper clipping folded inside, and Lily read the article from the *Salina Journal* dated June 10, 1957, four years ago. It featured a picture of her family's car, mangled and topless. Another picture showed the Aviator's brand-new, black 1957 Chrysler 300-C, which the caption said was a *production-line muscle car with enough power to reach one hundred miles per hour in second gear.* At the time of the accident, the Aviator was traveling an estimated 130 miles per hour.

Lily saw *decapitated* and *ten-year-old Dawn Marie Decker thrown from the car* and *the miracle of Lily Francine Decker's survival.* Sheriff Ingram was described as having hot tears in his eyes when he said that no one would ever know why the Buick had been traveling on the wrong side of the road. "Could be the Deckers swerved to avoid hitting a coyote," he'd said. "Maybe a raccoon or a skunk. But it'll be a mystery, always." Ingram said the thirty-seven-year-old Aviator would not be cited, although he'd been cautioned to watch his speed. "No one to blame," the sheriff concluded.

Decapitated. Lily felt the word as a sharp, unexpected blow to her solar plexus. She hadn't known. They'd kept it from her — the gruesome death of her parents. And the Aviator hadn't told her the truth, not the whole truth. The Aviator had let her believe that the accident was his fault, but Lily's father had been driving on the wrong side of the road.

Lily tucked the clipping and portrait back beneath the sheets and closed the cupboard door. She put it all back where it was supposed to be, buried and hidden away.

* * *

She licked her fingers and touched herself the way Uncle Miles had taught her. She wet her fingers in her mouth once more and sent them back as quickly as possible, not wanting to lose the sensation she was building, a skyscraper of guilty pleasure and release. She needed to keep the pressure steady and so had the idea to wedge the satiny edge of her blanket between her legs. She squeezed with her thighs, tightened, released and tightened her muscles until it arrived — that sensation of heat and freedom.

After Lily was done, she swore she would never do it again. She would stop. No one had told her it was a sin or bad or sick, but she knew it was. If it had to do with Uncle Miles, it was bad. The knowledge of her perversity was solid.

Lily didn't understand any of it — not the irresistible impulse to engage or any reason behind the pleasure. It was a disgusting need that Uncle Miles had ignited within her. Surely other girls didn't feel this way, know these things, do these things. Her very core was diseased.

"I've been looking forward to this all day," he said one summer night when Lily felt a soft, cooling breeze coming through her open window. The Sorensons' yippy little dog had just finished a protracted, panicked bout of barking. Uncle Miles pushed up her nightgown and ran his rough hand up her leg. "You're getting such long legs," he said. "Young filly." Uncle Miles' hand reached her crotch. "What's this?" he said. "Off. Get them off of you."

"But —"

"Then I'll do it." He slipped his hand into the waistband of her panties and yanked. The sanitary belt stayed with the panties, slid down with them as he tugged. He spotted the pad.

"You've got your monthlies?" he said, pulling back.

She was surprised that Aunt Tate hadn't told him, but she was instantly grateful that her aunt had kept it to herself.

"Since when?" Uncle Miles asked, and Lily realized that for some incomprehensible reason, Uncle Miles was suddenly worried.

"A few months."

"Oh." He reached for the bedcovers and

threw them over her exposed body. "Shit."

With the exception of a sporadic "damnation" when the wrench slipped and cut him or when the lawn mower refused to start, Uncle Miles rarely swore.

"Then that's that," he said, standing and looking down at her. He walked out of her room and actually closed the door completely, the click of the latch an unprecedented explosion of sound.

Lily lay there, trying to comprehend. Some part of her knew Uncle Miles was gone forever, that he wouldn't come back. But why not? What had she done? And why was even a fraction of her feeling sadly rejected, as if she'd failed? Why was she anything other than joyfully relieved? *Now* what had she done wrong?

Throughout Lily's early teenage years, the Aviator continued to pay her dance school tuition. Lily studied tap and modern dance, which Aunt Tate pronounced "a good deal of meaningless thrashing." Lily learned ballroom dancing and started to work on ballet positions (*à la seconde, effacé*), but Aunt Tate couldn't afford the toe shoes, and because Lily would never presume to ask the Aviator for more, ballet remained a dream. Still, she could jitterbug and do the

Charleston and shimmy and mimic Gene Kelly's easy, athletic leaps and Cyd Charisse's sexy, long-limbed elegance. *An American in Paris* and *Singin' in the Rain* instantly became her favorite movies when she watched them as reruns on *Dialing for Dollars* after school.

The Aviator faithfully attended all of Lily's *Tah-Dah!* dance performances, and Lily knew he'd be at the upcoming recital of *Enchanted Woodlands,* too. Some of the younger girls chose to be squirrels. One was a big, clumsy bear, and several flitted across the stage as chattering birds. This time Lily was nervous — largely (and as usual) because of the pressure she'd put on herself. With hard work, she'd earned a solo, which meant she could choreograph the final piece of the evening for herself.

Lily wanted to be different, to perform something that transcended childhood and matched the fact that she would soon be moving on to high school. In the library, she learned the word *diaphanous* and read the myth of Daphne, the beautiful nymph who spurned every suitor, even Apollo. When Daphne asked her father, a river god, to help her escape from Apollo, her father turned her into a laurel tree. It was an abominable, cruel solution. A daughter asked for help, and her father's incomprehensible response was to sentence her to eternity as a tree, with roots bound to the earth.

Lily wanted to free Daphne — at least for a while — and so Lily's Daphne leapt onto the empty stage and danced as if escape were possible. She wore a green leotard, chestnut brown tights, and she'd sewn lengths of pink, rose, and fuchsia ribbons to the arms of her leotard. A diadem of leaves interspersed with ribbons crowned her loose, flowing hair. She felt free, transported. And beautiful.

Lily covered every corner of the boards with her leaps, and she let her arms float in graceful, ever-moving arcs so that her ribbons wove patterns about her. She threw her head back, closed her eyes in rapture as if she were thrusting her defiant face into Apollo's sun. Then, in keeping with the myth's inevitably, Lily began to freeze. Mustering great dramatic authority, Lily stuck her feet to the floor of the stage. Inch by inch, with exquisite control and painful slowness, Lily stilled her body until only her fingertips quivered with musical breezes. The ribbons hung lifeless. She held her mouth to the audience in a silent, open O — an arrested scream.

There was a long silence, and then they applauded. Someone even shouted *"Bravo!"* Lily bowed, letting her ribbons trail on the floor of the stage, and as she calmed her breath, she felt the audience's energy lift her skyward. She kept her eyes closed as a beatific glow possessed her. When one of the younger dance students touched her arm, Lily opened her eyes to a bouquet of lilies and baby's breath. She cradled the flowers in her arms and made a final bow, hoping the Aviator knew her thanks — her debt — was to him.

In the hushed car on the way home, Aunt Tate said, "What do you call that?"

"What?"

"That kind of flailing."

"Interpretive dance. It was my interpretation of the character, through dance."

Aunt Tate sighed. "Well, I guess as long as we're not paying for it."

A voice inside Lily said, *Don't let her take this from you.* Still, it hurt. Wasn't there anything she could do that would make her aunt proud?

Back at the house, Aunt Tate said that lilies smelled of funerals, and so Lily gladly set the vase on the nightstand next to her bed, where the scent of the Aviator's tribute would perfume her sleep. Lying in the dark, still too fired up to sleep, Lily relived her performance, and she knew Aunt Tate and Uncle Miles had not succeeded. Lily had found a way; she'd done it. The audience had not only seen her, they'd loved her. Lily Decker was not invisible.

A couple days after her dance recital, Aunt Tate left a gift on Lily's bedside table, next to the vase of fading lilies. When Lily tore open the wrapping paper, she found a crystalline box with a butterfly suspended inside, its wings spread wide as if in optimistic flight. The creature's wings were a stunning sapphire blue — vibrant, even in death. A card written in her aunt's cursive read *To match your beautiful eyes, and because you have more spirit than I ever did.* And then, the most amazing, bewildering part of all — Aunt Tate had written, "Love, Aunt Tate." LOVE.

6

In high school, the bones of Lily's face emerged like the visage of a goddess rising from a deep seabed. She was no longer merely pretty or interesting; her beauty arrested. When she walked the sidewalks of downtown Salina, men spun in their tracks to look at her. Women eyed her with a mixture of studied curiosity and envy. Once, when she was grocery shopping with Aunt Tate, a complete stranger stopped to say, "Now I understand what was meant by 'the face that launched a thousand ships.' " To which Aunt Tate replied, "Well, we're in Kansas, and I don't see any ocean, do you?" At that, the woman walked on, but she turned briefly to shake her head and give Lily a secret, understanding smile.

Any baby fat that had dared to linger now melted from Lily's body. Standing five foot ten, she had a dancer's slim hips, abundant breasts, and she wore her hair bobbed and blunt cut with glowering bangs. Although it was already passé, Lily cultivated beatnik black, morose cool, and mystery touched by a hint of simmering, bedrock rage. She lined her eyes heavily in black, and the look suited her in a way that the perky flips, teased mountaintops of hair, and bright polyester fashions of the midsixties did not.

The Aviator remained in her life, a steady presence, a secret ally. For her sixteenth birthday in 1965 he gave Lily a light blue suitcase record player and fifteen dollars she could use to buy whatever albums she wanted. It was Dylan who spoke most clearly. She took to heart his advice that if you weren't busy being born, then you must be busy dying. She was a disciple of his cynicism, his challenges to everything from teachers to the president to God. Dylan was her fellow iconoclast; like Lily he distrusted absolutely everyone. With the volume turned down low to keep Uncle Miles from shouting at her, Lily dreamed of highways, of the infinite variety of mountains, of escape.

At age sixteen, Lily walked into Masterson's Grocers and applied for a job. She needed spending money for makeup and sewing supplies, and Uncle Miles had decreed that it was time she contributed to her upkeep, which he set at thirty-five dollars per month. The manager, an already obese twenty-year-old named Harold, had dense patches of acne on his cheeks and daubs of ketchup on his mint-green clip-on bowtie. He hitched up his pants and slowly eyed the curves of Lily's body, letting her know in no uncertain terms why he'd be hiring an inexperienced girl. Harold handed her two pink-and-white uniforms to try on for size, and as she undressed next to shelves of canned goods in a back stockroom, she wondered if he was standing at a peephole, watching. Lily imagined his gaping mouth, his widened eyes, and she took her time before choosing the shorter, tighter dress, the one that would best follow the contours of her body.

Harold assigned her to mark prices and stock shelves — an obvious ploy to have her bend over repeatedly, lean over cases with her box cutter and reveal her cleavage. She was on display, just like the towers of canned peaches and pyramids of apples and oranges on the *This Week Only!* promotions at the endcaps of the grocery aisles. But Lily didn't mind. The grocery store was merely another stage, another setting in which she could experiment, learn what effect her lush body had on men.

She watched Harold's face, the faces of

men who came in weary from driving a combine all day, their necks and arms dusted in wheat chaff. Lily learned how to signal bashful innocence, along with a sort of vulnerable availability. She learned how to encourage men to help her when she couldn't *quite* — not *quite* but *almost* — reach the shelves where the Corn Flakes, Froot Loops, and Alpha-Bits cereal boxes lived. She came to realize that men didn't want to see competent independence; they wanted to see a slice of need. So she gave them that. Lily knew, too, that none of them considered that she might be intelligent. Her agile mind was not something a single, solitary man cared to consider.

Everyone was reading Truman Capote's new book about the murders in Holcomb, just a couple hundred miles southwest of Salina. Even Uncle Miles had thumbed through the novel, afterwards puffing out his chest and announcing that those two killers would never have gotten through the door of *his* home. Lily imagined her uncle ineffectively bonking one of the killers over the head with his dusty *Hawaiian* ukulele, like the cartoon horse Quick Draw McGraw's alter ego, the masked and black-caped El Kabong. *Kabong!*

Lily also thought a lot about the killer Perry Smith, about his childhood, his longing for love and his constant leg pain. It threw her — that Perry could be the sympathetic one in the duo, the one with artistic aspirations, but the one, ultimately, who did the butchering. Lily also wondered about the murdered teenage girl who had hidden her watch in the toe of her shoe. The unfairness of it all. Even if you followed all the rules — got straight A's as Lily did — it was no guarantee against wanton destruction.

The state of Kansas had hanged the two men last year, in 1965. For so long, it seemed to be the only thing on the news. Perry Smith and Dick Hickock murdered Kansas' innocence. They killed the myth of idyllic, small-town safety far from the big cities with their slums, poverty, and drugs. Now, people in Salina locked their doors at night. And yet, Lily didn't share the titillating fears of the girls at school; she knew that danger didn't necessarily come from a stranger.

Lily stood with a towel around her neck and used the ends to catch streams of sweat. They'd been practicing flick kicks, falls, and recovers. Effortlessly, she folded herself in half, stretching her hamstrings.

"Lily? Might we take a few minutes to talk about your future?" Mrs. Baumgarten, the owner of the *Tah-Dah!* Dance Studio, leaned against a nearby wall.

Lily was still awash in the complete relaxation she felt after a hard workout, and her thoughts had been elsewhere. "What?" she asked. "I'm sorry, Mrs. Baumgarten, I didn't hear you."

"I was saying that I know you plan to dance, but what kind of dance career do you have in mind? Where do you plan to go from here, when you leave Salina?"

Lily took a deep, luxurious breath and tilted her neck to one side until her ear nearly met her shoulder. "I was thinking Hollywood or New York, I guess." It was the first time she'd ever dared to speak her dream.

Mrs. Baumgarten continued to watch Lily as she stretched. "Your forte is jazz. That's where I see your skill, your aptitude. And it's what best fits your body — you have to pair your body with the right movements. It's as much about a look as it is about technique. And, actually, I have an idea for you. Are you ready?" Lily's teacher smiled mischievously. "Viva Las Vegas!"

"Elvis? Ann-Margret?" Lily smiled.

"For you, for dance," Mrs. Baumgarten replied. "Las Vegas is where there's an exciting, growing jazz dance scene. You'd find it easier to break in there than L.A. or New York. You'd gain valuable experience, build your dance résumé. Then you can try for the more competitive venues."

"You think I should head to Sin City?" Lily could easily imagine her aunt and uncle's response to that particular plan.

Mrs. Baumgarten continued as if Lily hadn't spoken. "The casinos compete with each other for floor shows, dance numbers. And celebrities flock there to perform, to see and be seen." Lily's teacher began counting off on her fingers. "Debbie Reynolds. Liberace. Judy Garland. The Rat Pack. *Sammy Davis, Jr.,*" she said with great emphasis, knowing that Lily was wild about his tap dancing. "Think what you could learn, what you'd see. The exposure you'd have."

Before Lily left that night, Mrs. Baumgarten handed her a stack of *Dance Magazine.* Then she leaned close, and Lily felt her teacher's kiss on her cheek, a brief brush of tenderness. "We'll talk again," she said.

At home in her room, Lily used the photos in *Dance Magazine* to prod her body into new, more complicated movements and configurations. Looking into the mirror above her dresser bureau, she mimicked the professional dancers' hand gestures, the way they held their arms. She jutted her chin, narrowed her eyes, dared her mirror image the way that Nureyev dared the camera, and wished she had his boldness. She'd been twelve when Nureyev defected from the Soviet Union, and she remembered watching news footage of him striding across an airfield in Paris, hearing Uncle Miles say that the sissy's rejection served the commies right. "He can never go back? Never go home again?" she'd asked her uncle. "Never," Uncle Miles pronounced, his fingers dribbling flakes of tobacco into the fold of his cigarette paper. "He'll never see his family again," he'd said with an oddly self-satisfied smile.

Lily began to believe Las Vegas was the answer, and she started to plan. She pulled out the atlas in the school library, studied the route from Salina to Vegas, and counted the state lines she'd cross. She studied the figures in her savings passbook, totaled up how much more she'd be able to save between now and graduation, in just slightly over a year. She'd need bus fare, plus spending money to keep her afloat until she landed a job. Her columns of figures made the whole enterprise increasingly real, and Lily volunteered for extra shifts at the grocery store, just to see the totals multiply satisfyingly. Lily felt a burst of hope. The tallies told her she could do this — would do this. Escape was not only possible; it was within her grasp.

One evening when Lily, now a senior in high school, got off work, the Aviator was waiting for her. He leaned against the waxed black shine of his car, his eyes hidden behind dark sunglasses.

"You need to watch yourself," he said without preamble. "You're asking for trouble."

"What're you talking about?"

"What you're doing. With men. I've seen you," he said, dropping the end of his cigarette to the asphalt and crushing it beneath his boot. "You're playing a dangerous game."

She couldn't see his eyes, but the set jaw, the taut striations of his neck muscles, told her that he was dead serious.

"I'm not doing *anything* with men," Lily said. "I don't even date." High school boys stared at Lily but were too intimidated to approach her, and she did nothing to encourage them.

"Boys are one thing." The Aviator picked up the cigarette butt and folded it into his handkerchief. "Leading *men* on — men who would be only too happy to *take* what they see — that's another story entirely."

"You're talking about *flirting*? You're telling me not to flirt? Who do you think you are?" She paused and then daringly added, "It's not as if you're my father."

The Aviator moved to within a foot of her, and she felt the implicit threat of his height, his muscles. His shadow covered her. But there was a surprising tenderness in his voice when he said, "No, Lily, I'm not your father. I am your friend, and I'm trying to watch out for you."

Before she could come up with a sarcastic, dismissive response, he climbed into his car, started the engine, and left her there to decide.

Lily frequented the thrift store in the basement of the Episcopal church. She'd just this year discovered that the wealthier women of the congregation regularly donated nearly new clothing; some pieces even bore designer labels. Lily had found a pair of Balenciaga boots — black suede that came up and over her knees — for just five dollars. And, there was more: silk blouses, sunglasses, fringed leather purses. She found more fashionable pieces and at better prices than she could at J.C. Penney or Sears, and no one was the wiser.

When she came across a particularly pretty cardigan sweater in a lovely teal, she brought it home for her aunt who, standing before her bedroom mirror, said, "But with this open weave. It's a little impractical, isn't it? What will the girls in Bible-study class say?"

In that moment, Lily felt sympathy for the girl who'd been named Tatum, who'd endured a younger sister who was much, much prettier than she, who'd had to watch her sister marry well. And then who'd been saddled with a bewildering, cast-off child and a husband who night after night sat in his chair, adhered like fungus to the Naugahyde. Lily saw her aunt's stoicism, her self-defensive rigidity, how desperately she tried to conceal her confusion and fears of inadequacy. And Lily saw that her aunt would never, ever go anywhere. She would never leave Kansas.

It made Lily wonder. Would Mama be thick around the middle, and would Daddy be balding and forgetful? Would they still live in Salina, or would they have moved to a new town, to new sights? What would

Dawn be like? Would she be in nursing college or married to a farmer or a railroad engineer or an aircraft mechanic? Would she already have toddlers who would call excitedly for Aunt Lily when she stopped by with Popsicles? Would Dawn make Mama's Swedish meatball recipe and plan elaborate picnics next to the Smoky Hill River? Would she admire the dance costumes Lily designed and applaud when Lily stood on stage?

"Do you ever think about them?" Lily asked in her sentimental moment of weakness.

"Never," Aunt Tate said, pulling her arms from the sweater and heading for her bedroom. "And you shouldn't either," she added. "Pure self-indulgence."

Lily heard her aunt's closet door open and close with finality, and she knew Aunt Tate would never permit herself the treat of the delicate sweater. She'd keep it in that closet, undisturbed, and she'd instead relish her ramrod austerity. Lily nearly went to embrace her aunt. Tate was suddenly such a sad creature, believing that her habitual ferocity could protect her from loss and pain. *Walls,* Lily thought, *keep out the good as well as the bad.* She was determined to remember that, not to let fear overtake her, never to risk losing her joy.

For the First Annual *Tah-Dah!* Dance Studio Scholarship Fundraiser, Mrs. Baumgarten rented the Fox-Watson movie theater on South Santa Fe Avenue and managed to get ahold of a print of *Ocean's 11* with Dean Martin, Frank Sinatra, Peter Lawford, Angie Dickinson and — best of all — Sammy Davis, Jr. Lily sold all of the five-dollar tickets she could at school and work, and she bought a Simplicity pattern for a clean-lined, spaghetti-strap dress. She made it in dark gold satin and hemmed it so that it ended two thirds of the way up her thighs. Even though it was almost too warm for them, she paired the dress with the Balenciaga boots, and she tied a length of black satin ribbon around her neck as a choker. For added drama, Lily moistened her cake of black liner and outlined her eyes as usual, and then she added a third dark line along the crease of her eyelid, like Twiggy. Using an eyebrow pencil, she extended the outer edges of her eyebrows. She applied a pair of false eyelashes and a light-blue cream eye shadow, and finished with Yardley beige-pink lipstick.

"You're not leaving my house dressed like a whore," Uncle Miles said when he spied her trying to make a quick exit through the kitchen door. He put both his hands on her forearm and twisted them in opposite directions — a version of what the kids called an Indian burn. When he released her arm, Lily stepped back and accidentally smacked the back of her head against the furnace door.

She felt her upper lip reflexively lift into a snarl. "You're calling me a whore?" she said, and then waited a meaningful beat. "Quite a statement for a man who *Fucks. Little. Girls,*" she spat, and then caught sight of Aunt Tate standing in the entry to the kitchen.

Aunt Tate sagged heavily against the doorjamb as if her skeleton had been dissolved in acid and all that was left of her was limp, loose skin. Lily cut past Uncle Miles and reached for her aunt's arm.

"Stay away! Get away from me! I don't need your help!" Heavy-limbed, Aunt Tate kept a balancing hand against the wall until she reached the kitchen stool and dropped into it. She pressed her lips together, looked from Lily to her husband and then back again. In her aunt's eyes, Lily saw a teeter-totter of indecision, of weights and balances. And then, it happened. Lily knew before her aunt said a word, and so the words when they came were mere confirmation:

"Your uncle's right. You look like a hooker."

Lily closed her eyes, dropped her chin to her chest, and slumped against the wall. She wanted darkness. And tears. The release of ten years' worth of tears — everything she'd held back seemingly forever. But she would never give them that. Instead, she envisioned using her nails to pinch the soft skin inside her upper arm and thought about the relief of leaving half-moon bruises. Or maybe stabbing a fork into her thigh. Razor blades. Any kind of distracting pain.

A thick silence settled over the kitchen. Lily thought she smelled the garlic and onion of ten thousand meals, the sulfur of rotting eggs, hamburger meat gone bad.

Don't let them diminish you, Scallywag, she told herself, and then, wordlessly, Lily straightened her shoulders and left through the kitchen door. No one tried to stop her. When she reached the curb, she used trembling fingers to light a cigarette and stood in the spot where she habitually waited for her friend from dance class to come pick her up. Even though the evening was mild, she wrapped her arms around her shoulders and began shivering. Her whole body vibrated; she could feel her legs shaking, her lips trembling. She shuddered — big shudders that hunched her shoulders suddenly, made her throw her head back as if she were having a seizure. She stomped her feet, did a little softshoe to warm herself, tried to trick her body out of its inclination toward a state of shock. She felt as though she'd been hit, and hit hard, by something harsh and unforgiving.

Lily looked back at the scene that played out in the kitchen window. She saw Uncle Miles lower his bulk into one of the kitchen dinette chairs, Aunt Tate frozen in place on the pedestal of the kitchen step stool. They made her think of a brightly lit department-store window display — something some deluded romantic would call Domestic Bliss.

It had been coming, this revelation. Inevitable. Barreling down the pike toward them, for years. And now it was done. Anticlimactic.

She'd been right never to have told Aunt Tate. Look at her there, diminished, stalled on that kitchen stool. Aunt Tate wouldn't have stood up for a younger Lily any more than she did now. She wouldn't have protected Lily. She wouldn't have chosen Lily over her husband. No, instead she would have said, *No, no, no. I don't think so not the man I married.* There was too much Aunt Tate would have to admit to herself, were she to hear what Lily had to say.

Anger born of rejection bubbled up, and Lily was tempted to go back inside. She wanted destruction. She wanted to pull down Aunt Tate's curtain rods, leave craters where the bolts had once fit so snugly within the wall. She wanted to empty the kitchen cabinets of the china Aunt Tate had bought using the Green Stamps Lily had so faithfully pasted into booklets. Lily pictured hurling those cheap plates against the wall. She imagined shackling Uncle Miles to a radiator, holding the flame of a lighter beneath his chin, and making Aunt Tate watch it all. But mostly, Lily wanted to make herself bleed. To slice the tender, sweet skin of her forearms until red rivers flowed and her true wounds were rendered visible.

The Fox-Watson Theatre, where the *Tah-Dah!* fundraiser took place, was a wonderful art deco concoction of crystal chandeliers, a fantastic stairway, and luxurious, gold-leaf highlights. Still feeling an uneasy trembling in her legs, Lily stood in the lobby and leaned against the cigarette machine, taking it all in. Mrs. Baumgarten appeared in a silk caftan and turban, rings and bangles and long, dangling earrings. The silk was tangerine with a pattern of tumbling crimson tulips.

She kissed Lily on both cheeks and gently, inconspicuously, took Lily's forearm in her hands. She held Lily's arm between them, intimate. "Who?" she asked, indicating the bruise that was surfacing like lies long buried.

But Lily just smiled weakly into her teacher's face. She didn't want a scene, and it was too late for remedies. She just wanted out. Out of Salina in four weeks and six days. She covered her arm with the opposite hand, held it against her waist, and failed to come up with any response, even though her teacher's sympathetic gaze lingered.

The movie was disappointing. Sammy Davis, Jr., sang, but he didn't dance — not as he had in *Robin and the 7 Hoods,* when he twirled guns, tap-danced on and off of a bar and a roulette table, and exuded boundless energy. Still, there were Vegas dancers in the background in several scenes, and Lily focused on those segments, memorizing every detail. The girls' outfits were perfect — lots of plumage, bared legs with beautiful pointed heels and sky-high kicks.

After the film, people milled about in the lobby saying their goodbyes. Lily spotted a lovely woman standing beside the Aviator.

His date wore an aqua jacket and skirt, and the collar of a bone-colored silk blouse peeked shyly from beneath her short jacket. She had brown hair cut just below chin level and a delicate nose. *Rarified,* Lily thought, like Jackie Kennedy — sophisticated, simple. But maybe just a little bit dull and unimaginative.

The Aviator left his date's side and crossed the room to Lily. He took in the tall suede boots, the now much-wrinkled homemade dress, and he ran a hand across her hair, smoothing flyaway strands. His touch sent a shock through her. "You're beautiful," he said. Then he seemed to sense the intimacy of his grooming of her, and he shoved his hand into the pocket of his blazer. "You're so grown-up," he said wistfully before turning to find his date.

Lily stood there, becalmed, as she watched him walk away. It had never before occurred to her that the Aviator could have any woman in his life, other than Lily.

A few afternoons later, Aunt Tate found Lily at the sewing machine in the corner of the dining room and asked, "What are you working on?"

Other than perfunctory, necessary phrases, it was the first time Aunt Tate had spoken to her since the night of the fundraiser. Lily recognized the overture, released the pressure on the sewing machine's knee-operated control lever, and peered up at her aunt, who looked completely enervated, as if she hadn't slept in weeks. Aunt Tate was pathetic, Lily realized — a weak, albino stalk of a flower struggling to grow in the dark of a closet shelf.

I'll escape, Lily thought, *but this poor woman will never leave. I'm stronger than the both of them.* And so, feeling somewhat conciliatory, Lily said, "This is my final project for Miss Lambkin's class." She held up the deep rose brocade. "It'll be a lined evening-dress jacket, something I can wear over a skirt, maybe dress up with a piece of costume jewelry." She'd already sewn a pair of bell-bottom pants out of the material and loved the way the fabric stretched across what some of the other dance students referred to as "the Grand Canyon of your hips." That canyon took two hundred sit-ups a night on the rag rug next to Lily's bed, but it was worth it.

"Pretty," Aunt Tate said. "But it's musty in here. You should open a window." She touched Lily's shoulder fleetingly, so lightly that it could instead have been the minute brush of a passing moth's wings.

"Aunt Tate?"

Her aunt paused but kept her back to Lily as if she somehow knew that Lily was going to take that one, placatory gesture and use it to open a chasm in their lives.

"I'm not a liar. I never have been," Lily said and watched her aunt's back stiffen.

Without a word, Aunt Tate left the room, and soon Lily could hear her in the kitchen, putting together the evening meat loaf.

Lily sat with her hands in her lap. She picked a few spent threads from her jeans. It was only when she heard her aunt sniffle and then blow her nose that she knew Aunt Tate was remembering all the nights Uncle Miles had left their bed and made his way down the darkened hallway to Lily.

7

"But I do have a plan," Lily said as the Aviator stood beside her. Although it was her day off, she was in the produce section of Masterson's, doing Aunt Tate's grocery shopping. A couple of women who'd been poking at the pears and cantaloupes looked up, but the Aviator charmed them with a smile, and they returned to their quest for peak ripeness. "I *do* have a plan," Lily repeated.

"College?" He filled a paper produce bag with exactly seven Granny Smith apples and folded down the top with precision.

Lily snorted. "No."

"Why not?"

"For starters, we can't afford it."

"But you can."

"Right," she said, looking at her aunt's list, the one her uncle had added to in his left-handed, back-slanting cursive: *dow nuts, choclut Marshmello cookys.*

The radio station was playing the just released Beatles album, *Sgt. Pepper's Lonely Hearts Club Band,* and Lily heard the lyrics of "She's Leaving Home." It was as if the Beatles had written the song just for her. The girl in the song stepped outside her front door and was free. Soon, Lily would do the same.

Seeing her distraction, the Aviator said, "Let's talk in the parking lot."

Lily sat in the passenger seat of the Aviator's Thunderbird and double-checked the change the clerk had given her. She folded the receipt and shoved it all into the front pocket of her hip-hugger jeans.

"You're a bright, bright girl," the Aviator began, and she could smell his aftershave — a tart, citrus scent. He was wearing camel-colored khakis and a soft, white cotton shirt with the sleeves rolled loosely to his elbows. His fingernails were perfectly manicured, the nails buffed — a decided contrast to the decades of grease that accumulated beneath the nails of Uncle Miles' sliced and diced mechanic's hands.

"I'm a dancer. Not a college girl."

"With an IQ of 155."

"Who says?"

"Your guidance counselor." He pushed in the cigarette lighter when he saw her shake a Salem from her pack.

"You were talking to Mrs. Holcomb about me?"

"I was." He held the hot, orange coil of the lighter to the tip of her cigarette.

"*I* didn't even know," she said, rolling down the window and blowing smoke out into the parking lot. "I purposely did not go in to hear my scores." Lily noticed that the Aviator smoked Marlboros. "Come to Marlboro Country," she said, using her deepest voice to imitate the commercial. It fit the Aviator — the long, lean, isolated cowboy who was a man in every sense of the word. Took no guff, lived life his way.

He sighed. "I'm trying to have a meaningful conversation with you."

"I know," she said, pulling open the ashtray, tapping her cigarette. It didn't surprise her that the Aviator's ashtray looked as if it'd been washed clean in a sink. "You're a bit of a neat freak, aren't you?" she said.

"I like to do things right. Which is why I'm trying to talk to you." Together they watched a young mother pushing a baby stroller while trying to pull up the strap of her shoulder bag. "You realize that 100 is average. A score of 155 is in what's considered the very superior range."

She hadn't. All she knew was that when they took the test, she'd finished an easy twenty minutes before everyone else, and not because she'd put her pencil down and decided not to try.

"Let's go at it from another angle," the Aviator said, all efficiency and logic. "What *is* your plan?"

"To dance."

"To dance." He sighed. "A girl with an IQ of 155 should be capable of more specific planning. Even if she has been brought up by heathens."

"You know, that's what my dad called them. Heathens," she said, looking at the Aviator, his upright posture, his flat abdomen. She saw something flash across his face — a mixture of pain and memory. "I'm sorry," Lily said, touching his forearm. "I didn't mean . . ."

"Do you see the irony of this?" he pleaded. "You? Apologizing to me?"

A soft rain had begun to fall, dotting the windshield with drops that ran until they randomly joined each other. *Is that what people did, too?* Lily wondered. Fall and drift until they collided with one another, the way the Aviator had collided with her ten years ago?

As he rested his fingertips between his

brows, she realized her hand was still on his forearm, and she kept it there, increased the pressure. "You've been good to me," she said. "Better to me than anyone else. I've always known I could depend on you."

"Then let me help you. Let me help you with college. There's money," he said, now earnestly looking at her. "I've saved. You have a college fund. Please don't throw your life away."

She took back her hand, stared into her lap. "Thank you," she said. "I'm grateful, really. But if you truly want to help me, then help me get to Las Vegas. To dance. That's what I want."

"Vegas?"

"Mrs. Baumgarten says it's the best place for jazz dance. A place where I can learn from real pros. *Accessible,*" she said, coming up with the best word she could think of to summarize the perfection of her Baumgarten-assisted plan.

She watched him struggle with the idea, weighing his will against hers. Finally, he said, "That's what you really want? You're certain?"

"It's the one thing I do know," she said, simply.

"Well then. I won't stand in the way of your dream."

You can't stand in my way, she thought but did not say. *No one can.*

She thought about explaining to him that dance was something she needed. How it purified her body. How, when she exerted herself physically, she felt the strength of her limbs, that they belonged only to her. That for however long she moved to music, Uncle Miles' proprietary insistence became obsolete. But Lily didn't explain. She could not pass through that stone wall from shameful shadow to bright sunlight — not even for the Aviator.

The rain came down more insistently, and through her open window it wet the sleeve of her paisley-patterned blouse. "I have to get going." She used her sleeve to wipe water from the car upholstery. "Or I'll catch hell."

"That's exactly what I'm afraid of," he said, his voice soft, sad.

Taking the grocery bag into her arms and opening the car door, Lily pretended not to understand.

At dance class the next day, Mrs. Baumgarten delivered one of the Aviator's books to Lily. It was a gilt-edged 1942 edition of Walt Whitman's collected poems, and on a plain white strip of paper intended as a bookmark, the Aviator had written *"The hungry gnaw that eats me night and day." I understand this is your need to dance.* She saw the line embedded in the poem "From Pent-Up Aching Rivers." The gift, Lily thought, was not the book. It was his understanding.

In the wee hours of the morning after she graduated as one of the top ten in the class of 1967, Lily left a bouquet of daisies on the dining room table. She set it next to a blouse she'd made for her aunt, along with a card that said *Thank You* on the front in silver embossed letters. Inside, Lily had written a paragraph of gratitude for taking her in, teaching her, and providing for her. She signed it with *love* because the other options — *sincerely, fondly, best wishes* — all seemed needlessly cruel. And maybe — in fact, honestly — she did love her aunt, despite everything. It was no one's fault that they were mismatched, just as much or more so than Mama and Aunt Tate had been. And Aunt Tate really had done her best. She simply wasn't capable of more — or she might long ago have left her husband. Escaped Salina.

Lily didn't leave anything for Uncle Miles, certainly no forwarding address or information other than that she was leaving Kansas to dance. Then, Lily walked out of the house and climbed into the Aviator's waiting car.

It was barely after four A.M. when she stood with him in the bus depot parking lot. About her neck Lily wore a fine gold chain on which she'd strung her mother's engagement and wedding rings — a graduation gift from Aunt Tate. Lily pulled the rings from beneath her blouse, fingered them and thought of her mother's hands dusted in flour, sewing a button on her father's shirt, and teaching Lily how to tie her shoes. Had her mother braced those beautiful hands on the dashboard when she saw the Aviator's car coming?

"I'm sorry I didn't make you a gift," Lily told him. "But nothing would have been enough, and I didn't know what would say goodbye in the right way."

The Aviator took her chin in his hand. He lifted her face, and for a moment she thought he might kiss her lips. A part of her wanted that. Instead, he slipped his thumb into the cleft of her chin, let it rest there, calm and steadying. She saw that he might cry, and so she took his wrist, closed her eyes, and kissed his beating pulse.

Leaving the Aviator was like leaving her real family, once and for all. The finality of it hit her, hard, and she felt her knees threatening to drop her to the pavement. Instead, she turned and walked into the bus terminal.

At some point, every girl in Kansas dressed as Dorothy for Halloween. Pinafore, petticoat, simple white blouse, a straw basket for trick-or-treat candy, demure ankle socks, and red shoes. *Goodbye, Dorothy,* Lily thought, *good riddance to you and all of your "There's no place like home" bullshit.*

Lily remembered when a teacher had told them that Kansas was once a vast inland sea. She'd hunted fossils with Beverly Ann and tried to imagine how change could have occurred on such a massive scale. She remembered the tadpoles she and Dawn had caught and watched grow. If Kansas could go from sea to prairie, if a frog egg could radically transform itself from an almost-fish with gills to an amphibian that left water for land, then Lily could transform, too.

At the Colorado border Lily decided that her new self deserved a fresh name. Lily Decker would become Ruby Wilde. She thought it worked — her dark red hair, the elegance lent by that extra *e,* like *shoppe.*

Lily looked at her palm, studying the lines of influence on her Mount of Venus at the base of her thumb. The lines were said to represent the friends, teachers, enemies, and lovers who change and shape existences. Lily had countless fine lines on her palm, and many of the lines touched, even traveled across her life line. She recognized the deep lines of her childhood: Aunt Tate, Uncle Miles. The Aviator. Her parents. Dawn.

People come and go, Lily thought. Sometimes they vanish unwillingly, the resulting break adamant, like a sharp slap of the ruler across the palm — decisive, unequivocal. Others leave with as little thought as the tip of the finger that snuffs out the life of an ant crawling across a pantry shelf.

Beyond her window, Lily saw fence posts and dull-eyed cattle. Black hawks circled, eyeing the ground for deer mice and lizards. Clouds coalesced and broke into discrete puffs. It was June 9, 1967, exactly ten years since her family had dissolved like sugar stirred into iced tea. Lily settled back into her seat and relaxed. She'd done it. Ruby Wilde was on her way.

Ruby Wilde

1

She waited until the bus was safely within the boundaries of Nevada before opening the Aviator's envelope.

June 9, 1967

Dear Lily,
There is more where this came from, but this is a start. It should help you to pay your rent and eat decently for a few months, until you find your place in the limelight. You haven't seen much of the world, and I don't know if you realize what an unforgiving place it can be. Be careful and pay attention.
If you need anything, *call me.*

Yours,
Stirling

Unforgiving? He must be kidding. She had already plummeted into the depths of that word, deeper than the Aviator could ever imagine.

He'd enclosed four fifty-dollar bills that looked as if they'd never seen daylight. She discreetly tucked them into her pink leather wallet, wary of the prying eyes of the passenger next to her. Ever since he'd boarded the bus in Utah, she'd felt him watching her. She refolded the Aviator's letter and slipped it into her fringed leather shoulder bag.

Although they were excruciatingly close to her final destination, the bus pulled into a rest stop in Glendale, Nevada. After freshening up, she sat at the luncheonette counter, smoking and thinking that even though it was after ten P.M., she needed either a chocolate malt or a cup of coffee.

"Would you mind?" the watchful man from the bus asked, pointing to the stool next to hers.

"No." She crushed her cigarette and decided her first Nevada meal would be ice cream. She laid down the menu as a signal to the waitress. The man had shaved, and now he smelled of Right Guard and Aqua Velva.

"May I treat?" he asked.

Ruby spun her stool and looked at him. He was probably about forty, forty-five, wore a wrinkled gray suit, a burgundy tie, and a gold tie bar. His face was soft, round, and he was balding, with outsized red ears. The man's smile was friendly, and she decided to let him be gentlemanly. "Sure," she said, "but I'm a cheap date — just a chocolate malt."

"Make it two," he said to the waitress, who slipped the carbon paper between tickets in her book and jotted down their order.

There was a moment of awkward silence until the man said, "Mason." He held out his hand. "Mason Maddox."

She remembered to use her new name. "Ruby" — she smiled — "Wilde."

"Nice to meetchya, Ruby Wilde." He fiddled with the long-handled spoon the waitress set before him and unwrapped his paper straw. "Going to Vegas to spend all your hard-earned money?" he asked.

"I'm a dancer," Ruby said, feeling warm, easy, as she opened into her new self. She had a quick vision of a full-blown cabbage rose — pink, luscious, the scent of early summer before the heat set in.

"My daughter Rose works in Vegas. On my way to visit her."

"She dances?" The waitress placed two thick malts on the counter. Ruby plucked the cherry from the top of hers and dropped it into her mouth.

"Works reception at the new Caesars. She's been in Vegas almost two years now."

"Does she like it? Las Vegas?"

"Loves it. But to be fair, she's comparing it to Salt Lake City, and there's one hell of a difference." He laughed to himself, sipped his milkshake. "Mind my askin' how old you are, Ruby?"

"Eighteen."

"Tell them you're twenty. It'll be easier for work in the casinos. And" — he looked critically at her face — "wear more makeup. It'll make you look older."

"Okay. . . ."

"Do you know anyone there? Got a place to stay?"

Ruby hesitated.

"I'm just concerned about you," Mason Maddox said. "My daughter's only a couple a years older than you, and the stories she tells . . . Well, let me just say, Miss Ruby, that I know my Rose isn't telling me everything, but what she does tell me is plenty. You gotta watch out for yourself. Don't trust anyone." He stirred his shake. "Everyone's on the make. *Everyone.*"

Ruby quietly focused on her malt.

"How about I do this." Mason eased a napkin from the dispenser. He wrote out

Rose Maddox, carefully printed his daughter's address and phone number, and slid the napkin to Ruby. "Just in case," he said. "I'll let her know you might be callin'. She's a good girl. She'll help you out, show you the ropes."

"Thank you." Ruby folded the napkin and slipped it into her purse. "I mean it," she said. "You're kind."

"Pleasure's all mine," Mason said, standing. "It's what I'd want someone to do for my Rose."

She finished her malt, had one more cigarette, and climbed back onto the bus. Thanks to the ice cream, Ruby managed to doze until the brakes sounded and the bus pulled into Las Vegas just after midnight.

The Greyhound terminal was located within the Stardust Casino, and even though it was the middle of the night, people swarmed all about her. Standing with a heavy suitcase on either side of her, Ruby stalled, overwhelmed.

Slot machines were tucked into every nook and cranny, and most of them were occupied. Women's hips oozed from the backs of their chairs and flowed like slow, lugubrious lava over the edges of their stools. Their eyes were transfixed, glazed over, as they grabbed the levers. She heard raucous bells, the jangle of coins falling into metal trays, and she saw flashing lights. Men with cigarettes dangling from the corners of their mouths, neglected ashen tips grown long, rolled up their sleeves, inserted more coins, and waited for the spinning to stop and land on their futures.

Ruby thought she saw hope mixed with despair, longing brushing away reality's faint protestations. Their faces held an intense desire for something better, something else. She saw homeward-bound bus passengers standing in line with their emptied pockets, the light gone from their eyes. She saw insomniacs who let habit carry them someplace, nowhere.

With sudden clarity, she also saw herself, and she panicked. Her plan was inadequate. She was in the wrong place. This was a mistake. She would be consumed here, disappear like flash paper in a magician's hands. She'd been a fool to follow Mrs. Baumgarten's advice.

Moving to a wall, Ruby leaned against it, tried to catch her breath and force the encroaching tunnel vision to retreat. Her heart shouted. She cupped her hands about her nose and mouth, breathed. *I'm just tired,* she tried to convince herself. *That's all. Just tired, unwashed. Too many hours on the bus to sustain hope and optimism. Don't panic.*

"Looks like you could use a drink." A sinewy man, wearing a short-sleeved white T-shirt with a pack of cigarettes jammed into one rolled-up sleeve, started to reach for her arm. He had tight hills of biceps and his palms were suffused with blood, red hot.

Ruby pulled back. "No," she said.

"C'mon. Beautiful newcomer like you. Let me carry your suitcases." A rose tattoo lurked beneath the thick black fur of his forearm.

Ruby took hold of the handles of her bags, straightened herself. "Please go away."

"Bet you could use a place to stay. I got room." He grinned.

He was standing too close. She could smell grease and onions.

"Ruby!"

She heard the name, but it took a moment for her to realize that it was her name.

"Ruby Wilde!" Mason Maddox called again, stepping between her and the insistent creep. "Glad we found you." He gave the other man a hardened stare, and the man walked away slowly, looked back once, shook his head as if it were Ruby's loss, not his.

Ruby wished she'd had something more

sustaining than the milkshake, which now left her shaky and needful.

"Girl, this isn't good. I knew it. Shouldna let you go off all alone." Mason picked up one of her suitcases and added it to his own. "This settles things." He turned, motioned to his daughter. "Rose? This here's Ruby. Ruby, Rose. Now," he said, nodding at his daughter, "you get her other bag."

"But —" Ruby tried feebly.

"No ifs, ands, or buts. Rose's got one of those teensy-weensy VW bugs. We're gonna squeeze into it like a pack of sardines and give you a ride to wherever it is you're going."

Rose was elegant in tight jeans, with a bright red silk blouse, gold hoop earrings. She smelled good — something wistful, floral. Straight, golden-blonde hair was parted down the center and hung just past her shoulders. She had clear, grey-blue eyes that made Ruby think of rainbows and prisms.

"Daddy, hold on a minute. Let her talk." Rose smiled a warm welcome. "Sometimes you can't get a word in edgewise with Daddy. What do *you* want, Ruby?"

Ruby was tempted to say *Rescue,* or *To get back on the bus,* but she didn't. Instead, she pulled from her purse the AAA guide the Aviator had given her, flipped to the page where he'd starred several entries with a ballpoint pen. "Do you know how I could get to one of these motels?" She handed Rose the directory.

Rose ran her finger down the page. "Bombay Motor Court is the decent one. It's got kitchenettes and is close enough to let you walk or catch a bus between the casinos. While you look for work, I mean." Rose handed the book back to Ruby. "Daddy says you're a dancer. So cool. Why don't we drive you there? You must be beat."

"I'd be so grateful," Ruby said with relief.

"*Now,* Daddy. *Now* we can help her." Rose winked and picked up Ruby's other scuffed thrift-store bag. "On the way, we'll show you a bit of Vegas."

Outside the bus terminal, stupefying neon displays towered like mountain cliffs, and the superheated desert air burned her nostrils. The Stardust's marquee featured a globe of blue-and-green neon, surrounded by pink-and-white rays; blue-and-pink stars twinkled off and on. Two times over it said *Stardust* in white lights, and planets whirled about the earth as if it were the center of the universe. Another brightly lit sign said, *'67 Lido of Paris — Grand Prix 67,* and beneath that, a smaller sign read *In the*

Lounge: Kim Sisters, Big Tiny Little, and Lou Styles. Ruby recognized Big Tiny Little as the piano player on Aunt Tate's dreadful *Lawrence Welk Show,* but he also played for Dinah Shore. His fingers flew across the piano as if the keys were electrified. She'd seen the Kim Sisters performing on *The Ed Sullivan Show* in their tight, satin cheongsam dresses. Maybe she'd seen them with Dean Martin, too. It was unreal. Ruby really was in the land of the famous.

Wedged into what passed for a backseat, her knees bumping the back of the bug's front seats, she felt her flame reignite like a furnace's pilot light bursting from a tiny blue maintenance flame to a full bar of fire. She could do this. She could and would dance on the same stage as Big Tiny Little and the Kim Sisters. Ruby smiled. She sounded like the children's book — the little train. *I think I can. I think I can. I think I can.* Well, there were worse mottos.

Rose caught Ruby's smile in the rearview mirror. "Feeling better?"

"One hundred percent better," Ruby said, and looked for a handle so that she could roll down the window, stick her head out, and see more of the neon-filled sky. She found an ashtray but no handle — the VW's backseat window didn't open. She sat back, thought about how the neon kept night at bay.

"So, this is the Strip, obviously," Rose began. "The Frontier and the Desert Inn are behind us. Coming up is the Flamingo, and then across from it, my place. Also known as Caesars Palace."

The Flamingo had a marvelous bubbly champagne tower that lit up gradually, like neon effervescence. Ruby had never had champagne; it was one of the things she intended to do — to let bubbles tickle her nose, fizz and pop on her tongue. She started a mental list of never-hads: avocado, lobster, baked Alaska.

But it was Caesars Palace that took her breath away. "Oh my God," she said.

"Pretty spectacular, isn't it?" Rose turned to look at Ruby.

"It's giant!" Ruby gasped. A series of huge fountains and marble statues led toward a magnificent semicircle of columns that enfolded patrons in a generous embrace.

"Over thirty acres," Rose said, slowing down to give Ruby a better chance to gawk. "The theater-restaurant seats a thousand, and there are several dining rooms, two health clubs, even a beauty salon. See the trees? Well, if not, you will in the daylight. Anyway, they're genuine Italian cypress trees, imported. Several theaters — the Circus Maximus, Nero's Nook, the Roman Theatre."

"Good grief."

"I know."

"It literally leaves me breathless."

"That's what it's meant to do," Mason said. "You're in another world."

"Beauty salons and health spas?" Ruby asked.

"You never have to leave."

"Also on purpose," Mason pronounced, and Ruby heard the disapproval in his voice.

"Daddy doesn't like Vegas." Rose paused. "But what he doesn't seem to understand," she said, "is that people come here to escape. To get away. To feel a bit of magic for a little while."

"People come here to be robbed of their hard-earned wages."

"Isn't it the place of dreams?" Ruby asked.

"Oh, dear girl," Mason said, and then let it rest.

"Don't listen to him," Rose said. "Sometimes, Daddy can be such a square."

"Realist," he countered.

"No imagination."

"No delusions."

Ruby sat back, half heartedly listening to the father-daughter banter while she reveled in the fact that she'd done it. She'd escaped. And now here she was, in Las Vegas. Scallywag's stubborn determination had paid off.

Soon, the neon lights were spaced farther apart and the shouting edifices gave way to intermittent empty lots. Rose pulled into the Bombay Motor Court, and a reassuring neon arrow above a facsimile of a Moorish arch flashed VACANCY and FREE TV, HEATED POOL, IN-ROOM PHONES.

"We'll stay until you're checked in, make sure everything's set, all right?" Rose asked, and Ruby didn't bother to protest. She felt some of her misgivings return as she thought about facing it all alone. But the room was clean, with a bright pink bedspread and white walls stenciled in gold with images of East Indian statuary and twining vines. She was able to get a room right by the pool, and she imagined how refreshing it would feel to cool her burning feet, to float and let the ripples and sun relax her.

"We'll call tomorrow," Rose said, taking her father's hand to tug him away. "Not because we think you need us," she added quickly. "We'll call you because Daddy is a worrier, right?" She smiled at him.

"Right," he said and then gave Ruby a

brief hug. "I kinda feel responsible for you, kiddo."

"I owe you," Ruby said. "Big time."

"You don't," Rose stated firmly. "It's what people should do for each other, that's all."

Ruby waved to them from the doorway, and then she broke the paper strip across the toilet, peed, unwrapped the thin sliver of pink Camay soap, and took a long, hot shower before falling into bed. Feeling profligate, she dropped a quarter into the box next to the bed, and the Magic Fingers started up. "Ahhhhhh," Ruby said, keeping her mouth and throat open so that the vibration of the bed made her voice waver wonderfully.

At last, it was her future to define, to take. Her life belonged only to her.

Ruby walked over to the motel office and bought a pack of cigarettes from the machine, along with a copy of the *Las Vegas Sun* and two postcards. Seated in the sweet morning air beside the pool, she read that the war in the Middle East might be coming to an end and that the Monkees had appeared at the Hollywood Bowl. She went through the newspaper's want ads, found three promising-looking dance auditions, and circled them. Then she addressed the postcards. One, of a jackalope — some mythological jackrabbit with an antelope's horns — she sent to Mrs. Baumgarten, and the other, a sun-drenched pool scene with huge fringed umbrellas and women strolling in bikinis and carrying cocktails, she sent to the Aviator. She signed them as Lily, and she gave the Aviator her temporary address and the motel's phone number. Then, after going through the dollhouse cabinets of her kitchenette, she made a grocery list: coffee, cigarettes, cereal, milk, fruit, and a category she labeled *actual food.* Just after ten, she put on a pair of cutoffs and a cotton tank top and climbed onto the empty bus. She took a seat in the front, near the driver.

"Am I the only person who gets up before noon?" she asked the man, whose curly dark hair and bass-drum gut reminded her of Jackie Gleason's Ralph Kramden.

"Just you and me, honey," he said, looking at her in his rearview mirror. "Just us early birds."

Ruby tucked her hair behind her ears, looked out the streaked window, and saw her first palm tree. The bark reminded her of the rough diamonds of pineapple hide. She craned her neck, looking for coconuts.

"First time?" the driver asked, although it was obvious.

"Just moved here."

"Gonna work in the casinos?"

"I'm a dancer."

"Oh," he said, and this time he looked at her much harder, longer. "One of *those* dancers?"

Ruby wasn't sure what he meant. "Like the June Taylor Dancers," she said.

"Oh." He sounded disappointed. "With your looks and all, I just assumed you'd be one of the other kind."

What on earth? Did he think she was a stripper? Was that it? "I'm the kind of dancer who keeps her clothes on. A professional dancer," she added for emphasis.

"Beg pardon." He touched the back of his hand to his cap. "No offense intended."

In the long run, he turned out to be helpful, pointing out the grocery store, a Laundromat, and a drugstore where she could buy stamps. "Watch yourself," he advised as she left the bus. "Lotsa crazies out there, even before noon. Leftovers from the night before."

Why did everyone keep telling her to be careful? If there was one thing she'd long ago learned, it was that no one could be trusted.

After a few hours of exploring on foot and trying hard not to look like a tourist, she found slot machines lining a section of the grocery store and decided to try her luck. Ruby loaded ten pennies and pulled the lever. On her third pile of pennies, the three reels landed on the same image: a yellow bird. She smiled as the hopper filled with coins — a whopping three dollars. Feeling lucky, Ruby climbed down from the stool and stopped while she was ahead.

She'd never eaten TV dinners — Aunt Tate thought they were too expensive and designed only for self-indulgent, lazy people. Ruby bought a Swanson fried chicken dinner with mixed vegetables, another with chopped sirloin and French fries, one with sliced turkey and gravy, and another that had shrimp with cocktail sauce. She even bought Jiffy Pop — another forbidden extravagance — along with small jars of mayonnaise and mustard, and bologna for sandwiches. As she made her way down the cereal aisle, she caught herself humming Dean Martin's "Ain't That a Kick in the Head" and dancing the quickstep.

This, Ruby realized, is what happiness feels like. Freedom. Bubbling champagne, yellow birds, music and dance and neon and possibility. Ruby grinned at everyone she saw — the cashier, the women with bristled curlers and miserable, snotty-faced toddlers, the gawky boys stocking shelves, and the heavy-jowled butcher weighing out three pounds of ground chuck. She made her way back to the motel, put away her groceries, practiced her dance steps until she rained sweat and felt the cathartic release of physical effort, and then she did stretches beside the pool. She took a quick, late-afternoon dip before heating up her shrimp TV dinner, lifting the foil when it was finished and salivating over the six tiny battered shrimp. She turned on the *color* television that was not pinned under Aunt Tate's milk glass collection, and through her open window listened to kids released from the backseats of station wagons, mileage markers, license plate games, and highway rest stops, as they shrieked and played Marco Polo in the pool. Later, when the sun had gone down and the temperature relaxed below 95, Ruby sat on the lawn chair outside her room, savored a cigarette, and watched insects congregate beneath the lamps that lit the pool deck.

Tomorrow's audition was at noon. She was nervous, but she reminded herself that nothing worth having comes without effort, without overcoming fears and doubts. And this was all about her dream, the talent and hard work that would take her away from all that had been. She fell asleep lying on her side, watching the slit in the curtain where pale moonlight shone through.

2

Ruby wore a miniskirt over her cherry-red dance shorts, a sleeveless, white cotton blouse tucked into her shorts, and the necklace with her mother's rings — a good-luck charm she'd not taken off, even to shower or swim, since graduation night. In her dance bag, she carried a pair of flats and a pair of heels, since she wasn't sure which the managers would want to see her perform in. She'd thrown in her tap shoes, too — just in case.

Ruby walked beneath the fifteen-story sign that held aloft the giant gold Aladdin's lamp. Leaving behind the day's heat, she entered the mercifully air-conditioned lobby. The Aladdin was barely a year old, and Elvis had been married here just last month. She looked behind her, for a moment thinking she might see her footprints alongside those of Elvis, sunk into the carpet pile.

After asking for directions, she made her way through the cacophony of slot machines, blackjack dealers, scattered roulette and craps tables. She saw mostly middle-aged people, a lot of bow ties, women in simple A-line dresses or strapless cocktail dresses and permanent-waved hair. A sign announced that the Gold Room offered around-the-clock dining, and posters advertised *Topless Scandals of '67, Pussycats Galore Revue,* and the *Jet Set Revue.* As Ruby reached the Aladdin Lounge at last, she thought that this casino alone must employ dozens of dancers; surely the odds were in her favor.

Inside the lounge, two gray-skinned men sat at a table next to the stage, tapping their cigarettes into an overflowing ashtray. They looked up at Ruby, and one of the men thrust his chin in the direction of a door. Ruby made her way through that door, where she found less than a dozen other girls in their dance attire, stretching and warming up. She smiled nervously, but none of the girls returned her greeting. Chalking up their lack of friendliness to pre-audition jitters, she noticed that all of them were wearing heels. At least that question was answered.

Ruby was bustier than any of them, maybe

a little less adamantly muscular, and definitely longer-legged than most. Some — clearly ballerinas — were thinner, and others had washboard torsos beneath midriff tops, the tails of blouses tied beneath their breasts. One particularly thin, limber dancer displayed several medals from national classical ballet dance competitions on a ribbon looped through the handles of her gym bag. Ruby found a spot near the wall and began her stretching routine. She wanted to ask someone what happened next but knew better. This was no friendly competition.

Deacon, one of the men seated near the stage, identified himself as the choreographer's first assistant and called them all onto the stage to line up. Ruby found a spot second from the end, stage right, next to a thin-boned ballerina in a black leotard. The girl had pale, milky skin and a blue vein that beat stridently at her temple. While Ruby stood as if at attention, stiff, her feet together, her hands at her sides, some of the other girls posed as if they were being photographed. Ruby felt sorry for them, thinking that they'd confused a beauty pageant with a dance audition.

The assistant walked along the line, assessing. Ruby smiled a tentative smile, which Deacon either didn't see or ignored

— he wasn't spending a lot of time looking at their faces. He told the shortest girl she could go, and Ruby watched the girl's hunched shoulders as she left the stage without having danced a single step. To the remaining girls, he said, "Listen up and watch." Then Deacon stepped back, and keeping his cigarette in his mouth, pushing up the sleeves of his wrinkled oxford shirt, he clapped twice and executed a surprisingly swift, intricate floor pattern including a series of soutenus, piqué turns, chaînés, a curved walk, ronds de jambe, and kicks.

"Now," he said when he'd finished. "One at a time, starting with you." He pointed his cigarette at the milk-skinned girl next to Ruby.

Ruby was stunned. They were to perform the identical choreography he'd just completed, and after seeing it only once? She glanced left toward the other girls, thinking she'd see the same surprise on their faces, but they were impassive. The girl next to her stepped out from the line and flawlessly repeated Deacon's performance. Ruby watched, counting and saying the names of the moves to herself, trying to will her body to learn the movement combination by osmosis.

"Good, good," Deacon said, and then he

nodded at Ruby, who stepped forward. He clapped his hands twice, signaling the start of Ruby's performance.

Ruby found her spotting point, managed the soutenus and what she thought was the right number of chaînés, but she screwed up on the ronds de jambe and ended up by ad-libbing with her hitch-kick — her most impressive move. Heart pounding, she looked at Deacon and hoped he'd see her skill level, that he'd realize that once she learned a routine she could perform it.

"I need dancers who follow instructions." He gestured for Ruby to go, his arm like a broom removing dirt. "Dancers who pay attention," he added sternly. Mortified, Ruby avoided looking at the other girls and made her way off stage.

"Next," she heard Deacon say, followed by his quick double-clap, a sound she knew she'd hate forever.

Blushing with humiliation, Ruby returned to the dressing area and rapidly pulled on her skirt. She shoved her heels in her bag, covered her face in the enormous sunglasses she'd found in the church thrift store, and slunk out of the casino.

Back at Room 4 of the Bombay Motor Court, Ruby stripped off her sweaty, bad-vibe clothes and pulled a fresh razor blade from the package. On the bus ride back to the motel, the pressure had grown immense, almost unendurable. She leaned her hip against the cold porcelain of the bathroom sink and sliced across her mons pubis slowly, four times, keeping the cuts short and spaced closely together to minimize what she'd have to hide beneath a dance costume or bikini.

As soon as she saw the blood, relief put its hands to her heart, kneaded and pushed and pulled and relaxed her, eased out the toxins of shame and loss. She breathed deeply, set the blade on the glass shelf above the sink, and gently placed a gauze square over the fresh wounds. She gripped the edge of the sink and looked at her face in the mirror.

Don't panic, she told herself. It's only the first audition. Now you know how it works. At four o'clock, you will go to the Dunes, and you will pick a spot in the line where you'll have more time to learn the routine by watching the others. Then, you will perform flawlessly, you will show them. You can do this. You're not going to quit at the first little hiccup, are you? You're no weakling. C'mon, Scallywag.

Ruby turned on the room fan and lay back

on her bed. She read *Madame Bovary* in the nude until it was time to go, using a ballpoint pen to underline Flaubert's juiciest morsels.

Exotic, deep pink flowers elbowed each other in flower beds shaded by three thick palm trees. Like an omnipotent god, the Dunes' huge sultan stood above it all, hands on his hips, chest thrust out, simultaneously welcoming and challenging all visitors. Presumably, he owned the entire desert, maybe even the distant blue-gray mountains that rose so swiftly from the desert floor like an apparition. Ruby could hear splashing and shouting coming from the Dunes' pool, and on the asphalt beside the sharply pointed, space-age-looking valet parking hut she saw sparrows squabbling over pieces of someone's leftover hamburger bun. The marquee bragged of the *Casino de Paris* show, and another sign touted the Persian Theatre's production of *Vive Les Girls*! That was where she was headed for the open-call audition.

This time, there were close to twenty girls. Ruby slipped on her heels and didn't once try to smile or ingratiate herself with the others. She caught a glimpse of herself from behind in a full-length mirror, saw how perfectly her shorts hugged her curves. They zipped up the back and were as tiny and flattering as Ann-Margret's famous white shorts in *Viva Las Vegas.* Ruby eased into her splits against the wall, and she tied the tails of her white blouse so that her flat — if not chiseled — abdomen was evident, enticing. She buttoned only a single button, let her cleavage show. No other girl had breasts that even began to compare with hers, and this time she fully intended to use them.

But the other girls had impressive stamina and quick-fire muscles that let them snap crisp turns and skillfully execute the choreographer's combinations. Ruby got through most of the routine they'd been shown by yet another bored-looking choreographer's assistant, who never bothered to mention his name. She executed one of her best stag leaps and finished the final few turns, stopping directly in front of the table where the men sat jiggling the ice in their drinks.

"Not quite, honey." It was the older one — the one who didn't dance but likely financed the show, Ruby guessed. Still, he gave her the first real smile of her day. "But get your stuff and c'mon down here, Red. Don't leave without talking to me."

Ruby permitted herself a small smile as she walked offstage, feeling the sensation of her competitors' eyes boring into her back. *It's not over,* she told herself as she pulled her bag from beneath the bench, returned to her street attire, buckled her sandals. He's not saying *no,* and this is only my second audition. She used her powder compact to blot the sheen from her face before heading for the men's table.

"Robert — Bob — Christianson," the older man said, standing and extending his hand. "I manage the Persian and the Casino de Paris showroom."

"Ruby Wilde." She gripped his hand strongly, smiled.

"Sit down." Bob pulled out a chair, glanced quickly at the stage where another dancer was being sent home. "Drink?"

"Iced tea?"

He signaled to a waiter Ruby hadn't noticed standing in the shadows, and soon she had a fat-bellied aluminum pitcher of tea sitting before her, along with a sugar bowl and a saucer of lemon slices.

"Here's the thing, Ruby," Bob began after waiting for her to finish drinking deeply. "And I'm going to be brutally honest."

"Okay."

"Where're you from, honey?"

"Kansas."

"Jesus."

"I know. That's why I'm here." For reasons she couldn't identify, she felt she would be able to laugh with this man — maybe even laugh at herself.

"You know the perfect Vegas showgirl body?" He waited a moment and then continued. "Five foot nine, 129 pounds — but not too thin. 36-24-37." Bob winked at Ruby and watched the choreographer's assistant narrow the applicants to five. "Get my drift?"

Ruby shook her head.

"You're perfect showgirl material."

"Oh, no. . . ." Ruby picked up her glass, began examining the melting ice cubes as if they were unexplored mountain crags. "I'm not. . . ."

"Have you seen a show? How long you been in Vegas?"

"This is my first week, my first few days." Ruby tried to still the sudden shaking in her hand as she picked up the heavy pitcher and poured herself another glass of tea. "This is only my second audition."

"Which leads me to the brutally honest part, sweetheart." Bob was lean, somewhere in his forties, with curling chest hair and a gold necklace. On his left hand he wore a pinky ring with a deep, blood-red stone surrounded by a thick gold bezel. He smelled of an expensive aftershave — not the Hai Karate of Kansas boys but something more like what the Aviator wore. Between his fingers, Bob flipped a one-hundred-dollar Dunes house chip with a drawing of the sultan, muscular arms crossed. Ruby thought about how many groceries, how many nights at the Bombay Motor Court, that one chip would buy. To Bob, it was a plaything.

Ruby set down her glass. "Go ahead." She tried to add a teasing tone to her voice. "Let me have it."

"You're not up to snuff." He set the chip on the tablecloth. "You won't get a job on the Strip as a troupe dancer. It's not what you're suited for, and it's not what anyone who is doing auditions will see when you walk onstage."

"But —"

"Doesn't matter if you were the reigning dance queen of Kansas or champeen of the greater Midwest tractor-pull show, honey. Doesn't matter if you got rave reviews for your starring role in your hometown production of Mancini's *Pink Panther* revue. This is the big time." He leveled his gaze at her, and she made herself look back. "I'm saving you time. Tears. Disappointment. You cannot make the big time. Not as a troupe dancer. Shift gears, Ruby Wilde."

Onstage, the auditions had progressed to individual dance performances. The girls appeared to be performing prepared pieces, without benefit of music. So, this was what would come next, if Ruby could climb out of the first round.

"You're saying that to make a living as a dancer I have to take my clothes off," she said, still staring at the stage, trying to avoid Bob's directness.

"I'm saying you are the perfect topless showgirl. You have sufficient dance ability. You're strong enough to wear the costumes. Primarily" — Bob put his hand on top of hers — "you are drop-dead gorgeous. You could make a killing."

She fought the impulse to remove her hand from beneath his and looked at him. "Nude."

"Topless. Classy topless."

"Baring my tits," Ruby said.

"Ass, too." He smiled. "Take that girl." He nodded toward the stage. "Yes, she can dance. She's a regular ol' whirling dervish. But" — he paused, tapped the poker chip with his index finger — "she doesn't look like you. She will never look like you. She will never make a showgirl-level income, which is at least five times what a troupe girl can bring in. Sure, she can do the footwork, but that's not what men come to Vegas to see. She's part of a dying breed, the Debbie Reynolds gal. I'm telling you," he said, taking a deep breath, "you have a future. Just not the one you pictured."

Ruby let an ice cube into her mouth, cracked it between her molars, and chewed. She watched the girl on the stage, her chassé steps and impressive isolation abilities. She was awfully good — better than anyone Ruby had ever seen in real life.

"The washboard abs are impressive," Bob said, also watching the girl perform. "But she's not the stuff of men's fantasies. *Not* sexy. You, Ruby Wilde, are out-of-the-ballpark sexy. You look like a *woman,*" he said, leaning in and lowering his voice. "*That,* you can sell." He pulled a business card from his shirt pocket and wrote a short note on the back. "Here," he said, passing it to her. "Bring a friend. On me. See what the show's like. I guarantee it'll prove your assumptions wrong. This isn't some sleazy porn theater. It's a celebration of women, of beauty." He smiled broadly.

Ruby took the card but stared at the tabletop, focused on the ironed folds in the linen. She hadn't come this far to give up so soon, especially to cry *uncle* by taking her clothes off for money. Dancing topless couldn't be that far above whoring herself out beneath a streetlamp.

She stood, reached out her hand to shake Bob's. "Thank you," she said. "Sincerely. For the tea. For your advice."

"I want you on my stage, Ruby Wilde. You could be great. A real star."

"I'll keep your card," she promised.

Bob stood, put his hand on her shoulder. "You have the skin. The body. The looks." He shook his head. "Don't close the door before you see what's behind it. It's a limited window of opportunity."

"I'll think about it. Really. Thank you."

"You should be draped in pearls. Feathers brushing that lovely cheek." He touched her face with the back of his hand, familiar but unthreatening. "I'll look for you," he said, finally releasing her.

Ruby left the room, aware of Bob Christianson's eyes on her ass. On her way out through the padded doors, she turned, waved her fingertips in his direction, and thought about how wrong — how truly, utterly wrong — he was about her and her future.

She hadn't eaten since breakfast and was ravenous. Ruby looked at the lights of the

Aladdin across the way and told herself to go back to the site of her first rejection, get back on that particular horse of failure before she began superstitiously avoiding the place. *Face it down,* she told herself, and, dance bag slung over her shoulder, she walked to the casino.

Ruby sat at the bar, and after eyeing the various colored bottles behind the bartender, she ordered the only drink that came to mind — a daiquiri, her first. The fifty-nine-cent happy-hour price was right, and the bartender kindly refrained from nabbing her as underage. The drink was deliciously cool, sweet like a dessert, and she felt its relaxing effects immediately. Ruby ordered a second.

The man on the barstool next to her instructed the bartender to put her drinks on his tab. Ruby turned, saw a mouse-brown toupee and a weak, practically non-existent chin. The man introduced himself and said something about his huge johnson. Ruby leaned away from his stale breath, signaled to the bartender. "I'll pay for my own drinks, all right?"

"Gotcha," he said.

The man slurred his words. "Immafedral-judgeshaknow," he said, clearly expecting her to be impressed. All Ruby managed to dissect from his gibberish was *judge.* "Un-nidedstatesdistructuvnewmeshico."

"What?"

"Newmeshico."

"New Mexico?"

"Sright."

"Sure."

"Impordundecishuns," he continued, undeterred.

Ruby looked pleadingly toward the bartender, who mouthed, *Your problem* and smiled wickedly.

"Bill?" she tried. "Billy Artie Virgil Alphonse?"

"Johnshun."

"Yeah, well, here's the deal," Ruby said, thinking maybe she was starting to sound a little drunk herself. "I'm not interested. No matter how big and important you or your johnson might be. Okay?"

"Misshingout."

"My tough luck, your honor."

He started to slide off his seat, keeping his eyes on her.

"Sayonara," she said, and saluted.

"Semper fi." He returned her salute and staggered off toward the roulette tables.

Ruby ordered a third daiquiri.

"Judicial conference," the bartender said when he put the fresh drink before her.

"Not exactly rocket scientists."

"No kidding." She looked toward the gaming tables and imagined a room full of black judges' robes, gavels pounding. She giggled.

"Cuttin' you off," the bartender said when she raised her hand a fourth time. "You're gonna fall off the barstool, Red."

"Ruby."

"Ruby Red."

"Okay." Ruby reached into her purse, and her fingers found the surprise of the poker chip Bob Christianson had slipped into the pocket when she wasn't looking. She held it up, evaluated the sexy sultan's biceps. She had to admit — the sultan was pretty.

"You got lucky at the Dunes today," the bartender said, eyeing her chip.

"I'm not so sure about that."

"Looks that way to me," he said, and then waved off her money. "Just come back and see me sometime. And do me a favor before you hit the street."

"Yeah?"

"Stop by the buffet. Get some food in your stomach, soak up the alcohol." He must have read her face, because then he added, "It's only $1.99. All you can eat. Just do it, Ruby Red."

She stood, unsteady. And then she laid a

dollar bill tip on the bar and looked for the women's restroom. The earth was spinning faster than it did in Kansas. Of that — and maybe only that — Ruby was certain.

3

Ruby nursed her first-ever hangover by floating on her back in the pool, occasionally opening her eyes to watch clouds travel in wisps above her. The air held a noticeable layer of desert dust whipped up by overnight winds. She listened to the glug and slurp of the skimmers and tried to muster an appetite so that she'd have energy for the noon audition at the Sahara. When a child's beach ball hit her square in the face, she got out and quickly dressed to catch the bus for the trip to the Sahara, way on the north end of the Strip, past Caesars and the Flamingo, past the Desert Inn, the Riviera, and the Thunderbird.

As Ruby descended from the bus in front of the casino, she thought, *The Beatles played here,* and wondered if she would ever get used to brushing against the famous — or at least their wakes. Next to the tall, vertical sign that said *Sahara,* palm trees rose like huge lit torches, and the new, high-rise section of rooms towered over the city. She passed the camel sculptures with their Bedouin riders, thinking of the movie scene where Ann-Margret and Elvis stood beside the very same camels, talking. Bird of paradise flowers nodded their sharp, subtly threatening orange-and-blue heads at her as she crossed the parking lot. Inside, she saw signs for the Congo Room, where she knew Dinah Shore performed, but she was looking for the Casbar Lounge. Posters announced upcoming shows for the Smothers Brothers and Buddy Hackett.

Some of the girls backstage were familiar from previous auditions. Still, everyone kept to themselves, and no one uttered a word, although one girl had the hiccups.

Ruby broke the rules, smiled encouragingly at the girl. "Wish I had some peanut butter for you."

"Why?" The girl hiccupped again, covered her mouth.

"That's what my mother always used. A spoonful. And it worked."

"Stand on your head," another girl suggested.

"Hold your nose and drink a glass of water without stopping," someone else advised.

"It has to be sugar water," said another.

Every hiccup remedy known to mankind was mentioned, and for a few minutes, there was camaraderie amongst the competitors. It made Ruby feel good to think that she'd gotten the ball rolling, that being kind was still an option, even in this setting.

But the rest of the audition went exactly as the previous ones had: Ruby danced her heart out and was one of the first girls cut from the line. Afterward, as she finished dressing and cramming her dance heels back into her bag, the hiccup girl joined her.

"You got cut too?" Ruby asked.

"Story of my life," Hiccup Girl said, slumping into a folding chair beneath the wall phone.

"How long have you been at it?"

"Too long." She hiccupped.

"Don't give up," Ruby said, running a brush through her hair.

"No, this is it. I decided last night. No more after this."

Ruby sat down beside her, saw that the girl's roots were dark brown and her pink nail polish chipped. "What will you do?"

"Go home."

"Oh, no."

"It's okay. I have a fiancé," the girl confessed, looking into Ruby's face. "The deal was that I could try this for a month. And then, if it was a no-go, I'd come back."

"Where's back?"

"Colorado."

"I liked what I saw of Colorado," Ruby said. "From the bus."

"Where're you from?"

"Kansas. Salina."

"Cool."

They sat there, neither one inclined to work any longer at conversation. Finally, Hiccup Girl got up, stripped off her dance attire, dropped a Hawaiian-print muumuu over her head, and slipped her feet into mustard yellow flip-flops.

"Can I buy you a drink?" Ruby asked, remembering the poker chip in her purse. "At the Dunes?"

"Why the Dunes?"

"I don't know," she said, not wanting to reveal that that she'd been on the receiving end of such a huge gift. Or bribe. Or maybe it was bait.

"Actually," the girl said as she picked up her bag, "I'll buy. It's my last night here. Might as well." She sighed.

"Okay," Ruby said, thinking that the girl shouldn't be alone. Besides, it would be nice to have someone to talk to, other than a bartender or a drunk, middle-aged loser in a toupee. "Let's go to Caesars." Ruby was suddenly inspired. "I have a friend who might be working tonight."

"Okay, sure. At least I haven't bombed there."

"Me, either," Ruby said. "Yet." Then, thinking she might have jinxed herself, she quickly added, "And I've been wanting to see it."

"Georgia," the girl said, extending her hand.

"Ruby."

"Figures," Georgia said.

"What?"

"My hiccups finally stopped." Georgia gave Ruby a lopsided smile.

Ruby spotted Rose on duty behind the reception counter. She was wearing a short white toga, gold sandals, and a gold belt. Gracefully curved gold bracelets circled her upper arms, and her hair was piled into a gold barrette, with loose tendrils framing her face. Ruby felt tacky, sweaty, and considered skipping the hellos, but Rose saw her and waved her over.

"We've been calling you!" Rose said, giving her a hug. "Hey," she said to Georgia.

"Rose, Georgia. And vice versa," Ruby said.

"Daddy and I want to take you to dinner before he leaves town. And tomorrow's his last night."

"Oh, you don't have to."

"You don't have a choice. He was going to have me drive him over to the Bombay Court and camp out if we didn't get ahold of you soon."

"We're on our way to drown our sorrows," Ruby said, trying to bring Georgia into the conversation.

"No luck?" Rose looked genuinely concerned.

"Not yet," Ruby said, wanting to ward off pity. "But I'm learning."

"Hah!" Georgia blew out a breath, and Rose gave Georgia a puzzled look. "I just mean," Georgia said, fumbling. "Just . . . I just meant me. I was thinking about me. Not a comment on Ruby. She's good."

"Georgia's going back home," Ruby said by way of explanation. "She's getting married." Ruby tried to sound enthusiastic, as if she believed marriage weren't Georgia's consolation prize.

Rose looked back to the reception counter and nodded at one of the other toga-clad women. "I gotta go. Listen," she said, touching Ruby's elbow lightly. "We'll come get you at six tomorrow. Okay? Daddy hates eating any later."

"Sure."

"Dress up."

"Is that a comment about my present attire?" Ruby tugged at her cutoffs and grinned.

"He'll wanna take us someplace special. Steak. Prime rib. Prawns." Rose smiled.

"I've never had prime rib. Or prawns."

"Good." Rose kissed her on the cheek. "So glad you stopped by," she said, and Ruby felt a melting in her chest, as if distrust could take a break for a while.

Georgia was a talker. She didn't seem to expect Ruby to do anything other than listen, which suited Ruby fine. From their table against a wall in the bar, Ruby was enjoying watching people, imagining their stories and conversations. Awkward men in J. C. Penney suits, their wives with cultured pearl necklaces, scuffed handbags, sometimes an abbreviated fur stole despite the summer heat. The women had careful curls, mascara, and penciled eyebrows but no eye shadow — eye shadow was apparently too slutty for denizens of Minneapolis or Des Moines or Savannah. Ruby saw lapel pins on the men — Rotary Club, Masonic emblems, American flags. Women leaned in to have their cigarettes lit and trotted off in sadly dependent pairs to find the ladies' restroom. She saw the men in their wives' absence, easily won over by cocktail waitresses and cigarette girls flashing tan thighs and perky breasts from beneath their perfunctory Caesars togas. She saw them all so eager to glimpse glamour, their hungry eyes roving in search of even a minor celebrity — someone they could tell everyone back home they'd seen *In the flesh, this close!*

Ruby didn't want to live her life in anticipation of one precious, boredom-cracking week a year, a vacation planned for Vegas or Our Nation's Capital or Disneyland. She sipped tonight's foray into alcohol — a rum and cola — and squeezed extra lime into the drink before licking her fingers. She looked at Georgia as she nattered on about domesticity, clearly trying to convince herself that she was headed back to something she genuinely wanted. Ruby imagined Georgia in a few years, seated with her husband in the bar at Caesars or trying to spot Tony Curtis pulling up in his Rolls-Royce, telling anyone who listened that she'd danced in Vegas, that she'd lived the neon life before she settled down.

Settled. That was the key word, wasn't it? As long as I don't quit, everything will be all right, Ruby told herself as Georgia described her fiancé, Sam, the long-haul truck driver. Georgia was worried about having to endure her mother's *I told you so,* and she dreamed of owning her own Laundromat, maybe a children's clothing store. Or, she might manage a shoe store.

I'm not Georgia, Ruby swore to herself. *I'm not Georgia. I won't quit.*

Besides, there was nothing — no one — for Ruby to go home to. No Sam. No mother. No *home.*

Rose and her father seated Ruby between them at a table in the least expensive section, farthest from the stage. Still, it was the Sands' Copa Room, where Sinatra performed and an omni-tan, pomaded Dean Martin sashayed his way through "Volare," a tumbler of amber liquid perched atop his piano. This, too, was the theater where Red Skelton clowned, his hands animatedly flying about. But what Ruby could not believe was that she was on the verge of seeing — in person, live, sharing the same stale refrigerated air she breathed — *Sammy Davis, Jr.,* and the world's greatest drummer, Buddy Rich.

Ruby carefully laid the linen napkin across the gold of the dress she'd worn to her *Tah-Dah!* Dance Studio fundraiser, and she relished each mouthwatering bite of the prime rib that oozed deep red juices. Much to Mason's amusement, she blew clean her sinuses with a hefty dose of horseradish and dabbed at her teary eyes, laughing along with him. There were *haricots verts* — which turned out to be green beans in disguise — and a baked potato packed with butter and sour cream. She sipped a glass of the bold, nearly chewable cabernet sauvignon Mason had ordered, and when the lights dimmed and the band struck its initial chords, Ruby looked to Rose and Mason, sending pulses of gratitude to them for their kindness. She felt a near crazy grin on her face, and she whispered, "My dream come true. You made my dream come true." They smiled, obviously pleased by her joy.

Nothing could have prepared her for how small Sammy was. He was a constantly moving, high-speed sprite, with a sharply pointed chin and long, thin nose. Short, black suede boots that on him looked right. A gold chain circled one vulnerable, bird-boned wrist, and he peppered his conversation with *baby* and *dig* and *chick* and *cool* and *right on* and *that cat.* He held them spellbound from the moment he speed-walked himself onto the stage, through his verbal riffs, his über-cool slides and glides, and his head-nodding, thigh-rapping accompaniment to Buddy Rich's drum solos.

Cigarette in his right hand, microphone gripped in his left, Sammy sang "That Old Black Magic." Then, without pausing he grabbed a long shoehorn, slipped into tap shoes, and performed his syncopated version of "Me and My Shadow." Ruby tried to memorize the fluidity of his technique, to think of her feet flying at Sammy's Morse-code speed. At one point, the band cut out, and in the silence all she could hear, other than an occasional smoker's cough, was the rhythm he created. Sammy made it look easy. His skill, his sheer athleticism, fueled her love of dance. She felt her dancer's heart revitalized, despite the recent string of failures and disappointments.

Sammy Davis, Jr., was a hepcat seducer who lured with junkie, fast-talking patter. He fed on applause, attention, and like Ruby he was determined to take the audience captive.

He succeeded. They were his. A vast sea of enraptured white faces watched the Negro-Cuban boy who had climbed so high that he could audaciously, publicly caress and marry a gorgeous white woman. At the same time, Ruby knew that until just a year ago he'd been forced to enter and exit Vegas casinos through the kitchen — "with the garbage," as he put it. Tonight, in the middle of one routine, he used a falsetto voice to slip "Two, four, six, eight, we don't want to integrate" into his riff, and then he kept dancing as if someone else had spoken. Ruby heard nervous, scattered laughter, and she thought about his courage. Sammy Davis, Jr. was winning. Despite the odds.

Ruby adopted Sammy as her god that night. She had all the advantages he had not — she had her savings, her above-grade femininity and beauty, her peaches-and-cream skin, and her automatic, white-girl acceptability. How dare she contemplate failure? How dare she imagine following Georgia off of the stage, quitting?

No more doubts, she promised herself. No more.

When the lights came up and people started making their way out of the Copa and into the main casino for a night of serious gambling, Ruby couldn't stop talking. She hadn't felt this animated in — well, maybe forever.

"You made *my* day, kiddo," Mason said, patting her shoulder. "To see you smile like this. Rose said you were pretty down."

"I was."

"But we took care of that?"

"You and Sammy." Ruby grinned. "Baby," she said, cocking her head in imitation of the hipster.

"Dig this, chick." Rose pointed, à la Sammy.

Mason held out an arm to each girl. "Shall we?"

They linked arms and walked with Mason through the smoke of the gambling tables, the incessant clanging of the slot machines, and out into the desert night to stand in the parking lot where the asphalt exhaled an endless sigh of unrelenting heat. Ruby imagined the over-warm air filling her skirt, lifting her like a hot air balloon over the Strip.

"I'd miss the stars if I lived here," Mason said, looking up. "Can't see a damned thing with all this neon."

"No Big Dipper to scoop ice cream," Rose said, looking at her father's upturned face, sharing a childhood memory with him.

"I know you love it here, Peanut Blossom. But me . . ." He shook his head. "I prefer the real world."

Ruby lit a cigarette and watched them. She envied them their closeness, the fact that they could touch each other — physically, or with words, ideas. Rose could ask her father about his childhood or what he thought about the civil rights movement or if he liked ground pepper in his tomato juice. Or lemon juice. Or both. Despite her gratitude, her genuine like of the Maddoxes, Ruby felt a pang of envy.

The newspaper headlines screamed the sensational death: Jayne Mansfield, thirty-time *Playboy* playmate, film star, and beautiful blonde bombshell, was dead at thirty-four, killed in a horrendous car wreck on a Louisiana highway in the small hours of June 29, 1967. The article was accompanied by a photo of Mansfield, her light-blonde hair teased and piled high, her cleavage a joyous shout of sexual promise. Mansfield's car had rear-ended, and then traveled beneath, a tractor-trailer truck; the three adults in the front seat were killed outright. Mansfield's three children, who'd been sleeping in the backseat, survived.

Ruby dropped the newspaper, covered her face with her hands. There was *her* word, *the* word. Mansfield had been *decapitated.* It took her breath, made her chest hurt, a crushing pain as if a sledgehammer had struck her breastbone. Ruby could smell hot rubber, gasoline. She could smell blood. She could see Mansfield's rich mane, the blonde strands wedded to each other with clotted blood; she heard wailing, the cries of shocked children as strangers lifted them from the backseat.

Ruby opened her eyes, picked up the newspaper, and forced herself to finish the article. There had been several small dogs in the car, too. Some lived; others died. *Those poor children,* Ruby thought. *To lose their pets, too.*

Bereaved. Comfortless. She felt it all again. Time collapsed, disappeared, and she was back on that lonely Kansas highway.

There was a photo of the car, the top of it sheared off. Ruby could hear glass fracturing, the sharp, brutal sound of metal shearing.

She hadn't known it was there — the memory of that night. The sensations, the smells and sounds — they had lain dormant within her for all these years, to be coaxed to the surface by the eerily similar circumstances of a celebrity's unfathomable death.

A few days later the newspapers corrected themselves. Mansfield had not been decapitated. Someone had mistaken her abundant hairpiece for her head.

4

Three months of failure. Ruby paid for another couple weeks at the Bombay Motor Court. Counting out the cash on the countertop, she felt a ceaseless, dull throbbing at the back of her head. She'd grown bored with the formerly forbidden magic of TV dinners. The thrill of tossing a perfectly good waxed paper cereal box liner into the trash and imagining Aunt Tate's disapproval had not endured. Ruby was sick of the motel room and the Roger Miller lyrics that flowed pitilessly through her mind, Miller's litany of no phone, no pool, no pets, and no cigarettes. She was tired of television, bored by the interchangeable families that filled the pool every night. She was disillusioned. She was lonely.

Ruby got tossed off of the stage at eight more auditions. The Desert Inn, Riviera, Stardust, Tropicana — and more. She stopped trying to talk to the other girls and made eye contact with no one. She thought about Georgia in exuberantly green Colorado, about engagement parties, white satin and taffeta. Dimpled flower girls with rose petals and patent leather shoes.

She mailed another postcard to the Aviator and told him to hold off sending the things she'd left in his care. She told him she was looking for a more permanent address while she decided which casino to grace with her presence. She finished with *Hahahahahahaha!,* which she felt transformed the card from obfuscation to honesty.

She hadn't yet cashed in the hundred-dollar Dunes chip that Bob Christianson had given her. She'd pull that rip cord when she needed to jump from the burning plane.

When the phone rang, Ruby was sitting on the end of the bed, desultorily switching the channel dial back and forth between *The Dating Game* and *The Match Game.* The fan in her room had first screeched in protest and then broken. The front office had yet to send anyone to fix it, so Ruby was listless with the heat.

"Did I wake you?" Rose asked.

"Naw. Just hot." Ruby wound the phone cord around her bare ankle, pulled it taut.

"The girls at my apartment complex are

having a spur-of-the-moment barbecue tomorrow afternoon. I want you to come."

"I —"

"I know it's short notice."

"It's not that." Ruby hadn't realized how down she was — down to the point of feeling nearly completely antisocial.

"You'll have a good time. Margaritas and tequila chicken. Chips and guacamole. They're a good bunch."

"All right." Ruby knew she sounded less than gracious. Lately, she had to work so hard to make herself do anything at all. She squeezed her big toe between her fingers, realized she'd have to muster the energy to shave her legs and fix her toenail polish.

"I'll come get you so you don't have to take the bus. And there's someone I want you to meet."

"Please, not a guy," Ruby pleaded.

"No, no no. It's just us girls," Rose said, managing not to sound defensive.

"Sorry."

"Still no luck, hunh?"

"Still an abject failure."

"Well, be patient. And," Rose hurried to say, "I know it's easy for me to say, but I have a feeling about you."

"That makes one of us."

"Four o'clock?"

"Deal. And Rose?"

"Yeah?"

"You're a peach."

"And you're a jewel, Ruby. Don't you forget it."

Vivid carried a glass pitcher of margaritas richly beaded with moisture. She stopped in front of Ruby and topped off Ruby's glass. Vivid's eyes were hidden behind her sunglasses, but a knowing smile broadened her face as she used one hand to capture some of the droplets from the pitcher. She rubbed her wet hand across her collarbones and then, stretching, languorous, she ran that same wet hand up the length of her neck, circling like a secret beneath her shoulder-length, pitch-black hair. "Better." She sighed.

Ruby felt her lips part, unbidden, at the sight of Vivid's ripe, Ava Gardneresque sensuality. She'd never seen a sexier woman. Ruby watched as Vivid threaded her way through the other girls surrounding the tiny, kidney-shaped apartment pool. In her late twenties, Vivid wore tight, toreador pants that zipped up the side and were cut to sit just below her belly button. The material, a mod floral pattern in reds, yellows, and greens on a white background, had a sheen to it. A cropped, tight, sleeveless white T-shirt and no bra revealed the contours of Vivid's breasts, and her erect nipples were clearly visible beneath the thin cotton. She wore tall wedge sandals, and in her wake Ruby smelled a rich, heavy perfume that reminded her of her mother's Stargazer lilies.

Vivid's outfit made Ruby long for a sewing machine and yardage she could stitch into something just as provocative. At the same time, Vivid's lean, flat belly made Ruby realize that she really needed to get back to the nightly sit-ups that she'd let go in exchange for wallowing in front of the motel TV. She looked down at her legs in her cutoff shorts, the utilitarian Keds sneakers that needed to take a spin in the washer. She'd let herself go, as the Salina housewives used to say of each other when they were caught out at the grocery store in curlers or a rumpled blouse.

"Oh, good — you met Vivid," Rose said, perching on the lounge chair next to Ruby. "Scoot over." Ruby moved her legs to the side. Rose covered Ruby's kneecap with her palm in a familiar, friendly gesture. "I'll get her over here later so you two can have a chat."

"She's stunning," Ruby said, still stupefied. "Does she work with you at Caesars? And that's her real name — Vivid? Just Vivid?"

"Stage name. Her real name's Vivian O'Shea — pure Irish on both sides. Vivid's in the Folies Bergere at the Tropicana, but she's worked almost everywhere. That's why I want for you two to talk. She can help you. Really help you, Ruby."

"She's a dancer then."

"A showgirl. Topless. Yes."

Ruby tried to hide her surprise — that Rose would encourage her to strip for money.

"I'm not as innocent or as pure as you think," Rose said, accurately reading Ruby's expression.

"I didn't —"

"You've mostly seen me when I'm with my father. And, for obvious reasons, I have to stay on my toes around him."

So, it was an act. Not Rose's generosity — that was genuine — but the good-girl thing, that was a performance for Daddy. Ruby put her hand on top of Rose's. "You know what? It's a relief. I mean it — a huge relief. Takes the pressure off. You're not perfect, after all."

"I even say *piss* and *shit* and *fuck,* from time to time." Rose grinned.

"She's not telling the entire truth," Vivid said, pulling over a chair and joining them. "When properly inspired, Rose has the mouth of a sailor."

"A sailor on fucking shore leave." Rose laughed.

Ruby could feel the tequila's effects. And, maybe it was the company, too. She loaded a chip with guacamole — a taste she could add to her list of new experiences.

"Rose says Bob Christianson singled you out. At one of your auditions." Vivid leaned toward Ruby, and Ruby could see midnight-blue highlights in Vivid's hair. "Is that true?"

"He slipped me a hundred-dollar chip. And his card."

"You say that as if you don't know what it means."

"I guess I don't."

"Guaranteed job. Money. Clothes. Jewelry — for starters."

"A car," Rose added.

"Ha!" Ruby scoffed.

"Look over there." Rose pointed past the wrought-iron fence that separated the apartment pool from the parking lot. "That's Vivid's convertible."

Ruby spotted a 1967 Pontiac GTO two-door coupe painted a deep, almost navy blue with a white retractable top and a generous white interior. "Bob gave you that?" she asked.

"An admirer gave me that. But your Bob, or Donn Arden or Evan Brashear or Harold Minsky or Jack Entratter — those are the men who can and do put girls in the position where they can receive gifts like that car."

Ruby didn't say what she was thinking — that she wouldn't sell her body for a car, or the diamond tennis bracelet that clung to Vivid's wrist, or the emerald ring on Vivid's right hand.

"Stand up," Vivid said, her tone direct. Rose moved aside, and Ruby surprised herself by obeying. Vivid appraised her. "Bob knows his stuff. You've got it — I can see that — and you auditioned, Bob saw you dance?"

"Yeah. But he didn't hire me."

"Not as a troupe dancer. But I gather he told you exactly where you can make money. With that body, your beautiful features. You can make serious money."

"And," Rose said, "you'd get to wear the most incredible costumes."

"I thought I'd have to parade across a stage naked," Ruby said, sounding archly dismissive. She sat back down on the edge of the lounge chair.

"The vitals are covered — I wear a G-string, pasties. But the rest of the costumes we wear can weigh as much as seventy pounds. It takes strength, grace — *talent* — to be a showgirl." Vivid took a sip of her drink and moved her sunglasses to the top of her head. Her eyes were a clear, swimming-pool blue. "We're on stage to be admired. It's a long way from prostitution. I sleep with the men I want to sleep with — that's it. No different from any other woman, except I get far more offers than the average. So, Ruby, what I'd say to you is don't knock it till you've tried it."

"At least go see Vivid dance," Rose chimed in. "You need a job, Ruby. And I don't mean waitressing or cashier work."

Vivid stood, rubbed an unconscious hand across her flat belly. "I have to get out of the sun," she said. "I can't afford tan lines." She started to walk toward an empty spot at a table beneath an umbrella but paused to add, "I'm willing to teach you the ropes, and that's a generous offer in a competitive environment. Talk to Rose."

"Thank you," Ruby managed.

"I'm not doing this for you. I don't know you. This is for Rose," Vivid said. "I'm offering because Rose asked me."

Ruby could hear the defensiveness in

Vivid's voice. She regretted her judgmental attitude but didn't know how to take it back and so just looked helplessly between Rose and Vivid before noticing that her own fair-skinned legs had begun to turn pink in the sun.

Ruby sat cross-legged on her bed, counting out the remainder of her cash and tallying her projected expenses, including quarters for the dryer, dimes for the washers. She was living on breakfast cereal, canned beans, four-for-a-dollar frozen pot pies, and boxes of powdered macaroni and cheese — the cheapest things she could find in the grocery aisles. She needed deodorant, lotion, and the heels of her tap shoes cried for the attention of a shoe repairman. She calculated that she had about two weeks left before she'd have to cash in the poker chip. After that, she'd be forced to contact the Aviator. But she wouldn't — she knew it. Her pride would never let her fully confess failure to him. That's why she said yes when Rose called to say Vivid had complimentary Folies tickets waiting for them at the Tropicana's front desk.

The Folies Bergere costumes were beyond anything Dinah Shore could have dreamed of — skyscrapers of feathers, paste-jewels the size of golf balls, chains of bright, multicolored beads dripping in elegant curves from the dancers' outstretched arms. Perfectly choreographed lines of beautiful women lifting long legs, prancing like finely trained Arabian horses, with eyes that glittered from beneath birdlike swaths of bold color. They were utterly feminine, and the fact that their breasts were bare was practically lost on Ruby, so won over was she by their lavish costumes, the extravagant fans of floating ostrich feathers. The band was excellent, and she counted nine costume changes, including a different pair of sparkly, three-inch heels for each outfit. She watched the women dip, turn. Closefitting, bejeweled caps obscured their hair and made them all look alike, despite the differences in the curve of a waist, the shape of a breast. She had to look hard to spot Vivid during each dance number, but eventually she recognized the elongated muscles of Vivid's thighs, her broad smile and heart-shaped face.

"Over there." Rose pointed discreetly. "That's the lead dancer. Patricia La Forge."

Ruby watched La Forge, who did seem to possess a greater level of self-assurance than the others. Ruby found herself wondering if the lead dancer was paid more, what perks came with the title.

The dancers performed a number in which they were chess pieces moving about a giant checkerboard. Another number featured a film projected onto a screen behind the stage so that it looked as though the women were accompanied by a dramatically expanded cast. Ruby saw contortionists and even trapeze artists — a breathtaking display of excess that she never could have imagined. Then, in a new segment of the show, a pair of German magicians draped cheetahs across their shoulders as if the wild beasts were heavy fur stoles. Dramatic, handsome men with high cheekbones and hair combed back from their austere faces, they were named Siegfried and Roy, and Rose said they'd been with the Folies for only a few months.

Sitting in the dark, watching every turn, every step, Ruby quickly acknowledged the skill it took for a dancer to travel up and down dozens of stairs without looking down, all the while supporting an unwieldy tower of plumage. The numbers were finely choreographed, the floating and revolving formations novel, intricate. In the final number of the show, the girls formed a line and executed perfectly timed high kicks like the Rockettes. Ruby watched with respect as they twirled and yet kept their snow-white tail feathers from crashing into each other.

All of Ruby's preconceptions and prejudices fell away that night. She was won over, completely sold. Maybe she could hold onto her dream after all. If she could be hired as a showgirl, she could pay her bills, appear on stage — and dance. At a loss for words when the show was over, she managed only "Good grief!"

"Told ya." Rose grinned.

Back in her room at the Bombay Motor Court, Ruby let her excitement grow and dismissed the voice in her head that said it was shameful, baring her body to gratify men's greedy eyes. She told herself it was Aunt Tate's voice, not her own. This route was a reasonable adaptation to her plan, a way forward. It took courage, she told herself, to reassess, to know when stubbornness and drive were productive and when it was time to look at things from another angle. Besides, she quite literally could not afford not to try — not unless she wanted to give up, never be a professional dancer. And Scallywag was no quitter.

5

The Tropicana's showgirl application was short and sweet. Date, name, address, height and weight. Hair color, eye color, complexion. Measurements, dress size, bathing suit size, hat and shoe sizes. Where it asked for her present occupation, Ruby wrote *DANCER,* and she added two years to her age. The final few questions required a bit more thought, although the minimal response blanks hardly required an essay. For *Ambition,* she wrote *To dance professionally and bring audiences pleasure through entertainment.* In answer to *Why did you apply for a Folies Bergere position?* she skipped over the financial truth and instead wrote *Excitement and Glamour!* She thought it showed more enthusiasm to capitalize both words.

"You decided not to take Bob up on his offer? You're not going to use that connection?" Vivid asked with evident disbelief.

"I wanted to work with you," Ruby said. "To learn from you." She hoped Vivid could see how humbled she was, how grateful.

Still, Vivid should have warned her, better prepared her. That was all Ruby could think about as she looked at the long table of six men, some of them wearing wrinkled suits, others with rolled shirtsleeves, cigarette smoke flowing upward in thin streams from ashtrays that sat next to a stack of showgirl application forms. What Vivid should have told her was that the men would look bored by it all.

The man at the center of the table, apparently the one in charge, had a silver crew cut and hound-dog eyes that drooped, darkly shadowed. When he called Ruby's name, she quickly chewed and swallowed the remainder of her Certs breath mint. She stood before the line of men, keeping one leg slightly in front of the other, turning at an angle as Vivid had instructed her. *"Don't stand at attention!"* Vivid had said, sounding a bit like a drill sergeant. *"You're not in the infantry! This is about beauty, Ruby. It's about being a girl!"*

Ruby lit her face with a genuine smile, showing her perfectly aligned teeth and letting her eyes radiate both pleasure and interest in the men who held her future.

She thought about all the times she'd put herself on display at Masterson's grocery store, and she made sure she achieved eye contact with each man.

"Where're you from, Ruby Wilde?"

"The Midwest," she said, basing her answer on Vivid's advice to keep things superficial, general.

"And you're a dancer?"

"And a model — back home." Vivid said they'd never check and that experience as a model would add to her allure, lead the men to think she could walk a runway, know how best to show off her features.

They had her parade back and forth, but they didn't ask her to dance. She was wearing her tiny red dancer's shorts, a crisp white blouse tied beneath her breasts, and she'd made sure to do a nice job on her nails the night before — Revlon red. Vivid had lent her a pair of black, patent-leather stiletto heels.

"Turn," the lead man said, and Ruby stood with her back to them. She kept her shoulders back, lifted up through her abdomen, showing her full height. She wasn't sure what to do with her hands, and so she held them away from her hips, bent at the wrists, fingertips pointed slightly upward.

"Good. Face us again, Miss Wilde."

Ruby made an elegant turn, eased into a smile once more. She took the fingertips of her right hand and slowly, gently, pushed her hair back from her temple in a purposeful, sensual gesture. Remembering how Vivid had used her hands to cool herself at the barbecue, Ruby closed her eyes briefly and let her hand drift down the length of her neck.

"That's fine." The leader of the pack cleared his throat. "Now, if you don't mind." He nodded toward Ruby's breasts. The request came as no surprise — Vivid had warned her that there was no other way for the men to evaluate Ruby's true potential as a topless showgirl. Vivid had Ruby practice standing in front of a mirror, envisioning the men watching her. She'd stood naked, staring at herself until she could smile assuredly and know that what she had was worth displaying. Her body should be seen, appreciated, and enjoyed, she told herself. It was just an act.

She was Ruby Wilde — *performing.*

Despite all her preparation, Ruby's hands shook slightly as she began unbuttoning her blouse. She knew she should maintain eye contact while she removed her top, and finally she did, at last untying the knot beneath her breasts without fumbling. Vivid had told her not to wear a bra — *You want for them to see right away that you're not prudish.* She told herself she'd have to reveal her body to an entire audience, that this kind of scrutiny was only the beginning. But, in a way, an entire audience seemed easier, more anonymous. This was so intimate.

Ruby pulled her blouse open and let the cloth drop from her shoulders.

"Remove it entirely, please. And stand in profile."

Ruby held the blouse in one hand as if she were a model who'd just removed a jacket. She turned, keeping one leg slightly in front of the other, her knees relaxed, slightly bent. She could feel her heart pounding.

"Other side."

She spun.

"Nice," the man said. "Very nice. Everyone?" the man asked, his voice now sounding less like a physician's or auctioneer's, more like that of someone who had warmed to her. None of the others spoke, and Ruby fought the temptation to sneak a look, to see if they communicated with each other by raised eyebrows, nods, or even shaking their heads *no.* "Face us once more, Ruby."

They were no longer bored.

"Now I understand what Renoir was after," the lead man said. "That soft, subtle coloring. Pinks, whites. Of course no one will see those perfect, quiet areolas. You have amazing skin," he said. "But stay out of the sun." He pointed his cigarette at her for emphasis.

Ruby nodded, still smiling. "I will. I do."

"Good. You can get dressed now. See Miss Jenkins backstage. She'll get you scheduled. And, Miss Wilde." The lead man stood, gave a small bow. "Welcome to the Folies."

Ruby felt as if she'd just stepped off of a cliff. She stood outside in the hallway and tried to catch her breath. She could hear Aunt Tate's infinite disapproval, almost thought she heard her aunt whisper, *Be careful what you ask for. Good lord,* Ruby thought — what on earth had she gone and done?

She signed her first showgirl contract *Ruby Wilde, a.k.a. "Lily Decker,"* and dated it October 14, 1967. Then, there was a trip to the beauty parlor for a makeover with a Mick Jagger–thin man named Toby who had her stand in front of a full-length mirror while he narrowed his eyes, tilted his head first this way then that, pushed his chin in the air, and looked at her along the length of his nose. He was wearing a dark red shirt covered in huge white polka dots, a black leather vest, and tight, skinny-legged black pants.

"*SPLENDID* color!" He snapped his fingers. "*PERFECT* mahogany hair, glorious skin," he effused. "And yes, the Cleopatra look's fine, but let's try something different. Something *FABULOUS*. Sit sit sit." He wet her hair, took his scissors in hand, and began to cut before Ruby had a chance to protest. *Could* she protest? She rather felt as if she'd been bought and paid for.

"Your neck should be on display, and a short, layered cut will reduce some of the weight of your hair." At times using a razor blade, Toby cut her hair so that her ears were exposed, and then he used the tips of the scissors to create what he called wispies around her face. "It's a shag, honey. All the rage, and ideal with your features." When he was finished, Ruby had to agree that her eyes somehow appeared bolder, bigger. "Just fluff it up with your fingers." Toby demonstrated. "Easy peasy. No fuss." He had delicate hands with calluses on his index finger and thumb and he wore a polished silver cuff bracelet on his left wrist.

"You'll need hairpieces, for variety." He led her to another section of the salon and seated her once more. "First, a far-out, long piece." He opened a drawer, and then with his hand still in the drawer, he looked up at her, thinking. "Black?" He held up a long fall, placed it next to her face. "Too dark," he said, returning the hairpiece to the drawer. "Something wild, though. You want to make a statement." He rummaged through what looked to be the remains of an entire zoo population. "Bright gold." He decided at last. "I dream of Jeannie!"

Ruby grimaced as if she'd smelled decay.

"Just take it." He dropped the hairpiece in her lap. "You'll see. Toby! Is! Always! Right!" He smirked, and Ruby was won over.

After piling six hairpieces of different colors and configurations in her lap, he sang, "Makeup!" and led her back to the salon chair where they'd begun. "After today, you'll have to do your own." He opened a chest of drawers that reminded her of Uncle Miles' giant metal toolbox, except that it was hot pink. The drawers were filled with eye shadow, eyeliner and eyebrow pencils, foundation, mascara, blush, and powder.

"Extend your eyeliner like this," Toby said, expertly drawing the line up and out from the outer corner of her eye. "Go like this." He opened his mouth into a huge O, and

Ruby copied him while he flicked mascara onto her lashes. "The trick the girls use," he said, opening a package of false eyelashes, "is three pairs. *Three.*"

"But how does anyone see through that much eyelash?"

"You get used to it. It's the only way to have your eyes pop, even from a distance. And pile on the rouge. Like this." He showed her how to apply the rouge below her cheekbone and to angle it steeply upward. "Use a darker color of rouge and lipstick than you normally would. Overdo *everything.* That's my motto." He laughed. "And girl, I do mean *everything*!" Ruby smiled back at him in the mirror. He'd transformed her. She felt like some rare tropical bird.

"One more trick," he said, handing her a roll of flesh-toned tape. "Know what this is?"

"I haven't a clue."

"It's toupee tape. Okay — stop," he cautioned, as Ruby began to giggle. "This is dead serious." Still, he began laughing along with her. "So anyway," he said, finally catching his breath. "You use this to hold your G-string in place. It can't be seen, if you do it right — and shifts in the ol' G-string can be — well . . ." He smiled lasciviously.

"Plus, I need to do some serious hair removal," Ruby said, feeling daring.

"Daily."

Toby of the Bottomless Energy loaded her with a fully stocked makeup kit in colors that best suited her complexion and a set of soft-bristled brushes in an array of sizes and shapes, and then he passed her on to Gloria Jenkins, the Tropicana's showgirl manager.

"All the girls call me Mother J," Gloria said, beckoning Ruby into her white Ford Falcon. "I take care of everything, and you can come to me anytime. An-y-time. For advice. Or whatever."

Gloria took Ruby shopping — for evening gowns, cocktail dresses, miniskirts, blouses, brightly colored tights and fishnet stockings, bellbottom pants in audacious pinks and oranges as well as pale celery and aquamarine, and even lacy red and black lingerie. Uninvited, Mother J came into the fitting room with Ruby, narrowed her eyes and expertly tugged at bra straps, ordered clerks to bring different sizes. She had Ruby bend over to get her breasts firmly seated in the bra cups, and as Ruby dressed and undressed, Gloria took note of Ruby's sizes in a little black spiral-bound notebook.

"Shoes," Gloria said, and they were off to Hi-Style Footwear, a store that catered to the casino crowd.

"Miss Jenkins, Miss Jenkins. *Enchanté,*" a man with a thin mustache greeted them at the entrance. "This is the new girl you phoned about?" He bowed to Ruby and, like a maître d' at a fine restaurant, ushered them toward a row of chairs. "We'll take very good care of you," he promised, snapping his fingers until a clerk appeared at his side.

This clerk, too, took orders from Miss Jenkins. "One pair of flats. Plain, black. Some short black boots, moderate heel. Heeled sandals. The rest fashion heels. And the usual order of Capezios. Oh, what am I saying? You know," she said, waving a hand.

Mother J purchased ten pairs of shoes for Ruby. Ruby's favorite was a tall pair of minimalist heels with a strap that circled her ankle. The silver shoes were open-sided, open-toed, and the only thing holding the shoe to her foot, other than the heel cup and ankle strap, was a narrow band of rhinestones in the shape of a loosely tied knot. They were supremely elegant Cinderella shoes, and it was all Ruby could do not to plead like a little girl to keep them on her feet, maybe even to sleep in them.

"How're you feeling?" Mother J asked when they got back into the Falcon. She rolled down her window, and Ruby did the same. Once the car was moving, there was enough of a breeze to begin to cool them.

"I keep thinking I'll hear a clock strike midnight and everything will disappear."

"I hope Toby remembered to give you some good facial moisturizers. This dry air is murder on the skin. The singers all complain about desert throat."

"I think he put some jars in the case," Ruby said. "It's a little hard to keep track of everything at this point."

Mother J flicked the lever for her turn signal and pushed in the cigarette lighter. "Go ahead. I don't, but you go ahead. I know how you girls manage to keep those figures."

Ruby felt instantly calmer with the first lungful of tobacco smoke, and she settled back in the seat, looked at the blue mountain range lurking in the distance, across the desert flats.

Mother J broke the brief silence. "Understand please, Ruby, what we bought today — these are your work clothes, your uniforms. You're expected to entertain after the show. You keep the men gambling, buying drinks, food. Basically," she said, turning to look at Ruby, "you keep them spending money, and you give them a good time. Let them brush up against glamour."

"I was talking with Vivid —" Ruby began.

"Good. Good. She's experienced, a good girl to go to for advice." Mother J drove past the red lights of the Tropicana, on toward the Bombay Motor Court. "So Vivid probably told you you're not expected to sleep with the men," she said, taking a moment to be sure Ruby was paying attention. "Of course you can, if you want. But nothing requires that you do that." Her tone was matter of fact, as if they were still discussing makeup or shoe sizes.

Ruby thought about the church group ladies back in Kansas, how they'd describe a girl hopping in and out of bed with just anyone. A girl Aunt Tate would say was on the Path of Ruin and Despair. A slut. Whore. In Kansas, you held on to your virginity as if it were a pile of gold bars secreted away in the light-starved vaults of Fort Knox. You stayed *intact.* It was something that had always worried Ruby — the fact that someday she would have to explain to some man why she wasn't a virgin. She'd always thought she'd use the horseback-riding excuse. Apparently, men bought it.

Ruby remembered the girls from high school who gossiped about those slutty girls rumored to have let some boy get to first base. Second base. And — Lord above! — *third.* If you were a good girl, a marriageable girl, you remained wholly, blissfully ignorant until your wedding night.

Really, Ruby thought, that was the way things were supposed to be everywhere. On television, *That Girl* didn't have sex with Donald, and who knows how long they'd been together. How many times had she seen that in the movies — the sweet or clever virginal put-off, the good girl who reaps the rewards? And if you didn't tell him no, then you got pregnant and paid the price.

Maybe, Ruby thought, this was precisely why the hippies bothered everyone so much, with their freedom and love-ins. Their lack of shame. Hippies made love to each other and then went on to someone else, and someone else after that. Maybe even all in the same afternoon, if what she'd heard was true.

And now, here was Mother J not only giving "yes" a blessing, but she did it as if Ruby and the other showgirls had a right to desire, to pleasure. She could *take* pleasure. She'd never thought about it like that — that she could be more than a gatekeeper; she could be an instigator, someone who chose. Someone who wanted to sleep with a man and made it happen.

"You're not listening to me," Mother J said, pulling up to a stoplight.

"Sorry," Ruby said, shaking off her reverie. "You were saying we can — I can — go to bed with men or not. That it's not required."

"More importantly, I was saying that you are to show the men a good time, to charm them."

"Making memories," Ruby said, thinking that Mother J really did look like a mother — not a woman who created high-priced, *almost* call girls. She was rather dumpy, wore cat-eye-framed glasses, and her middle-aged neck was starting to lapse into a rubbery wattle. Gloria Jenkins could almost pass for a member of Aunt Tate's Bible-study group. It made Ruby smile to think of Mother J sitting in a flock of Aunt Tate's friends, sharing the finer points of seducing gamblers.

"Memories. That's it exactly," Mother J said approvingly. "You give them memories. You give them tales to tell when they get back to Dubuque or Cincinnati or Tuscaloosa."

Ruby had lunch with Vivid and Rose the next day, watching them yawn their way through chef salads poolside at Caesars. At two dollars apiece, the salads were expensive, but Ruby had already received a paycheck from the Tropicana. She was flush, and she was buying.

"You are far too bright and bushy-tailed at this time of day," Vivid said, using an index finger to push up her sunglasses. "Please tell me you're not one of those morning people." She speared a piece of chicken.

"Sort of. Yeah. And geez — it's past noon."

"That attitude'll change," Rose said, taking a sip of her iced tea. She waved away the bikini-clad waitress who stopped to offer a refill. "Still, your hair looks great."

"I'll have you know that Toby said it was *fabulous*!" Ruby sang out. "And I have costume fittings this afternoon." She tried not to sound as excited, as perky as she felt.

"They'll only put you in one or two numbers at first," Vivid said. "Let you get your toes wet, see how you do, then work you up to a full production set."

"I've got butterflies," Ruby confessed.

"Sheesh." Vivid sighed and looked at Rose. "She's actually got enough energy to have butterflies!"

"That'll change," Rose nearly moaned.

"Oh yeah," Vivid agreed.

"You two —" Ruby began.

"We're a couple of killjoys," Rose said.

"Well, you're trying to be. But there's no way you can ruin this for me." Ruby grinned.

"And no way we'd want to." Vivid touched Ruby's forearm lightly. "No way on God's green earth we'd take one moment of this from you."

Rose smiled. "You've earned this, kiddo. And, soon enough," she warned with a grin, "you'll learn that nothing in Vegas — *nothing* — happens before three, at the earliest. It's called *sleep.*" She rubbed her forehead for emphasis.

6

The next few weeks were demanding, full of frenzied learning for Ruby. Connie, a dresser, led Ruby through the Tropicana's backstage rabbit warren, where she met a team of seamstresses who were constantly repairing, altering, wiring, and cleaning the costumes. Over fifty stagehands moved the elaborate sets in between numbers, pulling ropes and pushing wheeled set pieces into place. Inside a vault called the Bird Room were countless boas of every color imaginable. She saw waterfalls and fantails of feathers, costumes loaded with plumes from ostrich, quail, pheasant, and other species she couldn't identify. Other backstage rooms held racks of jewelry — velvet cuffs with rhinestone cuff links, jeweled chokers. Bras that lacked cups or any form of support but instead merely served to outline breasts. Glitter and more glitter, outlandish hunks of paste jewelry. There were Carmen

Miranda open skirts, long dresses with trains and cutaway swaths that revealed shapely legs. Cabinet drawers filled with satiny, jeweled G-strings. Elizabethan collars made of stiff black feathers. And Connie said these were just the costumes currently in use. The rest were in storage.

Ruby spent hours in fittings with Connie, who stood on a stool to lower the unwieldy headdresses onto Ruby. "Sometimes these things are so big we actually have to lower them by pulleys," Connie told her. The dresser showed Ruby how to wrap her hair in a pantyhose cap so that she could easily slip in and out of the headdresses. There were no chinstraps — and while the caps fit snugly (another measurement recorded in Mother J's little notebook), they could still slip and slide, and so Ruby practiced maneuvering in the headpieces. Costume changes lasted only two to three minutes — one more thing at which Ruby would have to become proficient.

For two solid days Ruby worked one-on-one with Marnie, the showgirl coach. Marnie first taught Ruby the showgirl walk, beginning with the bevel stance. "Everything's closed up." Marnie demonstrated. "Nothing open. Always lead with your toe, chest up, radiating confidence. See?" Marnie stepped down a short flight of stairs. "Think of your legs as the stem of a champagne flute — long, together as one." Ruby began imitating Marnie's walk. "Cross, cross. Arch your back a little more. That's it. Chin up!" Marnie cautioned. "Eye contact with the audience at all times. *Engage* them."

Ruby posed for publicity stills and sweet-talked the photographer — a former war photographer who looked to be in his eighties — into giving her a set of prints she could send to the Aviator and Mrs. Baumgarten. How tempting it was to slip one into an anonymous envelope addressed to Aunt Tate. Ruby mailed the photos despite a niggling shiver of reluctance; she was determined to follow Vivid's lead, to treat the entire enterprise — her new career — as something she was proud to have earned, not some sordid little secret. Besides, she had to admit it: all done up, she looked stunning. Ruby imagined the Aviator sliding the photo from the envelope, reading her note with her new address — a poolside apartment in the same complex as Rose, Vivid, and other Strip employees. He'd see how grown-up she'd become, that she'd landed on her feet and found her place in the limelight.

On a warm November day before her first

performance, the girls at the Sunglow Apartments gave Ruby a showgirl party, complete with a cake in the shape of a voluptuous woman wearing nothing but a bright red G-string and gold pasties. Ruby opened gifts, which included a bottle of Visine from Vivid, and, from Rose, a giant bottle of Anacin. "Sure you have a headache, you're tense, irritable. But don't take it out on her!" Rose mimicked the television commercial. A girl called Dee (short for Dee-light, the group told Ruby), gave Ruby a pair of panties made from soft, white rabbit fur — "for when the G-string has dug a trench so deep up your ass that you can't even sit." Dee laughed. She was a brown-eyed blonde whose looks made Ruby think of a lioness dozing in the African sun, sated after gorging on some poor antelope. Dee's beauty was drenched in primal lassitude.

"Hey — I found out that Ruby reads palms," Rose revealed. "And I have first dibs." She sat cross-legged next to Ruby on the floor and held up her palms.

"I need better light," Ruby said, and Vivid opened the blinds to stark sunlight.

"Well, the first thing I notice is your career line — the line of fate," Ruby said, running her fingernail down the vertical line that fell in the center of Rose's palm. "It's broken.

See? Right here," she pointed. "You'll have a sudden, decisive change in career at some point."

"I should hope so," Rose said, looking intently at her palm. "It's called marriage."

The other girls huddled around them, lifting their own hands to see how their lines compared. Ruby checked their palms, one at a time. She kept the readings short, found one or two things per person to explain. Vivid waited until last.

"Shall I?" Ruby asked her.

"None of the women in my family live past thirty-five," Vivid said, reluctantly extending her hand toward Ruby. "So don't tell me I'm going to die young."

"That's not what jumps out at me," Ruby said, fudging. She could see that Vivid's life line really did end abruptly, long before it even approached her wrist.

"What does jump out at you?" Vivid asked.

"This," Ruby said, using her thumb to depress the Mount of Venus at the base of Vivid's thumb. "See how meaty it is? How plump?"

Vivid looked, and Rose, seated next to her, held up her palm for comparison.

"Geez. It really is giant," Rose commented. "Does Venus mean what I think it does?"

"It does." Ruby grinned. "Sensuality. Love. Actually, your name — Vivid — is appropriate."

"I'm a lover not a fighter?" Vivid joked.

"You're sexual and passionate. Desired," Ruby said, still holding Vivid's hand.

"Let's see yours." Vivid turned Ruby's palm up while the other girls clustered about. "Aha!" Vivid said, pushing at the cushiony Mount of Venus on Ruby's palm.

"Whose is bigger!" Rose joked. "Oh, we're just as bad as the guys!"

"Never," one of the girls said. "Not even close. For starters, we know how to measure *honestly,* without exaggerating." They all laughed.

"Ruby's is bigger," Vivid said, a wry smile on her face. "Look out, world!"

"Naw," Ruby said, fighting the urge to hide her hands beneath her thighs.

"Venus! Oh, Veeeeeeeenus!" Vivid began singing, and the others quickly joined her. "Venus, goddess of love that you are," Vivid sang, standing and bringing Ruby to her feet. She waltzed Ruby about the tiny living room.

"Frankie Avalon," Rose said. "Brought to you by Beech-Nut Gum!"

"You're all great," Ruby said, well aware of the blush that had brought heat to her face. "I've never had such good friends."

Rose gave Ruby's shoulders a squeeze. "And you're not nervous?"

"Oh!" Ruby laughed. "I am *really* nervous!"

"It'll pass," Dee advised. "The first couple of shows are the hardest, but after that, you'll settle in just fine."

"First *fifty* shows," Vivid joked. "After *that,* it's a piece of cake."

"You guys aren't helping." Ruby laughed.

"That's because you only *thought* we were your friends." Rose winked.

Her first number as one of twenty showgirls was not a topless performance. The girls wore spaghetti-strap micro minis made in a gold eyelash fabric that shimmered beneath the stage lights. The music was The 5th Dimension's "Up, Up and Away," done Vegas style at an amped-up pace with a lot of horns.

Just before the band began to play, Ruby joined the other girls peeking around the curtain, trying to spot celebrities in the front rows. She could hear the low hum of dinner conversation syncopated with the tinkling of cocktail glasses, the flare of cigarette lighters.

Onstage at last, her heart fueled by the

audience's applause, Ruby spun, kicked, and flung her black derby hat along with the other girls. Their hat tosses formed an increasingly complex aerial pattern that drew cheers from the audience. She was confident of her footwork and managed to keep any jitters from showing. At the end of the number, the dancers climbed into five hot air balloons and ascended into the clouds by means of numerous cranks and pulleys.

She didn't have long to relish the applause, but she grinned widely, feeling the adrenaline-hot exchange between performer and audience. This was exactly what she'd craved.

Ruby rushed backstage to her dressing area and began removing her micromini, searching the countertop for where she'd left her silver pasties. In the next number, the girls were dressed only in G-strings and giant, full-length, ruffled capes that attached to their arms. The capes, sewn in satin and patterned in bright, variegated colors, were wired to form arcs like rainbows high above the showgirls' heads. With their bold colors and frilliness, the costumes had a sort of flamenco air to them. Ruby loved how they caught the air and made her feel as if she could take flight.

She quickly applied several gold stars at the corners of her eyes and fluffed her hair so that it was no longer pressed into a derby shape. But where were her pasties? Maybe she just wasn't seeing them, what with the multiple sets of eyelashes and the sweat stinging her eyes. She ran her hand across the countertop, feeling for them. "Shit shit shit!" she said.

"What?" Vivid stood behind her, already fully dressed. "What the fuck, Ruby? You can't fall this far behind!"

"My pasties! I can't find them."

"Never mind," Vivid said, opening drawers in Ruby's dressing table. "Stealing pasties is an old showgirl trick." She raised her voice, "Only INSECURE BITCHES pull this kind of shit!" Vivid retrieved a plastic cylinder of silver glitter from the rubble in the bottom drawer. "Where's your eyelash glue?"

Ruby grabbed the tube of glue from her makeup case and handed it to Vivid. "What're you going to do?" she asked.

Vivid pushed back the edges of her cape in frustration. "Hold this back for me," she said, and Ruby tugged at the cape. Vivid squirted glue onto the tip of her finger and circled Ruby's nipples with it. "Now," she said, opening the tube of glitter, "help me get them coated."

They worked together, dumping glitter over the wet glue and completely covering Ruby's areolas in silver flakes. When they were done, Vivid helped Ruby into her cape.

"No one will be able to tell the difference," Vivid said as Ruby inspected herself in the mirror.

"I think you just saved my ass," Ruby said.

"No." Vivid grinned. "I think I just saved your tits." She pushed Ruby toward the stage.

The band played the first, halting notes of the Rolling Stones' "She's a Rainbow," and the singer began. Ruby bevel-walked her way onto the stage and smiled. She'd done it. She'd made it. She knew she was jaw-dropping gorgeous, and — at long last — she was precisely where she belonged.

Being a Vegas showgirl was a gas, just as Vivid had promised. Ruby loved taking an audience captive, knowing that her looks and talent made the casino guests covet her nearly as much as she coveted their attention. She'd never danced so well, never been so beautiful. She'd never before felt such a sense of accomplishment. She'd made it in Vegas. *Fuck you, Kansas,* she thought.

And she was *dancing.* The exertion, the

physical and chemical release made her body feel vibrant and capable. For those hours onstage, Ruby was unsullied, immensely alive, focused on the moment, and set free from her history.

She had trouble sleeping because she couldn't slow down, couldn't turn off the amped-up high. Ruby wore a silly grin on her face even when she was loading dimes into the washing machine at the apartment complex or sifting scouring powder into the tub, still alive from her performance the previous night.

What with frequent rehearsals and the nine or more numbers each night — often twice a night — Ruby found she could eat absolutely anything and still keep her figure. She inhaled steaks, French fries, butter-laden potatoes, and bread. She checked lobster and baked Alaska off of her to-try list, indulged in hot fudge sundaes, and no longer had to shun vegetables in cream sauces or pastas thick with cheese. She was in the best shape of her life, and she was eating like a horse.

Where she fell down, what proved a challenge of Himalayan proportions, was mingling with the big spenders after the shows. "Mixing," as the girls called the unwritten, nonnegotiable requirement of her job. The men were all much older than Ruby, and she could see the unabashed lecher in every single one of them. Starched shirts, pinky rings, gold necklaces, aftershave, and tinted eyeglasses. High-buck toupees or careful comb-overs, dyed hair and even permanent waves designed to mask thinning hair. Professional shaves, sometimes even manicures. The entitlement they carried with their fat billfolds, the certitude in their thin-lipped smiles, their presumptive possession of her.

"I don't get it," Vivid said when Ruby walked across the pool area to Vivid's apartment for advice. Vivid's hair was set in orange juice cans, and she was painting her nails a frosty white. "Ruby, it's simple: We're arm candy. You keep the high rollers gambling. You keep them from leaving the Tropicana and going elsewhere. They buy you food, drinks. Tasteful gifts." She laughed. "It's an exchange — they get to sit with you, believe that you want them as much as they want you. You get them all fired up so that they can go home to their wives or girlfriends or whatever and give them a night to remember. It's an *act,* for Pete's sake, Ruby. Why not just pretend you're still onstage?"

"It makes me nervous. Really, really uncomfortable."

"But why?" Vivid screwed the top on her nail polish and blew on her fingertips. She stood. "I'm getting myself a Tab. Want one?"

"Sure. Yeah." Ruby ran her fingers through her hair. It was time to see Toby for a trim.

"Glass? Ice?"

"No. I'm fine," Ruby said, accepting the cold can. She pulled off Vivid's tab for her and then her own, keeping the ring on her finger. Vivid sat cross-legged on the floor, set her can on the glass coffee table next to a beautiful red lacquer box with a painting of a geisha on the lid. Ruby eyed Vivid's silver coffee table lighter. Everything Vivid had was sophisticated, expensive.

"So, are you going to tell me?" Vivid asked.

"What?"

"Why it makes you nervous to sit with a bunch of men who worship you."

"Because they want something."

"Of course they do!"

"And that's what bothers me."

"It bothers you that men find you attractive? You're a showgirl, for God's sake. You're designed to be wanted. Good lord, Ruby." Vivid shook her head. "What woman wouldn't change places with you in a second? To have men with money who want to spend it on you!"

"They want to spend it on me because then I'll owe them. Tit for tat," Ruby said, taking another sip of soda.

Puzzled, Vivid shook her head again. "Ruby, you don't have to give them a thing. You don't owe them! They're doing what they want to do!"

"In expectation of receiving more. Of sex."

"But not if you don't want to! It's up to *you.* Don't you understand? You can say *no.*"

Ruby looked down at the carpeting, tugged at a few of the shag fibers. "A couple of nights ago, this putrid old man with chunks of dandruff on his collar leaned over to me and whispered, *'I want to stick my tongue up your asshole.'* "

"So, he's a classless prick. Just tell him to fuck off. That's the kind of guy you don't even need to be polite to."

Ruby shook her head. "But it's the whole thing, Vivid. In general." She blew out a breath, looked toward the ceiling for inspiration that wasn't there.

"Honey," Vivid said. "What is it? Really."

Ruby kept fidgeting with the carpet fibers. It wasn't simply that for the most part she felt either pity or revulsion for many of the men. The thing was, she found it impossible to articulate her fears, the bedrock certainty that she was truly vulnerable, that she felt threatened even by the innocuous ones. Finally, she said, "I feel safer when I'm onstage and they can't get close to me."

Vivid continued looking at Ruby as if she were an intricate filigree lock, something for which there was no longer any key. The two women were so quiet that Ruby could hear a dove cooing from its perch on a telephone line. When Ruby at last looked up, she saw comprehension begin to wash across Vivid's face.

"I think maybe I get it. How could I be so obtuse?" Vivid touched Ruby's forearm lightly. "Fuck, Ruby," she said, and her voice caught. "It happened to me, too." Her tone was soft, nearly a whisper.

"What?"

"You can't even say it, can you? Rape. I'm talking about rape."

"Oh." Ruby looked at her friend. "I'm so sorry. I didn't know."

"How could you? It's not something I advertise. But I should have realized that about you —"

"But I haven't been raped." Ruby bit her lower lip. *Oh good God,* she thought. She pressed her lips together hard. She'd never thought about it like that before — what Uncle Miles had done. But now, hearing someone else actually talk about it, say the word, it was, wasn't it? It *was* rape. She'd been raped. And raped. And raped. She looked up from the carpet and into Vivid's sympathetic face. "I guess —"

"For me, it was my older brother's best friend," Vivid said. "A guy I'd been around forever. Someone I trusted. I was seventeen."

"Fuck," Ruby said, wiping the beginnings of traitorous tears from beneath her eyes.

"Who?" Vivid asked, taking Ruby's hand.

"My uncle."

"Jesus fucking Christ. You were a *child*?"

"Eight. The first time."

"I want to kill the fucker. Where is he? Is the bastard still alive?"

"He was never alive," Ruby said, turning to look for a box of tissues.

"Hold on," Vivid said, heading down the hallway and shouting back at Ruby, "I ran out and haven't had a chance to get to the store. Here," she said, returning with a roll of toilet paper. "And give me some, while you're at it."

They blew their noses in unison.

"How long?" Vivid asked. "How long did it last?"

"Until I was twelve."

"Fuck me."

"Yeah."

They sat in silence, sniffling.

"Here's the thing," Vivid said at last. "You're not a little girl anymore. You're not helpless. Now *you're* in charge."

Ruby shook her head, dismissing Vivid's words.

"No, listen to me. Please." Vivid's voice grew stronger. "You *are* in charge. They get nothing — *nothing* — that you don't want to give them. *Nada. Rien de chose.* And something in German, but I don't know any German." She tried a tentative laugh.

"But I don't know how to convince myself that I'm in control," Ruby said.

"You can learn it, I swear." Vivid became more animated, a lawyer arguing her case. "You talk to yourself. You have to kinda retrain yourself, you know? You tell yourself that you're having fun, that you're safe. You say, 'I'm safe. I'm safe.' " She took Ruby's hand once more. "These aren't evil men; they're not your rat bastard uncle. They're out to have a good time, to travel in the same orbit as something beautiful, damned near untouchable. They're in awe of someone they never thought would give them the time of day, let alone converse with them or join them for a meal. Stroke their egos. You don't have to stroke anything else."

"God, I hope not."

"Look, focus on what your bank statement says at the first of each month." Vivid let go of Ruby's hand and drained the last of her Tab. "Start collecting." She wiggled her heavily ringed fingers meaningfully. "And you know what else?"

"What?"

"You take revenge. Sure, these guys are technically innocent, but c'mon. You say, *This, you owe me, motherfucker.* For all the others. *Payback.*"

"Payback," Ruby said, thoughtful. After a long pause, she said, "He was afraid of snakes — my uncle. A genuine snake phobia. So I taught myself not to be afraid of them. Well, more accurately, I wouldn't *let* myself be afraid." She smiled. "Once I managed to catch a garter snake on my way home from school."

"Ugh," Vivid said.

"Yeah, but it was great, really. Because I scared the shit out of him. I pulled the snake from the pocket of my sweater and just watched his face as he realized what it was and took off running. He was freaking out and yelling to high heaven — 'SNAKE! SNAKE!' " Ruby laughed. "I loved it."

"See? Revenge works. But don't you dare pull any snake tricks on me, Ruby Wilde."

Vivid stood. "So, tonight we double, all right? I'll be there, right beside you all night. Okay?"

Ruby released a huge lungful of air. She felt as if she'd been holding her breath for over a decade and had at last found a way to let it go. Suddenly, she was tired. "I think I need a nap."

"You never told anyone?"

"No one."

"You must be exhausted. Holding that in for so long."

"Please — don't tell anyone," Ruby begged. "Not even Rose, all right? I just —"

"Why would I? And of course not."

"I owe you."

"No, you don't."

"I do."

"It's not accounting, Ruby. It's friendship."

Walking back to her apartment, Ruby realized Vivid was the first person who had ever understood her. She thought about the difference between understanding and acceptance, and then she realized Vivid had given her both in the space of less than half an hour. So, this was what it felt like to have a true friend. Someone who had her back. Someone she could lean on. Of all the things Ruby had expected to find in Las

7

In the end, for Ruby it turned out not to be about payback. She couldn't quite do it Vivid's way, but eventually Ruby developed her own style of mixing. She searched until she found something to like in every man. Some small thing. It might even be as minor as liking the buttons on his coat. Maybe his smile, the curve of an ear, the scent of his aftershave. His neediness, his vulnerability.

Telling herself that she was safe, Ruby was gracious. The homely, awkward Don Knotts look-alikes who attended ham radio conventions got the same, velvety Ruby Wilde presence as did the members of Rotary clubs and The American Legion, the Veterans of Foreign Wars, and the men who came to play golf for days on end or to find distraction after a miserable, wallet-emptying divorce. The real and wannabe mobsters, faded but still flexing their biceps and flashing solid gold money clips. The polished, professional gamblers who wore just-minted Krugerrands on chains about their necks. Ruby soon realized that more often than not they simply wanted to be heard, to tell their stories without criticism or interruption. She treated them all well — even if they could only afford to buy her a martini. Practice made perfect, and soon her charm flowed naturally.

The high rollers bought her rubies and garnets, sapphires to match her eyes. They bought her designer clothes at the casino boutiques, and the boutiques paid Ruby a percentage of all the sales she brought in. Her bathroom counter was crowded with bottles of perfume, and a half a dozen French bath oils circled her tub. She owned silk negligees, and even a supremely soft cashmere robe dyed the peaceful color of a doe bedded down on a forest floor.

But there were gifts more extravagant than rings and necklaces. Johnny Litchfield, a high-stakes gambler from Chicago, offered to buy Ruby a penthouse in the Windy City, where he said he'd be able to keep an eye on her. In reply, she winked and said, "*'Put her in a pumpkin shell, and there he kept her very well.'*"

Ruby was learning to turn men down gently, with such finesse that they didn't feel rejected. They weren't losers — they just weren't getting exactly what they'd expected. And so she turned down Johnny's Peter Piper penthouse. Instead, she accepted a ten-thousand-dollar poker chip, and every time Chicago Johnny came to town he found her — and gave her more outlandish gifts. He was a hard-bitten man with a cratered face and pale blue eyes that were too small. But those eyes were surrounded by ribbed fans of wrinkles, the kind that came only with repeated laughter. And Johnny made her laugh. He told her stories of outrageous gambling wins and losses, of his days as a middleweight boxer and then as an MP in Hawaii, corralling World War II soldiers on leave.

She sold the jewelry she didn't particularly like at the jewelers all the girls used — Goldfarb's on East Twain Avenue. The owner gave her good prices, and she banked the money, earning eight percent interest on her savings. Although she'd never been given the same piece twice, she guessed that some of the showgirls had seen the identical, recycled emerald ring or pearl choker more than once.

When an enamored Saudi prince gave Vivid a boat, the Sunglow Apartment girls ended their nights by waterskiing on Lake

Mead as the sun rose. Ruby, Rose, Vivid, and Dee christened the boat *Siren Song* and for their naming ceremony piled caviar onto water crackers and emptied three bottles of Bollinger Blanc de Noirs champagne. Sometimes, they took men along with them; other times it was just girls. They scrambled eggs on the boat's little propane cookstove, ate crusty bread donated by the chef in one or another casino restaurant, and brewed dark, French roast coffee. Then, they went back to their apartments to crash for a few hours before work.

Ruby studied Vivid, saw how she touched a man's arm or shoulder lightly to let him know that he'd arrived in her inner circle. She'd also seen how Vivid would often pit one man against another when she wanted more; jealousy and competition led them to outspend each other in comical proportions. Vivid seemed to have an insatiable need for more — something Ruby didn't feel. She longed to ask Vivid what "enough" would look like, but Ruby knew that Vivid would refuse to answer, that she likely had no answer other than "More!"

Ruby gained more than luxurious possessions from the men she entertained. She was learning. She garnered knowledge from the high rollers in particular, gradually coating herself with layer upon layer of sophistication. Like a pearl forming about a grain of sharp sand, she used her newfound etiquette to further escape her rube beginnings. Now, she used her knife and fork the European way and knew to ask for either still or sparkling water. She ate more slowly, as if dining were an event, not a race or simple fuel. The big spenders taught her the attributes of different wines and vintners, and she memorized prices so that she knew what was in a given man's price range. She learned to let a man pull out a chair for her, open a car door, help her with her coat. She leaned in intimately, enticingly, so that a man could light her cigarette. Men walked on her left side — unless her right side was the side closer to traffic — and she waited for them to lead her through crowds.

There were the men who knew which football or baseball teams to bet on, who even placed odds on the outcomes of elections, and who sank unfathomable sums into the stock market. But to her surprise, a few of the men — gentlemen — were impressively well read; one even bragged of owning a precious hand-annotated draft of Fitzgerald's *The Great Gatsby.* Once these men discovered that she was an avid reader, they suggested books. Through them, Ruby discovered Sophocles and Euripides, and she even tackled Shakespeare's plays when one of her Manhattan gamblers sent her two beautifully bound editions of the Bard's comedies and tragedies.

Ruby Wilde evolved until she was refined, worldly. Sophisticated and celebrated, she increased the distance between her new life and the repellent odor of Uncle Miles' Saturday night bowl of Fritos, the chaos of her aunt's kitchen drawer full of spent, useless keys and remnants of parsimonious string tied together into an indecipherable pattern of dots and dashes.

And yet, from time to time Ruby couldn't help but think of her aunt. She still yearned to impress Aunt Tate, somehow to gain her approval. Ruby knew it was a reflexive longing, something she hoped to grow out of or conquer one day — that need to fit within the puzzle pieces of Aunt Tate's love.

And then there were the heartbreakingly sad men. The ones who seemed always to be searching for footing on the crumbling, unstable scree of life. Duane Mulroney was a wholesale carpet salesman who hopscotched across the country every few weeks. He was practiced at airports and rental cars, easily charmed by stewardesses, and thoroughly enthralled with Ruby. Duane had enough but not a lot of money; he was one of Ruby's regulars who probably went just a little bit into debt every time he wooed her with expensive wines and tenderloin steaks. And, although he couldn't buy her what the true high rollers sent her way, Ruby still made time for him. There was something about Duane, something sweet, almost untried. She warmed to his Oklahoma-bred innocence. Maybe, too, it was because he was drifting decidedly toward outright obesity, and that made him both safe and soft. Duane was easy.

Ruby never had sex with him. What grew between Duane and Ruby was a sort of chaste friendship that permitted Duane to indulge in a sinful fantasy without actually transgressing.

He wore permanent press checkered shirts with navy blue ties, Sears-brand oxford shoes, khaki trousers, and a navy blue blazer with brass buttons that seemed to scream "Help!" as they valiantly attempted to hold the coat's material together over his bulging belly. He wore his thick, black hair in a bristle-top crew cut and ran his hand nervously across it several times a minute while his jittery legs bounced beneath the tabletop. His gold wedding band dug into his fleshy finger, and his belt sliced cruelly into his pillowy middle. From time to time he'd twist his ring like a bottle cap, as if he were testing whether it could be removed.

His passivity eclipsed anything Ruby had ever known. They'd once sat in his rental car in the dark of a parking lot, and he'd said, "Would you do something for me?"

"I need more than that before I'll agree to anything, Duane." Ruby punched in the cigarette lighter and fished in her purse for her pack of Salems.

"It's not an easy thing to ask for."

"We've got all the time you want." The pop of the lighter was loud, jarring. She lit her cigarette and wondered what kind of weird sexual thing Duane might be into. "Just ask me, Duane. I promise I won't freak out."

She heard him take a deep breath before he asked, "Would you breathe for me?"

"What?" She failed to keep the surprise from her voice, although she hoped she didn't also sound judgmental.

"Like artificial respiration. Except that I'm conscious."

"I don't understand."

"I think it would relax me."

"To have someone else breathe for you?"

"Yeah."

"You've done this before?"
"No."
"Jesus, Duane."
"Forget it. Sorry I asked," he said, ready to turn the key in the ignition.
Ruby put her hand over his. "I'll try it." She rolled down her window and tossed her cigarette onto the asphalt. "Tell me exactly what you want."
Duane tipped his head back against the seat, opening his throat. "Just blow," he said, his eyes closed.
Ruby scooted across the seat until her thigh touched his. Duane exhaled audibly, releasing all the oxygen stored in his lungs. She sealed his lips with hers and blew, steadily, softly. It was an odd sensation — she could actually feel his lungs filling with her breath. When she leaned away from him, he let out a long breath, a sigh, really. "Like that?" Ruby asked.
"Yeah. Perfect."
"And is it what you thought it would be?"
"Better."
"Again?"
"Please, Ruby."
She did it several more times, until she told him she had to stop. "I'm getting dizzy," she said, honestly. "Okay?"
"Thank you."

"What about your wife?"

"I don't tell Millie about *you*!" he said, sounding shocked that Ruby would even hint at his doing so.

"That's not what I meant. I meant why don't you ask her? She could do that for you."

"She'd think I was a weirdo. I can't do that. I can't risk that. I mean, she'd divorce me for being crazy. She'd tell all her friends."

"Oh, Duane."

At dinner after her show the next night, Duane talked. He talked and talked and talked. And Ruby heard him.

"It's just that it's so dad-gummed lonely, sitting in that hotel room every night," he said, buttering his third Parker House roll. Ruby nodded toward the waiter, who quickly brought another saucer of iced butter pats. "I perform all day — sell sell sell." He took a bite of his roll. "I practically do a song and dance, like you, kiddo, and I'm still *on* when I get back to the empty room. I can't sleep, can't turn it off. Nothing's on TV. I pick up a copy of *True Detective* at the liquor store, read a story about a body tossed in the Utah badlands or a sex freak cruising for victims. Still can't sleep. Every few days I call Millie, let her know how I am, where I am. But after eight years of marriage, we don't have anything left to say to each other. Not a dad-gummed thing." He shook his head, finished off the roll, and licked his fingers.

Ruby took a forkful of her Waldorf salad — her new favorite dish. The apples were wonderfully crisp and tart. She said nothing; she knew she wasn't meant to comment.

"Millie," Duane started up again after emptying his wineglass, "she doesn't make an effort anymore. I mean, look at you," he said, using the stem of his goblet to indicate he meant Ruby. "Look at you," he said again, his eyes watering some.

"Be fair, Duane." Maybe she should tell the waiter to cut Duane off. "This is my profession. I'm paid to look my best."

"Yeah, well, you shoulda seen her. My Millie. She was homecoming queen, did I tell you that?"

He had, but Ruby merely smiled in response.

"I was so goldurned proud to have her on my arm."

"She's still the same person," Ruby said, gently scooting Duane's wineglass to where the waiter would see it and remove it. She poured the last of the bottle into her own glass.

"Naw. She's not." He sighed. "She's not the same. She goes on and on about her Avon sales. And I just want to say to her, 'Millie, why don't you try a little of that miracle cream on your own face?' "

Ruby wondered what Millie would say, if she and Duane changed places. Would Millie be telling Ruby that Duane had gone to fat, that he'd lost his football tackler physique, that it wasn't worth it for her to try, to care about her appearance, if Duane couldn't be bothered to skip a dessert or two, maybe forgo his morning cinnamon bun? Or would Millie say she loved him, that he was a good provider?

"If we'd had kids," he said, absentmindedly. "Maybe then, things woulda been different."

"In what way?"

Duane ran his hand across his flattop. "I dunno."

"If you'd had kids, what?" Ruby pressed him.

"Maybe we'd still talk to each other. Maybe we'd have something left to say to each other."

He might be right — Ruby didn't know. Maybe children glued couples together in a more permanent way than could any wedding vow or 24-karat-gold ring.

"Aw, wouldya listen to me," Duane said. "Boring you silly with my sad-sack routine. Sittin' here with one of the most glamorous women in the world, better'n any movie star, and I'm going on and on about my blah old marriage."

"You know better than that," Ruby said, reaching across the table to pat the back of his beefy hand. She signaled to the cigarette girl, and Duane bought her a pack of Salems. "Here," she said, expertly tapping the pack so that she could offer him one. "Live dangerously, Duane." She smiled before lighting his cigarette.

They moved to the roulette table, where Duane won several times in a row and handed Ruby a fifty-dollar chip.

"Feeling better?" she asked, slipping the chip into her black beaded purse.

"You're my good luck piece," he said, revived by his wins. He reached an arm around her waist and took a deep breath. "Man oh man. You smell so good — you always smell so good, Ruby. Maybe I could get that scent for Millie, remember you whenever she wears it."

"It's not Avon," Ruby said, smiling into his florid face.

"Yeah, well, I didn't think there was any way it could be." He sighed.

And yet, it wasn't enough. The other showgirls didn't understand Ruby's need to feel she belonged to something bigger than the dance stage or the neon of Vegas. She refused to become another vapid showgirl who only knew clothes and shoes, jewels, and which gambler was the most likely to whisk a girl off to the Virgin Islands. The world was bigger — so much bigger than that, and Ruby's mind craved a wider horizon.

She was rarely home or awake to catch the news, but Ruby read the *Las Vegas Sun* religiously, listened to the radio, subscribed to *Time* and *Life* magazines so that she could keep up with what was happening in the world. Sometimes, the magazines stacked up for weeks before she got to them.

The November 10, 1967, cover of *Life* pictured the Leningrad Music Hall Girls — women dressed in white-and-silver miniskirts with matching white-blonde pageboy wigs. They wore elbow-length white gloves and silver heels that came nowhere near the stilettos in Ruby's closet, but still — the dancers were far more glamorous than Ruby would have imagined. It was an image starkly at odds with the dumpy, black-and-white world she'd been taught was life in the USSR. This wasn't a dour, stingy world, and the animated lines of beautiful women told her sex was alive and well, even under Communist Party leader Leonid Brezhnev.

She put the magazine in an oversized envelope for the Aviator, along with a letter detailing the latest in her life at the Sunglow Apartments with Rose and Vivid. She didn't tell him about the after-hours part of her job, but she wrote about how different she thought her showgirl life was from that of the Russian women she saw pictured in the article. Ruby added a copy of the Theatre Restaurant menu from the Tropicana to the envelope. It was a lovely lilac shade, with an illustration of three topless women as statuesque Greek columns. Inside, she circled the Breast of Chicken Sauté entrée, and wrote *It comes with risotto! Now that's on my have-tried list — have you ever tasted it? Delicious!*

The Aviator responded with a letter telling her he'd never flown U-2 missions over the Soviet Union — not like Gary Powers, whom the Russians had shot down in 1960, he reminded her. As if he still thought she was a naïve young girl, he added *The Soviets have to be watched. They pose the greatest*

8

Mercury, Gemini, and Apollo. The astronauts descended on Vegas like gods. Bona fide heroes, they were paraded along the Strip, cheered on as men who had braved the great unknown and fallen back to earth to tell the tale. The disaster of January 1967, when all three astronauts of Apollo 1 burned to death, brought home the very real dangers of their work, and the nation felt it, honored it. No one else possessed anything close to the kind of charismatic mystery that clung to the astronauts as they rode in the backseats of convertibles and waved to adoring crowds. America needed its heroes more than ever; Vietnam was not providing much in the way of glorious victory.

Ruby was swept along, just like everyone else. And maybe only a man of astronaut caliber could pull her willingly into bed, at last.

Kyle had the gold pin that proved he'd

flown in space, and he knew all the constellations. He had the lean, muscled torso of an astronaut, the closely cropped hair with sharp spikes of silver and gray, the angular, clean-shaven face. He had the bearing that proved he was a man of rigorous self-discipline. And he had a brunette wife with a beehive hairdo and two small, well-scrubbed children — all of whom had appeared in a *Look* magazine color photo spread entitled "Take a Peek: Astronauts at Home."

Ruby was in the grocery store reaching for a carton of Salems when the man beside her said, "I had quit, but while in Rome —" She only glanced at him — another man hitting on her, even though she was off duty, just a long-legged eighteen-year-old in a black twill miniskirt, braless beneath a pale green tank top, and makeup free. She could feel him beside her — a physical presence that was so solid and steadying, it made her think of the Aviator. That was why she gave Kyle "Chip" Casperson a second look, why she spoke to him.

"Why deprive yourself?" she asked, smiling. "I gave that up for Lent and never looked back."

"Self-deprivation?"

"Any kind of deprivation. My motto is

indulge."

He laughed and reached for a single pack of Camels. His hands were beautifully shaped, with long, nimble fingers. He wore no ring. Later, Kyle told her it was because rings could get caught in instrumentation, and he wanted to keep all of his fingers.

But then, in that moment when she first met him, he looked to be a handsome man without ties — a man who was drawn to Ruby not as a feathered sex symbol but simply as a woman in need of a smoke. She dropped the carton of Salems into her handbasket, smiled and wished him a good day.

"Who are you?" he said.

"What?" She paused, turned back toward him.

"I know you."

"I don't think so."

"Don't you know me?" he asked.

"I don't think so," she repeated.

"No," he said, shaking his head. "We do know each other. Somehow." He stopped smiling, looked intently into her face, tilted his head in thought. Ruby felt a sunburst sensation in her chest. When he held out his hand, his grip was warm, satisfyingly firm. "Kyle Casperson."

The name was familiar, but she couldn't

place it. "Ruby Wilde," she said.

"A cup of coffee? Someplace close? Just to find out." He smiled once more.

"To find out . . ." she said, letting suspicion enter her tone.

"That we know each other."

Why not? she asked herself. A cup of coffee was easy enough, and she had the time. She double-checked her basket; there weren't any frozen items.

A flustered waitress in the diner recognized Chip Casperson, said the coffees were on the house. He grinned across the table at Ruby, who smiled back, pretending that her heart rate hadn't just skyrocketed.

"The astronaut and the showgirl," Kyle said when she revealed her profession. "Sounds like one of Aesop's fables."

"The moral being?" Ruby flicked ash from the end of her cigarette.

"Sparks. Ignition. Out-of-this-world sensations."

"Oh my."

"Indeed."

He came to her show at the Tropicana, watched her perform, and she put forth more of an effort than she had in some time. Her kicks were higher, her turns crisper. When she looked back over her shoulder as a Dean Martin stand-in sang

"Standing on the Corner," she caught Kyle's eye and widened her smile. At the end of the show, she watched him stand to applaud, saw him encourage the rest of the audience to rise. As people recognized Chip Casperson, they turned their applause to him.

Backstage, he sat and watched wordlessly as she removed her makeup. Usually, the dressing rooms were a riot of gossip, commentary, and tales of who was winning at the gaming tables and who'd jetted to Paris with some big spender. Tonight the showgirls were subdued, maybe a little awed by Kyle's presence.

He came up behind Ruby, and while the other girls looked on enviously, he circled her body with his hands. She felt the silk of her kimono warm to his touch. She tilted her head backward until it rested against his chest, and she closed her eyes. As always after a performance, she was physically tired, but it lent her a kind of languor that helped her to relax.

He put his lips next to her ear, whispered, "Please, beautiful. Let's get out of here."

The Sands had comped him a suite in the hotel's new, seventeen-story tower that boasted a lucky 777 rooms. Jack Entratter's Copa Girls performed in the Copa Room, and Sinatra and Farrow had married at the Sands in '66. The Copa featured Sammy Davis, Jr., Dinah Shore, the Everly Brothers, and more mundane events like a gin rummy tournament touted to be the richest card contest in the world. The casino also advertised widely that it had astronaut Chip Casperson as its guest.

Kyle's suite was bigger than three of the Sunglow Apartments combined, with what seemed like a football field's expanse of peacock blue carpeting and white modern furniture arranged in several groupings, as if conversation circles were a regular event in such a room. Wall sconces in the shape of candelabras glowed against the pale blue walls, and vast windows followed the curve of the tower. Ruby stood looking out at the lights of the Strip, and she stretched her eyes past the city's garish neon to the darkness that fell away to desert and wilderness.

Kyle offered her champagne — there were half a dozen bottles chilling, gifts from well-wishers. She shook her head. Ruby wanted to do this without numbing herself. She wanted to experience what was spooling out before her in the cavernous room with the biggest bed she'd ever seen, a bed decked in white as if it were an immense, virginal wedding cake.

"I feel as if I'm on my honeymoon," she said when he held her. She smelled a spicy aftershave, and beneath that the antiseptic scent of Dial soap.

"Let it be a honeymoon," he said. "Let this be whatever you want it to be." He bent and kissed her neck.

"I'm about to go weak in the knees," she confessed, and he sat her on the edge of the bed, knelt to slip off her simple black pumps. She'd dressed down for Kyle, dressed in defiance of her showgirl glitz in a simple black sheath dress with a minimal string of pearls. She stood so that he could unzip her dress, and he let it fall from her to pool about her bare feet.

"Good lord," he said, stepping back to look at her in her black lace bra and panties.

"Don't pretend surprise," she said, smiling. "You've seen more of me than this onstage."

"It's a sight I could never grow tired of." He slipped out of his perfectly polished wing tips and unbuckled his belt.

They left the bedside lamp on. She pulled down the covers, lay back on the bed in her lingerie, watching him remove his shirt, his boxer shorts. She saw a flicker of vulnerability cross his face and reached her arms up to him. He eased onto the bed beside her.

"Don't get lost," he said, referring to the absurdly huge bed, but Ruby understood him on a different level. She had to stay in the room, in this bed, with this man. She would not hover up near the glitter-spangled ceiling or sit in a chair, watching at a place of safe remove. She believed a national hero wouldn't harm her — of that she was certain. He was a patriot, a man who could be trusted. As long as you weren't his wife, that is.

"What are you smiling about?" he asked, catching her expression.

"Being here. With you," she covered.

"Good."

"Very good," she said.

She had only Uncle Miles to compare Kyle to, but she recognized Kyle as a gentle, self-assured lover. He took his time, worshipped her body, wasn't afraid to emit sounds of gratification. And, he was just as pretty as she was, Ruby thought — the muscle, the tanned skin, the jubilantly curling chest hairs. The scent of him, of them.

"Kyle," she said his name, arching her back and lifting her pelvis toward his lips and tongue. He ran his lips down the length of one of her thighs, and she trembled with pleasure. He crawled back up the length of her body, took one of her nipples into his mouth, and just barely set his teeth on her raised nipple. "Oh!" she moaned.

"Tell me what you like," he said, his breath warm against her cheek.

Ruby fought back a tinge of panic. *What I like?* she thought. Her experience to date was a mantra of pleading, *Please, make it quick; get it over with.* Fleetingly, she felt sorry for herself, that she would be surprised by the concept of sex as something pleasurable. "Anything. Everything," she breathed.

"You're on the pill?" he asked, and she shook her head.

"Diaphragm," she said, glad that months ago Vivid had told her to just go get fitted for one and learn how to use it. "Already in place," she added.

She was surprised when he entered her; it was not the traditionally dry, painful thing that it had been with Uncle Miles. She felt the curve of Kyle's penis hit her in precisely the right spot. He teased her, put just the tip in, withdrew, made her want to call out for more. Tip, withdrawal, tip and tease, withdrawal. It drove her crazy with want, and she pulled him to her with all the strength of her arms, said, "Stay. Don't go. Stay."

He began to move quickly then, no longer holding back, unable to hold back. She felt her orgasm take hold of her, practically deprive her of consciousness. She didn't know if she spoke or not, if she made any sound. She simply felt her body tense, consumed with heat, felt her thoughts evaporate, felt only pure, unadulterated physical sensation.

Kyle stayed inside her, still hard enough to begin moving again, to let her have another, less intense orgasm. This time she felt her nails dig in to the small of his back, and she managed to stop herself from leaving marks his wife would discover.

When he pulled out, she felt a pit open inside her. She felt intense, instant loneliness. She wanted to cry into the crook of his neck, say, *Don't leave me, don't leave me, don't go.* It was a sudden, unbidden, wholly physical ache of abandonment that she could not comprehend, could only feel. Ruby turned her head and buried her face in the pillow.

"Where are you going?" Kyle asked, taking hold of her shoulder and tenderly rolling her to face him. "What, Ruby? What have I done?" he asked, seeing her expression.

"It's nothing you've done. Or not done,"

she said. "I don't know what it is."

"But that was extraordinary," he said, kissing her.

"It was," she said. "It was, Kyle."

"So, what?"

"I don't know." She touched his cheek with her fingertips, ran the knuckle of her index finger along the seashell curve of his ear, thought about him splashing down into the ocean in a capsule that had traveled through blackness.

"Does it have anything to do with those pearlescent scars?" he asked.

Ruby blushed, fumbled for an answer she didn't have.

"You hide them well, and that can't be easy wearing only a G-string." He waited, and when Ruby remained silent, he said, "I had a girlfriend once. Before my wife." He reached for his Camels and offered her one. She shook her head. "She used to cut herself, too," he said, flicking a silver lighter with the NASA emblem engraved on its polished surface.

The last thing Ruby wanted to do was to explain herself. What would she say? *Uh, Kyle, it, um, er — it makes me feel better. It releases something, that's all I know.* She'd never spoken about it to anyone, and she didn't intend to start tonight. *Or rather this morning,* she thought, seeing by the bedside clock that it was after four A.M.

"I'm sorry," he said, moving the cut-glass ashtray to rest on his chest. "I shouldn't have pried. You don't have to talk about it. Not if you don't want to." He crushed the last of his cigarette and rolled to face her. "But you have to admit that I was right," he said, brushing hair from her forehead.

"About?"

"Us. About knowing you. About you knowing me."

"Yes. You were." Ruby took his hand, turned it palm up beneath the light from the bedside lamp. "Your fingertips," she said, squeezing them between her thumb and middle finger. "They're padded."

"Padded?"

"They're not flat or stingy. They're the fingertips of a sensitive person. And see this?" she said, pointing to the small mount beneath his index finger. "This is Jupiter. It's associated with ambition, pride, leadership, and honor. And yours is well developed." He pulled his hand from hers for a moment to take a better look at his palm. "But this is what most interests me," she said, taking back his hand and squeezing the mount below his ring finger. "This is the mount of Apollo. It's associated with creativity and artistry. And this is your most developed mount."

"Meaning?" he asked.

"Well, combining that with your sensitive fingertips, I'd say you were an artist of some kind. Not a man who hurtles through space." She laughed and let go of his hand. "So much for palmistry."

"Actually," he said, thoughtful, "that's my dream. I write — mostly short stories, nothing great, but it's what I truly love."

Ruby sat up, rearranged the pillows behind her, and Kyle joined her. "That explains *pearlescent.*" She smiled. "But stories about what? Space?"

"Mostly about nature, things I see when I hike or walk the seashore. Stories I see in the people I encounter."

"And what do you do with your stories?" She hesitated, afraid he'd tell her he read them to his wife.

"Send them to *The Saturday Evening Post,* magazines like that."

"I'd think they'd jump at the chance to publish something written by an astronaut."

"I don't use my real name. The same way I suspect you don't use your real name."

"But can I read one?" Ruby asked, ignoring the hint that he wanted to know who was tucked away behind Ruby Wilde.

"Not until someone actually publishes one." His disappointment was evident.

"You can send me one," she said. "Don't make me wait for a magazine."

"I could," he said, smiling. "But in the meantime —" He tickled her, and, giggling, she tried to capture his fast-moving wrists. "I'm here for a week, and I intend to see a great deal of you — whatever your name is." He grinned.

"How was it?" Vivid began the inquisition, but the others quickly joined in.

"Out of sight? Out of this world?" Rose asked.

"Far out?" Vivid grinned.

"What?" Dee asked. "What are you guys talking about?"

"You must be the only person on the face of the planet who doesn't know," Ruby said.

"Know what?" Dee asked again.

"Only person in the solar system," Rose said.

"Only one in the *universe.*" Vivid trumped Rose.

"Enough with the space jokes," Ruby said, feigning frustration.

"Will somebody please tell me what's going on?" Dee nearly shouted.

"Ruby slept with Chip Casperson."

"No!" Dee looked to Ruby for confirmation. "The astronaut?"

Ruby nodded, smiling.

"So, to begin where we started," Vivid said, grabbing Ruby's shoulders from behind and shaking her. "HOW WAS IT?"

"Earth shattering." Ruby grinned.

"Gawd!" Dee said. "When did all this happen?" The others dissolved into helpless laughter. "No one tells me anything," she said, pretending to pout and then grabbing a cushion from Rose's couch and pelting Ruby. "I need details!" she shouted, hitting Ruby while the others grabbed cushions and joined her.

"Yeah," Vivid said. "It's the least you can do for those of us who have not had intergalactic sex."

Ruby folded her hands as if she were a peaceful Buddha and began. "Okay. First of all, let me just say that he is extremely well endowed. I believe you mere earthlings would say his dimensions are *astronomical.*"

Over the years, gamblers bought her nearly a dozen furs. Yet, her all-time favorite was her first — an abundant, calf-length silver fox fur with an absolutely enormous collar she could stand up so that its softness caressed her cheeks. It was so supple that it rippled like water when she walked. The coat's lining was a hot pink China silk, and the buyer was Kyle, the day before he left Vegas to return to his suburban Ohio home.

Ruby leapt into the coat in the nude, and they drove the Karmann Ghia she'd bought herself into the desert outside the city, where the darkness was so complete she could barely see her hand held before her face. They parked in a desolate spot on a forlorn dirt road, lowered the car's top, and watched as the stars faded and dawn arrived in pinks, intense peaches, and deep roses. Ruby listened to the coyotes howling and barking; she heard the whoosh of an owl's wings as it swooped to grab an unwary desert rodent. Away from the bells and whistles of the Strip, its omnipresent clouds of cigarette smoke, she could smell desert sage and catch the eyes of jackrabbits in her headlights. She felt peace in the aching, lonesome stretch of desert sand. She felt at home in this inhospitable setting.

And, Ruby felt gratitude for the solid, real presence of Kyle as they leaned against each other, warm, easy, wordless. She felt what she knew would be an enduring fondness for him — for his tenderness, as well as his commitments that kept her from becoming attached. Kyle was a dance partner who'd helped her to disentangle herself from a sizable, dark part of her past. He'd go back to his wife. And Ruby — she would go on to others.

9

Kyle was the first, but not the last. Ruby was fondest of him by far, but their affair had lasted barely a week, and he had his squeaky-clean public image to maintain. After Kyle, if the man was handsome enough, charming enough, or if he made her laugh — then and only then would Ruby consider riding the elevator with him to his hotel suite. The nearly anonymous sex was, she thought, about the best thing ever invented. It let her experiment freely. The man — whoever he was — would be gone in a few hours or days, so why not? It let her demand. It helped her to drive out the demons Uncle Miles had bred inside her, to make them matter less and less as they were caught in the undertow of other experiences, other men. Ruby had her favorite times, her favorite men and sensations. She consciously let fade the lackluster performances, the times when she'd been wrong about the chemistry or when her partner for the night had been too drunk to perform.

Sometimes, she could hear Aunt Tate's voice shouting *"Slut!,"* and she knew that most of America would have called her that — probably even her parents, had they lived. But Vegas gave Ruby the freedom to experiment. And maybe things were changing.

As 1967 eased toward 1968, Ruby got up, got dressed, and left men while they slept. She left them, always. She left them and left them and left them, and she knew it was the perfect life for her. Meaningless, recreational sex allowed her to convince herself that she was somehow protected. That her heart was immune.

She sent the Aviator a jar of Tang — *the astronauts' drink!* — along with a photo of the showgirl and the astronaut Chip Casperson. The Aviator responded by sending her a copy of *This Side of Paradise.* Inside the book's cover, he wrote *To the girl who's been to outer space.* He never threatened to visit and check up on her, never mentioned her aunt and uncle, but Mrs. Baumgarten repeatedly promised visits. Her husband's busy surgery schedule always interfered, which was actually fine by Ruby. She had to admit a secret grudge against her well-meaning dance instructor, the one who hadn't given Ruby particularly informed or good advice, who'd pretended to know more than she did about Vegas and the dance world in general. *Big fish, little pond* — it was a saying her father had used, and Ruby thought it most apt when it came to Lenore Baumgarten.

On her days off, Ruby went to see other Vegas shows, sometimes with her friends but more often on the arm of one of the cigar-scented men who sought to charm her. At the Aladdin, she saw Tempest Storm, marveled at the woman's artful striptease, the finesse with which the queen of burlesque removed her clothing. At the Sahara, Ruby rubbed shoulders with Joe DiMaggio and Paul Anka, and during one of Buddy Hackett's shows in the Congo Room, she spotted Sonny and Cher in the audience, along with Michael Landon and his wife. *Eat your heart out, Uncle Miles,* she thought, knowing how much he'd have given to see *Bonanza*'s Little Joe in the flesh. On Chicago Johnny's arm, she passed beneath the Riviera's twirling neon star, through the nine-thousand-square-foot lobby, and in the casino's Versailles Room she saw performances by Louis Armstrong, Ann-Margret,

Sarah Vaughan, and Debbie Reynolds. Afraid of losing track, Ruby listed the shows and dates in the back pages of her cashbook.

"What are you up to?" Rose asked, entering Ruby's apartment and finding her setting up a card table.

"I bought a sewing machine." Ruby struggled with the legs of the table and at last got them locked. She scooted the table beneath a living room window so she'd have plenty of natural light.

"Why? I mean, you can afford to buy any clothes you want. Or have them bought for you."

Ruby had often wondered how Rose felt about showgirl perks — the clothes, the jewels, and in Vivid's case, the cars and boats and probably one day even planes. Rose kept her clothes on, and so she was earning a comparatively mediocre salary, supplemented from time to time by drunken, elated-gambler largesse. Still, Ruby had never broached the subject openly — it seemed like a possible bruise for Rose, and she had no intention of pressing it.

"I used to make almost all my clothes," Ruby said, lifting the sewing machine from its box and setting it on the card table with a heavy *thunk.*

"My point exactly. Used to." Rose began sorting through Ruby's pile of Hermès scarves with the purpose of borrowing one to wear on her date with a new man — a Caesars card dealer.

"You're wearing your linen sheath? The turquoise one?" Ruby asked, scrounging around in the cardboard box until she found the sewing machine's instruction booklet and box of accessories, including a newfangled buttonholing device. The machine was far beyond Aunt Tate's old, no-frills Singer. Ruby was excited, anticipating all of the things she could make.

"Yeah, the blue dress," Rose said. "Good God, Ruby. How many of these do you have?"

Ruby went to stand by Rose and sorted through the pile of silk until she found the scarf she thought would best complement Rose's dress. She unfolded it and held it up so Rose could decide. It was a pattern of greens, blues, and purples with black accents that reminded Ruby of stained-glass windows.

"Perfect," Rose said, taking the scarf and carefully refolding it. "So explain the sewing machine, please." She sat down in one of Ruby's new wingback chairs. Ruby had had them custom upholstered in hot pinks and whites, bold geometric patterns. The Sunglow Apartments, with their broad-bladed venetian blinds and shadowy interiors, looked as though they had played a starring role in some Fred MacMurray noir film, and Ruby was determined to brighten things up.

"I want to design clothes," Ruby said, opening the refrigerator and pulling out a pitcher of iced tea. "Want some?"

"You bet."

"Anyway" — Ruby pried up the lever on the ice tray and freed enough cubes for their glasses — "I have this new friend. Tawny. She's one of the Tropicana's backstage seamstresses, and just so talented. I mean, I've always used patterns, been careful to follow all the instructions to a T— but she can cut and sew free-form, just take a look at a garment and then replicate it, but with her own style. So, we got to talking —"

"Did you talk salary?" Rose interrupted, accepting the iced tea. "Because I can guarantee it would be a ridiculously big pay cut."

Ruby, who was wearing hugely belled bell-bottom pants dyed in broad vertical stripes of white, red, yellow, and blue, plopped down sideways in the other wingback chair. She looked down at her thigh on the pink-

and-white upholstery and thought about how jarring the materials were. They nearly screamed. "I can't dance forever, you know."

"You're nineteen! That's hardly old."

"But the lifespan of a showgirl — you know," she said, hinting at what they'd all seen in Vivid — prime fading toward the beginning of the end.

"I'm just saying you're not there yet. Not for years."

"Maybe not, but I'm thinking about my future. I'm thinking that maybe I could be a costume designer, here in Vegas. I want to learn — and Tawny can teach me some of the fundamentals. I'm already sketching," she said, nodding toward a portfolio she'd left open on the loveseat. "Just ideas I have, designs I could start with."

"That's all good," Rose said, sipping at her tea, thoughtful.

Lately, Ruby had been inspired by fashions from the twenties, from the F. Scott Fitzgerald novels the Aviator sent, and fleetingly she wished Rose had shown some curiosity about her design drawings. "What about you? What do you want to do after Caesars?"

"I don't know why I can't do what a showgirl does, if and when I get tired of Caesars. Just move to a different casino, change the scenery."

Vivid was on her third casino since Ruby had met her. The showgirls easily moved from stage to stage, and it kept the productions fresh to have the dancers move about. It also let a showgirl quit for a few weeks, jet someplace with some man hot off a big win, and then come back to work.

Ruby shook her head. "I mean your *future* future," she said meaningfully. "I'm talking about long-term planning, Rose."

"I'm not like you. I'm more of a spur-of-the-moment gal. Besides," she said, setting her empty glass on the floor beside her chair. "Isn't that what a husband's for?"

"Oh, please." Ruby rolled her eyes. "You can do better than that."

"Who says? And who says there's anything wrong with that? It could be that Matt's the one."

"Tonight's Prince Charming?"

"Yeah."

"Okay then," Ruby said, not wanting to make her friend feel as if she were selling herself short. It had never once entered Ruby's mind that marriage — or some man — would give her the kind of security she needed. As a matter of fact, life had taught her something entirely different.

"But what about you? Don't you want someone steady in your life? A true love interest?" Rose flipped her hair over her shoulder. "I mean — and I'm not judging here — it seems what you're doing could get pretty lonely after a while."

"I'm not lonely."

"Fine. But don't you want something more permanent? A man you could rely on?"

"The way I see it is, if it's meant to be, it will be. I think, literally, the man who's right for me will just show up on my doorstep. I'm not into all this girly manipulation."

Rose smiled and aimed her gaze meaningfully toward Ruby's record albums. Nancy Sinatra's *Nancy in London* album was sitting front and center. "So," Rose said, "you're gonna go with wishin' and a hopin'?"

Ruby grinned. "I'm certainly *not* going to follow that song's advice."

"You mean wearing your hair just for him, doing the things he likes to do?" Rose laughed.

"Lord, no." Ruby shook her head, thinking she might have to give Nancy Sinatra a rest for a while.

"I'll tell you what I really want," Rose said, now deadly serious. "I want children. And stop it — don't shake your head at me."

"I wasn't. I wasn't going to," Ruby objected.

"I want to build a home, create holiday traditions, teach my daughter to roll out sugar cookie dough. I want a man who will hold my interest and give me security." Rose paused.

"But what else?" Ruby asked. "You do want more than a *Leave It to Beaver* life, don't you?"

"There's nothing wrong with wholesome."

"Says the woman who wears a teeny-tiny toga to work."

"Says the woman who has a good job, who has gotten out to see the world, and who now has a better frame of reference. I've tested my theories."

"Which are?"

"What's meaningful. What amounts to a life well lived."

"So Vegas is your contrast? The black to your white?"

"Maybe. But you and I know it's a place where a girl can come to have a life of her own, before she settles down. Look at Vivid. She has her independence, her freedom. But it can't be all she wants."

"Who says?"

"She'll marry some tycoon."

"That's not what she tells me," Ruby said. "She told me she wants to be rich in her own right — not have some sugar daddy doling out gifts or making all the financial decisions. I mean, c'mon, Rose. If the man has all the money, he has all the power. Can you really see Vivid taking orders?"

Rose laughed. "Point made. But don't belittle my dream, all right? I'm entitled."

Rose's dream life was essentially the life Ruby had supposed her sister Dawn would have had, had she lived. Marriage, children, sunny-day picnics and rainy-day baking. It's what Rose had grown up knowing, what Dawn had known, and for that reason alone it made sense. But Ruby believed that the doors that led to such acceptability, such wholesomeness, as Rose said, were closed to her. And now, given her Vegas life, Ruby was far too tainted ever to kiss the pristine garments of wholesomeness.

"And what about you?" Rose interrupted Ruby's thoughts. "It's pretty obvious that one thing you're after is a big savings account. Right? I mean, how much have you got socked away?" Almost immediately, Rose apologized. "Shit. I'm sorry. It's none of my business. It's just that you don't spend anything. Well, practically nothing," she said, eyeing the new sewing machine.

"It's because you never know." Ruby stood to get more iced tea. "You never know what life will throw at you."

Rose followed Ruby and held her glass out for a refill. "Sometimes you act like you're forty." She took a sip of tea. "What happened to you? I mean, to make you so cautious? It had to be something big."

"I'm not cautious!"

"You're cautious with money."

"I'm careful."

"Whatever. You're avoiding the question."

"I'm refining the question." Ruby smiled.

"Still avoiding," Rose shot back.

"Let's just say I learned early on that the rug can get pulled out from under you. Like the Boy Scouts say, *Be prepared.*" Ruby set down her glass and put a foot up on the kitchen counter, stretched.

"You're not going to tell me," Rose said.

"No offense intended." Ruby paused in her stretch and looked at Rose. "If I told anyone, it would be you, okay? I just don't want to relive it."

"Okay," Rose said, picking up the Hermès scarf.

"If you like it, keep it."

"Sure you won't miss it?" Rose teased, looking toward the tower of scarves.

"We're going to want a full report." Ruby switched legs. "In the morning. Or whenever you decide to come home."

"Maybe," Rose said on her way out the

door, "but I can keep a secret too."

Ruby hadn't told any of them of her family's death. She didn't want the breadth of her loss to define her, and she didn't want to see anything different in the eyes of her friends. But what did her past matter, anyway? She was Ruby now, not Lily. When she'd last bought a new wallet, she carefully printed the Aviator's contact information on the emergency identification card and tucked it behind the plastic window. He was her family — all she wanted of family.

In the spring of 1968, Evan Brashear wooed Ruby from the Tropicana to the Stardust, where she became one of Brashear's Lido Belles. Brashear was a really nice man in a city that wasn't always particularly nice, and he had pomaded, curly hair, an omnipresent cigarette holstered in his right hand, and a pointed chin that turned up slightly, reminding Ruby of the curled toe of a Turkish slipper. He gave her a hefty raise and put her on the cover of the menu for the Cafe Continental, the lounge where the Lido de Paris show was performed. Ruby even won Vegas Showgirl of the Year, which was a huge honor, especially for someone who'd barely been dancing six months. "You stand out," Brashear told her. "Even in a line of girls meant to look alike. You're luminescent, Ruby Wilde. A phenomenon," he'd said, chucking her under the chin.

Her first starring role at the Stardust was in a performance meant to feed off of audiences' fervor for anything having to do with space exploration, particularly as the launch for the moon landing mission approached. Otherworldly, tinny music began playing as the curtains opened. Suspended far above the stage on nearly invisible cables, the Lido Belles were clad only in cellophane and G-strings. Against an indigo backdrop liberally sprinkled with flickering stars, they performed an ethereal spacewalk wearing close-cropped silver feathers meant to simulate space helmets. At the end of the number, brightly colored silk parachutes unfurled, and they descended to the stage in a Vegas version of a space capsule splashdown.

The switch to the Stardust bolstered Ruby. And yet, she could no longer completely hide from herself the fact that although she'd not been dancing for even a year, tedium was stealthily encroaching. The requisite mixing with men after the show had become work. Their enamored looks had grown stale, and she was finding it harder and harder to feel sympathy for them. Instead, they reminded her of insecure little boys, when what she longed for was virility.

Ruby had to drag herself to the gaming tables, muster the energy to put on a happy face, to charm and delight. Too, the novelty of applause and of the seemingly endless flood of cash — it was gone, somehow worn thin by repetition. The gaudy superficialities of the showgirl life were no longer enough to hold her. She wasn't sure where her dissatisfaction came from; she just knew it was there, tapping on her shoulder more and more insistently as the days passed.

And, she'd begun cutting again. Even though she tried to keep the slices beneath her G-string and used opaque makeup to cover the scars, it was difficult to hide. She experimented with cutting the bottoms of her feet, knowing shoes would always hide the wounds, but slicing into callus didn't call forth blood, and it was the relief of blood she needed. Putting a blade to the tender skin of her arches impacted her dancing; she tried that once, only once.

Ruby was certainly smart enough to know that the cutting meant something. She could almost hear the Aviator shouting about her superior IQ and her ability — if she would only try — to marshal her emotions and control all of this. She knew she needed to pay attention, to sit still long enough to come to terms with what caused the insistent hunger for blood and release. In some ways, it reminded her of Vivid's periodic, compulsive need to rush out and buy ten eye shadow compacts or six pairs of designer boots — sometimes, even a new car. Something hidden, subterranean, gave birth to the need. Ruby knew that the cutting was a symptom, and she could no longer pretend it was a release for something Uncle Miles or Aunt Tate had done — or not done. No, this current urge to cut was the *progeny* of a need born in her childhood, something she desperately wanted to extinguish.

Ruby had read an article in one of her *Life* magazines about the growing popularity of transcendental meditation in far-out California. There was something about Buddhism that called to her, even if it was simply the concept of such extreme internal quietude. So she tried navel gazing, as Vivid called it, thinking that maybe by sitting cross-legged on her bedroom carpeting with a lit votive candle flickering weakly on her dresser top, she'd somehow come to terms with the disease-ridden ghosts of her childhood. But Ruby could only sit for thirty seconds or less before a cacophony of thoughts interrupted. She couldn't plumb the darkness, couldn't extricate the threads that connected her past to her present. All she could fathom was that something was missing in her life — something that would drive her, thrill her, that would put an adrenaline-sharp edge to her life. If she had that, the kind of wholehearted purpose that escaping Kansas had given her, then she would be all right.

Miserable and seeking relief of some kind, Ruby went to her usual fount of wisdom and asked Vivid how she'd stood the life of a showgirl for so long.

"But it's a blast! I've never been bored. Not once," Vivid claimed. "I love being in good shape, *feeling* the beauty of my body, the power it gives me. There's no other life I want. But maybe I'm not as smart or as deep as you," she said, clearly intending to goad Ruby.

"It's not that, and you know it. It's just that it's not enough, for me. I think I need something more."

"Well, what, exactly?"

"That's just it," Ruby said, rubbing her forehead. "I don't know." She watched her friend pick up the red lacquer box Ruby had often admired. Vivid opened the box and held it out to Ruby. It was about three-quarters full of small white pills. "What's that?" Ruby asked.

"Amphetamines. Speed. You've never tried it?"

"Never."

"I get them from this doctor. He does a crazy business for all the housewives and teenaged girls who want to be skinny."

"They're weight-loss pills?"

"Not meant to be, although they do keep you from being hungry. They'll give you a boost, get you high, make you feel good so that you can get into the swing of things again. Think of them as little bits of motivation." Vivid handed the box to Ruby to hold and plowed through a kitchen drawer until she found a roll of sandwich bags. She filled a Baggie a quarter full, rolled the bag on itself, and then wrapped a rubber band around the cylinder. "Start with a couple, an hour before you need them. The buzz will last about three hours, max, so you'll need a pick-me-up after the show — take another couple then. You can always work your way up to more."

"They're not dangerous?"

"Hell no." Vivid laughed. "Half the girls in America — well, the rich ones, anyway — are getting these from their good ol' family doctor. Their *mothers* drive them to the appointments!"

Ruby tried them that night, following Vivid's recommended dosage — but upping it to three pills for sufficient inspiration to survive the after-show drudgery. She found she was better able to concentrate on whatever the men were saying, to listen more patiently or to find something to occupy her attention, such as cuff links shaped like dice or poker chips, scabbed-over nicks from a razor, or a roll of tan neck flesh above a too-tight collar. She created contests for herself, competitions in which she had to name six distinct attributes about a man within the first two minutes of meeting him.

Speed turned life's volume up — just enough. She was so wired, though, that she couldn't get to sleep until just a few hours before the next night's show — which meant that the following night she took even more. The night after that, she took more.

Over the course of the next several weeks, Ruby jitterbugged her way into the life of an insomniac. All of those hours when she used to sleep, freed up! She delighted in getting all of her ironing done. Although her fingers vibrated with near-electric voltage, she drew designs for everyday dresses and pantsuits, swimsuits, cocktail dresses, evening gowns, lingerie, and of course, costumes for the stage. She was getting so much done! She defrosted her freezer. She blew the dust off of her record albums and set Dylan's *Greatest Hits* to play, flipping the album over time and time again, sometimes moving the needle repeatedly to "I Want You" and "Positively 4th Street."

Feeling hollowed out but immune to hunger, rocketing through the night into the early dawn hours accompanied by Dylan's nasal tones, Ruby wondered what had happened to the fervor she'd felt just a few years ago. Where had she been for the past year or so? Where was her edge, the adrenaline fix of risk? Who was she, anymore? Just a fungible showgirl? Was she coasting, letting her ambition wither while she distracted herself with parties and possessions?

Her thoughts raced; there was a near constant buzz in her ears like a frenetic housefly ping-ponging, seeking exit. She'd been wasting time. *Wasting time!* But the speed was helping, helping her to *see,* to search for what she really needed.

She got the speed doctor's address from Vivid. He didn't listen to her heart, weigh her, or do any of the things Ruby expected. All he asked was that she tell him that she needed to keep her weight down for the stage, and *voilà!* she had his signature granting her over a hundred tablets of electric energy. The drugstore pharmacist didn't even blink when, feeling like a girl with a forged permission slip, she handed him the prescription.

The drug made her mouth taste like tinfoil. She started sucking on peppermints and red cinnamon candies to mask the metallic taste and help with what seemed to be an eternally parched mouth, no matter how much water she chugged in between numbers. She was fidgety, couldn't sit still to read, and she felt like one of the Aviator's cars running in top gear — smooth, perfect, but with the engine pushed to the edges of its design for speed. Each time Ruby popped a handful of pills, she envisioned a tachometer's needle touching the red zone.

She stayed up for days in a row, jotting down all the design ideas that came to her, certain that each one was brilliant, that she could outdistance any designer on the planet, once she had the right connections and got better at the technical aspects of sketching and making real what she saw in her head. She gunned the engine of herself and raced headlong toward her future.

10

Driving to work during the first week of April, Ruby listened to the news reports. She lit a cigarette, adjusted the tuning on the radio, rolled down a window, drummed her fingers on the steering wheel, and bounced with frustration at the delay imposed by a red light. She heard it then: Martin Luther King, Jr., shot dead in Memphis.

By the time Ruby reached the Stardust parking lot, she was sobbing, bent in half, clutching her middle. He was thirty-nine. Just thirty-nine. And all he'd wanted to do was lead a strike for poorly paid garbage workers. Could there be a worse job than picking up someone's rotting trash? Well, emptying septic tanks, maybe. Those men should be the best paid — they did something no one else wanted to do. Imagine being married to one of those guys. The laundry. How could you ever get his shirts clean? Talk about ring around the collar!

But wait — King. She was thinking about King. She'd been following the news stories of his peaceful civil disobedience, and she'd admired him — had even written to the Aviator about Gandhi and King. This couldn't be. It just couldn't.

Ruby fumbled and then dropped her keys, got down on all fours in the parking lot to search for them beneath the car. She was crying, still. Loudly, messily. She stumbled up the curb, pushed her sunglasses back up on her nose, and, standing next to a perfectly arranged flower bed, she took a deep breath. She couldn't work. Not today. It was the first time she'd ever considered missing a performance, but she felt helpless, caught up in the King tragedy.

Ruby made her way down the hallway of administrative offices, trying not to see the garnet-red carpeting beneath her feet, not to think of blood pooling beneath King's head. She was plain-faced, her gym bag whacking her hip, a baseball cap pulled over her hair. Wiping tears from her cheeks with the back of her hand, she knocked on Evan Brashear's office door.

"What's happened?" he asked, coming out from behind his desk. "Here." He pointed toward his couch. "Sit down. Talk to me, Ruby." He took a handkerchief from his pocket and handed it to her.

"I can't. Can't dance. Not tonight," she said.

"But what's happened? What can I do?"

"They shot him. He's standing outside his hotel room, and he gets shot!" She knew she looked awful, that her face was blotchy and red, but she didn't care. She couldn't remember the last time she'd gotten more than two or three hours of sleep.

"The Reverend King? You're talking about King?"

She nodded.

"Listen, honey," Brashear said, perching beside her and putting his arm about her shoulders. "It is a tragedy. It is. But your reaction is overblown." He paused for a moment. "And I think I know why. I've been watching you." He nodded as if confirming something. "You're not the first, and I've been at this a long, long time."

Ruby wadded his handkerchief into a ball. She took a deep, stuttering breath, felt her exhaustion. She needed to get a glass of water, down some more pills.

"You've lost a lot of weight. You have dark shadows under your eyes that are no longer hidden by that concealer you girls use." Brashear picked up her hand, held it. "You can't keep your hand still, not to save your life."

"I'm just a little tired." Her legs were vibrating, too, and she wondered if, seated so close to her, he could feel them.

"You're doing speed. And way too much of it."

"Just enough. Just enough to get me through."

"But I can't keep you on. Not if you keep this up."

Ruby felt the swift wings of panic. She couldn't be fired! It had never occurred to her that this kind man would kick her to the curb.

"Stop the pills," he said, standing to dismiss her, a firm father determinedly gritting his teeth and laying down the law. "You can have a few days off, but I need to see that you're serious about quitting. I know you can't do that overnight, that it will take some time, but nevertheless, next Monday you'd better show up ready to work, looking one hell of a lot better. Convince me that you're at least *trying* — or I won't have a choice. Go home. Get some sleep. Eat. Clean up your act, Ruby."

Ruby stood, his handkerchief still a wad in her hand. She felt as if she might start crying again, and she didn't have a clue as to how to defend herself.

"It's not that I'm unsympathetic. But, Ruby, you're ruining yourself. And I'm not the kind of boss who lets a girl do that." Brashear touched her shoulder briefly and then walked back behind his desk, picked up his pack of Lucky Strikes, and shook one free.

Ruby stood for a moment, watching him. And then she turned and walked down the hallway until she got to the drinking fountain. She dropped four pills into the palm of her hand, swallowed them, and took a long drink of water, tossing her head back to make sure they went down. She shoved Brashear's handkerchief in her purse.

On the drive home, while she was waiting for the drug to kick in and get her back on course, she felt increasingly angry. How could he so blithely think about dismissing her? Daddy Evan should bear in mind how much money she made the casino. He should remember who brought in the audiences and kept the gamblers hammered on expensive scotch. Who showed up at golf tournaments, kissed the cheeks of winners. Who glowed during the opening ceremonies for championship rodeos and posed for photos with every Tom, Dick, and Harry Brashear asked her to pose with. She'd even been promised the cover of the 1969 Stardust calendar. Brashear was taking her for granted. She'd just go elsewhere. She had the star power to do that. She could do it in her sleep. But first, she'd take a couple weeks off. She'd never taken a vacation, and it was high time she did.

For the next five days, Ruby stayed glued to the television coverage of King's assassination. She watched footage of the days of rioting in Baltimore, as well as other major cities across the country. The entire nation burned with outrage, grief, and indelible hatred and bigotry. She sat, cross-legged and crying, as Bobby Kennedy stood on the back of a flatbed truck in Indianapolis and encouraged forbearance. On April 9, she watched King's funeral service at the Ebenezer Baptist Church. She ran out of Kleenex.

The Sunglow Apartment girls must have taken a vote; on the sixth day of Ruby's isolation, they sent Rose as their emissary. When Ruby opened the door, Rose was standing there in a sleeveless flowered cotton shift, her hair tied back in the Hermès scarf Ruby had given her. She was holding a foil-covered pie tin, and she edged past Ruby without asking.

"I'm opening the blinds," Rose said without preamble. She set the dish on Ruby's countertop and began parting curtains. "It's cold roast chicken. Some cheese and pickles. Make yourself a plate of food," she ordered.

Ruby looked beneath the foil but went no further. She watched Rose find the on-off switch to the television set and silence it.

"The air is stale in here," Rose said, crinkling her nose and cranking open a window. "And you." She turned, put her hands on her hips, and looked at Ruby. "You need a shower. Wash your hair, for God's sake."

Ruby went and sat in one of her wingback chairs. She sorted through the clutter of her side table, trying to find a pack of cigarettes.

"What the fuck, Ruby?" Rose came to stand in front of her, took Ruby's chin in her hand, and forced Ruby to look at her. "This isn't you, this slovenliness. What the hell is going on?"

"Nothing."

"I don't have the patience for your bullshit. You've been avoiding us."

"No one asked you to come here."

"Someone had to."

"Did you draw the short stick?" Ruby sneered, feeling awful that she was behaving so badly toward the sweetest human being on earth and yet not having the slightest inclination to get ahold of herself. She felt supremely irritable.

"Vivid didn't do you any favors," Rose said. "I know she meant well, but really, Ruby. You have to pick and choose when it comes to following her advice."

"I don't know what you mean." Somehow, Rose was making her feel like a petulant toddler.

"You know exactly what I mean, and don't think for a moment that I'm that stupid. Please."

"Yeah, well . . ."

"Where are they?" Rose asked, looking about the disheveled living room. "Bathroom?" She headed down the hallway. Ruby could hear the door of the medicine cabinet open and close, the sound of Rose moving bottles around on the bathroom counter. She heard Rose head into the bedroom, then the *thunk* of the nightstand drawer opening and closing. "Where's your purse?" Rose said, returning to the living room. Ruby tried to kick her bag beneath her chair, but Rose spotted it and made a dive for it.

"You have no right!" Ruby yelled, managing to catch hold of the shoulder strap while

Rose grabbed the body of the purse and tugged.

"Have you looked in a mirror?" Rose asked. "Have you seen what you're doing to yourself? You haven't been to work in days!"

"I quit," Ruby said, still clutching the purse strap.

"Aw fuck, Ruby! What's going *on*?"

Ruby capitulated, let go of the purse. And then, completely without warning, she began yet another of her incessant crying jags while Rose dug through the purse and pulled out the huge glass bottle of amphetamines. She held it up, shook it as if it were a maraca.

"For this?" Rose asked. "You're fucking up your dream life for this?"

"It's not my dream life. I hate it."

"Dancing? But why? Why all of a sudden?" Rose sat at Ruby's feet, put her hand on Ruby's bare calf. "You haven't even shaved your legs," she said, rubbing her hand up and down the stubble. "This is not you. It's not you at all."

"There's no meaning," Ruby said, and a small kernel of herself was pleased at last to have found a way to say what was wrong. "This killing. The riots."

"Since when are you such a big civil rights activist?"

"I pay attention to what's happening in the world." Ruby rubbed her forehead. She felt an enormous headache coming on. "At least the marchers, they have a purpose. At least they have something they care passionately about."

"I thought you had dance."

Ruby shook her head, winced with the pain the movement brought on. "It's not dance. Not really. It's prancing. And it's not important. There's nothing of value in it."

"You give people pleasure. You take their minds off of their troubles. You show them beauty."

"It's not enough."

"So, what do you want to do? Protest? Throw rocks through plateglass windows? Set shops on fire? Link arms, carry placards, and have fire hoses trained on you? Tell me. What exactly is it you want? Because the Ruby Wilde I know doesn't sit around feeling sorry for herself. She doesn't drug herself. She deals with things."

"There aren't any black showgirls, have you noticed? None. Why not? Is Vegas only for white people? And as for *Ruby Wilde,*" she said, flinging her hands in the air as if she were tossing confetti, "it's not even my name. C'mon. Really. Have you even noticed?" Ruby looked into her friend's face.

"Nothing in this entire place is real. It's all fake. It's all smoke and mirrors, painted scenery. Silicone tits. Dyed hair. Fake eyelashes. Fake tans. I spent my entire childhood wanting to be anyone but who I was. And, man, I sure found that. I don't wear costumes — I wear *disguises.* I don't even know who I am anymore."

Rose sat listening as Ruby continued at full speed.

"You're the only one honest enough to go by her real name. Not Vivid. Not Dee for Deelicious or Deesire or Deelight — whatever the hell it is. I'm a fake. Faker by the day."

"You're real to me."

"You're the only genuine thing, the only real person in this whole fucking shithole. I mean, what are we doing? The real world is trying to stop a war, to find racial equality. Not us. Not Viva Las Vegas. We're living in la-la land. We're hanging on by our fingernails to the good ol' days. Dean Martin, Sinatra, Rosemary Clooney. Andy Williams!" Seeing Rose's expression, Ruby stopped with the list-making. "They're the *past*! I mean, it's *ridiculous.* Vegas takes the current hits — but only the ones that don't *say* anything. The ones that won't make people stop and think, that just tell them what they want to hear." She began humming Marvin Gaye's "Ain't No Mountain High Enough." "We'll perform those, dance to those. But 'Monterey'? Or 'All Along the Watchtower'? No, those songs might actually say something. Mean something." She took a breath in preparation for yet another verbal sprint.

"C'mon," Rose said, trying to pull Ruby up and out of the chair. "You're gonna go stand under the shower, and then I'm taking you out for a steak. Thick, red, juicy steak."

"Maybe it's just as well," Ruby said, resisting Rose's tug. "They'd take 'Purple Haze' and have us shout 'Kiss the sky!' while wearing headdresses in the shape of giant red lips." Ruby giggled at the image.

"Stand up. You have to eat."

"I can't eat."

"You're going to. So give up now."

Rose led her down the hallway, and then while Ruby watched, Rose lifted the toilet lid, unscrewed the bottle top, and tilted the jar of pills into the toilet bowl.

"I can get more," Ruby said. "Any time. All I want."

"I know that. But it's a start." Rose tossed the empty bottle in the trash and turned on the shower. She tested the water temperature with her hand. "Get those clothes off and get in," she commanded. Much to Ruby's surprise, she did as she was told.

Ruby had forgotten just how good a shower could feel, and she lingered beneath the flow of warm water. She inhaled the rose, sandalwood, and flowery scents of her Yardley Khadine perfumed soap and realized that something was trying to escape. Something that lived deep inside her, that had settled in the marrow of her bones. The speed was beckoning this ancient, lurking thing — this boiling, black anger and shame — to escape. Clearly, Ruby could not afford this. She'd go crazy. Rose was right. She had to quit the speed.

When she climbed out of the shower, Rose handed her a clean towel. "At least your bed was made." Rose smiled.

"I always make my bed." Ruby toweled her hair. "I cannot stand an unmade bed. It feels dirty. As if something's terribly, terribly wrong. In a really perverse way." She looked in the mirror, shouted down the pictures of Uncle Miles that had arisen, unbidden. In her steamy reflection, she could see the curve of each rib, the adamant jut of her hipbones. Rose stood behind her, watching Ruby's expression as she discovered just how wasted she'd become.

"Jesus, kiddo," Rose said. "You don't do a

single, solitary thing by half measure, do you?"

Ruby looked pleadingly toward her friend's reflected face. "I know it's making me crazy, that I'm not thinking right anymore. But I don't know how to stop. I don't know if I can."

"You can. If anyone can, it's you. I already talked to a doctor, and he told me what you can expect." Rose held up fingers, counted off the side effects of amphetamine withdrawal. "Fatigue. You'll probably sleep a whole bunch, then suffer more insomnia. For several days, he said. You'll either be hyper or dragged out, slow on the uptake. You might have nightmares. But," she said, holding up a final finger. "You'll be hungry enough to eat a horse." She grinned.

Ruby touched her hipbone. *A man could slice himself open on this,* she thought, before promising Rose she'd try. She would try.

11

A wash in Rose's kindness and humbled by her friend's love, Ruby got clean. It wasn't easy. As a matter of fact, it was far worse than Rose had predicted. For more nights than seemed possible, Ruby was both exhausted and insomniac. She grew increasingly frantic, watching the hours of two, three, and four A.M. slip past while she remained adamantly awake. In the daylight, her thoughts seemed sluggish, delayed. She would stand in the grocery store, staring into the pyramids of apples and oranges, and she'd wonder what she'd come to buy. She couldn't even manage to choose one variety of apple over another. Intense cravings nearly consumed her willpower, and all the while she could sense Vivid's cache of drugs, so close by.

But Scallywag held on, and once she broke free of the drug, Ruby found it unbelievable that she'd descended as she had. She paged through her frenzied design sketches and saw them for the crazy, drug-fueled failures that they were. She burned them in the apartment complex's barbecue pit, and as the smoke rose, Ruby decided she'd give up cigarettes, too. *My body is my temple,* she told herself, smiling.

"You sound like you've found Jesus or something," Vivid said when she came by with a bottle of wine and Ruby turned that down, too. "Get real," Vivid said. "You can't be a showgirl and refuse to drink. You just can't."

That, Ruby had to agree with, and so she'd drawn the line at banning booze. Still, as the days passed, she felt stronger, more herself than she had in months. She'd successfully mortared-in whatever darkness had tried to overtake her. And, she thought she understood something: Dance was enough when it served as the vehicle of her escape from Kansas, her childhood. But now that she'd left Kansas in the dust, dancing wasn't enough. Reading the newspaper, reading books — that wasn't enough, either. Was it love? Was Rose right — did she need a more permanent, reliable man in her life? Maybe the Aviator was right — she needed to use her brain, not just her body. But how? She told herself she'd find the answer, search for it. For now, she knew only one thing with certainty: It was time to go back to work.

Ruby passed the artist Constance Maxwell at her usual spot in the lobby of the Dunes, where she created pastel portraits of patrons. Finding Bob Christianson's office, Ruby laid on his desktop the hundred-dollar poker chip he'd given her.

"I don't know if you remember me," she began.

"Honey, everyone worth his salt knows who Ruby Wilde is."

"Well, I'd like to work for you. To dance for you, here, in the Casino de Paris show. The Persian Theatre. Wherever you'll have me."

"You want to wear costumes by the god otherwise known as Carlos Garcia Vargas."

"I do."

"You want to pose for photos on the racecourse, at card tournaments, if that's what I ask you to do. Even if the publicity job is set for ten A.M., and you didn't get to bed until three or four."

"I do."

"You remember I'm a straight shooter. I tell it like I see it."

"I do."

"Well then, Ruby Wilde. To dance for me,

you need to put on some weight." He looked straight through her attempt at disguise — a loose-fitting silk tunic top and black palazzo pants. "Men don't fantasize about fucking a coat hanger."

Ruby pressed her lips together. She'd been trying to regain weight; she'd have to try harder.

"Deal?" he asked.

Ruby extended her hand. "Deal."

"Start learning the routines. See Charlotte, backstage. Give her this," he said, writing instructions on the back of his business card, just as he'd done when Ruby first met him. "She'll fix you up."

"Thanks."

"Remember when I told you that you had the perfect showgirl body?"

"I do."

"Then get it back. Once you do that, we'll talk again."

"Okay."

"One more thing," he said, standing and stretching his back. "And this is non-negotiable. Stay off the speed."

She hid her surprise. Apparently, Bob Christianson did see everything. "I will."

Ruby slid her sunglasses back on and left the casino. She felt that if she'd said one more "I do," someone would have had to pronounce them man and wife.

She toed the line at the Dunes. Ruby ate at least six meals a day, gobbled mixing bowls full of pudding. She added avocados to nearly everything. She buttered and ate bread and more bread. Fully loaded baked potatoes. Entire cans of nuts. Slowly, the weight climbed back on, and she started to see soft curves replace forbidding bone.

Celebrating the dawn of 1969 with her friends, Ruby made a silent wish for love and inspiration in the new year. The Aviator sent her a Christmas card, letting her know that he'd been transferred to Kirtland Air Force Base in Albuquerque. He'd be that much closer, and she thought that one day she just might surprise him with a visit. In the meantime, Ruby dutifully replaced her wallet's old emergency notification card with a new one, including the Aviator's updated contact information.

Ruby thought about the passage of time, the changes she'd seen and made since she'd arrived in Vegas coming up on two years ago. Soon she would turn twenty, and the undercurrent of dissatisfaction she'd felt while drugged remained. To tolerate the superficialities she'd begun to refer to as *Vegas plastic,* she came up with a plan for escape. Ruby tallied her savings — which were substantial, given her income of just about sixty thousand dollars a year, including all of the gifts she converted to cash, the chips she'd been given by enamored men. She had nearly eighty thousand dollars in savings. She told herself she would dance for one more year, smile and charm and stomach Vegas life for that single year, and then she'd set herself up as a designer. She was thinking about L.A. And, if only he would mentor her, she was determined to get Carlos Garcia Vargas' help.

He'd been designing at the Dunes since 1963 and was known for his use of rich textiles. Vargas didn't limit himself to silks or satins — he used chinchilla, velvet, and fox. One of the first costumes Ruby wore of his design was made entirely of strings of hot pink beads that were held together by gold-toned cuffs located at strategic points — upper arms, hips, neck. Lacing meant to simulate a Roman soldier's footwear ran from ankle to calf, and Ruby's headdress was a complicated tower of black, knotted material that swiveled marvelously when she moved. There was a diamond-shaped cutout revealing her belly button, and rows of diamond cutouts marched dangerously low across her belly.

Vargas also created costumes with enormous, feathered back pieces that looked like sails and turned the showgirls into stately, bare-breasted birds that floated across the stage. The back pieces were unwieldy, and their size — as much as ten feet wide and eight feet high — made it difficult to maneuver and see the other dancers. Still, once the girls stopped bumping into each other and got the hang of it, the costumes really were impressive, if merely because of their overblown qualities. They were extravagant in Vegas, and that was definitely saying something.

"You can't just show up with some drawings and expect to be hired," Vargas told her. Seated in his studio, he was wearing blue, striped, flared pants with a neon-green silk shirt. A vibrant purple silk handkerchief bloused from the pocket of his navy blue blazer, and his black Italian boots had decorative straps that crisscrossed at the ankle.

He caught Ruby looking at the boots. "They made me think of Michelangelo's bondage slaves." He grinned.

"I don't —" Ruby shook her head.

"He carved the figures emerging from stone, but not fully. They're still largely encased. And they're chained, ropes across chests, tied down. Hint, hint," he said, grinning even more widely.

"Oh."

"That's my point, don't you see?" He crossed his legs, bounced the top leg as if to bring her attention even more fully to the boots. "That's exactly why you need formal training. In design school, you'd have classes in art history. You'd learn what's been done. You'd get context."

"That's necessary?" she asked, forcing herself to look away from his jittery leg. For a moment, she wondered if he was on amphetamines, but then she spotted the coffeemaker parked unobtrusively on his credenza, next to a spider plant that needed water. She felt her own dry mouth, longed for one of the butter rum Life Savers she still used to keep from smoking.

"Your work is okay," he said, using a flat tone to signal his ambivalence. "If you had mountains of talent, you might get away with skipping some kind of coursework. But even then" — he leaned toward her for emphasis — "you need a solid foundation in fabrics, in patternmaking. Draping, drawing — especially from models." He wore his dark, straight hair long, past his chin, and had pronounced, muttonchop sideburns. A mustache floated above his upper lip, and Ruby thought it looked pasted on. Well, why not? Women had their hairpieces, after all.

She looked at the wall behind Vargas, at the drawings he'd mounted there. She couldn't draw nearly as well as that — so cleanly. The sketches were elegant in their austerity. By comparison, her work made her feel like a fourth-grader, drawing Huck Finn standing in a stream so that she wouldn't have to try to get his feet right.

"Look, I'll help you some. Point you in the right direction. I'm willing to do that, when time permits. But, Ruby, girl — you can't just rely on your looks. Which is exactly what you did when you came to Vegas. Am I right?" He picked up a pen she'd thought was a joke — it was fashioned like an antique feather pen, but this pen's feather was a giant ostrich plume dyed banana yellow. Vargas used it to stroke his chin.

Feathers and bondage, Ruby thought. *Wow.*

"I came to dance," she said. "And yes, my looks got me hired."

"But they won't do a thing when it comes to fashion design. Your portfolio will get you hired. And to develop a portfolio, you need the background. Don't skip the necessary steps — you'll just regret it. Even then, what you'll get is an apprenticeship. This profession is far more involved than showing up with a few drawings." He pushed her portfolio across his desk toward her. *"Comprende?"*

Vargas let her have his design drawing for the hot-pink beaded costume, and he even autographed it. She saw that he drew in black ink and used watercolors. She'd been using colored pencils, and she could see how much richer the paint made his work. Even that little thing, she'd done wrong. Maybe he had a point.

Ruby took stock. She thought about the past several months, what she'd been doing with herself, how she could use her leisure time to pursue her dreams. Ruby began to scrutinize Vargas' designs more closely. She tried to discern his inspirations, his historical references. She devoured fashion magazines, tore pages out of *Vogue* and put them into a notebook. She dissected trends. Jane Fonda's *Barbarella* had latched on to the space craze and took everyone by storm — her tousled, just-got-out-of-bed curls, the boots that came up to her thighs, her cleavage. Fonda's rampant sexuality, her ability to project both vulnerability and availability, put Ruby's own efforts to shame. Ruby added Fonda to her notebook. She became a sponge, soaking up everything, from everywhere. Observing, learning, assimilating, and practicing. She was thinking about design schools, where she'd go, when she'd start applying.

She also made an even more committed effort to stay tuned in to the real world. So many changes, such upheaval had characterized the past year. Nina Simone was singing the desperation of the times, in response to King's assassination, asking "What's going to happen now that the King of Love is dead?" Sirhan Sirhan had gunned down Bobby Kennedy just two months after the King assassination, and Ruby remembered how overwrought she'd been when King was killed, how out of control. She felt such sadness over the hope that had been Kennedy, but at least when that killing happened she hadn't found herself driving around Vegas in a drug-induced state of hysterical mania.

Still, it was incomprehensible — the country's growing propensity for endless bloodletting, the winnowing of leaders with vision and optimism. Buddhist monks set themselves on fire in Vietnam. And in the August heat, the Democratic National Convention had erupted into unfathomable violence. Ruby had watched the footage of Chicago cops with clubs, beating antiwar protesters until they bled. Those kids were her age. They were out there, doing something. While she did nothing.

For the first time, she realized that Vietnam cast no shadows beneath the lights of Vegas; there were no flag-shrouded caskets, no hollowed, haunted eyes of returning soldiers anywhere near the casinos. How efficiently Las Vegas seemed to be able to keep hippies away from the Strip, where they might hurt business. The rest of the city was normal — trailer parks, grocery stores, shoe stores, schools, doctors' offices, and churches — but tourists didn't see those neighborhoods, and certainly Ruby had never been invited into any of those suburban living rooms. She'd been living in la-la land for far too long.

"Slut! Bitch!"

Up to that point, it had been a good evening. Ruby and Chicago Johnny were leaving Circus Maximus at Caesars, where they'd sampled Chef Laszlo Dorogi's famous sugar sculptures and sat back while Eartha Kitt purred her way through a performance. In one number, Kitt had worn a tight silver swirl of a cocktail dress, cut low, virtually strapless, and at last Ruby understood what Vargas meant about learning to drape — the dress had such superb folds; they followed the curves of Kitt's body as she sang "C'est si bon."

"Cunt!"

This time, the woman's shriek caught Ruby's attention.

"Yeah, you, bitch!"

Before Ruby could put up a defensive hand, the woman swung her purse at Ruby's face and struck her across her nose and left eye. There was an audible crunch, and then the woman hit Ruby again, this time harder, before Johnny managed to grab ahold of the purse. The woman didn't let go of the strap, and Johnny held on, too.

Ruby put a hand to her face, saw blood, and felt her eyes watering. Her nasal passages stung sharply, and it felt as if her nose had been shoved a good two inches into her skull. Still holding the crazed woman's arm, Johnny passed Ruby his handkerchief. She pressed as hard as the pain would permit and tried to stop the bleeding.

"She fucks other women's husbands!" the woman yelled, still in full battle mode. "Everyone! Everyone! Right here!" she yelled and pointed with her free hand. "This cunt here! Won't cost you much, but you'll have to get in line!"

Ruby overheard a man on the sidewalk say, "Who wouldn't want to sink his torpedo in that redhead?"

"Ma'am," Johnny said, using a calm tone to try to control the woman. "Please."

"Who're you? The whore's daddy? Maybe you're her pimp!" the woman sneered. "Give me back my purse. Thief! Thief!"

Ruby's vision had cleared some, but the woman — a middle-aged blonde with dark roots, a thick waist of undulating hills, and red lipstick run amok — wasn't the least bit familiar. God knows who her husband was, or if the woman even had the right show-girl.

Johnny twisted the strap on the woman's handbag until it dug into her forearm.

"Ow!" she yelled. "Quit it!"

"Cease and desist," he said, making Ruby want to laugh. Johnny sounded as if he'd been watching reruns of *Dragnet.*

"Let go of me!"

"I'll let go when you simmer down." He kept the purse strap twisted so tightly that Ruby could see the woman's skin folding. She couldn't help but think that it was yet another example of Vargas' draping lecture. And that's when Ruby started giggling. This whole night — what a night! Soon enough, she was laughing so hard that it was difficult to catch her breath. She was standing there, in the parking lot in front of Caesars, a bloody handkerchief held to her nose, blood no doubt sprayed across the front of her strapless white beaded gown. Some loony woman was accusing her of taking her husband, and an aging mobster was holding the woman hostage via her purse strap. Jesus!

"You think this is funny?" the woman spat at Ruby. "You think husband-stealing is a laughing matter?"

"I don't want your husband, whoever he is," Ruby said. Her voice sounded stuffy, her nasal passages were full of blood, and she felt more blood sliding down the back of her throat. She also had a massive headache. "Let her go, Johnny." Ruby sighed. "Let's just get out of here."

He gave the purse one last tug as if to make his point, and then he let the woman go. "I think you broke her nose," he told the woman.

"Serves her right. That whore broke my heart," the woman said, beginning to weep. "Took my Harry," she sobbed.

Harry, Ruby wondered. She didn't remember any Harry.

"Go home now," Johnny said, using a firm tone.

"What's left of it after that hussy home-wrecker," the woman said, turning her back to them. She was wearing a dress made of some sort of sparkly polyester, and there was a huge run up the back of one leg of her pantyhose.

The crowd began to disperse. Several of the women looked back at Ruby with disgust.

"So much for innocent until proven guilty," Ruby said, taking Johnny's arm.

"I'll get you to the doctor," he said, looking worriedly into her face. They stopped by a fountain, and he used the multicolored lights to inspect her injuries. "You're going to have a pair of black eyes. And" — he gingerly touched the bridge of her nose, which crackled — "a broken nose."

"Lord," Ruby said, and then she started laughing again.

"You're in shock," Johnny said, using his most paternal voice.

"No," Ruby said, trying to catch her breath. The bleeding had yet to stop, and she refolded the handkerchief and pressed it back in place. "This is all just so unreal!"

"Ruby!" It was Rose, jogging out the front doors of Caesars carrying a towel filled with ice. "Here," she said, catching up to the two of them, taking the soiled handkerchief from Ruby and gently putting the ice in place. "Hold it like that," she said, looking at Johnny as if he were the culprit.

"Rose, Johnny. Johnny, Rose," Ruby said from behind the towel. "How did you know?" she asked.

"One of the bellboys told me. Jesus, Ruby."

"I'm taking her to the hospital," Johnny said, sounding as if he were afraid Rose would steal Ruby and deprive him of his hard-won Sir Galahad role.

"There's a doctor inside she can see," Rose told him. "There's no need to drive her all over town."

"Now, you two. Don't fight over little ol' me," Ruby said, watching the two of them face off — Rose in her tiny Caesars toga, Johnny in his fifties mobster get-up.

They got on either side of Ruby and marched her back into Caesars, past the half-dozen people who were still milling about, watching the drama peter out. Johnny, ever the courtly gentleman, held the door for the two women, and Ruby lifted the ice from her face long enough to turn to Rose and say, "I think she had a lead brick in that purse. Or" — she paused, grinning — "maybe she managed to swipe a roulette wheel."

Ruby's face was in the final stages of healing when she met Tom Jones at a party in the Flamingo, where he was performing and getting ready to record his album *Live in Las Vegas.* He was still wearing one of his stage outfits — a white shirt cut nearly to his belly button to reveal a giant gold cross nestled in a frenzy of black chest hair. His shirt had French cuffs with jet black cuff links and was topped with a black sequined jacket. On his fingers, he wore large shouts of gold jewelry — a pinky ring on one hand, and on the middle finger of his other hand, a ring that looked as though it could knock out Muhammad Ali. Jones had clearly spent a good deal of time in a tanning bed, and Ruby couldn't help but wonder if he had done so in the nude. It was no act — the man exuded raw, animal sex. She could feel his energy from across the room, and as she watched him she smiled and imagined gliding over to ask *What's new, pussycat?*

Vivid introduced them, and Ruby found her eyes straying down to Jones' large silver-and-gold oval of a belt buckle, his narrow hips.

"Earth to Ruby," Vivid said, teasing.

"Hello, sweetheart," Jones said, wrapping Ruby in his arms.

He was damp with sweat from his performance, but it didn't bother her. It was the first time in a long while that Ruby had been starstruck.

"Show her," Vivid commanded, smiling slyly.

Slowly, as if performing a salacious magic trick, Jones reached into his pocket and pulled out a pair of pale yellow panties.

"I've heard," Ruby said. "I gather that at times you're literally pelted with panties."

"Yeah, but look closely," Vivid said, taking the panties from Jones and stretching them wide in front of Ruby's face. In black marker, a woman had written her phone number. "And they throw him their hotel room keys, too!"

"Ha!" Ruby laughed. She looked at Vivid. "How come that never happens to us?"

"Boxers or briefs!" Vivid grinned. The image of white jockey shorts with illegible scrawls of men's phone numbers was truly funny.

"I'd write my number out for you, honey," Jones said, looking intently at Ruby. They were just about the same height, and although he wore stacked heels, Ruby's heels were taller — so he looked up slightly to meet her eyes.

"Tom Jones, you are an incorrigible flirt," Ruby responded. "I know you're married."

"The whole world knows he's married," Vivid said.

"Come perform with me," Jones said to Ruby. "Even once. Just be on the stage with me."

"Singing?"

"The others will cover for you. Just mouth it."

"An ornamental performance?"

"Why not?"

Ruby looked toward Vivid. This must have been why she'd brought her here tonight.

"True confession," Jones said. "I saw you onstage, and Vivid and I are old friends." He put an arm around Vivid, pulled her close and winked. *Duh,* Ruby thought, realizing they must have slept together. "I asked Viv to introduce us. For purely professional reasons," he added.

"It'd have to be on one of my nights off. Is that worth it to you? To have costumes fitted for me for just a performance or two?"

"He writes his own ticket," Vivid assured Ruby. "He can do what he wants."

"All right then." Ruby grinned. "It sounds like a kick in the ass."

And it *was* a kick in the ass, just the kind

of jolt she needed. Ruby loved being onstage with Jones, the four backup singers lined up alongside her, and the enormous lit *TJ* hovering above them all like a constellation. The singers were surprisingly gracious, given Ruby's relative lack of vocal talent. She guessed their loyalty to Jones reigned supreme, and she was right — he was known to be a decent, thoughtful employer, someone who understood what it was to come up from nothing by dint of hard, concentrated work.

The women were eager to learn a few dance steps from Ruby, and together they concocted some minimal dance routines to add to the show. Jones was a tremendous performer — he genuinely enjoyed what he was doing, and in turn the audience responded enthusiastically. Sometimes he'd pull Ruby out front with him and force the band to ad lib while they danced together. Every pelvic thrust, every "Unh!" he uttered made Ruby grin. She was having fun again, and it was marvelous.

Things snowballed from there. Through Jones, she met Charo, who was starring with Xavier Cugat in Nero's Nook in Caesars. She met Mama Cass and Flip Wilson. Best of all, she met Sammy Davis, Jr., who told her he was planning a trip to entertain the troops in Vietnam. He asked if she'd join him, assuming he could pull it all together. Ruby screamed "YES!" and in her enthusiasm almost tried to lift the elfin man off of the stage. "Cool, man," was all he said. "I'll be in touch." His proposal was perfection — at long last, she'd be able to do something in the real world.

Ruby was well aware of the fact that no one wanted her for who she was, for what she read or thought. Other than the Aviator, they didn't care about her opinions or hopes and aspirations. They didn't care if she dreamed of becoming a fashion designer, or if — like Vivid — she dreamed of living in a glass-walled house looking down on the beach at Malibu. Not Tom Jones. Not Sammy Davis. Not Bob Christianson or even Daddy Evan Brashear, who asked her to think about returning to the Stardust. They wanted her looks, and to a lesser extent her talent as a dancer. To them, she was just like Vegas — all glitz and glamour. An anonymous blur, like a passing freight train.

"You're on fire!" Rose said. "Really, kiddo — you're lit again. It's the best thing I've seen in ages."

"Except that," Ruby said, pointing to

Rose's fourth finger. Rose and Matt, the card dealer, were engaged, with no firm date yet set. Ruby refused to think about it — what it would mean if she lost Rose in her life, if the couple moved elsewhere, which was a distinct possibility.

"Yeah, well," Rose said, blushing.

"But as for me, I'll never fall in love again," Ruby sang, à la Mr. Jones.

"I double-dog dare you," Rose said and punched Ruby lightly in the upper arm. "As a matter of fact, I triple-dog dare you!"

Ruby didn't foreclose the possibility of love. She'd never admit it, even to Rose or Vivid, but she fostered a secret, quiet hope that she might find someone. Or that someone might find her.

12

They landed on the moon, and the world stopped to watch — even Vegas. Ruby pictured Kyle at home with his family, viewing the same live television coverage. Was he envious? Was he glad for his friends? Was he still writing his stories? She sent him her fondness and hoped that — somehow — he sensed her.

In September of 1969, torrential rains pounded Las Vegas, and the weak desert sand could not hold the sudden abundance. Caesars flooded, leaving miles of saturated carpet a ready and willing breeding ground for mold. What had been carefully controlled landscaping flowed down the street in putrid gray gobs of dead and dying vegetation. Everyone made the easy connection to Noah, to God's need to wash the world clean. Next, maybe frogs would fall from the sky or clouds of locusts would scream overhead. After a few days the floodwaters dried up, and all that was left was the lingering sensation of a wrathful but incomplete apocalypse.

The year ended with arrests in the Manson murder spree, fatal stabbings at the Rolling Stones' concert at Altamont, underground nuclear detonations at the Nevada Test Site just sixty-some miles from Vegas, and John and Yoko sponsoring huge billboards that told the world *War is over! If you want it.* In November of what was Nixon's first year in office, 700,000 antiwar demonstrators took over the nation's capital.

Nearly oblivious, Vegas played on. Dean Martin's opening night at the Sands' Copa Room was a mob scene. At the new International Hotel, Elvis performed to sold-out audiences for $125,000 a week while in Mississippi, the median household income was just over $5,000 a year.

Ruby thought the center could not hold. How could it? After less than three years in Vegas, she was herself earning far beyond anything Uncle Miles ever could have dreamed of depositing in his Salina bank account. Still not knowing what else she could do and admittedly not giving the issue any genuinely concerted effort other than a wistful New Year's wish for 1970, she kept her head down, worked, and waited for the Fates or Sammy Davis to let her know when her life would hold some wider, less self-serving meaning.

Maybe Ruby was primed for love when she spotted the Spanish photographer standing at the foot of the stage apron that January night, when he refused to release her from his gaze. Perhaps Javier Borrero had been foretold all along, in the fine lines of her palm.

He didn't stare at Ruby in the lurid, covetous way of most men. He was immediately, obviously different. As she danced in the thrall of his powerful gaze, Ruby was flustered, had to watch her step and be conscious of her balance. She felt her headdress shift when she turned, and she had to resist the temptation to reach up and touch the sequined cap to be sure it stayed on her head. Each time she pivoted toward the audience, she saw him still transfixed by her, and only her.

A light meter was looped around his neck, but he held his camera forgotten at his side. Ruby had heard that the watchful Spaniard was the Dunes' new professional photographer, yet Javier Borrero hadn't once raised the viewfinder to his eye or clicked the shutter. Instead, he seemed mesmerized by the lengths of pearls softly lapping at her thighs.

A tendril of pink ostrich feather tickled Ruby's lower lip and then drifted to the corner of her eye. She swallowed a reflexive sneeze. The feather caught in her false eyelashes, and she blinked rapidly to try to free them.

With elegant precision, Ruby descended the calf-killing stage stairs, the other showgirls trailing in her wake like geese in flight. She turned in time with the music, revealed her G-string-clad ass to the man. She faced him again, performed several high kicks, her bare breasts bouncing. *Now,* she thought, *now is when a pastie will pop off, and his only reaction will be to stare impassively.*

The rhinestones of the showgirls' costumes pulsed beneath rainbow-colored stage lights, there was a crash of cymbals, and the dancers joined to form the pony line, beginning the grand finale of synchronized cancan kicks. The audience broke into enthusiastic applause, but still the photographer remained inert. At last, standing breathless with the other girls and taking a bow, Ruby stole a look at him and felt a trickle of nervous sweat meander down her back.

Ruby exited the stage and made her way to her dressing room, knowing that the insistent pull she felt for the Spaniard was chemical, uncontrollable. But it was more than lust. She was connected to this man — maybe from some distant, past life or maybe because they were one and the same. Who knew? And did it matter? She'd seen dozens of gorgeous men trail in and out of the casinos: Elvis, Warren Beatty, Harry Belafonte, even Richard Burton — a man made exponentially more compelling because Elizabeth Taylor walked on his arm. But Javier was the most beautiful man she'd ever seen.

He had thick, dark brown hair that fell in waves until its curly tips brushed the collar of his white Nehru jacket. His eyes were chestnut brown beneath heavy, dark brows, and his lips were generous, the dip in his upper lip pronounced. He had a substantial, dignified nose, skin the color of coffee generously dosed with cream, and the only movement he showed was to purse his lips and knit his brows, as if in thought, each time he took a pull from his cigarette and exhaled a stream of smoke toward the ceiling. Not one ounce of Javier Borrero pleaded for Ruby's attention, and she adored that. As she sat before her vanity mirror and her dresser carefully lifted off the heavy headdress, Ruby felt truly exposed, exquisitely vulnerable.

The rule was that whenever a showgirl loused up a number, the whole pony line had to show up the next morning at the ungodly hour of eleven A.M. to rehearse. It was like elementary school — one student screws up, and the entire class has to stay after school. No one was happy about it, but they all knew better than to punish the girl who'd flubbed her steps. Eventually, it happened to all of them.

Javier Borrero was there at the rehearsal the next morning, this time actually using his camera. The girls were in full costume, and it was a good opportunity for him to get action publicity shots without distracting an audience. Today, he wore casual clothes — bell-bottom jeans, a white poet's shirt, and a wide, brown leather belt cinched with a brass belt buckle that had a Renaissance flourish. His brown-skinned feet were clad in worn leather sandals, his hair was just the right amount of unkempt, and he wore a black scarf tied loosely about his neck.

The dance routine was punishing not for the steps, but for the props. The curtains opened to the girls hanging from the ceiling, each in her own see-through Lucite bathtub filled with clear plastic Ping-Pong balls meant to simulate a bubble bath. The number was set to a jazzed-up version of Bobby Darin's "Splish Splash." The costumes — tight, aqua-toned split skirts and armbands with fish fins made of ribbed gold, blue, and green satins — were great in theory. The problem came when the girls were to climb from the bathtubs out onto tiny individual platforms that hovered a good five to seven feet above the stage floor. The mermaid-tail skirts limited movement, and, inevitably, several of the Ping-Pong balls would escape the sides of the tubs as the dancers maneuvered onto the platforms.

High heels and small balls flying like erratic popcorn — it was a decidedly bad combination, and nearly all of the girls had fallen at some point. Despite all of this, the choreographer was unwilling to reconsider the number, and there was halfhearted talk amongst the showgirls that the insurance company should be notified. The danger was apparent, and it seemed inevitable that someone was going to get hurt.

The Spaniard moved below them, shooting upward. Ruby watched him move in closer until she could see the top of his head, his hands holding his camera as if it were holy, an offering bowl held before an altar.

Ruby noticed that there was something off about his right foot. Where toes should have extended from his sandal, there was only a single big toe. It couldn't be that they were folded under. *No,* Ruby thought, *they're gone.* His limp was barely discernible. She was both curious as to what might have happened to him and surprised that he wore sandals, that he made no effort to disguise his disfigurement.

She felt a sense of instant kinship with this Spaniard. The unshakable certainty that their flaws sang in harmony. Ruby longed to examine the details of his palms. She wanted to measure his life line, discover his childhood. She wanted to count his lovers, the horizontal lines secreted on the side of his hand beneath his pinky finger — and to see if, maybe, she could find herself there.

That was when Ruby slipped. The toe of her shoe slid over the edge of her tiny platform, and her ankle fought futilely for balance on the half-inch surface of her stiletto heel. Ruby fell six feet — directly into the arms of Javier Borrero. There was a shriek of pain in her ankle, a chaos of Ping-Pong balls in her peripheral vision, but all she knew was the musk of him — the deep woods scent, as if he'd been sleeping in a soft, yielding bed of decaying oak leaves.

Together, they tumbled to the ground. Javier's body cushioned her fall, and she immediately worried that she'd crushed his camera. He was splayed out on the stage beneath her, and she was struggling to right herself, to keep her heels from gouging him. Finally, the band stopped, and a couple of dancers rushed to help her. Each grabbed an arm, and when Ruby stood, she felt her ankle's unwillingness to hold her. The girls half dragged her to the lowest stage step, and Ruby unbuckled her shoe and gingerly began rubbing her ankle — all the while watching the Spaniard as he slowly gathered his wits and stood.

"Your camera!" she said when he looked her direction.

"Is all right," he said, neither smiling nor frowning. "I cover it with my hands, like dis." He demonstrated, clutching the camera to his abdomen, a running back tucking the football into his gut.

Ruby couldn't read him, couldn't tell if he was angry.

"We told you this would happen!" one of the girls yelled at the choreographer, who'd at last deigned to approach and check on Ruby.

"No more!" another girl said. "We won't do this number. Are you waiting for someone to break her neck?"

The others were nodding in agreement. They stepped down from their various perches and gathered about Ruby on the stairway, an impromptu sit-in.

"But your contracts require —" the choreographer said rather feebly.

Borrero knelt and gently took Ruby's foot into his hands. "Relax your foot. Your ankle," he instructed and then waited until she complied. He compressed her foot at the base of her toes with one hand while cupping her heel in the other. "Is painful?" She shook her head. He moved his hand up toward her ankle, increasing the pressure only as her facial expression permitted. He circled her ankle with his thumb.

"That's sore," she said, thinking the injury was well worth it, just to have his warm hands caressing her foot.

"*Flexiona* — uh, you must flex de foot."

She felt the muscles of her arch, tight and sharp, and she flinched. "I think I pulled the muscles, mostly," she said. "They're tender."

At her use of *tender* he took his eyes completely away from her foot, instead looked into her face. And he smiled — his first smile, the first emotion she'd seen cross his face. Carefully, he set down her foot and picked up her discarded shoe, holding it as if it were some rare captive bird.

"*Los zapatos de tacón.* Of course you have hurted your arch," he said, and in his accent she thought she could feel the noon heat in Barcelona, that she could smell oranges ripening in a silver, sun-struck bowl.

This close to him, with all the others disappearing like inconsequential dandelion fluff, she could see two tiny moles punctuating the outer corner of his left eye. A third strayed onto his cheekbone and rested there, a challenge.

13

Ruby was spending a quiet night at home nursing her wounds and reading a paperback when the doorbell rang. Javier Borrero stood in the glow of her porch light, a bouquet of pink roses in one hand, a can of Campbell's chicken noodle soup in the other.

"I skinned my butt." Ruby laughed. "Isn't chicken soup for a sore throat?"

"If you letted me in, I explain." He smiled.

"All right." She combed her hair with her fingers and thought maybe she should change out of her short black silk robe. Javier eyed her legs as he set the flowers and soup on the kitchen bar. "There's a vase in the cabinet beneath the sink," Ruby said, opting to pull on a denim miniskirt and T-shirt. "I'll be right back. Oh, and there's beer in the refrigerator."

Once dressed, she took an extra few seconds to look at herself in the bathroom mirror. She was makeup free, but ah, well. He'd come unannounced — surely he couldn't expect her to look her best.

"Thank you," she said, returning to the living room and accepting a bottle of beer. "For the flowers, too." He'd set them on the side table between her wingback chairs. "They're lovely."

Javier tapped the neck of his bottle against hers. "I am hoping for you to get bedder soon."

Limping slightly, an ACE bandage wrapped around her ankle, she led him to the couch. "So," she said. "The soup." She knew he watched her throat move as she closed her eyes, tilted her head back, and took a sip of beer.

"The word in Spanish for throat" — he moved his hand along his own throat — "is *cuello.* I had this American friend. Learning Spanish. He told me he was not dere for rugby practice the day before because he had an infection in his *culo.*" Javier began to laugh. "You see? Is very close, but is wrong. He wanted tell me he had an infection in his *cuello* — his throat. But he said *culo* — and dad means he had an infection in his asshole. I said to him that he should no be telling me all this. It was yust too intimate." He winked at her.

"Okay, that's funny!" Ruby grinned.

"I was only glad dad he said dad to me. Not to someone impoordant." Javier ran his palm up and down his thigh as if he were wiping his palm clean.

"So the chicken soup is for my sore *culo*?" Ruby asked, smiling.

"Yes. Dad was my joke."

"Very good," she said, again touching the neck of her bottle to his. "I like a man with a sense of humor."

"I like you," he said. "And I have come here tonight because I don't play de mouse and cat game." He shrugged his shoulders, looked down, and smiled shyly.

"I'm glad you're here," she said. He was wearing a white cotton shirt with the sleeves rolled up to his elbows — a look that on him was elegant. "I just wish I looked better."

He looked up, genuinely surprised by what she'd said. "Oh no." He shook his head. "You are so much more beauteeful without dad . . . *Cómo se dice*?" He rubbed his forehead. *"Maquillaje."*

"Makeup?"

"Yes, dad's it. For the stage is one thing. For the rest of your life, I say no. I say you must be your real self. Your true self."

He had a muscular neck and heavily

muscled shoulders — maybe from the rugby he'd mentioned. And, already, he'd zeroed in on what she'd been thinking about forever: What was real, what wasn't. Plastic, manufactured fantasy versus genuineness, truthfulness. He didn't want to play any "mouse and cat game"; he wasn't some slick gambler feeding her a line. He was a man struggling in a second language to tell her what he honestly thought and felt.

"Javier," she said, setting her beer bottle on a coaster. "Will you take me out on a date?"

"I had dad planned." He smiled widely, his eyes gold in the light of her table lamp. "Do you know Dinah Shore? She is at the Sands in the Celebrity Theatre, is called."

Dinah Shore! Who was this man? How did he know the child she'd been? *Lily,* planted in front of Aunt Tate's television set, fixated by Dinah Shore's even, white smile, and her exquisite costumes. This man sensed her genesis. Javier Borrero instinctually knew which pulse points to touch, where Ruby's heart beat loudest, cleanest.

It was a cliché, Ruby knew, but Javier truly was a breath of fresh air. He had limited funds, and so they didn't go out dressed to be seen, in excess finery. The Dinah Shore show was a stretch for him financially — this Ruby knew — and so she made it a point to tell him afterwards that she wanted to go to a diner for a hamburger and fries, not some expensive restaurant.

For their second date, they went to see Hitchcock's *Topaz* at the Las Vegas Cinerama, and in the dark Javier held her hand, almost innocently moving closer so that he could put his arm about her shoulders and let her rest her head against him.

They traded their histories like coinage. He was twenty-five "years-old," he said, running the words together. He'd grown up in Toledo, south of Madrid, the son of a man who still made swords and knives for a living. It was a medieval city, he said, one that had inspired some of El Greco's landscape paintings.

"Is not like this place. Is on a mountaintop. You can see the sky, the river below. The curve of de world. It has history," he said. "Not like this place dad was built yust yesterday."

She loved his accent. It forced her to listen carefully, and the degree of focus his words required made everything he said seem important, as if his sentences were dipped in gold.

"You want to know about this," he said as

they sat on the stone border of a flower bed outside the movie theater. He extended his knee and together they stared at his deformity. She hadn't asked about his wounded foot, thinking that her curiosity was, as yet, an unsolicited intimacy.

"Only if you want to tell me," she said.

"Of course you are curious. You should not pretend that you are not." He set his foot back down as if anchoring himself.

Ruby sipped her soda and waited. The ice had melted, and her Coke was weak, growing flat.

"You know about my country, about the ruler of Spain, yes?"

God, but her knowledge of world history was paltry. "Sorry," she said, removing her sunglasses so that he could see her sincerity. "I don't."

"Generalissimo Franco. El Caudillo — he rules my country. He is dictator."

"Oh." What Ruby knew of dictators was Hitler, and surely there could be no worse fate for a people.

"My uncle — my father's *hermano* — he died during El Caudillo's White Terror, before I was born. Franco had declared my uncle and others like him — the atheists, the leftists, and all of the intelligentsia of the country — he declared them enemies.

My uncle starved to death in prison."

Although the events Javier described didn't yet explain his misshapen foot, she immediately saw that the story was hers: It was a tale of early, cataclysmic death, a death close to home, reality too soon imposed upon a child. The unmitigated injustice of death and loss. Sitting next to him, feeling the heat of the immutable stone beneath her, she sensed the threads between them multiply and strengthen, as if a rope of immense tensile strength were being woven that would bind them fast, one to the other.

"I was studying art at the Universidad of Madrid. The students — like the students here in your country — we protest. *La revolución! Sí?*"

"But what were you protesting?" Spain had no Vietnam, and, as far as she knew, no civil rights movement.

"Many things. The *Policía Armada.* They have forced on the people the rule of the Catholic Church, all of those social rules. We were betrayed by these *grises* we call them, these police in gray uniforms. They spied on us. They knew our plans."

Here it was again, like a huge mirror held before her, one she couldn't ignore. He'd done what she'd only thought of doing:

He'd bravely fought against injustice. This foreigner had passion and meaning in his life, the courage of his convictions, while she merely danced on stages or made faint attempts at fashion design. She was decorative.

"And these *grises* police — they're responsible for your foot?" she asked.

"It is so much worse than what you see on your television. They have clubs, yes — but they also have guns and horses that trampled the people on the ground. They rode over us. The police, he look down at me. He smile, and he put his horse forward so that its hoof crush my foot. In the hospital, they cut them off," he said, now removing his sandal.

"I'm so sorry," Ruby breathed, feeling the inadequacy of her words. She took his foot in her lap, made herself look at the seam of flesh where his toes had been, a raised, uneven white line across beautiful, brown skin.

"This is why my father sent me here, to your country," Javier said, reaching to take hold of her fingers and squeezing. "So I would be safe. So I could know you."

Javier said he'd first gone to New York, but then he'd quickly grown tired of winter. He'd arrived in Vegas purely by chance, had actually been headed to L.A. to find work in the film industry, but his VW bus broke down thirty miles east of Vegas. Initially, he merely intended to earn enough to pay the mechanic for a new engine, but instead he'd stayed on, telling himself he'd continue on to L.A. in six months. He was five months into that plan when he saw Ruby on stage and decided six could easily become twelve.

She told him about Kansas, about her dream to escape banality and leap onto a stage. It seemed that they were both haphazard Vegas transplants — although maybe anyone and everyone who lived in the city was there only by chance. After all, Vegas was chance made tangible. She didn't tell him her real name or reveal anything more than superficial details of her childhood, like taking refuge in the public library or pushing tacks into the bottoms of her shoes when she mimicked tap dancers. She left out the Aviator. She failed to mention her parents and sister Dawn. She merely said she'd been raised by relatives, and she thought he could tell by her tone that it was as good as being raised by wolves.

It wasn't that she didn't trust Javier; she did — implicitly, instantly. He was so utterly, oddly *familiar.* Rather, it was that she didn't want for him to know the extent of her damage, just how faulty the product known as Ruby Wilde really was.

For their third date, she drove him out into the desert to watch the sunrise, drink coffee from a thermos, and eat flaky, marzipan-filled pastries from Freed's Bakery. That morning, it was just below 40 degrees. Somewhat embarrassed by her relative wealth, Ruby skipped her fur coat and instead wore a thick turtleneck sweater over bell-bottom jeans and old, scuffed boots. In the nebulous gray dawn, they sat on the back end of her Karmann Ghia, looking eastward.

"The sky looks wounded," she said. A thick band of deep lavender cloud sat like a heavy bruise on a meager sliver of red sky.

"Is like your painter Rothko. Those lines, those soft bands of color, how they blend into each other." He pointed.

"Will you teach me?"

"What?"

"About art. I don't know enough. I need to know, for design school, and I don't know anything."

"I can teach you dad. And other things, too."

He touched the angle of her jaw with his dawn-cool fingertips, turned her face toward his and kissed her deeply. His mouth tasted of coffee and cigarettes; she felt his bitterness on her tongue. Ruby slipped her own cold fingers beneath his hair, felt the heat at the back of his neck, and pulled him closer.

"I think maybe," he said then paused. "Maybe today is our day."

He was nearly featureless in the dim light, the sunrise still held at bay by the onerous bank of clouds.

"Yes," Ruby agreed. "Our day."

"We will have a lacy day," he said, and she realized he meant *lazy,* easy.

She didn't yet know where he lived, but she guessed that he must be ashamed of his circumstances, and so they went to her apartment.

His nipples were a dark maroon, and his uncircumcised penis had a slight purple tint to it — a decided contrast to the variety of pink penises Ruby had known. She imagined him striding across a savanna, all sinew and barely restrained power. As she stroked his body, she knew that he was capable of running at great speed, of sinking claws into the shoulders of his prey and bringing it down. Ruby was eager to be devoured, eager to succumb. And so, she did.

She lay wholly, completely naked beneath his gaze. Determinedly, she let go all artifice, all pretense of self-assurance. She'd touched his scarred foot, and so she let him see her scars without once attempting to hide them or distract him from them. She let his fingers caress their contours, let his tongue linger over their pearl borders. She let him see her face when he looked up from her body, when he tried to see behind her eyes, to learn the secret birthplaces of her wounds.

He waited until afterwards, when he lay on his back, staring at her ceiling and holding a cigarette between his thumb and index finger. Ruby was lying on her side, watching him, thinking she'd never before in her life been so relaxed, so "lacy."

"Why you hurt yourself?" he asked, crushing his cigarette and turning on his side to look at her. When he touched her face, she smelled the tobacco on his fingertips. "Such a beautiful wooman, and she makes those scars on her body."

Ruby took a deep breath that became a sigh. "I don't know."

"No," he said, shaking his head, still stroking her face. "Dads no true. We have promised each other to be honest and true."

She owed it to him to live up to their promise, as brief-lived as it might be. Ruby rolled onto her back so that she wouldn't see his face. She specifically did not want to know what emotions might cross his countenance — disgust, incomprehension, pity, fear. His wound was valiant; hers was shame incarnate.

"It builds," she began at last. "Something inside of me builds — a pressure, like floodwaters behind a dam. The pressure grows until I can't stand it anymore. I try to resist, I really do, but I can't. And so then I cut. Most of the time, I can barely feel it at first. It's the blood, primarily, that helps. When I do it, I let a little of the water out from behind the dam, and then the pressure subsides. The waters recede." A part of her thought about her vocabulary, wondered if she should choose different words, speak more slowly. But he kept up with her.

"Is pain, *sí*? You are talking about pain. Your words are all about pain."

Ruby nodded, keeping her eyes focused on the ceiling.

"There must be another way. A better way for you to let this pain fly out of you." He leaned up on an elbow so that he could see into her face. "You have had no one you can give dis pain to? To unburden your heart?" He pressed a hot palm over her breastbone. "Ruby?"

She shook her head no. "I haven't," she

said, simply, clearly. "Never."

"Then I am the one," he said. "I am the one you will give this pain to."

She reached and touched his face, let her thumb drift softly across his lips. She closed her eyes, and in that self-imposed darkness she felt the shift of tectonic plates, the collision of landmasses. She opened her eyes, and he was there, still. He was looking at her, and it was not with pity or even compassion. He looked at her straightforwardly, and she thought, *Yes, this man can handle my pain, my past.*

"I think —" she began. She closed her eyes, gathered her courage, and reopened them. "I think maybe you are the one."

14

They went to the library together — a place she'd not often gone since moving to Las Vegas. The moment they walked through the entrance, she realized how much she'd missed the sanctuary of libraries. They calmed her, and she remembered how thrilling it was to scan banks of shelves, to think about all the wonderful words there were to read, all the things there were to learn. She had to get back to that — and here was Javier, apparently heaven-sent, to inspire her.

They sat together at a broad, empty wooden table, and Javier opened large-format books with plates of collections from the Louvre, the Hermitage, the National Gallery in London, the Met, and more. He taught her about the span of Michelangelo's color palette, the sculptural quality of his paintings; he discussed the progression from Giotto's flatter works toward Mantegna, and the achievement of dimension in drawing and painting. Javier helped her to see more than she would have seen gazing at the reproductions on her own.

"Is fantastic, this painting. You see?" he whispered, presenting her with Mantegna's *The Lamentation over the Dead Christ.* "You see the perspective even in the wounds, yes? They have depth. And look at the shadows in these toes!" he nearly shouted.

She saw the animation in his face and wondered if he'd heard his own words, if he felt his war wounds. She felt her own omnipresent wounds like a steady, beating pulse. Did he not feel anger or some pang of absence when he gazed at Christ's well-rendered toes? Had he learned to live with the loss? Maybe Javier could help her reach that place in her own life, help her find a sweet, flat meadow of quietude about her past.

"You must see them one day," he said, and Ruby adored the wistful longing in his voice, the clear love of beauty that possessed him. "When you see the paintings, when you stand in front of them, you see the size." He demonstrated with his hands. "Is one thing to say, oh, this one is twenty-two inches by sixteen, *por ejemplo.* But to be there. And to step close, see the brush strokes. The thickness of de paint. The colors. These" — he gestured dismissively toward the books — "these no are right." He flipped through one volume until he came to Van Gogh's *The Church at Auvers.*

"I have seed this one. I have sitted and stared at this one. This sky here — is not right. When you are there, you see is much more vibrant. Is deeper. Cobalt. If you are there, you see what the artist *intended.*"

He pushed back his chair. "I will take you," he promised. "One day, I will take you to my country. We will go to the Museo del Prado, and you will see Fra Angelico's *Anunciacíon.* You will see the masterpieces of Alberto Dürer. And we will lie in bed for the siesta, and hear the church bells, the singing of the doves. And we will make love."

Ruby didn't want to wait another moment before boarding a plane to Madrid. "We don't have to wait until someday," she said. "I have the money. I can take us."

He shook his head vehemently. "No. No, I must be the one. Is the man's job. I will make the money, and then we will go, *mi amor.* Then we will go to my country."

He brought her pastries and hot coffee, fed her crescents of mandarin oranges while she soaked in a hot bubble bath. He evaluated her drawings, gave her critiques. "Less is more," he said, pointing to one of her best drawings. "I show you." He drew a woman's figure swiftly, with minimal lines — just as Vargas did. "Do you see? You do not need all those fussy lines. The brain will fill in the gaps." Next, he drew a leaf with a few scant lines, and Ruby could see what he was trying to say — her brain did complete the drawing, and that made the rendering so much better. Javier's instinct for simplicity, his self-assurance, inspired her to work even harder.

When she wasn't distracted by work, she was longing for him. She'd never before been this hungry for a man — for the timbre of his voice, the smell of him, the heat of his skin. His touch. The only other time Ruby had felt such intense longing was when she'd dreamed of hurling herself away from Kansas. But this was something wholly different; now, she wanted to pull something into her life, not escape it. She wanted to run headlong toward this man. At last she understood the songs where women sang about waiting frantically for the phone to ring or thinking they would die without a glimpse of their lover.

Javier also stood up for her. He listened to her complaints about work, about some of the other girls' lackluster performances or the inadequacies of the choreographer, and he rallied to her side.

How long had she yearned for shelter, for someone who could make her feel safe? For an ally, an advocate? How unwilling she'd been, until now, to trust someone enough to give up any of her tight-fisted control. She'd always adamantly rejected the concept of a knight in shining armor, and now, here she was — besotted, a believer.

When she awoke in the night, she reached for him, and sleepily he would open his arms to let her pillow her head on his chest. His presence was comfort, blissful comfort that had been so very long in arriving.

She imagined taking Javier to meet Aunt Tate and Uncle Miles. Javier would loom above Uncle Miles, size him up, instantly know that he could snap the old man's neck or strangle him slowly, letting Ruby watch as Uncle Miles' eyes caught sight of impending death. How long had she secretly fantasized about watching her uncle endure a measured torture and death? How long had she wanted for someone to exact revenge for her? Javier became her promise. A solemn vow of justice.

While her friends begged to meet him, she hadn't yet introduced Javier. They had been seeing each other for over a month now, but she kept him to herself, like a secret stash of Godiva chocolate. She needed it to be just the two of them, for them first to cement their relationship before she brought in others. Sometimes, she wanted to close the two of them into some secret forest den where they could live their lives as quiet, smitten hermits, their love undiluted by the world.

"You must be sure to have Thursday night off," he said.

"But why?" Ruby asked while swiftly trying to crush the immediate, reflexive hope that Javier was planning some sort of romantic surprise.

"I am taking you to a meeting. On the campus, with some friends of mine."

She hadn't known Javier had befriended any UNLV students, but in a way it made sense that he was hanging out on the campus. She remembered finding a copy of *The Rebel Yell,* the student newspaper, on her coffee table. Javier would fit in far better with the students and academics than he did with the slick denizens of the Strip.

"What kind of meeting?" Ruby reached for a pear and bit into it. She wiped juice from her chin with the back of her hand.

"Is for a protest. We are planning a protest."

"Oh!" Ruby was thrilled. "Against the war?"

"No, no. Is something else. You will see."

If it wasn't the war, it had to be something to do with civil rights. "I'd love to," she said, kissing him with her sweetened lips. "Thank you for including me."

She could hardly wait until Thursday evening. At last, she would be part of something meaningful. Javier was ready to tackle what was wrong with the world, and she would be right there at his side.

The meeting took place in the men's dormitory, and Ruby was one of only two women in the room. The other, Mary Alice Higgins, wore her brunette hair long, straight, and parted down the middle. She wore very little makeup and dressed plainly, in a simple cotton skirt and blouse. Holding in her lap a three-ring binder, Mary Alice nodded curtly when Ruby sat down next to her on one of the room's two twin beds.

"Everyone," Javier began. "Dis is Ruby, who will join us as I told you before."

Everyone — a total of six earnest and naïve-looking men — nodded to Ruby, who at nearly twenty-one, seemed much older than the others. She'd purposefully toned down her makeup and selected an outfit she thought would let her fit in on a college campus: flared, hip-hugger jeans, heeled sandals, and a loose-fitting, purple, translucent tunic top with a visible black bra beneath. Still, it was clear she was overdressed. Ruby waved her fingers to the group, which seemed focused, very businesslike. Javier had brought two six-packs of bottled beer, and he passed them around. The students shared a bottle opener.

Barry, who seemed to be the group's leader, started the meeting. "First of all, the plan is to meet up here, Saturday at eleven, sharp. By noon, we'll have newspaper and television coverage — at least that's the plan. Kevin, you're in contact with the news media?"

"Yeah. My roommate's doing an internship at KSHO, and he's given me all the contacts I need," another student said.

"Okay." Barry checked off something on his clipboard. He was lean, wearing bone-colored corduroy pants that hung loosely on his scrawny hips, and his chin-length hair was densely curly, like a wedge of uncooked ramen noodles. He didn't look in the least like the subversive SDS members or other radical protestors Ruby had read about in the newspapers.

"Barry's a poli-sci major," Mary Alice whispered to Ruby. "He knows how to get things done."

Ruby saw Mary Alice's comment as an opportunity and so asked, "What, exactly, are we protesting?"

"Javier didn't tell you?"

"He acted like it's top secret."

"Well, it is. Sort of. We're going after the test site." Mary Alice shifted into a more comfortable position on the bed.

"What for?"

"Hey, you two." Barry thrust his chin at the women. "I hate to sound like your third-grade teacher, but is there something you want to share with the class?"

Ruby felt herself color, and Mary Alice said, "She was just asking what we're protesting."

"Jesus. What a flake," Ruby heard one of the others say.

"Anyone else confused?" Barry asked, and the rest of the group laughed. "Well, then I'll give Ruby her own very special rundown." His sarcasm stung, just as it was meant to. "The Nevada Test Site is sixty-five miles from here. I don't know how long you've been in Vegas." He paused, waiting for Ruby to answer.

"Three years. Since '67."

"Okay then. By that time they'd stopped atmospheric nuclear testing." He paused again, assessing her expression and clearly deciding she was part imbecile. "That means they used to conduct nuclear detonations above ground." He raised a hand high, as if to show her what "above" meant. "Atmospheric shots, they're called. When I was growing up in Vegas, we could see the mushroom clouds rising in the desert. Now, they're testing weapons underground — which means you don't see the clouds, but you can still feel the seismic effects."

Ruby nodded. She'd felt the ground vibrations from a few of the explosions.

"So, anyway," Barry continued. "My father is a radiation biologist. He used to work out there, before he came here to the university."

This must be why Barry was leading the group — he spoke with some authority. But what Ruby didn't understand was why they were upset about the testing program. Wasn't it necessary to the country's defense, a way of ensuring that American weapons kept up with what the Russians were developing? She'd ask Javier later, since there was no way she was going to expose herself to more ridicule.

"Our protest is twofold," Barry continued.

"And, Jeremy and Adam, this is where you two come in." Barry checked his clipboard. "You guys are in charge of banners and signs. I have poster board over there." He nodded toward one of the built-in student desks. "There's tempera paint, and you guys can find a few old sheets to use, right? I have a list of slogans here." He eased a page from his clipboard and handed it to the two sign-makers. "For the rest of you, what the slogans will address is the environmental impact of the nuclear tests and the need to promote peace over weapons of war." Ruby heard a couple of *yeah, man*s and *right on*s from the others.

"Richard," Barry said. "You can get us some bullhorns from the football locker room?" Richard nodded. "Javier," Barry said. "You're set to take photos?" Javier nodded. "And you." Barry nodded toward Mary Alice. "You've got my speech drafted?"

Mary Alice opened the rings of her binder and removed several sheets of notebook paper. "I think it's good," she said proudly. "I've got quotes from parents who say their kids have leukemia, that they know about other kids with cancer, and about all the families who've been subjected to clouds of fallout for years. I've got some former workers who talk about their dosimeter readings.

And quotes from scientists who've been arguing since the late fifties that this whole thing is a public health catastrophe in the making."

"Good, good." Barry was skimming the pages, nodding.

When he looked up at last, Ruby stood and said, "I'd like to contribute."

"What? She's gonna do a nude protest dance?" Richard or Adam or Jeremy — she couldn't keep them straight — said, sotto voce.

Ruby hadn't ever imagined that student protestors could be such assholes. Weren't they supposed to be selfless, sacrificing themselves for the greater good? These were a bunch of spoiled rich kids, living off of their parents and pretending that they were courageous rebels.

Fuck you, she thought but didn't say. This was clearly important to Javier. But lord, these kids pissed her off.

And they were *kids.* They hadn't had to learn to pay bills, make a living, sign employment contracts, or get up every day and work their asses off. She'd grown up way too soon, that she knew, but these boys were lingering in some kind of candy land, a delayed, absurdly extended childhood.

"I came here to help," Ruby said, aiming

her gaze directly at Barry. "I thought I could help. I'd think you'd want all the people you could to show up, to impress the news media with the number of people who care about your cause. Is it just this handful of you, walking around with signs? Have you gotten the word out? I'm wondering if you've even thought about the fact that most of the television viewers won't side with you. You have to persuade them. And keep in mind that a huge number of people who work at the test site — and yes, I actually do know a thing or two about this — they live in Vegas and commute. So, you're asking that the government shut down the test site and take these people's jobs from them. Your protest, if successful, would result in families losing what may be their only source of income. So, you'd better have your ducks in a row, and you'd better be able to suggest viable solutions — not just protest."

Ruby stopped herself. She looked toward Javier and was surprised to see him grinning.

"My Ruby, she is right," he said, standing. "You have a lot to learn, for *estudiantes.* I could tell you about real rebellion, what it costs, but you will no listen. And so it is *adiós, muchachos, muchacha.*"

Javier took her arm and led her out of the overheated dorm room, into the hallway that smelled of too many males confined in too small an area for far too long. When they reached the exit, Ruby gulped fresh evening air.

"Sorry about that," she said, waiting for him to light his cigarette.

"No. No apologies," Javier said, exhaling smoke. "Those kids. They are ridiculous. The *grises* would have wiped them out in just a few minutes." He shook his head. "Dis is no for us."

"At least you tried," Ruby said, taking his arm. "You tried to do something that mattered."

"They will be gnats. Just this" — he clapped his hands together — "and they are gone."

"If what they're saying is true, about the leukemia —" Ruby began.

"Is shame, no?"

"It's a shame," she confirmed.

15

Javier kicked her, hard, and she awoke with a start.

"Ow!"

He kept kicking, and Ruby used both arms to push him away from her. "Javier! Wake up! Stop!"

"Augh!" He sat up suddenly, still groggy. "What is?"

"You were kicking me. In your dream. Geez," Ruby said, turning on the bedside lamp and rubbing her shin. "That really hurt!" There was a crescent of blood where one of his toenails had nicked her.

He rubbed his eyes. "I am sorry."

"What were you dreaming about?"

"I don't remember," he said, clearly lying.

"You don't want to tell me?"

"I don't want to remember."

"The soldiers? The police?"

"The crowds," he said. "So many people, all pushing to get away."

"Come here," Ruby said, and as Javier moved into her embrace, she thought about how the night stoked primeval fears. *We let our guard down in the dark,* she thought, *and that's precisely when the past knows it can come hurtling forward.* Ruby held him until he slept once more, and she left the light on.

Ruby's birthday — Valentine's Day — was just a week away. Javier had borrowed Ruby's car, and so Rose was dropping Ruby off for work.

"He's moving in with you? Already? After what, five or six weeks?" Rose asked. She flicked her turn signal. "You've been keeping him all for yourself, and I understand that. Still, none of us has met him. I mean, it's up to you, of course, but it seems a little fast. Don't you think?"

"It's mostly practical. Javier doesn't have a lot of money. No paycheck yet from the casino for his work — there's some delay, I don't know — and he's had the expense of all the film-developing, the printing," Ruby explained.

"Okaaaay," Rose said. "It's just — well, I've never seen you act this fast. Not with a man." Rose paused, and Ruby could see that her friend was trying to decide whether or not to say what she said next. "Has he asked you to marry him?"

"What? No, of course not! And I wouldn't say yes, even if he did!"

"That doesn't bother you?"

"That he hasn't asked me or that I wouldn't say yes, yet? Well, it doesn't matter. It doesn't bother me. Not in the least."

"I get the physical attraction," Rose said, smiling widely. "I've seen him coming and going. He's gorgeous."

"Isn't he?" Ruby grinned at her friend.

"Don't distract the driver," Rose joked. Laughing, Ruby pretended to reach for the steering wheel. "But seriously. What would your family say? I mean — living in sin and all. My father would disown me." Rose pulled into the parking lot of the Dunes.

Ruby rested her hand on the door handle. She was unwilling to discuss family or morality, and especially not in a parking lot. And while other women might believe they should save themselves for marriage, Ruby had nothing to save — and no family to object. Besides, Javier was different. Her friends would see that when they met him at her birthday party. She touched Rose's shoulder and said, "I realize you care."

"We all care," Rose said, spreading the blame for her motherly lecture.

Ruby opened the car door and stood. "We'll have a blast at my party. Now stop worrying!"

Javier stored most of his photographic equipment — the lights, the reflectors, and the huge rolls of backdrop paper — in his VW bus, and that helped some as they squeezed their two lives into Ruby's one-bedroom apartment. Ruby unplugged her sewing machine and stuck it on the shelf in the coat closet. She gathered her drawing materials, her watercolors, and she packed them away.

Ruby was excited about sharing her life; she felt ready.

But Javier hadn't told her about the red-and-royal-blue parrot, whose cage took up a large part of the living room and who shouted *"Oye! Elisa!"* every time Ruby passed his cage.

"What does that mean?" she asked Javier one day when she came home from rehearsal and dropped her purse on the couch. He was in the kitchen making her tapas.

"What?"

"Iago's greeting."

"Oh, dad. Well . . ."

"It's profane?"

"Is what? Profane?"

"Dirty."

"No, no no. Is no dirty." He stopped slicing fingerling potatoes, set down the knife, and stirred a pot with some sort of red tomato sauce. Wiping his hands on the towel he'd tucked into the waistband of his jeans, he said, "Iago is saying *oye,* and that means 'hey.' And then he is saying *Elisa.* Dad is a wooman's name."

"Elisa."

"Sí." He turned back to the cutting board.

Ruby stood behind him, put her hands on his shoulders. "Elisa is an ex-girlfriend?"

"Sí."

"Oh." She felt a flame of jealousy, which was an entirely new experience for her. If Iago had known some woman long enough to learn her name and call out for her, it must have been serious. "Okay," Ruby said, resisting the temptation to ask more. She didn't really want to populate her mind with images of the woman — women — who'd come before her.

After all, she told herself, she was Javier's here and now. The others were his past. And hadn't each and every woman Javier had known before Ruby made him the man he was now, the man she'd fallen in love with? The man who'd said he was willing to hold her pain in his hands, to carry it for her? Maybe Elisa taught him all sorts of wonderful things. Maybe Elisa even taught him to make tapas.

Ruby picked up a carrot and nibbled on it. "When I was in sixth grade," she began, leaning against the counter, "I asked my teacher to help me find a pen pal. Her name was Calista Salvador Rocha, and she lived in São Paolo." She grabbed another carrot stick. "Her letters came in envelopes edged in the Brazilian flag's yellow and green. I remember" — she laughed — "that Calista wrote with a fountain pen that left burps of ink in the middle of sentences."

"Is most beautiful. Her name," he said. "That is what Calista means in Portuguese. Most beautiful."

"I never knew that." Ruby used the tip of her tongue to dislodge a piece of carrot from between her teeth. "But what I wanted to tell you was that she had a pet jaguar that lounged beside her swimming pool. And" — Ruby paused for emphasis — "Calista had a parrot that sat on the back of her chair and taunted everyone at the dinner table by shouting *'Mas que otário!'* at each of them in turn."

" 'Loser!' That is funny," he said, stirring the sauce. But his voice didn't reflect any kind of true appreciation for Calista's charm, and so Ruby let it go.

"I need a shower before we eat," she said, kissing him on the nape of his neck. Rehearsal for the new show had been murder. She was sore in all kinds of new places.

"Oye! Elisa!" the parrot shouted as Ruby headed down the hallway to the bathroom.

After dinner, they sat on her couch, sipping a peppery cabernet and quietly talking. Ruby was excited about her birthday for the first time since before her family died. Vivid, Rose, and Dee were helping her put together a party, and Javier had agreed to make paella and sangria.

"It's such a luxury to have someone cook for me." She sighed, full of pleasure. "You're spoiling me."

"Is what you deserve," he said, just as the phone rang. Ruby started to stand, and he said, quickly, "Don't answer that, *por favor.*"

"It's probably Vivid or Rose. Don't be silly," she said, barely glancing back at him.

It wasn't until she'd finished discussing paper cups, plates, and utensils with Rose that she saw Javier was seething.

"What?" she asked.

"They call you all the time. They cannot live one day without you? They cannot give us one day alone?"

"Of course they can," she said, still standing and watching her boyfriend suddenly transform to a truculent child planted on her couch cushions. "Are you jealous?" Ruby almost laughed at the absurdity of her question.

"Is no jealous. Is matter of respect. They don't respect me."

"They don't even know you! Honestly, Javier, you're reading an awful lot into a phone call. Rose was asking about my birthday party. Really. Let's not be silly about all of this."

"Come sit down," he said, thumping the cushion next to him. "You spend all your free time with them. I am the one should be *número uno* in your life."

"You are," she said, touching his cheek.

"It does no feel that way."

"I'm sorry," she said, and apparently to show her that he, too, was regretful, he took her foot into his hands and began massaging it. "Lord." Ruby sighed.

"Is better, yes?"

"Perfect," she said. He was just insecure — for now — in their newfound love. Truthfully, so was she. She'd be careful to demonstrate her devotion, and soon enough he'd feel central in her life. How odd it was that such a big, strong man felt needful, uncertain. But how lovely it was to be needed.

She sighed deeply and laid her head back against the cushions. Ruby had planned to ask him for the change from the fifty-dollar bill she'd given him to buy wine and tapas ingredients, but at this point it seemed wise just to let it go. He was a little too sensitive this evening; she'd ask him tomorrow. Instead, she stretched until she could switch on the TV, letting Steve McGarrett and the men of *Hawaii Five-O* distract her until it was time for bed.

For her birthday celebration, Ruby was wearing a backless black sequined dress, and she'd applied a generous swath of turquoise-blue eye shadow to each eye. She lined her eyes darkly, emphatically. She wore a choker made of five strands of pearls interspersed with rubies, and a ruby cocktail ring. Still, she thought as she watched Javier orbit Vivid, Ruby could have been naked for all that it mattered.

Javier was transfixed, drawn to Vivid just as every other man on earth was pulled in by Vivid's powerful gravitational field. That night, Ruby's friend wore a zebra-striped micromini with silver wedge boots that rose to the middle of her thighs. Beneath the dress' thin material, Vivid's breasts proclaimed absolute freedom, and her silver hoop earrings caught the light, fractured it into a thousand pieces, and sent it spinning off to land on the faces of Ruby's guests. Ruby saw a piece of that light dance across Javier's cheeks as he leaned close to Vivid and whispered something.

"I'm sure it's nothing," Dee said, standing beside Ruby and holding a tray of stuffed mushrooms. "Vivid's just being Vivid. She can't help it."

"She could," Ruby said, surprised at how fervently she resented Vivid for not turning Javier away. Ruby saw Rose and Matt exchange a look as they, too, watched Javier and Vivid. "I'll take that." Ruby grabbed the tray of appetizers from Dee. She marched across the living room and inserted herself between the couple. "Canapé?" she asked, forcing a smile.

"Oh, honey," Vivid said, clearly oblivious. "Javier was just asking me —"

Ruby saw Javier shake his head, trying to stop Vivid.

"What?" Vivid asked innocently. "Ruby won't care."

"Who says I won't?" Ruby asked, the edge to her voice sharp, the tray of hors d'oeuvres tilting precariously.

"He just wants to photograph me," Vivid said. "I told him fully clothed," she assured Ruby.

"Here." Ruby shoved the tray into Javier's hands. "See if anyone wants any." She could see him decide not to challenge her, and she watched his back as he moved off. He was wearing a Mexican embroidered muslin shirt, jeans with frayed cuffs, and his leather sandals. His hair was getting longer, now past his collar.

"He's fucking gorgeous," Vivid said, still unaware of Ruby's mood. "And that accent. God, pure sex. Is he as good in bed as he looks?"

"I think he'd like to show you," Ruby said.

"Oh, come off it, Ruby."

"How can you, of all people, be so obtuse?" Ruby heard that her voice was too loud, and she fought for control. "He hasn't asked *me* to pose for any photos."

"Hey," Vivid said, finally noticing Ruby's distress. She held up her hands. "I'm sorry. Look, I won't do it. I mean, I'm your friend, and I would think you would know you could trust me, but if it bothers you this much, then I'll tell him to forget about it."

Ruby closed her eyes, took a calming breath. "I know I shouldn't mind —"

"Yeah, well, clearly you do. So it won't

happen, okay?" Vivid squeezed Ruby's shoulders, and Ruby saw that Javier was watching them. "It's your birthday, Ruby Wilde. Let's don't spoil it with stupid shit like this. All right?"

"I'm sorry. I'm acting like a child."

"You're acting like a woman in love." Vivid kissed her cheek. "Now let's light twenty-one candles and humiliate you with song."

Late in the evening, Javier cleared off the glass-topped coffee table and carefully opened a Baggie of white powder. He took a teaspoon from the kitchen and carefully spelled out RUBY, using his fingertips to coax the powder into the proper shapes. From his hip pocket, he pulled out a Sucrets throat lozenge tin.

"Okay, so that cost a fortune," Ruby heard Dee's date say. "That's a lotta coke."

Ruby hid her surprise. She hadn't known Javier used coke — or even dabbled in it.

"My Ruby, she is first," Javier said, kneeling next to the coffee table. He opened the Sucrets tin and pulled out a short metal straw, beckoned her to him. Ruby bit her lower lip, shook her head. "Is part of the celebration," he said, smiling widely. "Just a leetle bit won't hurt."

She could only think of how poorly she'd done with amphetamines. Cocaine would be the same — maybe worse. And besides, how could he afford it? The casino still hadn't paid him. He couldn't afford rent, and he still asked Ruby for grocery and gas money.

"Is my birthday gift to you, *mi amor. Feliz cumpleaños.*"

Everyone was watching them. She knelt beside him, whispered, "You first — show me," and so he bent over the stem of the R, closed one nostril with a fingertip, and inhaled sharply through the metal tube. He raised his head, sniffed again deeply, and ran his index finger under his nose. "Is *muy* simple," he said, handing her the coke straw.

Nervously rolling the straw in her fingertips, Ruby took a deep breath and then imitated Javier's ritual. It tasted bitter.

"Here, do this," Javier said, dipping his fingers in a nearby glass of water and snorting the water. "Is better for your nose and keeps powder from — I don know the word. Clod? Clump?"

"Oye! Elisa!" Iago shouted from his cage in the corner, and everyone laughed.

While the others took their turns inhaling her name, Ruby went to stand on her front steps and cool down. She felt the powerful blood rush of the drug. She stared at the stars and felt the return of the enthusiasm she'd had for her birthday, for this Valentine's Day, and for sharing it with someone she loved. She wanted to dance across the courtyard. She could do anything, be anyone. She was high on Javier's mountaintop in Holy Toledo, Spain. She could see for miles.

Leaning against the doorjamb and looking back into the heat of her living room, she watched him flirting with Jasmine, a petite bird of a thing Dee had brought along. She saw Javier use a move he'd used on her — the downward-cast eyes, the shrug of his shoulders as if he were feeling shy. She saw him lean close to Jasmine and whisper something. She could almost see tendrils of hair come loose from Jasmine's high ponytail as they lifted on the breeze of Javier's breath.

In her mind, Ruby could hear Etta James singing "I'd Rather Go Blind," and she thought, *Oh, Etta. I know.* She would rather go blind than to see Javier walk away with anyone — Vivid or Dee or Jasmine or some stranger. She'd give up reading, watching clouds skitter across the sky, the acid green of a Granny Smith apple, if only she could be sure she'd never have to watch the back of him as he walked out of her life. Javier could give her life and take it away — just like that.

And then a countervailing voice reminded her that *she* was the one who held this man. This man all the women wanted. This sexy man. He was with *her,* in love with her, living with her. Of all the women in this room, of all the women in Las Vegas, he'd chosen her. Ruby felt her precariousness, but she also felt alive. Her fingertips tingled with budding sparks.

She wanted Javier. In bed. Now. She wanted the party to be over, and she wanted for him to take her. With force.

He looked up from his halfhearted, knee-jerk pursuit of Jasmine and saw Ruby standing in the doorway. They locked gazes. She could tell the others were watching them as they continued to stare at each other. The look in his eyes told her she was the one he wanted. Forever. Now. He took a deep breath and began to walk toward her.

"Hoo-boy," Rose said to no one in particular. "I think it's time to go."

Ruby knew she should be a proper hostess, bid them all good night and thank them, but she was caught in the conflagration of Javier's stare. She was marginally aware of the others filing out, of brief hugs and fleeting kisses. She might have managed a "Good night" or two, but she wasn't certain, and it didn't matter. All that mattered was the man who stood in the center of her living room, put his palm to the back of her neck, and kissed her so hard that she knew her lips would bruise.

In her bed — their bed — he lasted forever. He pounded her mercilessly, and she felt the familiar rapture of complete submission. Her head banged against the headboard, and she relished the edge of pain brought on by his relentlessness. Pinning her arms to the mattress, he rose up and looked down between them, then into her face, and said, "I like to watch the place where we meet."

He flipped her over, laid his weight along the length of her back. He opened his jaws wide and bit, taking nearly all of the width of her neck into his mouth. Shivering, with her face pressed into the darkness of the pillow, Ruby became a doe in the forest. She was brought down, held down. Devoured. She reverberated with her secret annihilation.

16

Ruby wrote to the Aviator and told him she was in love. In her excitement, she had to fight the inclination to end every sentence with an exclamation mark. As usual, the Aviator answered her with a book. This time, it was *One Hundred Years of Solitude*. It did not escape Ruby's notice that the city from the book, Macondo, was a city of mirrors and that the author, Gabriel García Márquez, was Colombian. The Aviator was always full of subtle warnings, it seemed. But what could he possibly know about her lover? She'd studied the lines of Javier's palm; she knew that it was full of promise, that he had a solid, unbroken line of success, that his heart line was clear and true.

When she came home from a hair appointment, Javier was waiting. Seated in one of her wingback chairs, he patted his lap.

"Here," he said. "You come here."

Ruby stood before him, her legs bare beneath a white denim miniskirt. She wore a magenta halter top tied behind her neck, the loose ends of the bow trailing down her back, tickling. Javier slid his hands beneath her skirt and lifted it to her waist, exposing her black lace thong panties. He took hold of her hips and turned her so that she faced away from him, and then he ran his hands over her bare buttocks. Ruby sighed with pleasure.

"Come here," he said again and guided her so that she was lying face down, bent over his lap, her skirt still raised to reveal her backside. She felt one of his fingers slide beneath the crotch of her panties and bury itself within her.

"Oh," she moaned.

"Where you have been?" he asked, still running his hands over her body.

"Hairdresser," she breathed, her forehead pressed uncomfortably into the arm of the chair.

He kept one hand on her butt, holding her in position, and with the other he untied the halter top. He tugged it down so that it, too, lay scrunched at her waist. She felt him reach beneath her and pinch her nipples.

"I didn't know where'd you have gone."

She didn't answer him; she was caught in

the undertow of his caresses, his manhandling of her body, and her exquisite vulnerability.

Smack! He struck her butt hard, open-palmed, and it stung.

"What?" she said, surprised and trying to lift herself.

"Stay." His voice was firm. He pressed one hand into her lower back, pinning her in place, and then he struck her again, harder.

"Javier!" Again she tried to lift herself, but she was off balance, couldn't get her feet beneath her. She felt the growing heat of the skin he'd struck. He sent two fingers inside her.

"You have been very bad girl," he said. His mouth was near her ear, and his breath on the side of her face was hot. "Very bad," he said, smacking her.

He hit her again. And again. Although she squirmed beneath the stinging blows, she quit trying to stand. She surrendered. And with that, she felt the wet tide of her desire rising.

"You won't." *Smack!* "Go away!" *Smack!* "Again." *Smack!*

When he stopped punishing her and instead put his tongue to the red-hot handprints, murmuring *Mi amor mi amor mi amor,* she cried out and came, her moans seeping into the chair's pink-and-white upholstery.

Javier waited until she'd calmed, and then he led her by the hand as if she were a pliant child. He took her to their bed and slowly made love to her.

"You are Botticelli's *Primavera,*" he whispered. "This creamy skin." He sighed, pressing his cool cheek to her fiery, wounded skin. Her skin that sang of him.

Ruby felt a thin patina of shame coating her life. She hid from everyone — including herself. It was nearly incomprehensible that, for her, desire's heat was so solidly fused with fear and pain. It was also, she knew, incontrovertible evidence of her misbegotten soul. She was depraved. Somehow, Javier had seen that in her. He coaxed her depravity, blew upon the embers and grew them into a firestorm.

It was a terribly powerful secret to share with someone. More intimate than everyday sex, it bound her to him, irrevocably. And yet she hadn't needed to resort to cutting for weeks, maybe months now. Javier had cured her. She thought about tossing her box of razor blades into the bathroom trash basket, but she held off. That sweet box of sharpness was her safety net, and she wasn't yet ready to trust that she'd survive without its promise, any more than she could fathom surviving without Javier.

For the most part, Ruby stayed away from the cocaine, but she funded Javier's increasing habit. Sometimes, she spent nearly a thousand dollars a week to feed his need.

"We will create our world," he promised. "Just us."

Ruby stopped going out with her friends. When Chicago Johnny came to town and tried to take her to see Tony Bennett, who'd signed a lifetime contract with Caesars, she pretended she had to work. In truth, she wanted no distractions. She wanted only to inhabit their own, perfect universe.

Ruby began work on the forthcoming Dunes production, *Savage '70s!* There would be tigers onstage with the dancers — a frisson of danger for both the showgirls and the audience, and a huge draw. The rehearsals were long, exhausting. And after the show each night she still had to fulfill her commitment to charm the high rollers.

One night when she got home after three A.M., Ruby began undressing in the dark. As her eyes adjusted, she could see the hump of Javier's body beneath rumpled bedcovers. The ashtray on his side of the bed was spilling over, and several days' worth of his dirty clothes lay strewn across the bedroom floor like the jumbled carcasses of roadkill. *Not tonight,* she thought. *In the morning, I'll tell him to pick up after himself.* She climbed in next to him, felt his warm, sleep-infused skin touch hers.

He pushed his face into her neck and inhaled deeply. "I can smell them on you. You stink." Roughly, he shoved her away, backed himself to the edge of the bed.

"I smell like the casino. Nothing else."

"I don't belief you. You have been making love with one of those ol' men."

Dismissively, tiredly, she said, "Believe what you want to believe. I can't stop you."

Javier threw off the covers and abruptly sat up. With a dramatic flourish, he dropped his legs to the floor and stood. Ruby watched the outline of his body in the meager gray light, and she longed to bring him back so that she could touch the dips in the muscles at the tops of his hips.

"Don't do this," she said as he began pulling on his jeans.

"You don't listen. A wooman should show her man respect." He pulled a dirty T-shirt from the floor and slipped into his sandals.

"You're leaving?"

"Is what you want."

Ruby sat up and turned on the bedside

lamp. The light stung, briefly. "Of course I don't want that!"

"Then you must hear what I am saying to you."

She patted the bed beside her. "Come back and talk."

"I have said what there is to say."

"No! You announced your opinion," Ruby said, now angry, "and now you're throwing a fit."

He turned and looked at her. "You think you are better dan me. You think I am here to cook for you and take care of you."

"I thought you liked cooking!"

"I am no your servant. You make like I am your slave."

"Oh, honestly. That's not the least bit true, and I don't for a moment believe you really think that."

"You go with those other men. You are out all night. You come back to our casa and you stink of those men. You leave me here alone all night. That is a slave." He picked up his camera from the top of the bureau and looped the strap over his head. It bounced once on his chest. He drew his hand through his hair, and then, wordlessly, he walked out of the apartment.

Stunned, Ruby heard his VW cough to life and back out of the parking space out front.

What had just happened? He knew full well what her job entailed. He had even once insistently sat at the bar, sullen-faced, as he watched her charm the big spenders. Javier knew that was how she financed his coke habit. Recently, he'd finally confessed that when they met he'd only been auditioning as the Dunes photographer. He wasn't hired; all the work he'd done was on spec, and none of it had been up to the Dunes' standards. He had no income of his own. He was fumbling, tripping, and scattered, and he needed her help — which she was only too happy to give. She liked providing for him, turning the tables on the usual man-as-provider thing. They were a modern couple. She loved him! How could he possibly think Ruby was hopping in and out of a dozen men's beds? What was it about her that led him to think such things?

Endlessly churning, she couldn't sleep. She got up, made a pot of coffee, and sat waiting for him. Surely he'd drive for a while, calm down, and then come through the door, sheepish and apologetic. He'd realize his overblown reaction was based on a big, fat misconception.

Ruby listened to Janis Joplin singing "Piece of My Heart" playing on the clock radio and thought: *Yes, that's right.* Let him do his worst; I'll show him how strong a woman can be.

But in his absence the cavern inside of her, where her heart beat and where she truly lived, opened into a giant black maw of need and lonesomeness.

He stayed away for three long days. When at last he returned, Javier put his key in the lock, set his camera back in its habitual spot on the bureau, and didn't say where he'd been. Ruby was afraid to ask, afraid to learn that he'd been with another woman. Instead, she told herself he'd been staying with someone he knew on the UNLV campus, likely sleeping on the floor of some dorm room.

He gave her a conciliatory kiss as if it were a diabetic's rationed piece of candy, and she tried to ignore the fact that his breath smelled like mildewed shoe leather. But maybe that meant that he'd been sleeping in the back of his bus with his photography equipment pushed to the side. He was grubby, in desperate need of a shower. *Yes!* She nearly sang her relief. He's been camping out. Alone. Definitely alone.

In an effort to prove that she did not think of him as her hired cook, she made him a spinach and mushroom omelet while he showered. Running the kitchen faucet until the water flowed ice cold, she wet her fingertips and wiped the remnants of sleep from her eyes; she'd had only four hours of rest.

Ruby knew she'd have to be the first to apologize. It seemed a small enough capitulation; her ego could handle it. In the past, he'd told her she was overly sensitive, and she believed him. She was determined to love well, to accept imperfection.

"I'm sorry," she said, handing him his plate, picking up her toast and chewing, dryly. "I don't want for us to fight like that."

"I am missing you," he said, taking a bite. "This is good."

Ruby rubbed her forehead. There was only one possible solution to their impasse; she would have to cut back on the after-show mixing. It would reduce her income, and it would definitely tick off Bob Christianson and the powers that be at the Dunes, but what was she to do? Maybe Javier was only human to be jealous. Even Achilles had his weak spot.

When he finished eating, Javier picked up his billfold and slipped a couple of fingers into the far reaches of what appeared to be a secret recess created to hide bills. He withdrew a chit of paper, which he unfolded and gazed at for a beat too long.

"Here," he said at last, passing it to her.

In what was clearly a woman's handwriting, the note said *Rebecca Dunworthy,* and beneath that was a carefully printed phone number.

Ruby accepted the scrap of paper. "What's this?" she asked, although she knew exactly what it was. Men were constantly passing her cocktail napkins, business cards, all sorts of things inscribed with their hopeful phone numbers.

"I am giving it to you. To prove to you that I will no call her." He raised a hand as if swearing an oath. "I give it to you to destroy."

She knew that she was supposed to see just how enormously desirable he was, and she was supposed to believe that in relinquishing the phone number, he was presenting incontrovertible evidence of his faithfulness.

When she remained silent, he said, "I am putted myself in your hands." She could see how hard he was working to gauge her expression.

Ruby handed him the paper. "You can choose to be with me — or not," she said, feigning more confidence than she truly felt, "but I'm not going to be your jailer. I don't *want* to be your jailer." She watched as he struggled with her unexpected reaction. After a few moments, Ruby could see him decide to drop it and instead change direction.

"I have beened thinking." Javier began tearing the paper into increasingly smaller pieces. He'd not yet shaved, and Ruby thought she rather liked the rough look of his stubbled face. "Málaga, Spain. Is by the shore. The Mediterranean Sea. You know it?" He sifted the last of the torn paper into the ashtray.

Ruby shook her head. Her sense of geography was dismal.

"Picasso was born there."

Ruby wondered if he planned to take her there. "Is it far from Toledo?"

"No so much. But I want to tell you about his nudes. You say you want to learn about art, so I am teaching you," he said, pulling one of her feet into his lap and rubbing it. Ruby leaned back into the barstool, lifted her other foot to his lap, too. "Oh." Javier smiled. "She is greedy."

"I missed you."

"I miss you *también.*"

"Take me to bed."

"I can do that." He smiled. "But you go first. I had an idea."

When he came into the bedroom, he was carrying a bowl full of warm water. He'd poured oil into a tumbler, set the tumbler in the bowl, and was using the water to warm the oil. He pulled off the top covers, had Ruby turn onto her belly, and then he straddled her. She heard him pour the oil into his palm, and she felt bliss as it pooled on her back, warm and soothing.

"Is good, yes?"

"God," she moaned.

"I was talking with you about Picasso. His nudes."

Her eyes were shut, her vision closed off. She tried to focus only on his baritone rumble, the warmth he was kneading into her body, and the weight of him holding her down, preventing her from spinning off into some galaxy of loneliness.

"What I have beened thinking," Javier continued, now dropping his hands onto her buttocks, spreading more oil. "Was that I take photos of you, your body. When you are like this. For my portfolio." He slipped his oil-slick fingers into the crack of her ass, pushed two of them further, into her vagina. She clamped down, used her muscles to keep his fingers inside her. He began moving his fingers deeper, then withdrawing them. Ruby moaned.

"You like this."
"Yes."
"I thought you would. Now turned over."
She did as he asked, and she opened her eyes to look up at him as he pulled his shirt over his head, undid his jeans and removed them. He wore no underwear, and she could see he was hard, ready.
"Come be inside me," she said, but he shook his head and instead poured more oil into his palm. He let the warm oil drip onto her breastbone. She felt the slip and slide of his hands as they rode her breasts.
"With those photos of you, I capture your physicality." He pronounced it *feeseecality,* and the combination of his voice, his touch, made her shiver.
"Please," she said. "Please, Javier. Be inside me."
"Your body does not lie," he said. "Your body is no angry with me. Yes?"
"Yes."
He slid into her at last, slow, controlled, still withholding.
"Please," she said again, and in response he thrust deeply, stopped.
"You will let me take those photos. Yes, *mi amor*?"
"Yes." She sighed, realizing the idea of posing in the nude for him, of hiding noth-

ing from the unflinching eye of his camera, turned her on.

"Is good," he said. "You are my Ruby."

Inspired by Geritol ads, Ruby pleaded exhaustion and iron-poor blood when she approached Bob Christianson. She told him that if she could cut back on the after-show mixing for a while, she thought she could get her energy back.

"You're feeling weak and run-down?" he asked, parroting one of the television commercials.

"Yeah," she said.

"At your age?" he asked suspiciously and then added, "And you get enough sleep?"

"Well, that's what I want to do. To catch up on things like sleep," she said, avoiding his gaze by looking at the photo on his wall of Miss Atomic Bomb 1957. The woman wore a skimpy, white-feathered outfit in the shape of a mushroom cloud.

"Ruby." He waited for her to face him. She turned and focused on the lines in his broad forehead rather than his eyes. "It's not this Spaniard, is it?" She shook her head, but he continued. "A lot of boyfriends can't handle it, seeing their woman onstage, knowing other men watch her."

"I just —"

"I'll give you a month." Her boss sighed. "But, Ruby." He closed his eyes briefly in frustration. "Don't let this man make your world small. Someone who makes demands — well, he's just not the right kind of man for a woman like you. Don't risk your career, all right?"

She nodded, looking down at the surface of his desk, pretending great interest in the polished wood grain.

"One month," he said firmly. "That's it."

"Thank you," she said, looking up at him briefly before making a quick exit.

Without the late nights spent mixing, Ruby was able to get up earlier. She and Javier used the time to do things together, and she felt their union solidifying, their intimacy deepening. She bought a pair of bicycles, and when the wind wasn't whipping up sandstorms, they rode in Red Rock Canyon, away from the Strip. She brought along her Instamatic camera and tried to capture the beauty of the rocks' colors against the startlingly blue sky. Ruby sent some of her best snapshots to the Aviator, told him of picnics she and Javier enjoyed on a rocky escarpment, watching a mated pair of red-tailed hawks soaring overhead. She told the Aviator that the raptors made her think of him, how she envied him his flights, his bird's-eye perspective.

Ruby found time to draw again, to use some of what she was learning from Javier about the world's great artists to practice techniques like foreshortening and proportion. When Javier took off on his own to develop film and print his photographs in the darkroom he rented by the hour, Ruby used the time to think. She came to the conclusion that relationships were like the variations in classical music, full of tempo changes, crescendos, and pianissimos. The variety of tempos served a purpose, held the listener's interest. If everything between her and Javier were smooth, how boring would that be? She determinedly pushed and pulled their union into the exact musical score she wanted to hear.

17

Rose waited for Ruby to come offstage and then cornered her in the Dunes' dressing rooms. "We miss you," she began. "*I* miss you. And I need for you to help me understand. You can't come to my bridal shower because Javier said you couldn't? He's telling you where you can and can't go?"

"Not in so many words."

"Then what?" Rose demanded.

Ruby took a quick look at the clock on the wall above her mirror.

"Now you're going to be late getting home. Is that what you're worried about?"

"Rose, I —"

"You what?"

"It's just that he's sensitive."

"You mean he acts like a spoiled child if he doesn't get his way. He's controlling, Ruby."

Ruby looked around, well aware that some of the lingering showgirls were eavesdropping. "Maybe we can go get a drink? Just one."

"I'll take what I can get," Rose said.

Ruby ordered a daiquiri and remembered the first time she'd tasted one, seated at that long-ago bar in the Aladdin. It seemed like decades ago.

Rose flipped her long blonde hair back over her shoulder and sipped from a glass of chardonnay. She was wearing her usual off-work outfit of tight, low-slung jeans with a silk blouse and gold hoop earrings. "So talk to me."

"What is there to say? You all seem to have made up your mind about Javier — a long time ago."

"Oh, Ruby." Rose sighed. "There's everything in the world to say. First of all, I haven't seen you — alone — in about a million years. You isolate yourself. You say you can't go out with us anymore."

They all wanted too much from her. Of course she didn't have as much time for her friends as she used to, not with a boyfriend in her life. They should understand that.

"And then there's this," Rose said, pointing to a bruise that circled Ruby's wrist. "What the fuck?"

Ruby covered the wrist with her other hand, shoved the whole mess into her lap, and looked at the kaleidoscope of colored glass bottles reflected in the mirror behind the bar. It had happened during rough sex. That thin, shaming line between pleasure and pain.

"Why do you put up with it? With him?"

"I love him. I need him."

"No. No, I won't accept that," Rose said firmly.

"Well, that's my answer." Ruby almost cringed at her peevish tone.

"Tell me what you see in him. And don't tell me he's good-looking. There has to be more."

"He's different. Exotic."

"So's his idiot parrot."

Ruby couldn't help but smile. She did hate that parrot, although she'd secretly begun trying to teach Iago to say, "Hel-looooooo, Ruby!"

"So you've not completely lost your sense of humor," Rose said. "That's one good thing."

"Javier helps me — in ways you can't see, and in ways I can't explain," Ruby said, thinking of the unused razor blades in her medicine cabinet. "He gives me comfort and protects me. And Javier needs me. No one's ever needed me before."

"He makes you *think* he needs you. Oh,

God, Ruby, I know you don't want to hear this, but someone's gotta say it. He's using you, plain and simple."

Abruptly, Ruby stood and began looking in her purse for her wallet.

"Don't," Rose said, putting a halting hand to Ruby's forearm.

"You don't understand," Ruby said. "You can't understand. No one understands what goes on behind closed doors, in relationships. Don't presume to know."

"I'm trying to understand," Rose said, countering Ruby's strident tone with a soft, nearly motherly voice. "Help me understand."

"He tells me the truth. I tell him the truth. We're honest — unlike everything else around here. Everyone else around here." Ruby gestured.

"The truth? You tell each other the truth?"

"Yes."

"All right, then tell me this: Where does he go when he disappears for days at a time, when he's gone off to pout? Do you know?" Rose paused, but not long enough for Ruby to find an answer. "And you. Have you told him the truth? Does he even know your real name?"

It was like a punch to her gut. Deflated, Ruby sat back down on the barstool. It wasn't just her past — her childhood and Uncle Miles — that Javier knew nothing about; Javier didn't even know her real name.

"Honey, no one is ever really honest at the start of a relationship. We all put on a show, hoping to attract someone. And then we get trapped by that person we've pretended to be. We try to be the one who's never jealous, never petty or smelly, who's always sunny and cheerful. But sooner or later, the blinders come off, and we're forced to see the other person — really see them. That's when you find out whether or not it's love. Not before then. You can't really love someone if you don't even know them."

"So, you and Matt are perfectly honest with each other."

"Maybe it'll take our entire lives to really know each other. But we took the time to get to know each other fairly well before we decided to get engaged, to even contemplate a life together." She patted Ruby's knee affectionately. "Kiddo, I love that you were brave enough to jump feet first into this thing — literally." She smiled. "But I'm worried about you. We all are. Any man who tells you to give up your friends — well, that's a dangerous man. Possession isn't love. And a man who does this" — Rose pulled Ruby's wrist onto the top of the bar, put it on display between their two drink glasses — "that's a man to run fast and far from. Pronto."

"I can't —" Ruby began. "I don't —"

"He talks about the truth a lot, that man," Rose said, slapping a five-dollar bill onto the bar and nodding goodbye to the bartender. "But I don't think he's ever met the truth."

Rose was wrong, of course. And Javier had been through so much in Spain. He'd lost not only part of his foot, but also his homeland. He was a wild, wounded dog Ruby had managed to coax from a cave. It was entirely reasonable that he be fearful of humans. Over time, with patience, she'd save him, bring him back into the world. But she couldn't — wouldn't — reveal all of this to Rose. This was *their* relationship — her and Javier's. She knew Rose cared — that was obvious — but Rose was also intruding, and Ruby resented that.

Rose took Ruby's elbow and led her out of the bar. At the curb, she said, "Look. Women give their all for a man. But have you noticed how men stop short? They save themselves. They have a sense of self-preservation, not self-sacrifice." Rose sighed.

"Ruby please, *please* come to my bridal shower. I don't want to have it without you."

"I'll try."

"Well try hard. Because, Ruby Wilde, I also want for you to be my maid of honor."

She gave Ruby a solid, long hug, and Ruby said, "I love you, Rose," while looking over Rose's shoulder into the blinding neon glare.

"You are saying is not negot— that word. You are saying that to me?"

Purposefully, Ruby kept her tone neutral but unyielding. "She's asked me to be her maid of honor. So yes, it's nonnegotiable. This afternoon, I am going to her bridal shower." Ruby had set up her card table and was wrapping a pink silk robe for Rose's shower gift. She loved feeling the fabric's graceful slide.

"Then I won't be here. When you comed home, I won't be here," Javier said, his hands on his hips.

Determined not to take the bait, Ruby calmly folded a sheet of crisp white tissue paper over the robe. What could possibly be threatening about a bridal shower? Still, she didn't look up. She wasn't the least bit certain that she'd be able to withstand the pull of her empathy for him.

"You are listen to me?" he demanded.

She reached for the Scotch tape.

"Maybe you wan that I keep you here? Maybe that is the game you wan play?" She felt more than saw that he'd taken two steps toward her. His shadow fell across the card table.

Ruby felt her self-assurance wane. "No, I do not want to play games," she said, hearing — almost as if it were a memory — how small her voice sounded.

"I can do that," he promised. "I can keep you here." And then when she refused to look at him, he smacked the gift box from beneath her hands, sent it flying against the wall. Reflexively, Ruby cringed and hated herself for it. Javier grabbed the top of her shoulder, dug in his fingertips until it felt as though he were trying to lift muscle from bone. She gasped with surprise and pain. Her wild dog had bitten.

There was a knock at the front door and Vivid called out, "Ruby?"

"You don answer that."

Vivid knocked again and tried the doorknob, which was locked. "Ruby," she said, and it was obvious that Vivid's lips were close to the door, emphatic. "I heard you. So open up," she said. "Or I call the cops."

Javier let go of Ruby, and she literally

ducked to get away from him. She held a hand to her shoulder, which burned.

Once Ruby unlocked the door, Vivid reached inside quickly. She aimed a look of disgust at Javier and grabbed Ruby's hand. "You're coming with me. Now," she said, tugging.

Ruby pretended helplessness in Vivid's grasp when all she really felt was a blend of shock and relief. She glanced back at Javier but let Vivid pull her out of the apartment as if her friend were a lifeguard, yanking her from turbulent waters. Javier crossed to the door and kicked it closed behind the two women. The sound was sharp, like a rifle's report.

She'd angered him, and now he'd leave again. How could things fall apart in a matter of seconds? In a matter of a few sentences? At the same time, how could a woman who'd survived her family's swift, complete destruction even ask that question or be the least bit surprised? Life could turn on a dime.

Vivid's apartment wasn't far, but Ruby's legs were rubbery and weak. Vivid put an arm around Ruby's waist, held her up, and once inside, she grabbed a bag of frozen peas and draped it over Ruby's injured shoulder.

"Thanks," Ruby said, seated on Vivid's couch. The radio was playing the the Guess Who's "American Woman," and before coming to sit beside Ruby, Vivid turned down the volume.

"He has to go," Vivid said. "Honey, he has to go."

Ruby shook her head, looked into her lap, and began crying. Why was she crying? It was the surprise of it; that's all.

"I'm just saying what you already know." Vivid lit a cigarette with her beautiful silver lighter. She blew the smoke away from Ruby.

"Let me have a drag," Ruby said. "Just one." She closed her eyes, let the smoke fill her lungs, and then handed the cigarette back. "Fuck me."

"You're already fucked, honey."

"He doesn't mean it."

"Come off it, Ruby! He's a sadistic, manipulative bastard. Don't pretend otherwise. And don't expect the rest of us to participate in the lie you tell yourself."

"You're making too much of this," Ruby said almost wishfully. She collapsed against the back of the couch and pushed the bag of peas back into place. She grimaced. Vivid was wrong, plain and simple. Yes, Javier had scared her. But Javier lashed out with violence because it was what he knew. Changing how he related to the world, helping him to learn trust, would take time. She'd be patient.

The two women sat quietly. Ruby knew her love for Javier was fat with desperation, a needfulness she'd never before known. She didn't completely understand it herself, the addictive nature of Javier, so how could she help anyone else to understand? The frozen peas were making her cold, and she shuddered before pulling a finely knitted purple afghan from the back of Vivid's couch and wrapping it across her bare legs, beneath her cutoff jeans.

"We can call the cops. Get them to remove him." Vivid crushed the last of her cigarette in an ashtray.

"It's not a big deal. The drama's unnecessary. Besides, it'll just make him angrier."

"Who gives a shit what scares him or pisses him off? He hurt you, Ruby! What if I hadn't come over? What then?" Vivid's voice was raised, but over it they both heard the squeal of tires. Vivid stood and parted her venetian blinds, looking out to the parking lot. "There goes your car," she said.

"I don't mind." He'd drive out to the desert, think about things, calm himself, and then in a few days, he'd return and apologize. And she'd apologize, too.

Vivid walked into the kitchen, grabbed a couple cans of Tab, and returned to sit by Ruby.

"I'm too cold right now," Ruby said, setting the can on a coaster. "But thanks." She was starting to shudder in earnest — uncontrollable pitches of her body as if she were having a seizure. It reminded her of something, another time when she'd gone into shock. Another time when something in her world had come crashing down. But she couldn't quite grasp the memory — it was like chasing a leaf blown in unpredictable patterns across a courtyard.

"I've been thinking about all of this. A lot," Vivid said, now scooting close to Ruby, lending her body heat. "I'm trying to understand the attraction, why you'd do this to yourself, this thing with Javier. And I think I get it." She waited, but Ruby just shivered; her shoulders hunched up suddenly and then a chill swept up her spine. "I'll get you another blanket," Vivid said.

When she came back from the bedroom, Vivid arranged a soft, sea-green blanket around Ruby and tucked it beneath her. "Better?" Ruby nodded, reached under the blanket, and removed the bag of peas. She took a moment to look beneath the strap of her tank top.

"Let me see." Vivid gently tugged down the strap. "Jesus fucking Christ." They both saw the deep purple fingerprints blooming on Ruby's shoulder.

"I'll be okay." He hadn't purposefully hurt her. If Vivid would just let things alone, they could go back to normal.

But Vivid was undeterred. "I couldn't figure it out. None of us could. But now I know why you're with him." She reached beneath the blanket, took hold of Ruby's hand. "He's familiar, isn't he? Javier is extremely familiar territory for you."

Ruby shook her head. "No. He's exotic — that's part of the pull. He's different."

"No, he's not." Vivid squeezed her hand once more, as if by doing so she could transmit insight. "Think about it," she said adamantly. "Think about it, Ruby."

Ruby did think, but again it was like that elusive, windblown leaf.

"Your uncle —" Vivid said, as if coaxing a game-show contestant toward the right answer. "The one who brutalized you. The one you spent your childhood enduring."

"Oh, God no," Ruby said. "Uncle Miles was a pig. He had no education, no refinement. And, he was the ugliest man I've ever seen."

"Right," Vivid said with certainty. "And now you're doing what's familiar to you. Granted, this time it's a prettier package, but it's the same. Repetition."

Uncle Miles? Javier? The same? They were worlds apart. Javier could talk knowledgeably about Renoir, Titian. He knew which utensils to use when eating dinner. He fought for what he believed was right, even nobly sacrificed for his beliefs. Uncle Miles spent his life in a recliner, farting and watching television. There was no comparison.

"Do you trust Javier?" Vivid asked. "I mean really trust him. Enough to tell him things? Enough to reveal yourself?"

She thought she did. He knew about the cutting.

"Does he know about your uncle?"

"Oh, God no. Vivid, you're the only one who knows. Unless you've told —"

"I haven't. Cross my heart," Vivid said.

Ruby sat there, making a genuine effort to comprehend what Vivid was saying. At the same time, a part of her said, *Get up and leave.* Who were Rose and Vivid to talk about her behind her back, to analyze and judge her? How dare they? Who made them all-knowing, all-seeing?

"You spent your childhood being punished," Vivid began again. "And we do what we know, I think. I know that I stand back. I keep myself distant from men. I don't trust them, not one iota. And so I make them into toys, playthings. I make sure they never matter."

Ruby nodded, only half listening. The concept that had pierced her cloud of incomprehension was *punishment.* She was used to being punished for some unspecified sin — any sin — and she'd tried to achieve impossible perfection so as to avoid punishment. Uncle Miles. Aunt Tate's flyswatter. The way they belittled her. She still deserved punishment — that feeling had never gone away. Was Vivid saying that Javier was now her punisher? She tried to think.

Vivid was watching Ruby's face intently. She started smiling, nodding. "You see. I know you do. You see, don't you?"

Ruby nodded vaguely, still deep in thought. That night of the *Tah-Dah!* fundraiser, when she'd inadvertently revealed the truth about Uncle Miles to Aunt Tate. When he'd called Ruby a whore and bruised her arm. When Aunt Tate had chosen that pathetic loser of a man over Ruby. Ruby had shivered and shuddered then, waiting in the front yard for her ride. That was the familiar bit — that memory of another betrayal. And now Vivid was trying to save her from a perceived danger. But Vivid was dead wrong.

Ruby's shoulder hurt, and she felt wrung out. She sucked in and bit the insides of her cheeks. She didn't want to cry, but God, it would be such a relief. Really to sob, hiccup, have her breath stutter and her nose run. All the times she'd kept from crying, when Uncle Miles would beat her bare bottom with the hairbrush and say, "Cry, girl! Cry! I won't stop until you cry!" That vow she'd made at her family's funeral, never to cry. Such a huge part of Lily had died then, along with Daddy, Mama, and Dawn. And she'd kept dying by increments over the course of that long decade with her aunt and uncle.

Ruby reached for the box of Kleenex. She blew her nose, wiped the wells of her eyes. Maybe Vivid was right about one thing: Her past was all over her, sucking her under like quicksand. "How do I climb out of my past?" she asked.

"I'm not sure," Vivid said, shaking her head slightly. "But I have the feeling that once you've seen the light, you can and will. And you do see, don't you?"

Ruby nodded, although she still wasn't

sure. She remained convinced that Javier was her teacher, something Vivid just didn't and maybe couldn't understand. Ruby had the sense that true comprehension would have to percolate through the soil of her, take its time before it reached her heart and she gained a true, complete grasp of things. For now, all she felt was confusion and exhaustion. And fear. Fear that he'd abandon her.

Vivid insisted on coming along to keep watch while Ruby showered and dressed for Rose's party. With a towel wrapped about her, Ruby slid the hangers along her closet rod, still so numb she couldn't decide what to wear. In the living room, Iago shouted *"Oye! Elisa!"* Finally, Vivid took over and pulled out an emerald-green, halter-necked catsuit sewn in supple, silk velvet. To go with it, she chose a chain belt that stretched languorously across Ruby's hips, leopard-patterned heels, and pearl-and-onyx chandelier earrings that swept the tops of Ruby's shoulders. She searched Ruby's bathroom drawers until she found a cake of Ruby's opaque makeup, and with gentle fingertips Vivid covered Javier's purple fingerprints.

All the while, Ruby watched and felt her friend's ministrations. As Vivid brushed Ruby's hair and picked up a can of hair spray, Ruby knew that Vivid was capable of understanding the kind of pain that had woven itself into the warp and weft of Ruby's being. Like Ruby, Vivid had no one. Rose had that adoring, doting, kind father. She didn't have a past — as far as Ruby knew — that included a rapist. Or a pedophile.

"There," Vivid said, putting down the last of the beautician tools. "That's the Ruby I know and love. Now let's go celebrate our asses off."

18

It had been nearly three weeks — the longest Javier had ever stayed away.

"You have *got* to get rid of that fucking parrot," Vivid said when she found Ruby cutting up strawberries and mangoes for the bird. "I take it you haven't heard from him."

Ruby shook her head.

"You should at least file a police report. Try to get your car back."

"Maybe he's gone to L.A."

"Not without his bus and photo equipment. Not without *Oye Elisa* here. No, he's just proving a point. He's the boss. *El queso grande.*" Vivid laughed at her own joke and grabbed a strawberry before heading for the doorway. "He'll show up soon enough," she said.

And that was precisely what Ruby both longed for and dreaded — the reappearance of Javier Borrero. During Javier's absence, she'd practiced conversations with him in her head. When he came back, she'd tell him he could never, ever, physically harm her again. He could not slam things, throw things. She'd tell him that she understood that he had been afraid, that his past had controlled him, and that maybe he'd even been unaware of his physical actions, but he could not ever again frighten her that way.

She would accept her proper share of the blame. Ruby knew that she hadn't approached the whole issue of Rose's bridal shower in the right way. She'd overplayed her hand by announcing her decision to go, rather than discussing it, listening to Javier's concerns, and appeasing them. Still, she'd have to think of how to phrase it all. What she had to do was use empathy, tell him that she understood, that she would help him learn more productive ways to express disagreement or strong emotions.

And Ruby would improve on her own ability to translate Javier Borrero. Up until now, her interpretations of his behaviors and intentions had been flawed. They could both do better. This was all about learning.

Still, she remained uneasy about his return. It was, she realized, one thing to have attained some minor psychological insight; it was another to follow through. He'd bred such a need in her. Was she in over her head?

Six tigers stalked Cleopatra's gold barge and loitered beneath ten-foot potted palm trees. On board the golden Egyptian ship, Ruby and the other dancers fed grapes to oarsmen or posed seductively against the boat's figurehead — an elaborately painted bust of the Queen of the Nile. Vargas had designed wonderful black braided hairpieces threaded with gold drum beads and topped with gold cobra headbands. The showgirls wore hip-skimming skirts sewn in a gold fish-scale material that shivered beneath the lights as they danced. Their eyelids were spread with gold and silver glitter, their lips vermilion. Minimal brassieres made of gold chains held their breasts captive, and emerald- and ruby-eyed creatures twined about their upper arms and calves. It was all performed to Shocking Blue's "Venus," and no one seemed to notice the mismatched references to queens and goddesses, the conflation of eras.

When a torch on the boat suddenly flared, one of the tigers roared, and the audience gasped. Ruby smiled out into the sea of people, wondering how many of them were in town for some championship bowling tournament, how many had come to celebrate a twentieth wedding anniversary or been married that day at one of the on-the-fly wedding chapels. She fought hard not to feel empty and unloved, but those were the abiding emotions she felt in Javier's wake.

At the conclusion of the number, the showgirls held their arms above their heads with their wrists bent away from their bodies at sharp right angles. They slid their heads left and right in line with their shoulders, and asked the audience, "What's your desire?" before bowing to the applause.

Backstage, Ruby found a vase of pink roses on her dressing table, along with a large manila envelope. She sat and opened it. *Have you locked me out of your heart or will you come start again with me?* Javier had written on a plain white card. Accompanying the card were two tickets to San Francisco.

With shaking hands, Ruby poured herself a glass of water. She drank thirstily and, on autopilot, unscrewed the lid to her Pond's face cream and began removing her makeup. Above the elated and confused pounding of her heart, she only half heard the other girls as they chattered about their plans for the rest of the night. Behind her in the mirror, she could see the approach of an arrangement of white mums so enormous that it hid the flower-delivery man's entire upper body.

"For me?" she asked and then leaned aside so that he could set it on top of her vanity. She looked amongst the pom-pom blooms; there was no card. Turning, she started to tell the delivery man that the card must have gotten lost, but then she stopped.

"Is me." Javier smiled tentatively. "I am back."

He was wearing the white Nehru jacket he'd worn the first time she'd seen him staring up at her from beneath the stage apron. She took a deep breath, looked down into her lap, and tried to slow her heart.

"You have open that envelope," he said, reaching over her shoulder to pick up the airline tickets. The scent of him, that familiar musk that was Javier, compelled her to turn in her chair and face him.

"Javier —"

"You must forgive me. I am just a passionate man. That's all."

"We —" she tried to begin again.

We what? she wondered. We can't? We shouldn't? We're wrong for each other? But looking at the sheer beauty of him, perceiving repentance in his face, she knew how hard he was trying.

The way Ruby had made it through life

was by focusing her willpower. Scallywag's determination had gotten her out of Kansas, into the featured showgirl spot. She put her shoulder to the grindstone and she pushed. And now she knew — she wouldn't quit Javier.

Besides. She loved him. *Loved him.* And he'd come back to her.

In San Francisco, Ruby fell in love with the crush of the city's flamboyant hippies, the street musicians, the psychedelic posters, and the narrow Victorian houses of the Haight. She reveled in the sight of a black man in a crosswalk dressed in a charcoal-gray stingy-brim hat with loud purple pants and a purple sweater. She was charmed by the steep hills, the crystalline water of the bay, the benevolent kiss of humid air on her face. The unbridled hair of young men's heads and faces, the girls' silver bangles, flowing skirts, and peasant blouses. The corner liquor store that sold loose tobacco and greasy tacos, the unabashed smell of marijuana in public parks, and the fresh sourdough bread that she and Javier tore apart and ate sitting cross-legged on an unmade bed. From their Bush Street hotel room window, they watched as antiwar protesters marched in the street below, heard the drums and horns, the megaphones and the shouts of "Make love, not war!"

Javier took her to see the Grateful Dead at The Fillmore, and once again Ruby couldn't help but feel she'd been living in a sort of fairytale Disneyland for too many years. She was so out of it. These kids weren't coming to Vegas; Rotarians and pallid mobsters came to Vegas. Hippies didn't have money for the Strip. Ruby had been dwelling — stagnating — in the music of her parents' generation. She'd been operating within their world definition. Ruby feared she was becoming just as passé as Vegas.

"They have fashion design schools here," Javier said, using a pocketknife to cut off a hunk of salami and slide it into his mouth. "We must come here, live here. We have a life here."

Ruby poured another couple inches of red wine into each of their glass tumblers, and lying back against the pillows, they smoked one of the joints Javier had bought in the Haight. She pictured herself in some shady grove in Golden Gate Park, flowers painted on her cheeks, a sketch pad resting on her raised knees. She could wander along Maiden Lane, duck in and out of fabric stores, loiter in the galleries of the Legion of Honor and gain a better understanding of how sculptors and painters created the drape of a sleeve or skirt, the folds of a sleeping dog's skin.

They used finger paints to decorate each other's bodies, weaving peace signs with curlicues and flowers, leaves and butterflies and birds. Moons, stars. The paint dried quickly. It cracked and shattered into colorful shards that drifted across the hotel sheets like spent confetti.

Make love, not war, Ruby thought as Javier moved inside her. She wanted love with him, not war. No more battles. Not even a skirmish. She hadn't asked him how he got the money for this trip, but she didn't care. He'd found a way to apologize on this grand scale, and she appreciated his efforts. This trip was a tangible symbol of his love for her, of his remorse.

Ruby wasn't stupid. She knew these few California days were just an idyll, but she also believed in change. She and Javier could put her savings to good use, draw on her funds to keep them going while they found new, meaningful lives. She could be a different, better person, here in this place — she knew it. The city of San Francisco was jubilantly pushing open every door and window; it had thrown out all of the tired old locks and laws, the reflexive, habitual ways of living. She'd escape again. Together, she and Javier would heal.

As they walked from their hotel room down to Union Square, Javier pulled her into a doorway and kissed her deeply. He held up his right hand as if taking an oath and said: "You see? I am cutted this for you."

The pinky nail he'd grown to use as an ever-ready coke spoon was cut to the quick.

"You've stopped?" Ruby asked. "Completely?"

"Sí."

It was the final piece of evidence she needed. Javier had changed.

On their second, ultimate night in California, Ruby asked him about his father.

"Already, I have told you about him," Javier said, gently brushing flakes of spent finger paint from her cheek.

"But who is he? Does he sing in the shower and cook like you do? Is he a good dancer? What does he like to read?"

"He took care of us, when my mother died. She had the stomach cancer," he said, his palm flat against Ruby's belly.

"How old were you? When your mother died —"

"Eight yearsold." He pressed his thumb

into her belly button.

"So young." She still couldn't bring herself to tell him of her eight-year-old self, wrapped in a blanket in the backseat of her parents' car. And he didn't ask.

Finally, Javier looked from her body to Ruby's eyes. "Without her, he was sad and angry."

"Did he hurt you?"

"Sí."

She wasn't sure she should press him, but maybe this was part of the answer she'd been seeking, the genesis of Javier's spontaneous-combustion furor. "Did he hit you?"

"*Sí.* He was always sorry, always sad. After."

"But he lost control?"

Javier nodded. "Then he would buy us a treat. I don't know what you call it. Ice, ground very small, with lemon or cherry syrup. Sometimes mango."

She felt compassion overtake her. It all made such abundant sense. Their cells must sing choruses of understanding to each other — two ravaged children grown to adulthood.

"I will be a good father to my children. I will love them as much as my father loves me — more — but I will never hurt them.

Not like what I had," he vowed. "You need to know that, my Ruby. I am done with that. *Nunca más, mi amor.*"

"Nunca más," Ruby repeated, feeling hope and faith twining, a sturdy vine that would let her scale the roughest wall. She'd climb to joy, to a future thick with promise.

The next morning, Ruby stood in the hotel bathroom listening to the faucet's drip. She was wavering. She wanted, for once in her life, to make a leap of faith. And so, after taking a deep breath, she used her fingernail scissors to cut an open heart into the center of her diaphragm.

"Is true?" Javier asked, grinning hugely. "You will do it? Live with me, have babies with me, come to be here in this place?" He looked down at the ruined diaphragm cupped in his hands, and when he looked back up at her, she could see tears in his eyes. "You still love me?" he asked, needlessly.

She thought about saying, *Yes, but you'd better keep your promises,* but she didn't. She didn't want to spoil the moment. She didn't want to spoil their future. No, she'd taken that leap, and now she intended to let go of the past, to see everything with eyes that dared to believe.

■ ■ ■ ■

"I didn't know how to tell you, and so I kept putting it off," Ruby said, seated in the shade of an umbrella by the apartment pool with Dee, Vivid, and Rose. Rose's wedding was in two days, and they were having one last get-together before Rose moved into married life.

The silence was decidedly uncomfortable. Vivid tapped a spoon on the tabletop, and Dee escaped to get more ice for the pitcher of margaritas. Rose was the only one who held her ground, refusing to look away from Ruby.

"It's like you're an addict or something," Rose said. "I mean, Jesus, Ruby. What does it take? Does he have to put you in the hospital? Rob you blind?"

Vivid set down the spoon and picked up a fork. "So, let me get this straight," she said. "Your plan is to quit your job, move to San Francisco, and live in some hovel with a complete and total asshole."

"He's not —" Ruby began, but Vivid spoke over her.

"Don't forget. I *know,*" she said, her jaw clenched. "That kind of bullshit behavior does not go away. Poof!" She raised a hand, looked up as if she could see a puff of smoke.

"He's passionate. We both are. We're like Taylor and Burton," Ruby said, desperate to convince her audience.

"Taylor and Burton?" Dee was back with the ice. "You're comparing yourself to Elizabeth Taylor and Richard Burton?"

"Oh, for fuck's sake," Vivid said. "This is your logic? Really?"

"They have a tempestuous kind of love," Ruby said. "They have their ups and downs, their dramas. Their breakups and their make-ups."

"So you think you and Javier are what — Antony and Cleopatra?" Dee asked.

"At least Liz Taylor gets sixty-five-thousand-dollar necklaces for her pains," Vivid said.

"And she can just jet off to Monaco when she wants to escape." Dee poured herself another margarita.

"I hear she gives as good as she gets," Rose said.

Ruby stood, angrily. "I knew you wouldn't understand," she said. "But it doesn't matter. I'm going with him."

"Then get ready," Vivid said, pinning Ruby with her gaze. She pushed the prongs of the fork into the tender skin of her own forearm. "He'll start like this." She pushed harder, deepened the indentations. "He'll push until he makes you bleed. And one day" — she paused — "he'll kill you."

"Oh, no!" Rose said, disbelieving.

"Oh, come on, Vivid," Dee said.

"I already tried breaking this particular horse the gentle way." Vivid set the fork down and patted it as if to make it stay in place. "It didn't work," she said, looking meaningfully at Ruby. "And so now I'm changing tack."

"I'm sorry you don't understand," Ruby managed before turning away and walking back to her apartment. She was breathing fast and could feel the adrenaline threading through her veins. They didn't understand. She knew they wouldn't. Vivid was exaggerating what she'd seen with Javier — pure drama. He'd barely hurt her. And Vivid hadn't seen Javier's behavior in San Francisco. He'd been a different person, away from the stresses of his life in Vegas. None of them had seen the promise in his eyes, how chagrined he was by his previous poor behavior, how much her "yes" had meant to him. They didn't understand devotion, what it was like to believe in another person. Vivid, in particular, with her admitted distrust, her purposefully shallow love affairs — she could never comprehend real love.

They all behaved politely, if somewhat distantly, at Rose's wedding. And then, on the following Monday, Ruby found a telephone message waiting for her at the casino. It was from Sammy Davis, Jr. Shaking with excitement, she called the number, and his manager answered. At long last, the week-long trip to entertain the troops was set. They'd leave for Vietnam on July 29 — in just over three weeks. The manager had already spoken with Bob Christianson, who was willing to give Ruby time off in exchange for publicity photos the Dunes could use to take full advantage of Ruby's goodwill gesture. All ten members of the troupe — Sammy and his wife, a four-piece band, three backup singers, and Ruby — would participate in the photo shoot. Was she still willing?

"Yes!" she screamed into the phone, not caring one bit that she might sound like an overeager teenager. "God, yes!" she added.

Davis had married for a third time, this time to Altovise Gore, who had worked as a dancer in London and on Broadway. With her permanently surprised eyebrows, her luscious lips and body, she was stunning.

Altovise choreographed the shows, and two brief rehearsals were held at the Sands, where Davis performed. A USO officer also met with the troupe, telling them what they could expect in Vietnam. He kept using the word *primitive,* and Ruby thought that of course war-torn Vietnam would be a rough trip.

Sammy and Altovise would be paid a hundred dollars a day; Ruby and all the others would receive twenty-five. The trifling pay hardly mattered. At last, *at last,* Ruby was contributing. She would be part of something that actually mattered, and heading to Vietnam was head and shoulders above a group of prima donna college students marching in circles with placards. Too, she knew that this adventure would serve as her perfect last hurrah before she retired as a showgirl.

In the past, she'd inadvertently triggered his rage. This time, she would control the situation. Ruby told Javier about Vietnam while they were standing in the checkout line at the grocery store, where he'd be less likely to cause a scene. She was right; Javier maintained his self-control. But only until they got to her Ghia and began fitting grocery bags beneath the hood.

Ruby bumped into him as she jostled a bag on her hip. "Sorry," she said.

"Are you?"

"Don't start." She tried to sound firm, in control.

"You want that I be quiet? That I no embarrass you?"

Ruby wedged in the last bag, reached up, and got ready to slam the hood.

"Wait," he said, gripping her wrist. "Not yet." Javier reached into one of the bags and pulled out the carton of eggs.

"What —" Ruby began.

He removed an egg, balanced it in his palm. "You want go off and be with these other men. To shake your *culo* for them. These men in the jungle who have no seen a wooman for too long. You want to do this to my heart." He slammed the egg onto the asphalt, and the yoke bled out. "That's my heart."

She almost laughed. Throwing eggs? Really? Ruby tried to grab the carton, but he thrust it behind his back where she couldn't reach it.

"You want to go with this black man. Travel with him ten thousand miles. And his band, those other men." He began nodding, convincing himself of his veracity. "That's it. You want to go fuck these other men. What is you always say? Oh, yes. You want fuck your brains out. With black men with big dicks."

"Let's get in the car," Ruby said, aware that other shoppers were stopping to stare. "Javier, let's talk about this privately."

"Oh," he said with a mock grin. *"Now* she wants private. This wooman who shows the whole world her tits and her *culo.* She wants *private,"* he sneered.

Ruby took out her car keys. She hated his childish high drama, but just now there was no point in trying to reason with him.

She didn't see it coming. The egg hit her squarely on the head. She felt it dripping, viscous and slow down her forehead, and she used the back of her hand to try to keep it from running into her eyes.

He came around to her side of the car and began pelting her in the back with one egg after another. "Fuck you, Ruby!" he screamed. "Fuck you, you cunt!"

She turned and faced him. She would do this differently, refuse to yell back. She would stay calm, and that would bring him under control. He'd quickly see that he was behaving like a child throwing a tantrum. "Your English is getting much better," she said, rather pleased with her self-control.

He'd run out of eggs, and that stalled him.

Javier stood there, empty carton in hand.

"Have you finished?" she asked, almost daring a smile. Over his shoulder, she saw a middle-aged man with black-plastic-framed eye-glasses gesture to ask if she needed help, and she shook her head no. "Javier?" she asked. "Shall we get in the car and go home now?"

It took a moment, and then he looked at the empty egg carton as if it were some foreign object he could not for the life of him identify. She saw a shift in his eyes. He'd released his anger, and he seemed deflated, pacified.

Ruby searched her purse and found a packet of tissues. She pulled out several and cleaned off the egg as best she could. When Javier touched her arm, she flinched.

"Let me." He took the tissues and cleaned the areas of her back she couldn't reach.

Slowly, she thought with satisfaction, she was learning how to manage him. This would take time, practice. She sighed with relief. He wasn't stalking off, leaving her. He hadn't hurt her. This time, he was swiftly conciliatory.

Once they were in the car, he rolled down his window, and Ruby started the engine.

"You knowed that saying?" Javier asked.

"What?" Ruby moved the gearshift into reverse.

"You can no make the omelet without first break the eggs."

"Ha!" Ruby let out a laugh. "Well, we're fresh out of eggs, *mi amor.*"

"Is true," he said, placing his hand over hers on the gearshift. "No more eggs. And I am sorry, my Ruby."

From then on, she included him in her preparations, thinking it would help him adjust. It seemed to work. He went with her while she chose a long wig in her hair shade, and he helped her find small gifts for the soldiers — candy that wouldn't melt in the heat, Oreo cookies, cigarette lighters, paperback mysteries, and a stack of the August 1970 issue of *Playboy,* featuring a pictorial on *Myra Breckinridge,* which had just come out.

Bob Christianson gave her a box containing five hundred copies of her Dunes publicity photo so that she could autograph them and pass them out; she was to encourage the soldiers to come see her perform on a real stage, once they got back to the States. Ruby hadn't yet told Bob of her retirement plans. That would all come later, when she had everything arranged.

The night before she was to leave, Javier

asked her to wear the new wig in bed, along with a red garter belt and thigh-high stockings he produced from the bottom drawer of the nightstand. And when she counted the *Playboys* before packing them in a duffel bag, there was one missing. She was glad of his small rebellion.

19

"One week. That's all," she said, standing with Javier on the Vegas airstrip, inhaling jet fuel and watching shimmering waves of heat hover above the pavement. "Then we start our new lives."

"I be here. *Siempre,*" he promised, folding her into his arms for one last, strong embrace. "You don't worry. And come back safe."

They flew in an army transport plane with box lunches balanced in their laps, and they stopped in Hawaii, Guam, and then finally Vietnam. Ruby had a headache, likely brought on by the rumble of the engines and the noxious smell of jet fuel, and she felt slightly nauseated. The band members sat together, Sammy and Altovise were huddled up, and Ruby sat with the backup singers — Darlene, Misty, and Yvonne. The singers were all nervous, jittery, and extremely unsure of themselves.

Dozing off and on to the drone of the plane's engines, she lost track of time, but well over twenty-four hours had passed by the time they at last landed at Tân Sơn Nhất, Saigon's airport. As Ruby descended the ramp, she was hit by a heavy, sweet smell that lodged in her nasal passages. She immediately recognized it as decay, death. She didn't really feel the heat until they were standing inside the claustrophobic makeshift customs building, but then she sensed how flushed she'd become. She felt dizzy, enervated. Uneasily, she answered a few questions posed by a surprisingly small, delicate Vietnamese officer. She swore she had no guns or knives, all the while thinking that everything — absolutely everything — seemed dirty, in need of paint and repair. Long trails of ants crawled up the wooden shack's dirty white pillars.

Their first meal was fried chicken. Sammy joked that they must have heard that black people love fried chicken, and he wondered if they'd be served watermelon for dessert. Ruby picked at her meal, as did Darlene — a big-hipped girl with startled eyes and severely bitten nails.

They performed their first show within three hours of landing. Sammy wore a silk, thigh-length Nehru jacket in a pink-and-orange paisley print; a huge gold medallion bumped against his chest as he sang "You've Made Me So Very Happy." He introduced Altovise, who sat with the bigwigs in the front row of the audience, and the crowd of thousands of soldiers cheered wildly when she stood. She thrust her fist in the air, and the black power salute was echoed by hundreds of black soldiers.

Dressed in a white shell top that buttoned up the back, a single set of false eyelashes, a pair of sapphire-blue hot pants, and her long wig flowing nearly to the middle of her back, Ruby whirled and kicked and swayed her hips to "Lucretia MacEvil." She and Sammy played off of each other, and he invited soldiers to come on stage to take turns dancing with Ruby. Darlene, along with Misty and Yvonne, sang backup and snapped their fingers, wiping sweat from their foreheads with army-issue white handkerchiefs. Disoriented birds flew about the stage, and soldiers stood to take photos of Sammy in action.

Movement revived Ruby, as did the contrast with her Vegas performances. The stage was small — not as small as many she'd perform on in the coming days — but it was not the grand expanse that she was used to. She loved the friendly informality, which let her interact with the band and Sammy, the other girls, and the audience in a more intimate way.

She smiled at the sea of soldiers seated in waves of folding chairs, the men who hooted and whistled and called out for more, as well as the ones who made their way onto the stage to take her hand for a few moments, shyly, to twirl her. She felt a shared history with these men — a childhood of the Lone Ranger, Superman; Malt-O-Meal and Campbell's soup TV commercials. They'd all grown up singing the Libby's jingle on playgrounds in Kansas, Wisconsin, along the Eastern seaboard, and in the desolate, wintry plains of South Dakota. They shared the dashed hope of the Kennedys, the strict, disciplined parents whose worlds had been so severely shaped by the austerity of the Depression. They knew fractured innocence.

As Ruby danced, the men answered with their enthusiasm. It was a fueled exchange. Back and forth. Back and forth. It was a conversation she never wanted to end.

The men gave Sammy a fatigue jacket sewn with patches from different units. His finch's body swam in the voluminous coat, which he wore proudly, with the sleeves rolled up. One of the men put a floppy boonie hat on Ruby and told her to keep it, said that he knew it would bring him good luck. He'd drawn on it in blue ballpoint ink: a peace symbol, a crude dove with an olive branch in its beak, and the name of his girlfriend, Chantelle.

In the audience, she saw a Vietnamese girl, maybe eight or nine, incongruously seated in a row of men. One soldier held a frantic monkey on a leash in his lap. She saw crosses and dog tags. Some men were shirtless, wearing headbands to keep back long, decidedly unmilitary hair. And she saw bandages — wounded arms and legs, crutches, gauze covering a man's head as if he were a mummy.

With his hip black mustache, dangling cigarette, and the worried-looking inverted V of his eyebrows, Sammy called upon his vaudevillian roots and charmed them all. He told jokes; he sang. He tap-danced speedy, intricate rhythms to standing ovations. He wore plaid bell-bottomed pants, never once tripped over the microphone cable, and never, ever complained about the abysmal sound systems, the slapdash stages, the dust, the dirt, the bugs, the food, or the fear. As if he were a tourist, he took hundreds of photos. He posed in hundreds more.

Da Nang, Vũng Tàu, Freedom Hill, China

Beach, Golden Gate, Liberty Center. Càn Tho Army Airfield. Long Bình and Cam Ranh Bay. In the streets of the bigger cities, a cacophony of horns sounded; motorcycles and scooters, bicycles and Citroëns and cars from a bygone era zoomed noisily past; advertisements touted beer, cigarettes, Coca-Cola, and even photocopies. The scent of exotic foods and spices mingled with the odor of shit.

Some of the locations where they performed were relatively plush, with air-conditioning and hot meals; in others, Ruby could see burned buildings and evidence of recent skirmishes with the Vietcong. She saw beautiful, mist-topped mountains, rice paddies that stretched for miles, hills and rivers. She learned about elephant grass with razor-sharp edges that grew up to fifteen feet high and was so thick it dropped men's visibility to less than a yard. She danced on hastily constructed wooden stages as small as six by eight feet, beneath corrugated-tin shelters, and to the twanging of pianos that couldn't hold a tune.

Often emulating Ann-Margret, Ruby wore a turtleneck with nothing but black tights and high-heeled boots, and she gave all she had to young men who sat cross-legged in the dirt beneath a merciless sun. One afternoon, she splashed and laughed and swam with an infantry squad in a crater that had been made weeks earlier by a two-thousand-pound bomb.

She was surprised by the men's sweetness, their quiet respectfulness. They called her miss and held doors for her. They eyed her with lust and longing, but not a one ever said anything stupid or insulting. These men didn't own her. They took her presence as a gift and a privilege, not a purchase made.

She saw *young* men. Not privileged, escapist college students. Not fading middle-aged men. They were eighteen, nineteen, and twenty — and she saw lean, muscled men with honest tans. She didn't see a single basketball-sized gut or ratty toupee. She saw men who'd come to realize what mattered in life, and it was not a gold pinky ring or a trip to the Bahamas.

She glimpsed the ghosts of the French in the food she ate, the architecture and faded signs.

And she wondered why the United States was fighting for this country — a place so impoverished that people squatted by the side of the road to defecate, not caring who watched. Children not even seven years old would run up to her and beg for cigarettes.

Ruby felt guilty about everything she had back home — her fur coats, her savings account balance, and her jewelry — even her modest apartment with running water. People passed her pulling overloaded carts as if they were beasts of burden. She saw malnourished children, children who were missing legs and who hobbled along meager dirt paths using homemade wooden staffs.

They performed at camps and fire support bases, hospitals and rehab centers. Some of the audiences were ten thousand strong; others numbered under fifty. Their helicopter would land, and Sammy would immediately jump out, start strumming his guitar and singing as he walked through the soldiers who came to greet and thank him. He took to wearing a canteen on his belt and was seemingly tireless.

"They're lonesome," Sammy would say to Ruby. "Go mingle." And mingle she did. Those were the times that meant the most to her, when she could sit and actually converse with the soldiers. They drank lukewarm beer together in air so thick with humidity that Ruby felt it could be stirred like a chowder. Some of them talked willingly, needfully, about their lives. Others stared at nothing and moved in a world inaccessible to anyone but themselves. She memorized it all, collected stories to bring back to Javier. And then, at night, Ruby lay awake and listened to the distant boom of artillery.

"You want to know what it's like?" a staff sergeant with the 9th Cavalry said, sitting on an overturned wooden crate, dirt lining the creases of his neck like the halting beginnings of a misbegotten tattoo. "Then do this. When you get back to the world, load a pack with eighty-five pounds. Strap it on. Step into the shower with all your clothes on. Stand there under the water for three days. Shut off the water every few minutes and stay there. Before your clothes can even think about drying out, turn that water back on. Keep standing there." He was tall, lean, and he had sharp, unambiguous features that made her think of the Aviator. His helmet said *SGT Ben*.

"Your feet will rot," he continued. "You've got a good forty-five mosquito bites on one arm alone. You've got the shits. You haven't bathed in months; you wash your clothes by walking through a muddy river."

Ruby didn't know what to say, but soon enough she realized he didn't need or want a response. Sergeant Ben was just talking. Just talking.

And she listened.

■ ■ ■ ■

"Maybe you should drink more water," Darlene said. "You could be dehydrated or something. The men told me if you mix it with Kool-Aid, it disguises the bad taste."

They were sitting in the oven-hot shade of a tent, and Ruby was so nauseated that she didn't feel she could safely stand.

"When'd you last eat?"

Ruby shook her head. Even the thought of food made her ill. The putrid smells were getting to her — the omnipresent rot of the place. She was ready to go home. She missed Javier.

"At least let me ask one of the USO girls for some saltines," Darlene said, already parting the tent flaps.

Ruby lay back on the cot. Flies hovered mere inches from her face, and she swatted uselessly at them.

She knew what this was. There was no more fooling herself. She was pregnant.

She covered her eyes with her forearm and begged the world to stop spinning.

She was back in the dry Vegas heat. Ruby thought she'd treat them both to a steak dinner and tell Javier then. She pictured candlelight, holding hands across a nice linen tablecloth, the weight of quality silverware, an obsequious waiter. They'd celebrate, even though she thought that maybe once she got back to the apartment she would fall into bed and sleep for weeks. She was so excited to see him again, to touch him. Mostly, she looked forward to seeing his face when she told him. Everything was on track, their dream on the cusp of fulfillment.

She'd brought him a souvenir white T-shirt with a drawing of a plane in navy blue ink. In a sardonic take on the United Airlines slogan, it read *Fly the Friendly Skies of Vietnam!* For herself, she'd bought a skintight satin cheongsam in deep rose-and-pink tones with lilting green leaves and white blossoms. The dress fit Ruby's skin tones perfectly. Maybe she'd wear it to their special dinner — and then likely have to put it away until after the baby was born. She'd have to stop dancing soon enough, but pregnancy was a fitting end to her showgirl career, a perfect start to their San Francisco plan.

Ruby waited for over forty-five minutes in front of the airport, her suitcase at her feet. She had to pee, but she was afraid of missing Javier when he pulled up to get her. She waited another fifteen minutes and at last gave up, picking up her bag and returning to the interior of the airport to use the restroom.

Sitting on the toilet, she thought about what a relief it was to be back in modern America, with flush toilets, running water, and essentially clean floors. But as she tore a strip of soft toilet paper from the roll, she worried: Was Javier sick? Had he been hurt? If he was all right, wouldn't he have called the airport, had her paged to one of the white courtesy phones? Or he'd have asked Vivid or Rose or Dee to come get her. Something was wrong. She pushed down a growing ball of panic, told herself that maybe it was a flat tire. *Don't borrow trouble,* she cautioned her reflection in the mirror over the sink. Everything will be all right.

When the cab dropped her off at the Sunglow Apartments, she noticed her Karmann Ghia parked out front. Javier's van, however, was nowhere to be seen. It made sense — if any vehicle broke down, it would be that dilapidated thing.

Ruby took the spare key from beneath the mat and pushed open the door. The apartment smelled musty, unused, lonely. She dropped her bag beside the couch and opened the blinds, and then she walked into the bedroom.

Javier's camera wasn't on the bureau. There were no dirty clothes on the floor. Ruby opened the closet. His blazer, his spare pair of jeans, his boots, and his Nehru jacket were all gone. So were her furs.

She opened the dresser drawer where she kept her boxes of jewelry — the necklaces, rings, bracelets, and earrings of gold, platinum, diamonds, rubies. It was empty.

She walked back into the living room, realizing Iago had not yelled *"Oye! Elisa!"* when she came through the door. The cage was gone. And so was Javier.

"I haven't seen his van for a couple of days," Vivid said when Ruby knocked on her door. "Come in and have a drink. I'm making G and T's."

Numbly, Ruby followed Vivid into her kitchen. "I think he's gone for good this time," she said.

"Sure it's not just another one of his fits?" Vivid squeezed a wedge of lime into each tumbler and handed a glass to Ruby. "Maybe he's just letting you know you shouldn't have gone off without him?" Vivid walked into the living room and sat on the couch, and Ruby followed.

"The parrot's gone."

"Oh. Well . . ." Vivid hesitated, took a sip of her drink. "I guess that pretty much says it all, doesn't it?"

Ruby nodded mutely.

"Well, listen, kiddo. I know you don't want to hear this, but maybe it's for the best."

"I'm pregnant."

"Shit."

Ruby took a deep breath and then swallowed half her drink.

"I know someone," Vivid said. "I mean, if you want to take that route."

"I don't know." Ruby shook her head. "I mean, on the flight back, all I was thinking about was cute little baby clothes and cribs and bottles and walking along the wharf in San Francisco, carrying my baby in one of those slings." She squeezed her eyes shut, took another deep breath.

"You can't dance pregnant."

"I know. But I would have a couple months left to earn a little more, save more money. Before I start to show."

"And then what?"

"Oh, Vivid, I don't know!" Ruby's voice rose with panic. "I don't know about San Francisco without him. I mean —" She stopped as her voice broke, and she fought for control.

"I'm sorry. It's too soon for me to be asking all these questions. Of course you don't know. But as you say, you have a few months — to dance, to make up your mind about keeping it. Her. Him. Shit. 'It' sounds awful, doesn't it?"

"That motherfucker," Ruby said.

"Total fuckwad."

"You warned me."

"Yeah, well, I wasn't in love with him."

"He pretended he was okay with it, with Vietnam. He promised me."

"One more Javier Borrero lie," Vivid said.

"I'm a total fucking idiot."

"Well" — Vivid smiled — "you're not a *total* idiot."

"Fuck me."

"No, fuck *him.* And the boat he came in on," Vivid said, raising her glass for a toast.

Ruby sat on the floor of the shower, letting the water run over her as if she could cleanse herself of Javier. He was gone. She tried to think *Good riddance,* but she couldn't quite believe that. She felt crushed, abandoned. Lost. Stupid. Humiliated. She'd dismissed her friends' opinions as ill-informed, thought they just couldn't see what she saw. He'd thoroughly played her.

At least she hadn't ever posed for the nude photos he'd wanted to take. She shook her head, imagining what he would have done with them.

But now, what would she do, who would she be without him?

Maybe he'd come back. *Maybe, maybe, maybe,* as Janis Joplin sang. He always had. This time, he'd just made it look as though he'd gone for good — that was how angry he'd been, hiding it all beneath a veneer of understanding and good humor. Or maybe he'd truly tried to change but found himself unable to carry through. After all, the truth was that she'd pushed him too far. She knew how much he needed to be the man, the top dog — and she'd emasculated him by heading across the world to be with thousands of soldiers. She'd left him behind. She'd abandoned *him.*

But if he came back, could she forgive him for the furs, the jewelry? Had he maybe even been pilfering her jewelry all along, hocking it? Was that how he'd paid for San Francisco? At least she'd kept her mother's rings on the chain about her neck — her good-luck charm in Vietnam. She held the rings between her fingers now, feeling their reassuring solidity.

When the hot water ran out, she stepped out of the shower. Feeling hollowed out, Ruby crawled between the sheets that still smelled of Javier. Much to her amazement she slept deeply, dreamlessly.

The next afternoon, Ruby forced herself to run errands. Her first stop was the bank; she needed to get some cash before picking up groceries. She stood at the cubbyholed desk in the lobby, filled out a withdrawal slip, and waited in line for the next teller.

"Hi, Kate." Ruby slid the withdrawal slip across the counter.

"Hey, Ruby," Kate said, looking over the slip. "Hold on, all right?"

The teller walked over to her supervisor, a man who wore bow ties and wing tips and looked as if he was and always would be a fussy bachelor living with his neurotic, widowed mother. He returned to the window with Kate.

"Miss Wilde?" he asked.

"What is it?" Ruby was only pulling $125. Her savings account held well over $75,000.

"You don't have this much in your account," he said, pointing to Ruby's figures on the slip.

Ruby laughed. "Of course I do! You know that! Kate?" She looked pleadingly at the teller's familiar face.

"Maybe we should go into my office," he suggested.

"No," Ruby said, standing her ground despite the sharp drop she felt in her stomach. Had *everything* gone to hell in the short time she'd been gone? "Please," she said. "Just tell me what's happened to my money."

"Kate, get the file off of my desk, would you?" Kate scurried off, obviously glad to be out of the line of fire.

Ruby drummed her fingertips on the counter while the flustered little man fiddled uselessly with papers, stacking them, making sure the edges were even. When Kate returned, he took the folder and pulled out a document. Pushing it across the counter, he said, "You'll see this is a notarized statement. With your signature."

The document was titled "Change of Account Status," and it indicated that Ruby was converting her account to a joint account, with Javier Borrero as the second signatory. She could feel the raised impression of the notary's seal, and at the bottom of the page was a nearly perfect rendition of her signature.

Ruby looked up into the faces of the two bank employees. "I did not complete this form."

"It's notarized," the little man said, as if

notarization meant God himself had blessed it.

"So what? It's a lie. This document is a lie, a forgery."

"We had no reason to distrust it." He adjusted his bow tie as if it had suddenly become a garrote. "Everything was in order."

Kate took a cautionary step back from the counter and then said, "You came in with him all the time, Ruby. You sent him to cash your casino checks. We saw you here together." Her voice was plaintive, wheedling. "He said you were all the way in Vietnam, that you needed for him to cash in your account. We left fifty dollars, just to cover any outstanding checks."

"You have to make this right! Someone has to make this right." Ruby closed her eyes briefly. Someone needed to make her entire life right, to undo all that Javier had done.

"It's out of our hands. We followed bank procedure," the little man said. "You could try filing a federal complaint for theft. But I don't know —"

"You let him take everything!" Ruby said, and although she could hear herself talking, she couldn't really feel her feet or her legs. This wasn't real. It wasn't possible.

"I'm sorry," Kate said.

"Yes," the supervisor added as Ruby turned and walked away, across the lobby. She felt dazed and weak, as if she were stumbling through some awful dream world. This was not happening.

She pushed open the glass doors and stepped onto the hot sidewalk, shading her eyes from stark, piercing sunlight. *Lord, I've seen the light,* she thought, coming to the street corner. *Now, please let me be,* she begged. *No more.* Coming home to the empty apartment had dropped her to her knees; this theft of everything she had worked for felled her completely, left her crawling. Were the gods laughing? Was she sufficiently entertaining? She could go no lower. She was scraping her belly along sharp gravel.

I am the stupidest woman alive, she thought. *Record-breaking stupid.* She opened her shoulder bag to find her sunglasses.

The 1968 Dodge Dart sedan struck Ruby's legs and tossed her up onto its hood. Her head hit the windshield, sending cracks across the glass like splintering ice. Ruby bounced off of the car and onto the asphalt, where her now unconscious body rolled for another fifteen feet before coming to rest in front of Vernon's Olde Time Ice Cream Parlor.

20

She swam in a warm soup of morphine. Slow, viscous. She could feel her pain whispering, ready to shout as soon as the drug's power began to wane. Both legs had multiple compound fractures surgically repaired with metal plates and screws. Her scalp had been split open, and she'd suffered a concussion. Her entire body was tender with bone-deep bruises.

She dreamed. Horrible, drug-laced dreams, some kind of hell specially designed for Ruby Wilde. She was the girl in Hans Christian Andersen's "The Red Shoes," one of the books the Aviator had given her so long ago. In her dream the red shoes were Dorothy's ruby slippers, but just as in the story, once the shoes were on her feet, they would not come off. They had become part of her, and as long as she wore the shoes, she was forced to dance, nonstop. She danced along the Strip, past neon displays and gawking tourists. She skipped up and down curbs, wove through rows of slot machines, and circled roulette tables, tap-danced past Rose at the reception counter in Caesars. But Rose couldn't catch her; no one could.

She danced until her ankles buckled, but still her feet whirled, her legs pranced. Finally, she found the Borrero cabin, hidden away deep in the woods. Soft-shoeing on the front stoop, she pounded on the door, shouting for Javier. He was the only one who could do this, she knew. He was the executioner, the one with the ax. Javier would be strong enough to cut off the shoes, to cut off her feet. Without his blade, she'd dance herself to death.

Whenever she started to swim toward the surface of her dreams, whenever she began to see golden light flickering and thought there might be fresh air within reach, she'd remember. She'd remember what he'd done, what she'd let him do. And she'd remember that she carried his child within her. A child who might be just as felonious, just as coldly devious and heartless as his father.

And then she'd stop swimming. She'd stop dreaming. She'd stop trying to reach air. Instead, she'd let her legs go lax, let her arms dangle. She let her body sink once more into the muck of decay. Into rest. Into oblivion.

She felt his presence beside her hospital bed. Ruby turned her head away from him, kept her eyes closed. How could she possibly face him? How could she endure the pressing, boulder-heavy weight of her shame?

He took her hand, grasped it firmly, and kissed the back of it. "Lily," he said, simply, softly.

She bit her lower lip, squeezed her eyes tightly shut.

"I'm here," the Aviator said, squeezing her hand.

"I know." She squeezed back.

"I'll take care of you."

"He took all my money."

"I know."

"How — ?"

"Your friends called me. You had my name in your wallet."

She nodded, still reaching one arm behind her body to keep hold of his hand.

"I want to take you home."

"Home?"

"My home. Albuquerque. You'll get better

there. Then you can decide what you want to do."

"I can't face you," she whispered into her pillow, not sure if he could hear her.

With his free hand, the Aviator brushed her hair from her temple and kissed her there, where her blood hummed just beneath the thin surface of her skin. "Lily, please look at me. Please."

He waited. She struggled to find just one more ounce of courage, to face her unutterably altered world and the man whose opinion meant the most to her. Slowly, she turned her head and opened her eyes. At fifty, he looked tired, careworn, and there were strands of gray threading his short, dark hair. But he was still her handsome, steadfast Aviator, and she forced herself to meet his gaze.

He smiled crookedly. "I know a lot about mistakes," he said. "And, yes, some mistakes have dire consequences. But it's not as if you killed someone." He paused so that she'd remember the depth of his sin. "You trusted someone. You loved someone, and he broke your heart. There's no shame in that."

Always and forever, he was her guardian angel. She pulled his hand to her lips and held it there as she drifted back into a drugged slumber.

Ruby could not get over it — the man who flew at supersonic speeds, who regularly broke the sound barrier, was driving a blue station wagon with fake-wood side paneling. It was the funniest thing she'd seen in ages.

As the hospital personnel transferred her from the gurney to the back of the station wagon, she began giggling.

"What?" the Aviator asked, smiling with pleasure at her laughter.

"A station wagon?" Ruby grinned. "You?"

"I'll have you know," he said, helping Geri, the private nurse he'd hired, to adjust the blankets around Ruby, "this is a Chevrolet Kingswood Estate wagon."

"Oh, an *estate* wagon. Well, then." Ruby smiled.

"It has a 350 V8 Turbo-Fire engine."

"Ha!" she laughed.

"You wait. Once we get out on the highway, I'll show you what this car can do." He squeezed one of her big toes where it emerged from thick white plaster.

Vivid, Rose, and Dee arrived just then. Vivid stalked to where the Aviator stood, her heels putting her at eye level with Ruby's rescuer.

"First we said champagne," she announced. "Then Rose — ever the voice of caution and reason — said we couldn't do that, that you couldn't mix painkillers with booze." To this Geri nodded. "Flowers are out, because they'll just die. And you got enough of those from all of your admirers." She smiled.

"Balloons wouldn't do, either," Rose added. "Bumping around in back with you all the way to New Mexico."

"So we did this!" Dee shouted, no longer able to bear the long, drawn-out introduction. She passed a large wrapped box to Ruby where she lay propped up on pillows against the rear of the backseat. "Open it!"

Ruby tore into the paper and pulled the lid off of the box. Her fingers touched it before she actually saw it, and she stopped, looked out the back end of the car toward her friends. "You didn't," she said.

"That rat bastard took all the others," Dee said.

It was a silver fox fur, calf length, nearly identical to the one Kyle had given her. "Oh, lord." She sighed with pleasure, feeling the soft fur in her hands. She shook her head. "You know I'm going to say you shouldn't have. This is terribly extravagant."

"Of course we should," Rose said, and

Ruby knew that for Rose, the cost had been budget-breaking.

"This way you won't forget us," Vivid said. "Or Vegas."

"As if I could." Ruby ran her hands along the coat. "You know it's the one I most regretted losing."

"We know," Vivid said, smiling. "Cosmic sex and all."

Ruby glanced quickly at the Aviator, but she couldn't tell if he'd heard Vivid. "There is another gift I want," she said, noticing that the lining of this coat was not pink as Kyle's had been, but instead a lovely aqua blue.

"Aren't you the greedy little bitch," Dee joked. "What else does Her Highness want?"

"A promise," Ruby said. "That you'll come see me."

"It's already in the works," Rose assured her. "We'll be talking with this lovely man," she said, putting her arm around the Aviator's waist and with surprising familiarity pulling him in until their hips touched. "When he says you're ready for a visit, then the three of us will take a road trip."

"But I'm only coming if he promises to take me up in one of his planes," Vivid said, flirting.

Ruby saw the Aviator's cheeks flush beneath his sunglasses.

"We're still going to call you Ruby," Dee said. "I can't get used to Lily."

"I'll answer to just about anything," Ruby said, still stroking the fur coat. "I'm going to miss you like crazy," she assured her friends.

"I'm going to check the trailer," the Aviator said, diplomatically removing himself for their final goodbyes. He'd rented and packed a U-Haul trailer with what he, along with Vivid and Rose, had decided were Ruby's essential possessions. They'd sold what they could, including her Ghia, and Ruby had a thin envelope of bills in her purse.

Vivid crawled into the back alongside Ruby, careful not to jostle her. "Did you decide?" she asked, and Ruby could smell Vivid's subtle Arpège perfume.

"Not yet," Ruby said as Rose, too, climbed in to be closer to Ruby.

"You call if you want to talk," Rose said.

"Call no matter what," Vivid said.

"Does he know?" Rose asked, indicating the Aviator.

"Not unless you've told him," Ruby said. "Or maybe the doctors said something to him."

"Geri knows," Vivid said. "So he probably

knows, too."

"Just get well. Take care of yourself, kiddo." Rose gave Ruby an awkward hug. "I love you," she whispered.

Ruby's nose stung with suppressed tears. Vivid kissed her cheek, and then both women crawled back out of the station wagon.

"*Sayonara,* sweetheart," Dee said, leaning on the trailer hitch and trying not to cry.

Ruby's friends stood there in the Vegas sun as behind them patients and their families flowed endlessly through the hospital's revolving door. The Aviator started the car and slowly pulled away from the curb. From her backward perch, Ruby waved farewell.

"You all right?" Geri asked.

"I'm okay," Ruby said, trying to convince herself. "But let me know as soon as I can have another pill."

"You're hurting?"

"On so many levels," Ruby said, burying her face in the soft, silver comfort of the coat.

Lily Decker

1

The Aviator predicted that they'd be on the road for about nine hours, including stops and starts. Lily spent a good deal of time staring out the rear window at the U-Haul trailer. With her wheelchair stowed in the backseat, the Aviator and Geri up front like Mom and Dad, she felt like a child or inanimate cargo. And although she'd imagined that the altered perspective of riding backward would be fun, Lily discovered that it only made her woozy. Fortunately, Geri fished something out of her medical bag that kept the nausea at bay.

Lily hadn't felt she had any choice other than to go with the Aviator. Vivid and the others would have tried to take care of her, but it was too much to ask, and they had their own lives. The last thing Lily wanted to be was a burden — she'd had enough of that as a child — but she was also determined to accept the Aviator's kindness, to remember what it felt like to be cared for, truly cared for. And she realized how desperately he wanted to try to whittle away at some of the guilt he felt over her family's destruction. Still, she knew she would work hard to become independent, to find a path out of this fearful no-man's-land in which she'd been marooned.

Lily slept off and on, and aside from pauses for food, gas, and restrooms, the Aviator drove straight through. He hadn't exaggerated; the estate wagon had a powerful engine that when fully engaged let them fly past nearly everything else on the highway. Their route took them far south of the Grand Canyon, which was just as well — she couldn't have seen much from her perch.

They picked up and lost radio stations along the way like Hansel and Gretel's breadcrumbs. Lily learned that a slew of hijackings had been orchestrated by a group demanding the liberation of Palestine.

"Is there any good news?" Lily asked, and the Aviator found a station that played Neil Diamond's "Cracklin' Rosie," Eric Burdon's "Spill the Wine," and a really sappy song called "Patches." When Dean Martin came on singing "My Woman, My Woman, My Wife," Lily was instantly flooded with regret. What was she was doing, leaving Las Vegas? She was running away when she should stay and face things! She was losing her plush world of martinis and high rollers, sophistication, and glamour — and exchanging it for what? Who knew?

She picked up the fur coat and, despite the September heat, buried her face in it. The last thing she wanted was for the Aviator to know her wretchedness, to think that she didn't appreciate what he was trying to do for her. But misery was gaining on her.

"How about some classical music?" Geri suggested, and the Aviator obliged. Lily sank back into the pillows, listening to a soothing Chopin melody and trying to distract herself by thumbing through the issue of *Newsweek* the Aviator had bought for her. The cover pictured a joint, smoke curling from the tip, and it posed the question *Marijuana: Time to Change the Law?* Fat chance, Lily thought.

She laid aside the magazine and closed her eyes, overcome by memories of Javier's *lacy* days of San Francisco. The hippies with their ribbons and embroidery, their bare feet. The smell of eucalyptus leaves and the fecund bay. How could he have lulled her into belief in him — a belief so strong she'd been willing to risk pregnancy? Admittedly,

Javier hadn't had to work very hard at it, given her growing misgivings about her life in Vegas. But still — to think of the fantasy she'd so readily bought, hook, line, and sinker.

Drifting behind closed eyelids, she tried to decide if Javier's actions amounted to purposeful, conniving manipulation. He'd strewn her path with pretty petals of lies, but how much had he planned? How much was effortless, simply part of who he was? Was he a natural liar? A natural thief? Had he ever intended to live with her in San Francisco, to make a family with her? Had he cared for her at all?

He hadn't carried her pain for her; he'd multiplied it like breeding bacteria. She shook her head. All those things he'd said. She'd believed him. Why was her vision so imperfect, so horribly nearsighted? The old saying was true, wasn't it? *Actions speak louder than words.* Love is not a thief. Love does not bruise and serially, finally abandon. Love doesn't lie. He hadn't loved her.

The very thing Javier did to her was what native peoples feared would happen if they were photographed: he took her soul captive. Until now, the nebulous haze of hospital morphine had kept her from feeling it all. And even now, in many ways it still didn't seem possible or true — that she'd become a veritable buffet of crippled loss. Maybe it would take months, years, or a lifetime to feel all of this, to understand. Not to understand Javier — she was determined not to give him any more of her time or energy — but rather to comprehend why she'd done what she'd done. What she needed now was to learn who Ruby — Lily reawakened — really was.

She opened her eyes to watch the sky peeling away from the back of the car. It was almost painfully absurd that she was forced to stare relentlessly at her past. In the distance, a solid brick of clouds appeared to Lily as though someone had taken the handle of a paintbrush and drawn it through the whiteness like a plow, creating a stark furrow of bright blue sky. It was, she thought, creation through removal — like a sculptor subtracting stone to reveal shape and form.

Her whole life felt like a welter of subtractions. Her family, her innocence. Her dream of being a real dancer. And now her savings were gone. She could forget design school, at least for the foreseeable future. And she would not dance again — the surgeon had been quite clear, even predicting that her legs would be permanently misshapen.

How on earth could she support a child? She'd be twenty-two in several months, but what skills did she have that would help her earn? She put a protective hand to her belly. It wasn't the child's fault his father was a deviant. The child had hung in there, survived her flight over the car and her raucous tumble down the street. The heartbeat beneath Lily's palm was that of someone who wanted to live, to be born. Maybe even to dance.

But to do it alone? In her head, she heard Diana Ross singing "Love Child." Things were changing, but there was still a huge prejudice against unwed mothers. And she wasn't going to be living in permissive Vegas anymore, as Ruby Wilde. No — she was, once again, Lily Decker.

Geri was surprisingly strong for her size. "It's from swimming," she said, helping Lily into the wheelchair and maneuvering her into a stingy gas station restroom. Lily could only imagine how unwieldy and heavy she must be, with two huge leg casts, but Geri never complained.

In Winslow, Geri and Lily sat in the sun while the Aviator went inside a diner to get them burgers and fries.

"That man's a gem," Geri said.

"He's perfect." Lily lifted her face to the sky. She was beginning to realize how good it felt to breathe clean, fresh air, to be away from the neon clutter of the Strip. And not to have to worry about sunburns or tan lines.

"I take it you've known him a long time."

"Since I was a little girl."

"Well, he cares deeply about you. I mean, that man's devoted," Geri said, pushing one of her springy strawberry blonde curls behind an ear.

Lily guessed Geri was in her midthirties. Her freckled hands were bare of any wedding ring.

"Does he know?" Lily asked.

"About the pregnancy?"

"Yeah."

"He does."

"Okay then," Lily said.

They both turned at the sound of the door banging. "Let's eat," the Aviator said, motioning toward a picnic table lodged beneath a pathetic excuse for a tree. With obvious effort, Geri wheeled Lily across uneven gravel.

Sparrows quickly grew bold and dropped from the tree's lower branches to scour the ground for crumbs. Lily watched them — indistinguishable bits of brown and black, hopping here and there. It had been ages since she'd watched birds, since she'd luxuriated in the sun or lingered anywhere that included much of the natural world.

"I didn't realize how much I've missed this." Lily looked toward the sun traveling low in the sky and softened by a skim of milky clouds. "Just being outside feels heavenly."

"I believe that nature is essential," the Aviator said. "Everything supernatural is in nature."

"Are you a transcendentalist?" Lily smiled.

"Devotedly so. You'll find a very long shelf of transcendental writings in our library."

"Books." Lily smiled at him. In many ways, books represented their most precious link to each other.

"You have to eat," the Aviator said noticing that she'd left her burger untouched.

"Because I'm eating for two?" she asked.

He stared at her from behind his dark green sunglasses, and Geri abruptly volunteered to go inside to get more napkins despite the obvious pile sitting in the middle of the table.

"I don't really know what to say." The Aviator dipped a French fry in a puddle of ketchup.

"There isn't anything to say, I guess." Lily

reached for one of his fries.

"I don't know if abortion is legal in New Mexico. I haven't had occasion to know," he said, his true feelings still hidden behind the dark lenses of his sunglasses.

Lily looked past him to a small grocery store that advertised a sale on pork chops and fresh roasters. A woman wearing a flowered housedress and pink sponge curlers was coming out of the door, carrying a brown paper grocery bag in each arm.

"Do you ever hear anything about my aunt Tate?" Lily asked.

"Maybe you know your uncle had a massive heart attack. About a year ago, I think it was. I didn't know whether I should tell you, and then I decided you'd ask, if you wanted to know."

"Dead?"

"Yes, I'm sorry."

"I'm not."

He carefully folded the paper that had covered his burger and pulled a handkerchief from his pocket. It was perfectly pressed, with knife-sharp creases.

"You're still fastidious." Lily smiled.

He smiled back at her, refolded the handkerchief, and then said, "You'd be a much better parent. A loving, caring, thoughtful parent. If that's what you're worrying about."

"They didn't set the bar very high."

"Someday," he began, and then stopped as Geri approached.

"Someday what?" Lily asked.

"Just someday," he said cryptically, unwilling to go on with Geri seated at the table.

The Aviator stood and walked to the station wagon. Lily watched his erect back, his faultless posture. She realized his carefulness was camouflage, his carriage a perfect cloak for his well-pressed secrets.

There was a lot, she thought, that the Aviator kept hidden. But would he ever share those secrets with her?

Arizona's Petrified Forest was eerily beautiful in its desolation. Lily gazed at the colors whirring past and thought about Aunt Tate, how she would be as a widow. Would she still sit on the couch and watch television at night, Uncle Miles' empty recliner next to her, a silent, obstinate memorial? Or would she have taken hold of her newfound freedom, rearranged the furniture, painted the walls, begun an evening class in tatting? Maybe she'd sold the house and moved into a nice apartment where others did much of the work for her. Or maybe Aunt Tate roomed with one of her Bible-study sisters, ate mashed potatoes and fried chicken for Sunday dinner.

Lily didn't feel hatred for Aunt Tate. She didn't feel anger — not anymore. She felt pity. Pity for a woman who had lived such a truncated, tightfisted life. A woman who'd allowed herself such minimal love, who'd foregone passion. Aunt Tate had been absurdly loyal to a man who didn't begin to deserve her devotion. Had she ever really seen him? Known him for who he truly was? Had she worn blinders throughout her marriage, or had she felt that she had no other viable option? No means of escape?

Love is blind, Lily thought. And then, immediately, *Good Lord.* She was criticizing her aunt for the very thing she'd done. For nearly a year, Lily had loved a man who was unworthy of her; she'd failed to see his mutinous heart.

Well, Aunt Tate hadn't paid the price Lily had. But then again, she'd paid a different price, hadn't she? Maybe we all pay a price, Lily thought. Maybe love is always costly.

She thought of Uncle Miles' shrouded raspberry bushes, lined up like the ghosts of murdered children. She thought of the ghost of herself and realized she didn't know who she'd been before Uncle Miles.

Who she was *during*. She didn't know who she was now, either.

They passed into New Mexico, winding through the vast desolation of the Navajo reservation and Gallup's red rock formations. After the sun set, they stopped at a line of malapropos, stuccoed Plains Indian tepees, and bought one last tank of gas and used the restrooms. Geri begged a little extra time to peruse the tacky gift shop for arrowheads and moccasins, and while Geri shopped, Lily and the Aviator lingered beneath adamant stars.

"How are you doing?" he asked, leaning against the station wagon's paneling.

"Truth?" Lily said, keeping her face toward the India-ink night.

"Yes. Always."

"I feel naked. And I know that sounds bizarre, coming from someone who makes her living parading around on a stage in a state of decided undress." She cast a smile toward him in the dark.

"So explain it to me."

"I think it's because this is all so intimate," she said finally. "I mean, we don't know each other that well, you and I, not really." She pushed on before he could disagree. "And now you're seeing me helpless, not even able to go to the bathroom by myself.

I'm completely dependent — physically, financially. And you've seen my folly, my ruin." She sighed. "Does it get more intimate than that?"

He'd kept his eyes focused on the heavens, as if by doing so he could lessen their mutual discomfort. But now he looked down at her. "I can't pretend to know what you're feeling," he began. "But I can say that I know what it's like to feel exposed. That's what we have those awful dreams about, isn't it? The dreams in which we're naked, walking down some hallway with everyone pointing and staring."

"It's true. One of our greatest fears is in being seen without the safety of our costumes. Of being revealed for what we really are, right?"

"So the experts say. But, Lily, I want for you to know you can trust me. Oh, hell." He slapped his thigh in frustration. "Just as soon as I say that, I realize how ridiculous and empty it sounds. You must feel so little trust for anyone at this point."

"Actually," she said, reaching from her wheelchair to touch his arm. He squatted so that his eyes were on a level with hers, and she continued, "I trust you more than anyone else on the face of this earth." Then, feeling oddly emboldened, she added, "And

I love you."

"Sweetheart," he said, leaning across the arm of the wheelchair to kiss her cheek. "You are so loved."

He smelled of perspiration and that old, familiar citrus aftershave. Lily was tempted to think of him as a soft blanket in which she could wrap herself. At the same time, she felt the stirrings of her old adolescent longing for him, his physical attraction.

The Aviator stood and looked one last time at the emerging night. "You and I — we met under some very different stars." His voice was solemn, sepulchral, and she had no response. He cleared his throat. "Over there." He pointed. "The bright one — that's Venus. Venus rising in the night sky. It's the only planet named for a female, you know," he said, placing a hand on her shoulder and squeezing. "And she's no easy, dull female. Venus is alive with storms, lightning-shot clouds of sulfuric acid. They think she may even have cyclones."

Lily tried to picture Venus' storms, and then she thought about trust. She remembered that as she stood on the precipice of her bus trip to Vegas, the Aviator had told her to trust no one. His advice had been prescient. And yet — she had to trust someone. How else to negotiate the rapids of life? Her error was in trusting the wrong person — that was more than obvious now. Her compass was broken.

But she'd trusted Rose's father, and then Rose. Vivid and Dee. Even Evan Brashear and Bob Christianson. The Aviator, now. Those people were not mistakes. The mistakes came when she fell in love. That's where her instruments failed to register properly. She'd so purposefully, obstinately defined the context in which she saw Javier — choosing to see him as her rescued, wounded creature rather than someone bent on using her. But why? What led her to fall so hard for him that she refused to see?

When they were moving again, she could glimpse the night sky from her makeshift bed. She was tired of thinking. It was exhausting, this fruitless, circular analysis and puzzlement. Maybe it was the painkillers that muddled her thought process, blurred all the edges. She shifted, trying to loosen her caftan, which had become bunched up beneath her. Vivid had given her two caftans that could easily be slipped over her head. They were a paisley flurry of bright colors, and one had gold piping circling the belled sleeves and hemline. Vivid had ensured that Lily was a very fashionable invalid, although her hair definitely needed a trim.

After over eight hours of driving, they came to what the Aviator called Nine Mile Hill, on the western outskirts of Albuquerque. Twisting to look out the windshield, Lily managed a brief glimpse of the jeweled lights of Albuquerque spread along a broad valley, a great hulking backdrop of mountains, and a fat moon hoisting itself up and over the peaks.

2

The main house was a hundred-year-old, low-slung adobe with sensuous, undulating walls that were nearly two feet thick in places. A sunroom with a red brick floor had been added to the south side of the house, its windows filled with wandering vines of pink bougainvillea. Two bedrooms contained heavy, carved wood furniture. A third bedroom had been made into a library with built-in bookshelves lining all four walls, a generously sized Persian carpet, and a chestnut-brown leather couch with matching chairs. The hacienda even included a small indoor swimming pool, around which swooped two dozen relentlessly cheerful yellow, green, and blue parakeets.

Geri and Lily were staying in what the Aviator referred to as the casita, a separate, modern guesthouse set back behind the hacienda. The casita was larger than Lily's Vegas apartment, with two bedrooms, a full kitchen and pantry area, a bathroom with a walk-in shower, and a living room. The plastered walls were the color of melted chocolate ice cream, and generous windows opened onto a view of the Rio Grande and the cottonwoods that rimmed the river. From her bed on that first morning, Lily spotted a roadrunner stalking lizards in the leafy debris beneath a peach tree in what the Aviator referred to as "our orchard."

Our was the operative word. Because on that first morning, sitting in the Aviator's kitchen and being served a breakfast of French toast and fresh strawberries, she'd met Jackson "Jack" Powell.

At six foot three, he was a big man, powerfully built, who nevertheless gave the impression of being an easygoing teddy bear. He wore tattered blue jeans, a loose-fitting Mexican shirt of thin vanilla cotton, and despite Albuquerque's early autumn heat, Birkenstock sandals with socks. His mussed, light brown hair flew in every imaginable direction; he had pale blue eyes, and a pronounced Fu Manchu mustache.

Jack made them all breakfast and then settled in beside Lily. She could smell the cinnamon and vanilla he'd used for the French toast. As he poured a generous flow of maple syrup over his toast, Jack looked up and caught her staring.

He smiled and said, "I told him not to say anything until you got here. About us, I mean."

"I —" she began, at a loss for words. What did he mean, *us*? She looked between the two men. The Aviator sat across the table in a baby-blue, crisply ironed oxford shirt, the sleeves rolled to his elbows. A crease was pressed into the legs of his khaki pants, and his short hair was, as always, carefully combed. Lily looked at the angles of his fingers as he held his silverware, the way he cut his French toast into precise rectangles, the way he tried to ensure that each piece soaked up an equal portion of maple syrup.

And Jack — the crow's feet at the corners of his eyes, the light emanating from his features, the promise of nurturance she saw there. She tried to comprehend the yin and yang of the two men. They weren't living together to save money — it was clear that wasn't the case. But . . .

That was it, wasn't it? When the Aviator looked up from his breakfast plate and smiled across at Jack, Lily saw it. She saw the Aviator's shoulders relax, his jaw muscles loosen. In that brief moment she could see they were a couple, that they loved each other.

"You didn't know," Jack said, reading her expression and grinning widely. "Don't fret, Lily. No one knows." He looked across the table toward the Aviator. "For obvious reasons," he added, still gazing across the table. Lily saw the Aviator's cheeks color, and he looked down, focused on slicing a strawberry into four pieces.

"I just —" Lily tried again. She laid down her silverware. How could she have missed it? The Aviator was a homosexual. She said it to herself several times over, trying to take in yet another dose of the Elixir of Lily's Eternal Blindness.

They hadn't had homosexuals in Kansas when she was growing up. Well, certainly, no one she'd known. She'd met some effeminate men in Vegas, especially in the costume design rooms, but it had never entered her mind that the Marlboro Man Aviator was — oh, *God.* This was insane. He'd had that petite girlfriend — that Jackie Kennedy wannabe Lily had seen at the *Tah-Dah!* fundraiser.

Lily couldn't take this in. Buying time, she took a sip of her fresh-squeezed orange juice. "This is delicious," she managed.

"It's a truly lovely feast, Jack," Geri added.

"Do you want to tell our story, or shall I?" Jack asked the Aviator.

"Go ahead," the Aviator said. "I think you're better equipped."

"Ah," Jack said, accepting the Aviator's dodge without comment. "Well then. 'The Ballad of Stirling and Jack.' "

Lily had almost forgotten the Aviator's real name: Stirling Sloan.

"I was hired to give a training at the air force base," Jack began, his gaze alternating between Lily and the man seated across the table from him. "To a bunch of cocky test pilots," he said, grinning. "I'm a psych professor at UNM — the University of New Mexico — and I was told that these fine men needed to learn about stress reduction." He picked up a strawberry, bit off the top, and dropped the remainder in his mouth. "Stirling and I had lunch afterward, and we got to talking. Primarily about chess, as I recall. The strategies of warfare, more generally, yes?" he asked the Aviator.

"And you challenged me to a match," the Aviator said, his eyes softening, a corner of his mouth rising with humor.

"We discovered that we both love books, philosophy in particular. Antiques. A nice glass of port," Jack said.

"Quiet contemplation," the Aviator added. "Emerson. Thoreau."

"And each other," Jack said, without embarrassment.

Lily looked down into her lap. She felt a fist grab hold of her heart and squeeze. She tried hard to calm herself, to hide her confused feelings.

"I already owned this house," Jack continued. "And then we added the guesthouse so that if the federal government chose to check on Stirling in connection with his security clearance, we could easily persuade them that he lived as my tenant in the guesthouse — not here with me."

"Lily?" the Aviator said, clearly worried. "What's wrong?"

Lily shook her head. She was losing again. Another removal. Now she'd lost the Aviator. And yet she knew that she was being horribly selfish — wanting him all to herself. She felt as if she couldn't breathe.

"I've been an idiot," Jack said, scooting his chair so that he faced Lily in her wheelchair. He cupped her shoulder in his hand. "Lily," he said softly, as if he might frighten away a skittish horse. "I didn't do this well. Not at all. I've been insensitive."

She shook her head. "No. It's not you, Jack. It's me." She was still unable to meet anyone's eyes and so instead stared steadily into her lap.

"You've had so much to deal with, in such

a short time," Jack said. "Too much."

"Jack," the Aviator said. "Why don't the three of us go talk in the library. No offense, Geri."

"None taken. I'll earn my keep, get the dishes cleared," she said, standing.

The Aviator came around behind Lily's chair and took hold of the handles. "Okay?" he asked, and in response Lily took her napkin from her lap and set it beside her plate.

Jack opened the library's French doors, which looked onto a small, flagstone patio with an old stone fountain. Shadows flickered across the stones, and birds dipped into the fountain's waters. "There's no air-conditioning," Jack said. "The house is too old. But these breezes help."

"I've had to be careful — still am careful," the Aviator said, sitting on the end of the couch and facing Lily in her wheelchair. "My career depends upon it. If anyone found out, I'd be tossed out of the air force. Actually, I'd be prosecuted. Criminally."

"But you had that girlfriend," Lily said, her hands gripping each other as if in prayer. "The one who looked like Jackie Kennedy."

"Oh, you mean Judith. No, Lily," the Aviator said. "She was my beard."

"Your what?"

"Beard. You hide behind a beard. She was my disguise, in case people started to ask questions — like *Why isn't he married?* And *Maybe my sister Mary would be a good match for him.*"

"Oh."

"She was a willing accomplice. Judith had her own reasons for wanting to throw people off the scent."

Lily had projected all of her longing, her need, onto the Aviator. She'd made him into her answer to loneliness, to the lack of a loving family. She'd seen only what she wanted to see — a man she could trust, love. "I guess I just always pictured you a certain way. And now I'm finding out I was wrong about you, too. I've been wrong about every single man in my life. Jesus. I'm a complete idiot."

"But you weren't wrong about me," he said, pulling her hands apart and holding them in his own. "You know I care about you. You must know that. And, Lily — I've just had to be very, very careful. Jack has tenure, but I don't have any protection. If anyone asks, we say I live in the casita, which means I can't even answer the phone in the main house — because then someone might figure it all out."

"He'd do anything for you," Jack said from where he'd come to stand behind the couch, a literal backdrop to the Aviator. "Stirling has talked about you from nearly the first moment we met. Hell, there was a point where I was even pretty jealous," he said, and Lily thought she saw Jack resist resting a hand on the Aviator's shoulder.

The stack of *Playboy* magazines she'd seen in the casita — they had to be a prop. How hard it must be for them, she thought. They couldn't acknowledge their love. They couldn't hold hands across a restaurant table or as they walked down the street. They couldn't use any of the endearments other couples used without thinking. Could they even grocery shop together? Would that generate too many questions? If Jack were hurt, in the hospital, the Aviator wouldn't be able to touch him or show tenderness.

And the names — the casual cruelty and ignorance of *pansy* and *swish, fairy* and *faggot. Pillow-biter.* She'd heard them all, never once connecting the venomous words with someone she loved. *The secrets we carry,* she thought. The heavy, shot-put weight of shame.

"This is horrible," she said, and caught a look of disappointment on both men's faces.

"Oh no — not you!" she quickly added. "I'm thinking about how you have to live. That you have to treat your love like some enfeebled cousin who's locked away in an asylum. I'm so sorry!"

"Then it doesn't bother you? Now that you know about us?" the Aviator asked, still gripping her hands in his.

Lily lifted their joined hands and held them in the air as if she were swearing a vow. "I don't care," she said, and then thinking that she'd again put her foot in her mouth, she added, "I don't care that you're homosexuals. I do care that you love each other. And that makes me very, very happy — for both of you." She looked up at Jack to be sure he knew he was included.

The Aviator stood and kissed her forehead, and Jack came from behind the couch and rested his meaty palms on her shoulders.

"We're going to get you back on your dancing feet in no time," Jack said from behind her. "But you stay here as long as you like."

"Stay forever, if you want," the Aviator said. "Jack and I want you here."

"I owe you," Lily said to both of them.

"No." The Aviator shook his head. "No,

Lily Decker. I owe you a debt I can never repay."

"Just tell me one thing," Lily said, wanting terribly to lighten the atmosphere in the room. "When did you stop smoking?"

"Jack made me."

"I told him I had no desire to lick an ashtray."

Lily blinked, hard. More unbidden intimacy. She tried again. "And the parakeets are Jack's, right?" She smiled.

"They make an unholy mess of the deck," the Aviator said, confirming her suspicions. He grinned widely at his lover.

"I'm trying to loosen him up," Jack said, bending to pretend-whisper in her ear. "Someday, I'll get the crease out of those pants."

"Ha!" the Aviator scoffed. "And I'll get you to put your gardening tools away."

They sparred just like any couple, Lily realized. "Do you two need a referee?" she teased, thinking that maybe, just maybe, she'd landed in a real home — a place that would hold her gently, securely.

The weeks that followed fell into a pattern. Doctor's visits, physical therapy, exercises and more exercises. The Aviator reported back to duty at Kirtland Air Force Base, and Jack spent his days at the university — with a good deal of free time, in between classes, at home, where he cooked, cleaned, and gardened. He even made peach jam, ladling the sweet, rose-gold preserves into mason jars that he carefully labeled in black ink.

"Have you always liked to cook?" Lily asked, watching Jack work from a sunny spot she'd found at the table.

"Always," he said, licking sugar from his fingers and then rinsing them in cold water. "Do you want a taste?"

"Absolutely." Lily accepted a teaspoon loaded with jam. "Wow," she said, feeling her mouth fill with saliva. "Nectar of the gods."

Jack sat down opposite her, sliding the morning newspaper out of the way. "My little sister and I cooked together. We baked cakes, and I actually got pretty good at making roses." He mimed slowly squeezing an icing bag with both hands, and Lily burst out in laughter.

"You have a salacious sense of humor," she said, grinning widely.

"Don't tell Stirling."

"I suspect he knows."

"Oh, that he does," Jack said, grinning back at her. "He just prefers that I not do it in public."

"You wouldn't."

"With a few martinis in me, I would. Have," Jack confirmed, his eyes narrowed by his smile. "I remember once there was a nine-inch pepper grinder . . ."

Lily burst out laughing again. "Jack, I'd like to go out on the town with you. Ever been to Vegas? Oh, we'd have a blast. I mean, maybe you could be yourselves there. Could you, do you think?"

"No," Jack said, shaking his head, suddenly serious. "Not even there, my sweet."

They were quiet a moment, and Lily could hear the vibrant, hopeful chirping of the budgies drifting in from the poolside.

"I grew up in Nebraska," Jack volunteered. "My father was a farmer. Corn."

"So we're both flatlanders."

"Oh, honey, don't I know. Talk about mind-deadening."

"It must have been hard," Lily said. "Growing up there. I mean —"

"Mostly, I was confused. Horribly confused. Not about whether I liked men or not — that I always knew. More about why I was that way, what I could do about it. I will say this" — Jack picked up the newspaper sections and ordered them like some puzzle he needed to solve — "it pretty much guaranteed that I'd never believe in God. Not a god who did that to me, who made me something to be despised."

"Your parents?"

"I'm banished. Shunned."

"Oh."

"Yeah. My sister, on the other hand, she tries. She married a dairy farmer — as uptight and conservative as they come, a Barry Goldwater man for God's sake — but she loves me, and we share a lot of memories. I used to help her climb out her bedroom window so she could go to dances."

"Do you see her at all?"

"We talk on the phone. That's pretty much it — and only when Drake is out in the barn or something."

"That's awful."

"It is. But it's also better than nothing." He finally stopped fiddling with the newspaper.

"And what about Stirling?" she asked.

"Well" — Jack smiled across the table at her — "he has you."

"He's pretty much always had me," Lily said. "In a way, I don't think we've ever been apart. At least not in my head, my heart." She touched her fingertips to her breastbone. "He's always been right here.

Right here."

"There's nowhere else he'd rather be. Of that, I'm certain."

The estate wagon turned out to be Jack's, which solved that puzzle for Lily. Far more in character was the Aviator's burgundy, soft-top Camaro with black upholstery that seared bare skin in the strong, autumn sun. He often wedged Lily's wheelchair into the backseat and took her for drives out along the western edges of Albuquerque, on traffic-free stretches of an old highway that paralleled the interstate and let him open up the throttle. They rocketed across impossibly sparse ranchland dotted with yucca and cacti, alongside remnants of extinct volcanoes and billboards advertising Acoma Pueblo, the sky-high Indian village.

In the men's shadowy, hushed library, Lily read as voraciously as she had when she was a child. She knew she'd found sanctuary with Jack and the Aviator, and while she sometimes missed the charged pace of her Vegas life, she could sense that for once she was exactly where she belonged. She read some of the Aviator's Emerson and Thoreau, found that numerous passages resonated with her. She could see what meaning they might have held for the Aviator, too, who'd underlined a passage in Emerson's *Nature:* "In the woods, we return to reason and faith. There I feel that nothing can befall me in life, — no disgrace, no calamity, (leaving me my eyes,) which nature cannot repair." Lily hoped it was true that nature could repair her the way Emerson and the Aviator believed — or hoped — it could.

Still, she found that she preferred fiction, and when she told the Aviator, he smirked and handed her a copy of *The Scarlet Letter.*

"Oh, very funny," Lily said.

"Hawthorne was a transcendentalist, you know. You'll have to read about Brook Farm. The hippies aren't the first to try communal, utopian living."

"Nathaniel Hawthorne lived in a commune?"

"Keep reading from that shelf" — he pointed — "and you'll see. But be careful. It's a topic that Jack can't get enough of. He'll go on and on and —"

"Will I now," Jack said, coming into the library. It was their traditional after-dinner reading hour, a time when Geri tended to borrow a car to do her own thing, which apparently consisted of yoga and folk-dancing classes. "I thought maybe tonight we'd have a little opera," Jack said, going to their shelves of record albums and pulling out Puccini's *Tosca.* "Do you enjoy opera, Lily?"

She was secretly cringing, thinking how much she'd prefer Crosby, Stills & Nash or Creedence. "I know so little about it," she said, honestly.

"Jack's on the board of the Santa Fe Opera," the Aviator said with evident pride.

"It's set in Rome, in 1800," Jack said, placing the vinyl on the turn-table. He blew across it to remove invisible dust and lifted the arm, keeping the needle suspended over the first track while he spoke. "It has all the drama you could want. Torture and murder and suicide."

"And some of the most beautiful arias ever written," the Aviator added.

"Vissi d'arte," Jack said. " 'I lived for art; I lived for love.' "

They listened for two hours, the men sipping their glasses of port, Lily drinking apple cider. To her surprise, she was enchanted by the music, raised up and sent spiraling by the melodies and the singers' exalting or cascading emotions. Geri came in toward the end, flushed from whatever exercise class she'd attended. She stood behind Lily and rubbed the aches out of Lily's shoulders and upper back.

When the music ended, the four of them let the silence spool out. Finally, Jack stood to lift the needle. "This opera season is over, but next summer, Lily. Next summer, we'll take you up to Santa Fe. It's an outdoor theater. You'll sit in the cool night air, and if you're lucky, there will be an electrical storm flashing in the distance. You'll see fabulous scenery and costumes, and hear world-class performers." Jack held the box for the LPs in his hands, his thoughts elsewhere.

But what Lily heard had set her heart racing. "Costumes?"

"Magnificent costumes. Innovative designs," Jack said.

"Oh." She sighed. "That's my dream."

"You've already worn some of the best, I would think," the Aviator said.

"To design costumes. Did you see, when you were packing up my apartment?" she asked him.

"Skimpy costumes?" he joked.

"My sketchbooks, with my designs."

He smiled. "I'm teasing. Yes, I saw your sketchbooks, along with your watercolors. Quite a pile of them, as a matter of fact. Vivid made a point of paging through them with me before we boxed them up for the U-Haul. Your passion was evident."

"Passion, yes, but I don't know if I have any talent. And besides, dance has defined me for so long. I mean, I've just always been a dancer in my heart, you know? And now I'm not sure who I am, who I can be."

"Then you've defined yourself too narrowly," Jack said, his voice kind but authoritative. "First of all, you're young. Second, we're all more than just one thing. Stirling is more than a test pilot. A great deal more. Geri is so much more than a nurse. And you, my dear. While you're no doubt a fine and talented dancer — and a great beauty — you are far, far more than that."

Lily felt tears begin to well in her eyes. "I'd planned to go to design school. I'd been saving for it."

"You still can," the Aviator said. "I've kept your college fund."

"Which you're spending now," Lily said, looking down at her casts.

"Stop," the Aviator said, and the stringency in his tone surprised her. "Just open your hands, receive. Let me do this without a fight."

"Save your energy for your recovery," Jack added.

"Which is going along so well," Geri chimed in. "It helps to have a patient who's motivated. And who was in such great

3

Lily liked to wheel her chair into the pool area, where she'd sit listening to the calming brush of the water against the pool tiles, the pump cycling off and on. She felt herself soothed, bathed in the thick warmth of humidity tinged with the clean scent of chlorine. The parakeets would abruptly stop singing when she entered, their hush telling her that she was — at least for a few moments — an intruder in their private world. She liked to wait for them, to watch for when they tilted their heads in response to a call from a bird outside the windows, and then to listen as they replied to that free bird's voice with such strident optimism.

This Saturday morning, she was watching the Aviator swim laps. Not surprisingly, his strokes were crisp, purposeful. She gazed at the water streaming along his sides, the white froth of his kick. He finished his habitual mile, which seemed to be composed mostly of turns at either end of the small pool, and then he shunned the ladder, instead easily pulling himself up and out using only his arms.

Lily handed him his towel. "You have a beautiful body," she said without self-consciousness — merely as someone appreciating a lovely creation.

"Shall I tell Jack that you've been flirting with me?"

Over the course of a couple months, they'd grown easier with each other, able to tease. He pulled a patio chair close to her and sat, dried his legs, and then draped the wet towel across his shoulders.

"Jack says you were brought up Quaker, in Pennsylvania."

"I was." He used the back of his hand to remove a drop of water that had traveled from his hair down his neck.

"They do that silent worship thing?"

"They do."

"And they're nonviolent?"

"Yes."

"Conscientious objectors, right?"

"Right."

"So what did your parents think when you joined the air force?"

"They objected."

"Even to World War II? To Hitler and all?"

"They object to violence across the board, and war is violence, no matter the impetus."

She wanted to ask if his parents had also disowned him for being homosexual. Or if they'd disowned him for going to war. Which came first. Or if they'd disowned him at all.

"We've had a rough go of it," the Aviator volunteered. "But we keep trying, we keep talking to each other — sporadically."

"They know about Jack?"

"They know about Jack."

"And me?" Lily asked, surprising herself with her frankness.

The Aviator stretched his toes, flexed his feet to stretch his calves. "They know everything," he said.

"The crash?"

"Yes."

"So, do you mind my asking?"

"About?"

"What they think about you and Jack."

"Well, it's interesting." He paused, gathering his thoughts. "They actually sent me a copy of a statement made by the Society of Friends in Great Britain, in 1963."

"And?"

"It said that any act that expresses true affection between two individuals and gives pleasure to both individuals did not seem to them to be sinful."

"Really? Wow."

"It's called 'Towards a Quaker View of Sex,' and it says that the fact that an act is homosexual does not, by itself, render it a sin."

"That's amazing. And your parents sent it to you, which must mean —"

"That they continue to wrestle with it, that they want to understand."

"They sound pretty cool."

"They are." He smiled at her. "So, now it's my turn to ask a few personal questions."

"Okay," Lily said, wondering what might be coming.

"Have you made a decision? About the pregnancy."

"Yes. I think so. I mean, I have. I have made a decision."

"And?"

"I'm going to keep it." She caught a quick flash of relief — maybe even joy — in the Aviator's expression. Still, she could tell that he was trying hard not to influence her. "This is a child," she said, quite purposefully placing a palm over her belly, "who has determinedly clung to life. I have to respect that. And, it feels like so far my life has been a long string of subtractions. This baby is a plus," she finished, feeling long-winded. It felt good to say out loud the conclusions she'd reached alone. It felt good to have someone to tell, to escape the isolated rumblings of her head.

"What about him? Javier?"

"He doesn't matter."

"You're certain? We could try to find him for you."

Lily shook her head. "He's out of the picture, and that's where I want him to stay."

"All right then," the Aviator said, standing. "I need to shower. Do you want to stay out here longer, or shall I wheel you back in?"

"Wheel me," Lily said, feeling like royalty. "And then let's tell Jack over lunch."

"He'll be ecstatic. And, frankly, he'll also be a fussbudget. That's my prediction." The Aviator circled behind her and began pushing. Lily reached a hand across herself, placed it on top of the Aviator's, and kept it there in steady, wordless gratitude.

Lily took delicious afternoon naps, and beneath her caftans and loose-fitting cotton shifts her pregnancy began to show.

She ached for Javier, for what she'd imagined him to be, what she thought she'd had with him. But she'd talked herself into so much with him, reasoned away his unpardonable flaws, and trumpeted the virtues she'd strived to discover in him. She'd mistakenly believed that her childhood method of dealing with the world — her stubborn, Scallywag determination — was the way to make her relationship work. But now she realized that as an adult she had more options than sheer obstinacy. True strength, she concluded, came from knowing when to change direction; stubbornness was not the same as strength.

And, strength came from wrestling with the past's wounds — just as she was doing, just as the Aviator and Jack did. Javier hadn't mustered the fortitude to do more than give lip service to overcoming his father's brutality. Instead, he repeatedly succumbed to the reflexive temptation to hurt her, to lash out every time he felt vulnerable, every time he was fearful. By contrast, Lily felt the beginnings of pride in herself, for what she was trying to do with her life. For how much she'd already accomplished and overcome.

The Aviator took her to a bookstore in a shopping mall close to the foothills of the Sandia Mountains, and Lily chose three volumes from the motherhood shelf. Ever the good sport, the Aviator even endured a fabric store, where Lily's wheelchair didn't fit down narrow aisles and he had to ferry bolts of cloth back and forth for her approval. She cut out patterns for maternity tops and daydreamed about the baby blankets and tiny outfits she'd gather in preparation for the birth. The obstetrician gave her a due date of March 1971, and the Aviator didn't dissuade the doctor when he assumed that the Aviator was Lily's husband. It weighed on Lily that the child would be expensive. Giving birth would only add to her existing hospital bills. But the Aviator assured her he wanted to do this, and she was trying to unclench Scallywag's stubborn, independent fists.

As for Jack, he was beside himself with glee at the thought of being an honorary grandfather. "I will dote and dote and dote," he told Lily over dinner one evening. "And Stirling will be silly and talk baby talk. Which means that you, Lily Decker, you will have to be the disciplinarian." Jack winked.

It was October, and Geri was flying back to Vegas in the afternoon. In just seven weeks since her arrival in Albuquerque, Lily had progressed to two far less bulky walking casts, and crutches had replaced the wheelchair. She could now take care of herself successfully, alone. She'd even managed to paint her own toenails and shave her legs above the casts, a bit of grooming she never expected to enjoy so much.

The four of them were seated on the flagstone patio off of the library, eating fruit salad and Jack's cheese soufflé, watching Albuquerque's skies. The early morning temperature was perfect for the flight of hot air balloons, and several of them touched down briefly in the shallow waters of the Rio — a baptism ritual for first-time passengers. The balloons were wonderfully cheerful, with bright colors and varied patterns, and when the burners fired, they roared like dragons, setting off dogs for miles around.

"It's my favorite time of year," the Aviator said. "The skies are a deeper blue, and the cottonwoods are just starting to turn."

"Perfect temperatures," Jack added before going inside to change the record. In a few minutes, Kay Starr's voice drifted their way.

"I shared a magazine with her." Lily grinned. "But I had the cover."

"Really? What was it?" Geri asked.

"The casinos have those weekly newspapers — they put them in the hotel rooms and around town. Maybe you've seen them," she said, directing her comment to Geri. "Anyway, I was on the cover of *The Saharan.* The caption was *Showgirl of the Year Ruby Wilde Is Ready for Summer!,* and I was posed — demurely, of course — on a beach towel, with nothing more than a minuscule bikini and a big-ass smile."

"And poor, neglected Kay Starr?" the Aviator asked. "Where was she while all this was going on?"

"On the inside pages, with the other acts. She's a beautiful woman, really," Lily said. "Perky brunette flip. And she was definitely a rose amongst thorns when it came to the other performers."

"Who?"

"Don Rickles, for one."

They all laughed and then quieted as Starr began singing "You Were Only Fooling."

Lily listened to the lyrics. It was her love life, in a nutshell: the man was lying with kisses while the woman was falling in love.

"So, the woman in the song," Lily said after it ended. "She believes his lies. Maybe he's even lying to himself; maybe he believes what he tells her. Whichever. How does she protect herself from men like that?"

Jack smiled. "Oh, Lily. Girl, the only way to protect yourself is to stop living."

"If you're not vulnerable, you can't love," Geri said with an impressive amount of confidence. "You have to be willing to risk heartbreak." She began stacking their plates. "As for me," she continued, "I'd rather trust than not. And I know that means sometimes I'll get hurt. But to walk around thinking everyone's out to get me? No thanks," she said. "And now I have to finish packing."

Lily wondered how much of Geri's speech had been a prescription aimed directly at her.

The holidays were coming, and with Geri gone, Lily had even more time to herself. She often found herself daydreaming, seated outside in a patch of sun, or taking increasingly steady, exploratory walks in the woods along the river beneath a flickering gold canopy of cottonwoods.

The casts were gone, and she walked with a cane. She'd sewn long granny dresses and skirts with elastic waists, and she'd let her hair grow. Her skin seemed fresher without the plaster of makeup. Maybe, too, it was all those pregnancy hormones, but she felt more beautiful and certainly more real than she'd ever felt parading around Vegas.

Lily took her time on her walks, often sat on a stump simply to watch the world.

Sometimes she looked up to find a fleeting white chevron of migrating snow geese high above, and she thrilled at the trilling of sandhill cranes headed south along the river's flyway. She thought maybe Emerson was right about nature's healing powers, its ability to lend perspective. At the same time, she knew that the lightness she felt was due to the family she'd found, the acceptance and safety she felt with Jack and the Aviator. And, she knew it was the expectation of new life that brought such a steady peace to her. Her child. Her child!

Jack and the Aviator converted the casita's second bedroom to a nursery. They wrangled about colors and painting techniques just as any familiar couple would. Jack teased the Aviator about his specially purchased painting coveralls, and at one point he dabbed sage-green paint onto the Aviator's cheeks while Lily laughed. The Aviator wanted to read all of the instructions for the crib assembly, and he laid out the parts to be sure everything was included. Jack, meanwhile, began putting the crib together, dismissing instructions as "a crutch for the incompetent." They bought her a changing table and a mobile modeled after an old-fashioned carousel, with rabbits, horses, chariots, swans, and elephants. One day, the

Aviator came home with a new turntable and a pile of children's records — recordings of the stories of Peter and the Wolf, Cinderella, Snow White, and Muffin, the dog who got a cinder caught in his eye and had to spend several days blind, traversing a city only by sound and smell.

Jack monitored her nutrition, making her special protein shakes, and the Aviator went through a book of baby names, placing stars beside his favorites, much as he'd identified appropriate motels in that long-ago AAA guide to Las Vegas. Her pregnancy was an idyll more enduring, more real than what she'd had in San Francisco with Javier. This time, she felt a permanent foundation beneath her feet — not dreamy, wishful clouds. Lily had not ever felt this sense of ease. She'd not ever before felt this kind of faith in her future. It surprised her — that she could feel this way despite a minimal bank balance and no job or income. How little contentment had to do with money.

In Javier's wake, she still hadn't felt the compulsion to draw blood. At first, she assumed it was because of the shouting pain of her injuries, a substitute for the pain she created with her blades. Then there had been the struggle of physical therapy — something she'd thought would consist of relaxing massages but was instead more about traversing fields of pain to regain function and balance.

But something had changed, and Lily couldn't quite touch the essence of it. She felt as if she were chasing the lovely lavender skirts of Change, forever nearly always within reach of catching hold of that beautiful dress material and stopping Change so that she could ask, *Why? Where has the need gone?*

4

"I was remembering something," Lily said one mid-January evening as they sat in the library after a meal of chicken cacciatore and lovely, crisp salad greens. She'd tried to tell Jack that she should cook for herself, let the two of them resume their private lives, but he'd been insistent: Lily was part of their family. If they wanted a private evening, they'd tell her. Until that happened, and as long as she wanted to, she should be at their dinner table.

She fingered the long fringe of the silk piano shawl Jack had bought for her on one of his monthly forays to an antique store in Santa Fe. It was embroidered with pink roses and Stargazer lilies and made her feel utterly feminine, like a true mother-in-waiting.

"What's that?" the Aviator asked, looking up from his well-thumbed copy of *Main Street*. "What do you remember?"

"In Winslow. You said 'someday,' and I had the feeling that there was something specific you wanted to ask me. And right now, today — tonight — I think I can answer whatever question it is you wanted to ask." She looked at his face bathed in the warm lamplight and thought about how much more she'd come to love him in these past few months. Sometimes, the breadth of the love she felt for him, for Jack, made her feel as if her body had no boundaries.

"Oh," he said, sliding his bookmark into place and setting the book on the cushion. "I think maybe it's none of my business, Lily."

"What? What could possibly be off limits between us? After all we've gone through? With all that's coming?" They'd shared her baby's movements, even touched the bump of an elbow or knee pushing at her skin. Now, she noticed Jack warily observing the Aviator's face. "And you?" she asked Jack. "Why are you looking so worried?"

"Because I'm afraid of what Stirling will do with whatever information you give him. I'm afraid he will use whatever you tell him to fashion yet another whip with which to beat himself."

"I won't," the Aviator assured Jack.

Jack shook his head. "You will. It's what

you do, my love."

It was the first time Lily had seen them let down their guard to this extent. She glimpsed their circumspect, private life as a couple. She felt Jack's fear — and his love; both were palpable.

"I think one thing I've learned living here with you two is this," Lily said. "It helps to get things out into the open. So let's just clean the wounds. Let's do what we have to, to get them to heal. I want my child to live without so much secrecy. Without the shame I've known."

The Aviator stared at her for an uncomfortably long time, as if he were waiting for her to backtrack and come to her senses.

Lily held her silence.

"Tell me what happened," the Aviator said, finally. "Tell me what those people did to you. What I set you up for."

Lily nodded once. She pressed her lips together, felt her eyes filling with tears — not for herself, but for him, the person she loved best in this world. Jack was right; the Aviator would use her story to add pallet after pallet of bricks to the burden he already carried, the guilt that gripped every fiber of his being. "I feel myself wanting to exact a promise from you first," she said. "But I know that's useless, because you're going to be exactly who you are. You're going to take the blame. And it's not your blame. I don't know how to make you believe that."

"But it's not yours, either," he said. "And yet you've carried it. I can see that. Jack can see that."

"Oh, fuck." She sighed, looking toward the ceiling. Careful of the shawl, she instead took the hem of her maternity top and used it to wipe her eyes. "Don't get up," she said to Jack before he could go for a box of tissues.

A strong gust of wind made the wooden garden gate behind the house bang suddenly, and all three of them jumped. Jack stood and fiddled with the logs on the fire.

"I'm trying to think of how to summarize," Lily began.

"I want to know it all," the Aviator said as Jack picked up *Main Street* and sat in the book's place, close to the Aviator. He put his arm about the Aviator's shoulders, a rare display of affection that gave Lily just one more clue as to how worried he was about the direction of their conversation.

"She was strict, Aunt Tate. Maybe no more so than other parents would be, but there was little warmth. She didn't know tenderness. Kindness was a weakness, to her. And, I realize, too, that she'd never been a parent. She didn't know — really — what to expect of an eight-year-old child. How much to require of a child. Or a teenager, for that matter." Lily took a deep breath. "To put it simply, even though she tried, I don't think she knew how to love me."

The Aviator nodded; he'd clearly made a decision not to interrupt.

"I know she tried, but she was limited. I see that now." She glanced at Jack, the Nobel Prize winner of caretaking. "Aunt Tate knew how to manage a household, so she managed me. And she hid in her religion." Lily took a deep breath. She could feel a trembling beginning in her hands, and she folded them together beneath the shawl to conceal them. "She blamed me for things I didn't do, and she readily, eagerly, punished me. She would belittle or punish me and then the next day leave me some gift as an apology. It was very confusing. She just always saw me as guilty, and I came to believe her. I think she took out all of her jealousy and envy — what she'd felt about my mother — and put it on me. Especially as I began to receive attention for my looks." She looked intently toward the Aviator, tilted her head to make her point. "The books you sent were a balm, but it was dancing that saved me. You gave me that." She smiled tenderly. "It saved my life." He nodded, his face still grim, anticipating. "It let me use my body, feel my body — in a good way. Unsullied."

It had to come now. Lily could feel her swift heartbeat. She wasn't sure she could do this. She wasn't sure she could tell anyone, let alone a couple of men — even a couple of men who had such unmitigated, accepting love for her. She heard the snapping of the fire, the wind howling its way across the patio. *A storm is blowing in,* she thought, *in more ways than one.* She swallowed, steeled herself.

"He came into my room at night," she said, seeing Jack's hand tighten on the Aviator's shoulder. "He did things to me." Lily paused. "No. That's not good enough," she said. "That's not sufficiently honest." She shut her eyes momentarily. "At first he touched me. Then he had me touch him."

The Aviator put his forehead in his hand, and then she saw him brace himself and return his gaze to hers.

"He forced me to perform fellatio. Eventually, he fucked me." Lily swallowed her tears. She took another deep, stuttering breath. "He did it for years. He was a foul, disgusting brute of a man. But the worst — or maybe the worst," she said, "was when my aunt chose him over me. She took his side."

"God," the Aviator said, and in that one word was immense, distilled anguish.

"Lily," Jack said. "Oh, Lily."

"He said he was teaching me. And that I was irresistible." She held her chin up, defiant now. "It wasn't his doing. He was helpless. I *made* him do it."

The three of them sat there, saying nothing. No one moved. A profound stillness held them all in place.

"I don't know what to say," the Aviator said at last.

"There isn't anything to say," Lily said.

"I can't fix it. I can't make it better." The Aviator's voice was subdued.

"What would that even look like?" Jack asked.

"I don't know, Jack! I want to put my hands around his neck and strangle him. Slowly. But it's too late. I can't promise that he'll pay for what he's done. I can't kill a dead man," he said, looking at Lily. "I can't ever give you justice."

"It's over," Lily said, more a prayer than a statement.

Finally, Jack spoke, as if he felt a professional compulsion somehow to intervene, to instill insight. "You're a phenomenally resilient woman," he said. "In large part — and horribly so — because of what you've survived. And," he added, "it tells me that you had a very good family life, people who loved you, before you went to live with your aunt and uncle."

"My fault," the Aviator said, nearly a whisper.

Lily left her shawl behind, picked up her cane, and stood to give herself more authority. She moved across to where the Aviator and Jack sat, and she looked down into the face of the man she so loved. She searched for magic words, knowing all the while that there were no such things — no more than there was a curative draft he could concoct for her. All they could do was love each other, as best they could.

"You make me happy every single day," she said. "Every single day you make my life beautiful. I have never — not *ever,*" she emphasized, "been as happy as I am living here, with you two. You are my home." She drew herself even taller, and then she said, "It was an accident. *An accident.* And if I tell you I do not blame you, then you have no right — none whatsoever — to blame yourself. That's my call, and I've made it."

Jack turned from her to watch the Aviator's expression. Lily could see the effort it took for Jack not to comment, to let the Aviator make the trip on his own.

"What will it take for you to hear me? To believe me?" she asked.

The Aviator looked up at her, beseeching, struggling.

"Scoot over," she said, and Jack obliged. Lily lowered herself between the two of them, leaned her cane against the couch, and took the Aviator's hand in hers. "I want you in my life. But not as a guilty man who feels obliged. I want you in my life because you love me for who I am. For who I will become. Just as I want you in my life because of who you are — and that's the reason I've always wanted you. Because of who you are — not because of what happened on some godforsaken highway."

"But everything that's happened —" he said.

"Is life," she finished for him. "That's what I've learned lately. Javier. My accident. Everything — it's just life." She thought a moment and then added, "And I am determined — so thoroughly determined — to see the beauty of life, to give it the power to overcome everything else. I mean, just look at what I have! I have Vivid, and Rose, even

Dee. I have you two — oh, I have you two. I have the future," she said, briefly putting a hand to her belly before letting it rest on the couch cushion. She felt Jack take that hand, and then the three of them sat holding on to each other as the firelight flickered across the library shelves, making the hundreds of hungry books dance with possibility.

5

Her ankles were swollen, her breasts were tender, and she had trouble sleeping. But Lily was in the home stretch.

Hearing the television's low-volume blur, Lily knocked softly on their bedroom door and pushed it open. She'd ironed the Aviator's shirts and wanted to put them away. Jack forbid it for himself, saying his style was rumpled and that he liked the natural look, as he called it. The Aviator was seated on the end of the bed and focused on the television screen; it took him a moment to register that Lily was standing there, holding a handful of hangers with his freshly pressed shirts.

"Oh," he said, clearly embarrassed. He went to where she stood.

"What are you watching?" Lily handed him the hangers.

"Nothing, really."

She made her way across the Navajo rug,

careful not to trip. "Oh ho!" she said, and let out a big belly laugh as she alternated between looking at the television screen and the Aviator's reddening face. "You watch roller derby! Oh, man," she said, sitting where the Aviator had been. "Roller derby!" she nearly shouted.

He hung his shirts in the closet, keeping his back to her longer than necessary. Then, a chagrined smile on his face, he came to sit beside her. "I like the female teams best," he confessed, almost as if he were revealing his favorite sexual position.

"Damn," Lily said. "These women are tough! And just a little scary."

"Yeah. Watch them use their elbows. Or the overhead, two-armed hatchet chop. They're wicked."

"And all while chewing gum," she said, watching one woman blow an audacious bubble and eye her opponent. "Do you have a favorite team?"

"I like them all, really. And I love the names. Bay Bombers, Cincinnati Jolters. Detroit Devils."

"Whoa!" Lily said. "That one just came out and hit her. They can kick each other when they're down?" she asked as one player stomped another with her heavy, wheeled skates.

"It's like wrestling — but with skates on. Different players have different functions, though. There are blockers, jammers —"

"This is brutal!" Two referees struggled to pull a couple of players apart. "They have *got* to be covered in bruises!"

"Yeah. Jack hates it. That's Joan Weston," he said, pointing toward one skater. "She's called the Blonde Bomber."

"I had no idea."

"It's the only game I know where men and women play by the same rules. They're equally violent, equally agile, and skate at some pretty high speeds."

Lily watched as a woman grabbed another skater's ponytail and hung on, whipping the ponytailed woman's neck backward and tossing her over the railing. "Jesus. So, this is your secret vice, huh?"

"Yeah." The Aviator grinned at her. "But you can join me any time you want. We have to watch back here, though. Jack doesn't even want to hear it."

"Some Quaker you are. You crack me up," Lily said, lightly nudging the Aviator with her shoulder.

"Well, good," he said, nudging her back. "I like to make you laugh."

"And now I hate to say it, but we should probably head out," Lily said, standing.

They were taking Lamaze classes together. The married couples who dominated the class stared openly at the two men and their pregnant — what? Daughter? What? Lily smiled freely at them all. She wanted to shout, *We are the amoral outcasts! The homosexual lovers and the Vegas showgirl!* Instead, the three of them kept to themselves and took full advantage of the relaxation and breathing techniques they were learning. The Aviator's huffing in particular made Lily giggle, sometimes uncontrollably.

She'd stopped walking in the woods, afraid of slipping on ice. Instead, she spent languorous, quiet days performing stretches, listening to opera, sewing teeny-tiny bibs, and reading. Today, she was reading a book Jack had given her — a volume from his university bookshelves entitled *Child Abuse and Its Sequelae.* He'd marked the chapters on sexual abuse and told her he would be happy to talk about anything she might want to discuss — or not.

Lily was approaching the book slowly, trying to take it all in and master the new vocabulary. She read of Freud's repetition compulsion, of an abused person's tendency to reenact and repeat a trauma in an attempt to master the event and redefine it. It was so close to what Vivid had said to her — that she was doing what was familiar, that Uncle Miles and Javier were conflated. She found it nearly impossible to believe how unerringly she'd gravitated straight toward a sadist to replace the sadist of her childhood.

It fit with what Jack had told her about trust — that she had to look at actions, ignore words. Less and less did Lily chastise herself for her failings. How could she criticize the Aviator for the same behavior, if she didn't try to change her own approach, reduce her own self-blame?

But the key passage in the book, the one that reached into her Pleistocene layers of shame, was the one about physiological reactions to sexual abuse. *The body can respond even to a sexual assault in a purely physiological manner. A victim can be aroused, even if the act is forced. A rape victim can have an orgasm while being raped.*

Lily held her place with a couple of fingers, looked out the window at the leafless trees and blustery gray February day.

That was precisely what had most shamed and confused her. It was the thing that had haunted Lily. Despicable, repugnant Uncle Miles had made her come. His tongue had brought her to orgasm. Her body had disobeyed and betrayed her. She had believed that she was that sick, that she actually *liked* having Uncle Miles touch her.

It wasn't her fault. Her body had simply responded, even if her heart, her soul, had begged for him to stop. It was an autonomic response; it wasn't her fault. It wasn't her fault. It wasn't her fault. It wasn't her fault. She was not depraved. She was not.

She opened the book and began reading once more. It said sexual pleasure and sexual aggression could become entwined as a result of sexual assault, in particular with repeated sexual assault.

The burning shame she'd felt when Javier hurt her and she came. When she wanted to be hurt. When she felt pleasure braided with pain.

Lily closed the book once and for all, thinking, *Bless you, Jack.* She felt herself buoyant, nearly weightless, despite the bulk of her advanced pregnancy. She was freed from the worst of herself. *Absolution.*

Lily and Sloane

Santa Fe

1979

Sloane Decker wore an unfettered outfit of her own, bold creation. Turquoise cowboy boots with silver-tipped toes. Purple tights beneath a wedding-cake skirt made of tiers of white lace. A ruby-red polyester blouse with enormous belled sleeves, a black velvet choker with a tiny bell sewn in the center. And on her head, a tightly knitted purple cap with multicolored ribbons dangling like long locks of hair. The eight-year-old's dark brown hair — Javier's hair — was stuffed beneath the cap. When set free, it tumbled down her slim back in heavy, undulating waves.

When Lily named her daughter for the Aviator, she hadn't realized the perfection of her choice, that in Ireland *sloan* had been used to refer to a warrior. Although Lily's warrior no longer permitted her mother to hold her hand, that September morning Lily was allowed to walk beside her daughter along the dirt road leading from their lot in the Yucca Terrace Trailer Park to the bus stop. Lily carried Sloane's mug of hot chocolate and her own cup of coffee. Sloane carried the framed photo wrapped in layers of protective newspaper.

"I'm so happy this morning," Sloane said, the bright polish of her boots' toes catching the sun with each step. She twirled, and her skirt lifted like flower petals in a breeze.

They waved at arthritic Mrs. Henderson, who slowly descended the shaky metal steps of her trailer in her pink chenille bathrobe, headed to retrieve her morning newspaper.

"I'm happy, too," Lily said, taking a sip of her coffee, which was cooling quickly. "Here," she said when they reached the spot by the long line of mailboxes where the school bus paused each morning. "I'll hold the photo. You drink your hot chocolate."

Lily had felt a brief flutter of reluctance when Sloane announced that she wanted to take the photo to illustrate the essay she'd written about her mother. Still, Lily resisted the impulse to squelch Sloane's plans. She didn't want for the girl's enthusiasm to be in any way diminished. Sloane was proud of her mother, and Lily's daughter would not be made to feel shame for any innocent act — ever.

It was an eight-by-ten black-and-white portrait of Lily in full showgirl regalia, standing next to Tom Jones. His arm was about her bare waist, and his fingertips pressed into her soft flesh. Ruby Wilde wore cuffs of rhinestones, a wide fan of feathers at the crown of her head, a silver beaded G-string, fishnet stockings, and heels covered in a mosaic of mirrors. The photograph was autographed: *For my favorite pussycat. LOVE! Tom Jones.* At least Lily's breasts were covered; it was an outfit that had been designed for less risqué performances and public appearances.

"They won't know who Tom Jones is."

"Then I'll tell them," Sloane said with a kind of confidence Lily could only envy. "I can even sing one of his songs! And besides, he's famous!" Sloane added. "And you are too, Mom."

The bus brakes shrieked, and Sloane traded her mother an empty mug for the photograph. She even let her mother kiss her cheek before she bounded up the steps. The driver saluted Lily.

Lily watched until the bus disappeared around the corner, and then she walked back to their trailer to finish getting ready for work. At first, Lily and Sloane had stayed on at the hacienda, where Jack and the Aviator could help with childcare. Then, when Sloane was ready to enter kindergarten, Jack's connections had won Lily a job at the Santa Fe Opera. Lily and her daughter moved sixty-five miles north, to the outskirts of Santa Fe.

She worked as an apprentice in the costume department, researching, designing, and creating costumes, wigs, and props. She'd traded applause and power-packed casino bands for backstage creativity, and it suited her. As a lowly apprentice, Lily wasn't paid much, and Santa Fe was exorbitantly expensive. Nevertheless, she hoped eventually to rise to a level at the opera where she could afford to move herself and her daughter out of the trailer park and into a small house. For now, she was satisfied.

The textbook for Jack's Friday afternoon graduate seminar in deviant behavior sat squarely in the middle of Lily's coffee table, next to her mother's palmistry book. When she could, Lily drove with Sloane to Albuquerque for the weekend, and although Lily was nothing close to a graduate student, she enjoyed sitting in on Jack's lectures and classroom discussions.

The Aviator was unabashedly pleased that

Lily was "using her mind," and although she wasn't yet ready to admit it to him, she was considering applying to the university and taking at least one class each semester. It was psychology that intrigued her — if only as a means of trying to comprehend the players in her life, those people represented by the myriad lines of influence in her palm.

Lily refilled her coffee cup and went to sit on the steps. She wore her hair long, caught up on the sides with a length of creamy lace, and at most she briskly, scantily coated her eyelashes in mascara. Lily listened to the soft tinkling of her capiz wind chime, watched the Nelsons' fluffy gray cat amble across the road. The house finches chimed in with their intricate arias, and the scent of dinner sifted through the screen door, making her mouth water. She'd filled the Crock-Pot with chicken, celery, onions, and carrots so that when she got home, there would be a rich broth waiting, tender meat falling from the bone. Simon would join them, bringing Sloane's favorite dessert of rocky road ice cream, and Lily would steam some rice. And then the three of them would sit down to dinner and share the news of their days.

Simon worked as a carpenter in the scenery department of the opera, building elaborate sets from often sketchy, incomplete plans. He could literally make dreams reality — this, Lily knew from having watched him over the course of the past year. His wildly curly, sun-bleached blond hair threw sparks as he worked, and his lean limbs were accustomed to hard physical labor. Simon could fix anything. Anything. Maybe even Lily.

He smelled intoxicatingly of freshly sawn wood. His fingertips when he touched her were wounded, rough from labor, and he'd introduced her to Tom Waits' guttural, blindingly beautiful poetry masquerading as song. And Simon made Lily laugh. Laugh until she begged for mercy. Laugh until it felt as though she'd done five hundred situps. He made up stories — wild, exuberant, improbable, and outlandish stories. He was easy with Sloane, and she was easy with him, journeying alongside him through the vibrant colors of his imagination, worlds populated by inanimate objects come to life, animals who stumbled about just as badly as their human counterparts. He'd also taught Sloane to hammer and drill, and together they were building a sled for when winter draped a thick blanket of snow over the shoulders of the Sangre de Cristo

Mountains above Santa Fe.

Lily hadn't read Simon's palm. She never would, although she knew he was there, a finely etched line in her own palm. When Lily had first spotted Simon's interest in her, she told him that before anything could begin, they'd have a long conversation. "Full disclosure," she'd called it, and then she had watched as Simon tried to hide his trepidation.

She gave him honest Lily, not a mirage. He was her first, after Javier, and she hadn't hidden anything — not her past's freeway pileup of death and loss, the serial rapes, the confused push and pull of Javier. And then she'd told Simon to go, not to see her or speak with her for at least a week.

Lily had waited. Waited for her words, the images they carried on their backs, to bleed into the soil of Simon. She waited until Simon truly knew who she had been, if not who she was.

When he came back to her with clear-eyed certainty, she hadn't quite known how she felt about it. He was absurdly convinced that he understood her, said he'd known pain too, that everyone was damaged in some way. But Lily knew that he couldn't possibly understand her. Not this early in the game, if ever, and not any more than she could ever understand him. Who understood anyone, truly? But she was willing to try — to take a risk, as Jack had coached her. And, Simon had received the approval of both the Aviator and Jack, which gave her a sense of hopefulness.

Lily longed for the respite of a man, the abiding sense of acceptance and belonging she hoped a lover might give her. But she was also afraid. Lily was afraid that Simon was *nice.* And she was afraid that, for her, nice would always be dull. Nice would be placid waters, cloudless skies, temperature-controlled rooms, and cookie-cutter housing developments with well-maintained lawns. Nice would not thrill; nice would not possess her, make her lose herself, starve her of breath. Nice would not be enough.

A few nights ago, she'd put Joni Mitchell's *Blue* on the turntable after dinner, and the three of them danced free-form to Mitchell's splendid, soaring voice. When the needle reached "A Case of You," Lily had slowed her steps and let go of the others' hands, left Sloane and Simon to dance together. She stood against the wall, watching them and listening as Mitchell sang of her fear of the devil, her attraction to men who weren't afraid. That's it, Lily had thought — the menacing, rumbling, lightning-filled thunderhead of Javier. When Simon lifted Sloane off of her feet and spun her, giggling and red faced, Lily had feared she didn't deserve him.

She drained the last of her coffee and set the mug on the step beside her. This weekend was the party at Jack and the Aviator's, in celebration of their tenth anniversary. Vivid was leaving Wild!, her Vegas dress boutique, in competent hands so that she could come for a week-long visit, and Rose was driving out with Vivid, bringing her twin three-year-old boys. Dee was flying in from Oregon with the husband none of them had yet met, and Jack was in seventh heaven, wholly consumed by the marvelous press of preparations. He called practically every night to tell her of changes he'd made to the menu or decorations. Last night, he'd proposed individualized marzipan sculptures for each guest. Lily could easily imagine the Aviator's patient, put-upon expression.

Sloane had made Jack and the Aviator a card, since store-bought cards didn't celebrate the anniversary of two grandfathers, and Lily sewed rich, satiny vests for each man. Jack's had pearl buttons and was made of a midnight-blue brocade patterned with white cranes in flight. For the Aviator, Lily had chosen a conservative emerald-green material with a pronounced basket weave, and she'd found black, leather-clad buttons to give it a subtle zip. Sloane threaded plastic beads that looked like throat lozenges onto lengths of red yarn for each of her grandfathers, and Lily knew that the Aviator would wear Sloane's bracelet proudly.

Lily stood, opened the screen door, and paused, looking into their cozy dollhouse home. Floating in one corner of the living room ceiling were angel's wings Lily had made of papier-mâché and white feathers. They were a firm reminder of the power of guardian angels — of the human variety.

Lily rinsed her mug and set it in the sink. Despite all of her uncertainty about her future, she felt a steady sense of peace. Peace came from this home, her home. A home filled with Sloane's effervescence and full-throated potential. A home that held the sheer beauty of the parts of Sloane that were so clearly Lily, unscathed.

AUTHOR'S NOTE

The summer after my father's death, my brave, adventurous mother loaded her four children into our station wagon and drove us all from New Mexico to California. It was 1966, I was ten years old, and we stopped for the night in Las Vegas. I recall being far more enamored of the motel's cute kitchenette and our decadent TV dinners than I was of the towering neon displays we saw while exploring the Strip, our heads tilted up and up and up toward the grandeur of those immense billboards of light. Still, my little-girl's heart knew I was in the land of true glamour — of feather-clad dancers and crooning singers, of fast-paced comedy routines and sophisticated celebrities. Something about that oasis of money, of titillation and sin, of fame and heat, stayed with me — still remains with me.

When I set out to tell Lily and Ruby's story, I wanted to explore what are, for me, some of the more intriguing puzzles of life. Which childhood events alter the way we see the world? What is "family," and how do we navigate the limits of those into which we're born? How do we create the groups of people who support us through life? Finally — and by no means least of all — how does our culture see the lives and bodies of women? Have things changed for the better? Or at all?

That now vanished, classic Vegas seemed such a fitting setting in which to pose these questions. After all, although arguably the culture of Las Vegas allowed for greater social freedom (it was, after all, Sin City), the Strip was essentially a movie set, all façade.

The more I worked on this novel, the more I became aware of the contrast between what happened in Vegas and what was happening in the rest of the country at the time — the Vietnam War, civil rights protests, the growing women's movement. The city seemed a microcosm of an America so obviously in flux: the growing divide between the values of an outgoing generation and those of the up-and-coming youth. There was Sammy Davis, Jr., dancing on the stage every night, but when he entered and exited the theater, he was forced to use the kitchen door. This was not the real world. It could not be the real world and still promise escape, both for its tourists and for its very own performers.

The most iconic Vegas performer, the showgirl, seemed to me the ideal figure to illuminate issues surrounding women's bodies — how they're simultaneously idolized and exploited, celebrated and taken for granted. Lily/Ruby also provided me with a way to write honestly about sexuality, that secret ignominy of a woman's life. Her fears about the accuracy of her internal compass of love. Her fears about men, about how to know which ones can be trusted and which should be avoided. I let this smart, ambitious heroine grapple with the question my friends and I have long discussed: What leads us to the choices we make in love?

It was important to me to explore love and attraction in many forms. The Aviator and Jack are born of two men I loved dearly, who could never reveal their feelings for each other, except within their closest circle of friends. I remember the surprise on their faces when they realized I knew their secret and nevertheless accepted them, loved them still and always. I very much wanted to honor them. I thought about what it would be like to be unable even to answer a telephone in your own home, for fear of unveiling what was considered sick and perverted behavior. I wanted readers to know that the military used to *prosecute* men in homosexual relationships.

A great deal of research went into this novel. I read numerous books on the history of Las Vegas, as well as biographies of famous figures who passed through the town. I created a map of the Strip for myself because so many of the glorious casinos and hotels of yore were destroyed to make room for the new, and I wanted to be sure that Ruby traveled in the right direction when she went from one casino to another. The Internet also provided me with marvelous resources, including UNLV's impressive digital collection of casino and showgirl memorabilia, right down to menus with prices and original design drawings for showgirl costumes. I altered some things to suit my fictional purposes. For example, Sammy Davis's trip to Vietnam took place several years later than is depicted in this novel. At times, I got lost in the research; it was a fascinating culture and time, and the variety and numbers of celebrities who passed through Vegas were astounding.

Several years ago, I returned to Las Vegas to attend a conference on special education law. It was no longer the place it had been when I was a child, and I felt a sense of disappointment — that I'd not been the right age to enjoy classic Vegas. I've remedied that disappointment by using my imagination to travel back in time. Now, I've walked with Tom Jones and Sammy Davis, Jr. I've sat next to Sonny and Cher in an audience, and I've experienced what Ruby felt when she stepped onto a lavish stage set. I had a great time in the Vegas of my mind, plowing this landscape for all it offers — light and dark — to illuminate the life of Ruby/Lily, to find a terrain that suited the challenges of my indomitable heroine, and to confront what we believe about ourselves and the world we inhabit.

Although I no longer practice law, I still find the need to fight for a cause (or two, or three). In my fiction, my characters become my clients, and I am their advocate. After all, the issues that define the lives of Lily, Ruby, Vivid, Rose, Dee, Aunt Tate, the Aviator and Jack — they endure, for all of us. And if I can hope to accomplish anything, it's to create a more expansive sense of justice and to urge understanding.

ABOUT THE AUTHOR

Elizabeth J. Church is the author of *The Atomic Weight of Love,* a #1 Indie Next List selection and Target Club Pick that was shortlisted by the ABA Indies Choice Book Awards for adult debut book of the year and the Reading the West Book Awards for best adult fiction. *All the Beautiful Girls* is her second novel. Church lives in northern New Mexico.

Find Elizabeth J. Church on Facebook.
Twitter: @ElizJChurch

The employees of Thorndike Press hope you have enjoyed this Large Print book. All our Thorndike, Wheeler, and Kennebec Large Print titles are designed for easy reading, and all our books are made to last. Other Thorndike Press Large Print books are available at your library, through selected bookstores, or directly from us.

For information about titles, please call:

(800) 223-1244

or visit our website at:

gale.com/thorndike

To share your comments, please write:

Publisher
Thorndike Press
10 Water St., Suite 310
Waterville, ME 04901